Time of Isolation

Book One of the Survival Trilogy

F. D. Brant

F.D. Brant

GRESHAM, OREGON

F. D. Brant
P O Box 522
Gresham, Or 97030
www.fdbrant.com

Book Layout © 2017 BookDesignTemplates.com

TIME OF ISOLATION/F. D. BRANT. – 2nd ed.
ISBN 978-1-946179-06-7

This story is dedicated to, as always, family, and to my friends Keenan, and Ellen. To all members of my family who have supported and encouraged me to continue through to the completion of this project, and the suggestions made to improve the story, my friends for direction in other areas and their continued friendship, and my wife Audrey who has to live with this writer.

CHAPTER ONE

Sampson hurried along the thoroughfare trying to move as fast as his overweight body would allow. He needed to find his supervisor now. Unfortunately she was located completely on the opposite side of the communications complex. While he was in charge of his section, an underling, the news he had needed to be brought to Shana's attention personally and could not be sent over the circuits. So by avoiding eye contact with the many others he passed, and breathing quite hard from the exertions, he continued to move with strong determination. It had happened again. This was the fourth time in the past annuals, and he was shocked when it had happened on his shift, with his team. Just what was going on? Finally nearing his destination he found that he was raising a sweat. He just hated sweating, but this time he had to endure it as well as making this contact with his boss. He had never liked Shana, but knew that he could never become a supervisor of her level. First, he was not one born into the proper order, and second he knew that he could never match the intelligence necessary to oversee such an operation as this.

Finally reaching her entrance he stopped, caught his breath and tried to calm down. These meetings were rare, and he preferred it that way. Then gathering his courage he entered and encountered Susan, the one who ran interference for the boss. Again he had never liked her either, as it seemed that she always put on an air of superiority around any who were lower or worked under Shana. "Susan, I need to have a conversation with Supervisor Shana, and no before you ask, this cannot wait."

Looking down at him she said, "Who are you to just barge in here? You do not have any right to demand anything, ah . . . let's see . . . *underling* supervisor Sampson. Do I have it right?"

When she said these things it seemed as if she was attempting to get something out of her mouth such as a bad taste. Shaking his head he could tell that things were going from bad to worse. But what could he do? What he had was critical and they had been told that if another incident happened that he, or any of the under supervisors, had to go to their supervisors immediately and inform no one but them. He wasn't even supposed to inform the underworkers for the lead supervisors. It was to be for their eyes and ears only. Carefully holding his anger in control he gritted his teeth and said. "Yes, you have it right. I must see Lead Supervisor Shana now without delay."

"Without delay? What is it that could be so important from your *minor* position that could even require a minute of Supervisor Shana? Her time is always filled, so, if you please, make an appointment and come back later. You are interrupting my work and I for one will not allow you to interrupt hers. Now get out of here before I report you!"

About this time Lead Supervisor Shana hearing the loud conversation in the outer office went to investigate. Catching the ending conversation from her underworker, and seeing one of the under supervisors from the communications section, she became curious. Underworker Susan catching the gaze of Sampson turned and saw Shana there and started apologizing for interrupting her work and that she had everything in control and this minor supervisor was just leaving. *Why was he here?* Then she saw that under supervisor Sampson was looking intently at her. She also knew that he had never liked her, so again why was he here? Looking directly at him Shana asked. "Under supervisor Sampson may I inquire, why are you here?"

Again looking directly at her, he was at a loss for words. The directive had been explicit, nothing could be said to any others just his boss. "I have something that must be given to you, but only to you." He stammered.

"What's so important that it couldn't be communicated over the circuits?" Then she saw a troubled look on his face, and indecision there. Yet at the same time a look that said that he would not give up on this.

"Ma'am, this has to do with the most recent directives that said that if a specific circumstance or event happened that I or any of the other under supervisors must report in person, immediately without delay, and I for one am not going to violate such a mandate. I am here as it requests."

Shaking her head, she had really never liked this under supervisor. She had never liked people who had let themselves go like this. He seemed fat and lazy, and seemed to be the type that used the rules and regulations strictly as written – never bending or thinking outside what was there, one with little imagination, yet one who did what was necessary and kept his underworkers to task – one which caused as little friction as possible. "Which of the many mandates would this one be, under supervisor Sampson?" With so many coming out she never had time to read many of them anyway, depending on her staff to keep her informed.

Now what, Sampson thought, the mandate had been specific. No one but his supervisor could hear what he had to say. Then he remembered that if there was situations like this that he could specify a color to let her know. Now if only he could remember the color. Blue! Blue was that color. "Ma'am, ah color it blue", was all he said.

When he stated the color, she immediately paused. He had given her a code color that reflected an emergency of some kind and could be private and for her eyes and ears only. She then turned to her underworker and said, "Under Supervisor Sampson may enter." She then turned around and went back inside of her office wondering now what could be so important for him to have used that code. She didn't have to wait long as he entered her office right behind her. "I don't have much time, what is it that is so important?"

"Ma'am, do you have this room secured for silence? The directive said that before this information was to be given that all security features must be activated."

Sitting back down at her desk, she motioned him to a seat, and then pushed a few buttons. "Okay, I have activated the security. Again what is it that required you to use the code word?"

Not quite sure how to continue he hesitated and then said. "Ma'am we've lost communications with another city. It has gone silent without warning. We have tried for the required amount of time to reestablish contact, but like the others it is like it never was."

Silent and shocked at what had just been relayed to her, many questions went through her mind. *Was it just a temporary loss or is this going to be like the others? Which one this time and what truly is going on? If it is confirmed then this will be the fourth city lost.* She slumped her shoulders and then asked, "Which City have we lost contact with?"

"Terra ma'am. It is one of our larger cities and had many a backup, especially in communications. But without warning it went silent and we have been trying now for hours to reestablish contact, but all we get is silence and static."

After minor supervisor Sampson had left she sat for a short time defeated by the news. Something was happening to their cities, but with no information there were no answers. She knew that right now she would have to drop whatever had been planned for the day and head out and find the other department heads to see if the information that she had been given was confirmed there. If so then they would have to inform the council. *Four gone now, that's a frightening thought. Just what's happening to them?*

If they are being destroyed, why were there no refugees – again if a disaster had befallen them why no contact? Yet, when one looked at the order of loss, it appeared that something else was going on.

* * *

When the information reached the council they immediately called an emergency session. When one city had disappeared off the grid it had been a major concern – but now with four gone it had become something unthinkable. They knew that they were vulnerable to the primitive tribes and clans that existed here. But so far they had just warred among themselves, more concerned with each other. As far as these tribes and clans knew, the cities did not exist, and if they thought that they might, it was more legend than reality. So what had changed? Why were their cities disappearing?

Because of the low populations, they knew that there was no way for them to fight or go to war against these people. So instead technology had been developed that blocked the cities from view. It required a lot of power to maintain the illusions that they created. So, most of the funds and work, went into maintaining and upgrading the power units. They even had created large backups just in case something happened to the main units. Over time they had been able to create both holographic images of the lands around them to give the illusion that where the cities were located was desolate useless lands – to further the chance that the primitives would not be interested in investigating the areas. Plus a minor force field that required a device worn by the citizens to be able to pass through. With all of the city's needs existing inside of these protections there was very little reason to leave. They also kept devices in the cities that allowed them to monitor the few entrances and exits into the cities.

They had depended on these protections for generations and it had always worked. So they had grown complacent. Because of this complacency they had few that could even fight, as it had never been necessary in the past. Yet something had changed, and now the cities were disappearing. With no hard evidence they did not even know why. So with the loss of this fourth city they, the council, had almost panicked. They spent half a day uselessly arguing back and forth coming up with no answers or solutions. Until finally the head of the council called a break realizing that until they had some answers there would be no solutions. Sione, the council head then summoned the *underworker to the council* Sayvon to his side and said, "Sayvon, I need you to get in contact with Shayne. Have him report immediately to my chamber. We need answers and we can sit here all day debating and still have nothing in the end. Do not waste any time, I am calling a recess when I go back into the council meeting area. If necessary give him the code color yellow. It will let him know that this is most serious."

"Where would I find this Shayne, sir? This is someone I am unfamiliar with. In fact I do not ever remember this person ever mentioned at all."

"Not surprising really. You see he is the leader of what we thought was a program that we would never use. He has been before us many times a long time ago, imploring us to keep what he works on . . . his life work really, alive. I must admit that there were a number of times we almost cancelled his section, but that is old history. You will find him and the ones who work for him at the edge of the city close to the wilderness that lies beyond. The compound is actually blocked off from the city and those who live within this compound are trained from their youth to be what they are. They usually work in teams of two, and if siblings so much the better. Here, if you look at this map of the city they are located there." Taking Sayvon to a picture on the wall he flipped a switch, which then revealed the map. He pointed to an area that seemed almost unused. There appeared to be no major structures, nothing to indicate industry or farming, just a few minor structures and that was all. It could have been one of the many parks, but was so far out of the way that it would be one that no one would ever have need of visiting.

Looking closely at the map Sayvon asked, "I don't really see how you even travel there. And why would anyone want to live and work there anyway?"

"Understand this, if anyone is going to solve this puzzle and what is happening to our sister cities then it is he or one of his teams. Remember we have become a people that have depended on our machines and as such probably could not survive on our own without them. Shayne is a throwback to an earlier time when we were just beginning to bring our machines on line. He and any of his many teams could survive out there in the wilderness and among the primitives. Something neither you nor I, and I suspect the rest of this city, or any of the other cities could do. You see we are the last city to even allow this program to continue. So he and his teams may be our last chance to keep what we have. Or become like those other disappearing cities leaving not a trace of whom we are or what we did behind. I suspect we are dealing with a change within the primitive world. And somewhere along that line they have learned of our existence and worse have found a way to penetrate our illusions and protections. We are not a warrior race, and I suspect that we are an easy people to conquer if an attacking army can get past our protections. So please hurry, and if you look closely you can see that you actually have to go this way, away from this compound before you can work back to it." Then pointing again at the map he traced out the route that Sayvon would have to take. "Now here you should find some signs that actually will direct you to the compound. The signs will simply say The Wilderness Space."

Sayvon shuddered at the thought of having to go into a space like the wilderness outside the city. He was a citizen of the city and had no wants or desires to be even close to a place that simulated the wilderness. But he had been given a directive and he would follow it to the best of his ability. What Sione had relayed to him worried him more than this trip he had to take. Now once he found it could he convince this Shayne to follow him back? He had never been given that code color before. The highest he had ever used was blue. He did not know that there was one higher than blue until now. Now he wondered if there was any that was higher than yellow? He did not know. While he looked at the map he also realized that it would take him the rest of this day to reach this compound. It would be dark and if this area simulated the wilderness what was in there? He never considered himself brave but now had no choice but to face this unknown.

CHAPTER TWO

Sayvon had gotten lost a couple of times, as this was part of the city that he had never been in before. It seemed to be much older than the portion he worked and lived in. In fact one of the major signs he had come across stated "Old City". It seemed to be poorer and more run down, but that could be an illusion since you could see the age in the buildings. The pathways and sidewalks were worn and narrow in comparison to the main city, and as dusk approached it appeared that even the lighting was dim and dungy making the area appear to be unsafe. Yet he knew that it was illusion since there was little crime. At times he would pass couples arm and arm paying him little or no attention. And then there seemed to be many children running around playing their many games. He with his nervousness just pushed on until he reached the edge and saw one of the signs pointing him in the proper direction. It was fully dark by the time he had reached the area and was immediately blocked by a wall that had to be twice his height. *Why the wall?* Walking along the wall, it just seemed to go on forever.

Eventually he reached a small door that had a light above it, and what he guessed was a monitoring device. Looking closely he saw what appeared to be a summoning device. It showed little use and left him wondering if it actually worked. So he pressed the button and found that his initial assessment was accurate. The button had not been used in who knew how long, and was resisting his effort to push it in. Finally it seemed to loosen up enough and appeared to function. He waited what he considered was adequate time and with no response tried again and he decided to knock also. Again waiting for what seemed a long time and again without response he gave up and started to leave, then jumped when he heard the grating of the door sliding open. Turning around he saw a youth, but one who was dressed strangely. There seemed to be an air about him that made Sayvon really *look* at him. He couldn't place the difference but it was there. The youth stood there silently waiting for Sayvon to say something. "Ah, I'm Sayvon; I have been directed by the head of the council Sione to seek out Shayne. I have something for his eyes and ears only."

The youth only nodded, and then signaled Sayvon to follow, turning around and immediately headed back inside expecting Sayvon to follow him. Realizing that was what the youth wanted he finally got himself moving and as he entered the compound the door closed behind him with a heavy thump causing him to jump and cringe. It sounded so final. Then the sounds within the compound started to assail his ears. It was too dark to see, and he found himself stumbling as the youth, sure footed, continued and was actually outdistancing him. The youth seemed to have an easy flow to his movements like he was a part of this world and not the one Sayvon had just come from. There seemed to be a confidence, a quiet confidence that spoke of tests and trials that had been overcome. *What is this place anyway? Who is this youth?* He had never said a word or offered him his name. Again why did this place even exist? From the signs he knew that the area was not a secret, yet in all of his life he had never heard of it or what its function was. One thing for sure he was learning quickly.

As his eyes adjusted to the darkness he could now see that they appeared to be walking on a dirt path that led up to some small structures just ahead. He then noticed that the youth leading him was barefoot. The structures in the distance seemed to be lit, but the light emanating from the windows were weak and seemed to flicker. Why was that so? He was so out of his element that he could not come up with any satisfactory answer at all. Eventually he was led to one of the units in the center. Here the youth that had brought him here pointed to this one building. On the door he could barely make out the name Shayne. That was all it said. There was nothing to identify that he was even the one in charge. Why was that so? It was something else that did not make sense. Turning around he saw that the youth was leaving and heading towards one of the other buildings leaving him alone. *Were they all this way here?* Shrugging, he went up to the door and started to knock only to have it open. A man stared at him seemingly sizing Sayvon up immediately. Sayvon saw someone who was only a little taller than him, but his skin appeared to be brown, and if he guessed right this man had to be lighter than he in weight. There seemed to be no fat on this man at all. *Didn't he eat?* The next thing that registered was this man was not young. There were streaks of gray in his dark brown hair, and he also had facial hair . . . something that was never seen within the city at all.

Smiling Shayne said in a soft voice. "Come in, come in! I don't get too many visitors from the city here at all. And to have one from the council is so rare that it has only happened once in my lifetime." He then signaled Sayvon up the short set of wooden steps and inside the small building. Once inside he saw why the lights seemed so dim and flickering. Instead of the lighting that was powered by the power units of the city, what was here appeared to be lamps and candles. The lamps had some type of clear oil inside of them with a wick and a chimney. Everything within glowed under the flickering yellow light. Nowhere that he looked could he find anything of the city. The furniture was rough and seemed to be made from natural things. Even the cooking appeared to have been accomplished over an open fire type conveyance. As his eyes continued to search the room he found nothing in it that was familiar. Then looking back at his host he realized that the clothes he was wearing also appeared to be made by hand. There absolutely was nothing of manufacture here. It appeared that someone's hands had made everything here. Then noticing the floor he saw what appeared to be an animal skin laid out like a rug. Stammering he asked, "Is . . . was that real?"

Smiling Shayne said, "Of course. It at one time was a living animal. By watching you, I believe that you have searched this whole area and, I assure you that you will not find anything that you commonly use in the city. Everything you see was either living or was constructed from natural materials. You see, here one must be able to live in the wilderness beyond. That means that what you take for granted does not exist here. So one must learn to use what is available. If you do not then you have *no* business here."

That last statement seemed to be directed at Sayvon. And in truth if it wasn't, it would have been easy to interpret it that way. This Shayne had a way of looking at a person that appeared to look to your very soul, judge you, and then if found wanting, ignore – or at least give no signs of trust. *Why had he agreed to come here?* He was so far out of his element that he was even at loss as what to say. He again stammered, "Sir, I have been sent by Sione to have you report to him immediately."

"Sione? I am afraid that name does not seem familiar. I assume he is of the council since I can see on your shirt the badge identifying you as the underworker to the council. Who is he anyway?"

Somewhat affronted by this revelation and question, he became indignant. "He, sir, is the head of the council!"

Laughing Shayne said, "Did I ruffle your feathers? You must remember that here you and your city do not exist. We do not keep up with the policies or politics, and who may be in charge at any certain time. As I said earlier it is rare that any city member visits here, and rarer still when someone from the council puts in an appearance. So why would it matter to us?"

Sputtering now with a deeper indignation Sayvon said. "Because it is the generosity of the council that has made sure that your section still exists. If it were not for them keeping it alive, then like in the other cities you would not have been able to continue!"

"Is that all? Gee, and to think that because of the council, which, by the way, this operation has cost them little to nothing, that I have a job. Gee, I just don't know what to say."

To Sayvon the sarcasm was so thick he could have cut it. "It . . . it's true! We are the only city left that still allows this to continue. With just a stroke of a pen you and your section could be gone like everywhere else."

"It's the other cities' loss. And if this council were stupid enough to eliminate the only section that could give them intelligence on what is happening outside of the cities then it, in the end, would be their loss. Oh, I'm sorry; I've not even offered you anything or a place to sit. Where are my manners? By the way, are you finished with your worthless threats? And can you tell me why you are here, especially since it is after dark. You have me curious, as no one comes here after dark."

One thing for sure this Shayne had continued to keep him off balance since he had arrived here. He thought that his political savvy and the ability to spar verbally were pretty good. But he was finding out that he was no match for this Shayne. There was nothing he could use as a weapon against him. It just seemed that he did not care, and it appeared that he was being toyed with. Not by some amateur, but someone who appeared to be more amused by his attempts. Something like a cat playing with a mouse, and he was that mouse. It made him more uncomfortable. To be out of his league here was an understatement. How did one attack someone that seemed not to care? "Look, I know it is unusual for someone from the city to come here. In fact I did not even know that this existed until today. As far as what you do here I don't know that either. But I was sent to get you. Sione, who is the council head, said that it is urgent, and to not wait until the morning when it would be daytime here. So I am here because of that request. At least you could honor it and come back with me and find out what it is he wants to discuss with you. I was told that this had to be a face to face meeting, and he directed me here."

Again laughing Shayne said, "You fool. Here, other than what you saw at the gate into this place, there is nothing of the city, which means that there are no devices or such that allows me to talk over the airwaves to anyone. If anyone wants to talk to me they have to talk to me in person. So you, thinking that it will show some importance, by showing up here to talk with me really means nothing or anything at all. Yes, there is a part of this facility that has those capabilities, but they are mobile units – off limits except during training . . . normally shut down and inoperative. Here, everyone learns that it is important to have direct contact. There is much that can be learned from another when you do that. For instance you are both extremely nervous and have a fear of this place. Plus I can read that you have an overblown view of yourself, where you work, and whom you work for. It is there for any to read." Then shaking his head he sat down in a chair that was next to a table. He signaled for Sayvon to do the same.

Now sitting across from Shayne again he asked himself, *who is this person? He surely did not have any proper respect for the city and its leadership. So why would Sione want to speak with him?* Personally it appeared to be a lost cause. Shrugging his shoulders he then said, "I see that I have wasted my time and yours. I will go back and report to Sione that you are not interested."

"Interested in what? You have yet to even present anything other than the leader of the council wants my presence. With so little presented you have yet to give me a reason. For all I know he wants to show me off to some of his political friends. I do not have time for such nonsense."

What Shayne said was true. He had only said that the leader of the council wanted to see him. But since being here he had been so out of his element that he had been completely off balance. He had never faced anyone like this – someone who could read him like an open book. After all he had prided himself in the ability to hide his true feelings and motives. Yet here before him was someone who had just proven that premise to be false. "Look, I was sent to get you. There is an emergency and he, Sione, felt that you and your teams were the only ones who could help."

"Ah, now that's better. Was that so hard? What kind of emergency are you talking about here anyway? I haven't sensed anything unusual happening within this city . . . not that I get into it very often."

"Nothing has happened to our city, but that does not mean that something isn't going to happen."

Curious now Shayne asked. "And what do you mean by that statement?"

"Look I am not at liberty to say, but I was told that if I was unsuccessful that I was to say yellow."

That stopped him. Yellow was the code for most serious. Once he heard that he did not say anything else. He stood up, grabbed a coat and headed for the door. "Aren't you coming?

After all you needed to get me to come along. So I'm coming along. Lead away!"

Shocked and still off balance, this sudden change left him even more unsure. "Okay, you're not planning on doing something are you?"

Shaking his head Shayne said. "Now what would give you that idea? You gave a color code and it answered my most immediate questions. I will now go see your Sione. So lead away. And do not worry I'll protect you from the dark."

* * *

Back at his cabin now after being with the head council member all night, he remembered that as he had begun his walk to the council chambers if the quoting of such a high emergency color had been appropriate. After all, there was only one color higher and that was black. Between blue and yellow there were also two others with green being the one just above blue, and brown just below yellow. White was all clear, and red the first towards emergencies. So the order began with white, then red, blue, green, brown, yellow, and finally black. When Sione brought him up to date as to what had been happening he knew that it could have been very easy for this Sione to have used the final emergency color, yet, by not doing so showed him that maybe this councilperson might actually have some common smarts. Something that appeared to be lacking in most politicians and one of the many reasons he normally tried to avoid them.

Four cities gone! What had happened? At least this Sione knew who to turn to, to find out. He and his teams were the only ones equipped to live outside the cities, and having heard that his teams were the last to exist in any of the cities left him sad. Had the cities progressed so far in both their ego and ignorance to think that something like this could never happen? The answer was obvious to him, *yes*. Now it would fall on him and his teams to try and find out what was going on, and who was responsible. He suspected by the way they disappeared that it had something to do with the primitive tribes. Somehow through a failure or something similar one of the cities became known, and once known was then destroyed. And if some of the tribes had united, these combined tribes would be a force to reckon with. Since they had to survive in the wilderness, and the many skirmishes that happened continually between them, they were a strong wily enemy, while the cities would be a weak easy target. Once a tribe got beyond the outer defenses then the rest would fall quick with barely a whimper. This enemy would barely raise a sweat. Then by seeing how the cities were hidden, these primitives would seek out other such areas. And each time one was found they would learn more and it would become easier. In truth the facts supported this. There had been a large amount of time between the disappearance of the first city and the second. But then the times became shorter and shorter as the third and fourth city vanished.

It was time to bring in his second and then get some sleep. He knew with the information that he had that there were to be many sleepless nights ahead of them. Time was short, and the longer it took to find out what was going on, the more chances other cities would fall. So heading back out to the middle of the compound he rang the bell with three short rings signaling assembly and waited. Within a few breaths the compound filled with the students and teachers of the wilderness. He waited until the restlessness left the crowd and silence followed. Looking around at his teams he felt proud to be a part of them. Now they would be tested to the fullest. Had there been enough done? Or would he find, like the cities disappearing, that they were lacking. Looking around at the gathering crowd he said. "After generations of work here where everything was just simulation and scouting, we now are to face a real test." He could see the smiles on their faces as they anticipated actually doing something. "I would like the leaders and trainers to remain here. The rest of you are dismissed, and shortly after I talk with this group they will pass on to you what we have discussed. Be prepared, our time is short, and our very existence may come down to what we learn and do. Other than that, it is all I can relay to you at this moment. This will involve everybody, so there is no need to fear that any of you will be left behind. Thank you." He turned and headed for the common eating area where the teams would meet as a group. As he left he saw that the trainers and leaders were following him and the rest heading back to whatever assignment they had before the call to assemble.

CHAPTER THREE

He had gone over in his mind, as he was walking back to the compound, what needed to be done. But fatigue had clouded his mind, and while he had some ideas it was important to use the whole team to lay out a plan of action. Once he entered the common eating area he signaled the leaders to sit at any of the many long tables. "I've just spent the night with the leader of the council. I can see from your questioning looks as to why I did such a thing, since you and I know that we rarely see anybody here let alone someone from the ruling class. In fact, as you know, I have only seen one here in my lifetime up until last night. I figured that most likely it would be bad news, something like, they had finally decided that we were to be closed down as the costs of running something like this, even though it's not much, was not worth keeping it in operation. In fact I had a confirmation that the other cities have already shut down this operation and we are the only one that is remaining." Letting that soak in for a moment before continuing he then said, "Fortunately for us that was not the reason for the visit or the request that I return to the chambers of the leader – I was given yellow." He could see the reaction from the group when he had given them the color. Watching them he could see them looking at each other and with concern in their very beings showing through he said. "Yeah my very reaction – I know that many of you have relatives, and loved ones living in the city as I.

They in the city do not understand what it is that we do here, and as you know I have a sister and her family there also. We, like you, and yours, are very close although we do not get to see each other very often. I find it necessary to live here to maintain the edge that we must have if we ever have to use these skills that are taught here. And now, I for one will be happy that I have done just that. Getting back to the color, when I was given that, I dropped everything, even the conversation that I was having with this official and immediately went to see this Sione. I did not know him, but for your information, he is the head of the council. He relayed to me that within the last couple of annuals that four of our sister cities have vanished, period." At this point he paused to see how that had affected them. He could see disbelief in their eyes and actions. Something like this had never happened. They couldn't even remember when one city had disappeared. Four was unthinkable, and to have them disappear in such a short time brought worry to all of them. "This information can be passed to everyone here with the admonishment that it must stay here. No one outside of this compound will be allowed to know this. So gather your teams and students and give them this information and start preparing for an exit from the city. We do not have much time, and we do not know which city may be next. I am not opening this for questions at this time. I want this information out to the teams as quickly as possible. I need feedback and ideas. That's all for now, Skylar, I need you to remain behind."

He watched them as they quietly left. It was obvious that they were in deep thought about what had been revealed. Looking back at the tables he saw Skylar waiting patiently to see what he wanted of him personally. He headed over to the table where Skylar sat and joined him by sitting across from him. "So what are your feelings on this?"

"Are you sure what you have presented us is accurate? No, if you went and were shown the information, and I think I know you well enough, then, it probably is correct as far as it goes. If what little we know is true, then I have to agree I think all of the cities are vulnerable." Looking down at the table and thinking a little before he continued Skylar said, "Okay I did not see the data as you, and I know that you gave us a very short version of what was found since as you say you were gone all last night. That must have been some session. Hmm, so what is the plan? I mean I have so many questions, and very few answers. I guess the important one is, are we ready to face what this threat represents? So what is it you want me to do?"

"As I said I need to get some sleep, but this will not wait so with you second-in-charge here, you need to get moving on some type of plan. I said this would involve everyone and that is the way it must be. I feel with this unknown threat that all of us will be needed to come up with some solution. I talked long with Sione and he said that they on their end would be attempting to find a way of changing and improving the defenses. We on our side must find out how they found out, and somehow neutralize the threat, and as I said we do not have much time. Of course we are assuming that the tribes are responsible, but it is the most logical conclusion. Plus without any additional assistance from the other cities, we overall, are a small group and there's a big world out there. Here let me give you this." He then handed Skylar a stack of papers and continued, "Normally they, the ones in the city, do not use paper. But Sione knew that we did not have the devices here to read the information that way and had this printed out for us. Read up on it, this is everything that I know at this point. I should be back at it around mid-day and at that time I'll join you. Once you read through this stuff I think you will agree that our time is very short."

With a troubled look Skylar asked, "How much of what is in here can I reveal?"

"Everything. We do not have time to play games here. And who knows any one of the members here may have something that we would not have thought about. Right now, as you will see, we are lacking any real hard facts. But the conclusions from what has been gathered are hard to dispute. Okay then, I'll catch you a little later or maybe sooner, if I am unable to sleep." He then bid Skylar a goodbye and headed off to his cabin to try and catch a few hours of sleep.

After Shayne had left Skylar remained sitting for a little while. He scanned the many pages, and as he did he became a little more alarmed. As Shayne had said the information was sketchy, but the conclusions made in the report appeared to be correct. Included with the papers was a map showing the cities and when he studied this he saw that the ones that had disappeared were north of them but on a direct line to their city, which had the name Sequoyah. Again if accurate, the times between the cities disappearing were shortening tremendously, and if the timeline shown here continued, it would not be long before another city vanished. Could they act in time to prevent it? When he truly thought about it the answer was probably not, as there just wasn't time. Smiling, although it was a grim smile he said softly. "Yeah, time was something that we had on our side. We wished for something to happen to go and try ourselves against the real world, and now with this crisis we have it." Shaking his head he continued, "So now what? Now that we have gotten what we wished for, now what?" He didn't have an answer for that one. So sighing he got up and headed out the door. There was a lot of information that needed to be passed around and sitting here thinking about it was not going to get it accomplished.

The next few hours he moved from group to group, passing on the information and stating that after the evening meal that there would be a gathering there in the eating hall to discuss further what their actions would be. And yes, what Shayne had stated was true. Absolutely everybody would be involved – from the rawest members up to and including Shayne who is their leader.

Then Skylar thinking about how the area was laid out began to go over in his mind the shortest route around the facility. Except for the mated couples, strict discipline and separation was maintained. There were barracks for the single males, and barracks for the single females, and these were located on opposite sides of the compound. Between these two locations sat the mated couples' cabins. During the days and of course during the night exercises they worked side by side, but the idea of cohabitation between unmated members were discouraged, as this could lead to problems at a critical time and put more than just the couple at risk. Many of the exercises they were involved with could cover many weeks at a time. One group would establish a village in their compound area within the wilderness that had been created within. They would try as best they could to appear to be no more than any other of the many tribes and villages that existed in this world. During the exercises a second group then would become a rival tribe and attack the first to see how well the first group had set up their camp, taking in the factors of location to the necessities, and defensibility, followed by how well they guarded their area, and then how well they would fight to protect their site from a rival village. The simulations were to be as close as to real as they could make them.

Some of the older teams of two had, carefully in the past, gone out into the real wilderness and observed tribes as they lived, fought, and died. Everything had been recorded so that not only would the observations made by the teams be known, but also there was a visual record that went with the narratives. These observations were something that periodically they would perform. So that any changes in the way the tribes interacted could be viewed and studied. Yet, again, something had changed, for the cities now seemed to be the targets, and very easy targets. Skylar hoped that other cities had picked up the alarm and were doing something to improve or change their defenses. The report overall had concluded that what had been working in the past was no longer. If rapid changes were not made, then there would be no cities left, and they and their way of life would be gone forever. What had happened to make that first city vulnerable? Then, what was it that revealed the others that had fallen? What was it that the primitives had learned that allowed them to penetrate the veil that had hidden them from their sight until now? As he thought about this the biggest question of all entered his mind. How had they succeeded in bringing down the cities so that not a word could get out that they were under attack? These people were not technologically advanced so how would they know what to do to make sure that nothing ever got out of the city once they attacked?

Before he knew it Shayne was standing next to him appearing blurry eyed. "Shayne, you know after reading what you handed me, and then going around and bringing all up to date with this data, I've become more alarmed by the minute. There appears to be more going on than when you first start putting the pieces together. Oh and did I mention it, you look like hell."

"Thanks, I feel that way too . . . and yeah, you too. It's the same with me. I really am worried. From what I can see, it has become easier for these primitives to get inside our cities, and to keep anything from getting out to warn the other cities, they have to be well organized. I mean we know that they can organize for the hunts, and attacks on other tribes. But this is something far beyond such a thing as this. Our smallest cities are larger than five of the tribes combined. Of course if you were to look at only the fighting element of these tribes then it would increase to probably twice that many. We have seen over the years that a couple of tribes would get together to put down a particularly troublesome group, but rarely more than that. It's like they can only stay aligned a short time before they begin to fight each other. These actions show a change and one we know absolutely nothing about. Because of this, we now are paying the price of this ignorance. I had really thought that we really were keeping track of what the primitives were doing, but this has left me knowing that our intelligence gathering is truly lacking."

"Yes, that's obvious. But we were unaware that the program that we are under no longer exists in the other cities. There is no way that we could cover this whole world from here. It is, or was the responsibility of each city to provide intelligence from their local area. It now appears that as time went on that such a thing was no longer considered necessary, except here. So now we are paying the price of complacency and of dropping our vigilance."

"I couldn't have said it better. I never realized that we were it either. I've been sending out reports as required as long as I've been in charge. And I know my predecessor did the same. Who would have guessed that this information was going nowhere, and it had been a waste of time to submit these reports?" Shaking his head Shayne continued, "Now what? We are up against something unknown, and obviously quite dangerous. How are we with our small group going to be able to defeat what is causing this? If we had other teams from the other cities there would be a better chance of solving this. But it's just us." With that stated it shook him to his very core. He had always thought that there would be additional help from the other cities if some major crisis developed. Well, a major crisis had developed and there would be no help, absolutely none at all.

Now deep in thought the two walked the compound heading for commons to make contact with others. It would be a few hours yet before they met at the meeting after the evening meal. Looking around they could see the serious worried expressions on all that they passed. With the weight of decision lying upon them, the afternoon drug by slowly, but eventually it was time for the meeting. This was to be a fact-finding session, attempting to come up with some ideas as to how to tackle this with such a small group overall.

* * *

As he prepared for sleep, Shayne felt that after the meeting that they had made a good start, but knew that was all. There had been many a good idea thrown out. Now they had to find the best of them that fit the circumstances, as they knew them right now. But, be willing to make adjustments on the fly as new facts and situations became known. This was not going to be easy at all. Just what was it that had revealed that first city to the primitives? And then what had these primitives found that revealed the other cities to them? He had no answers at all and it worried him, and even the assumption that it was the primitives causing this was just a guess. Tomorrow they would be sending out an advanced scouting unit to see if anything could be learned. At least the way out of the area for him, and his teams, was well hidden.

There was a cave system that lay to the south edge of their manmade wilderness. It was well hidden with a door that appeared to be nothing more than any of the many boulders and rocks that covered the hillside. What had surprised the ones in the past who had discovered the cave complex was the sheer size. It appeared that the whole small mountain was hollowed out sometime in the distant past. It could have been the results of ice or maybe an extinct volcano. Whatever had caused it, it had left at least one large grotto somewhere towards the center. They had found three points that one could enter or exit and these had been disguised and hidden well. It was the way the teams who researched the wilds left and entered. They had explored the whole region to make sure that there was no place that someone on the outside could observe a team leaving one of the two exits that lay outside the city. At those two exit points there had been some observation ports cut in the past that allowed anyone from inside the caves to observe the outside areas.

The grotto area housed their special equipment and was large enough to hold the entire force. So if the unthinkable ever happened then they could hide until they could then leave safely. Speaking of the equipment, it was probably time to check the portable units completely. He thought that, most likely, they would be using everything that was stored there. This was to be an operation that involved all, and that had never been done before. How had they gone from being comfortable and secure to this state, and all in one day? And why had it taken so long for this information to get to him? He thought that if they had received this information after the second city had gone silent that there was a chance that they could have discovered what was going on, how they had been discovered, and then been working towards a solution – leaving the possibility that the last two cities would not have gone silent at all. Sighing, he knew he wasn't going to solve this tonight, and if he was to be coherent tomorrow he needed to get to sleep. So finally climbing into bed he tried to relax.

But his mind just would not stop. So for what seemed to be an eternity he tossed and turned, and then somewhere during all of this mental turmoil finally fell asleep.

* * *

Something awoke him and he did not know what it might have been. It was still dark out but he could tell that dawn was just about to arrive. Questioning himself again, just what had awakened him? Then he realized that something just did not feel right, but he did not know what it was. Now alarmed he jumped out of bed, quickly dressed, and went out into the courtyard. When he arrived he found that he was not alone. He was not the only one who felt that something was amiss. Then it hit him. It was the silence. There was always a background hum coming from the city and now it was silent. Then it hit him hard. He suspected that this city was about to be attacked and somehow the enemy had shut down all the power to the city leaving it completely open and vulnerable. Now there would be no time for planning, and with his small force, he would not be able to help any in the city. He first thought of his sister and their close ties, and knew he could do nothing to help her or her family. Shaking his head he grabbed the nearest person standing there and told him to wake everyone and to head for the grotto. If they were going to help any of the citizens of this city or the other cities that had gone dark, they would need to survive. Now being a hero and charging into this city would only bring them death and expose the rest to capture.

He admonished the people he grabbed to keep it quiet and to get to the grotto as quickly as possible. He could see shadows as his teams began their near silent exodus out of the compound to the caves – his only hope that they would be there before they were found. As the sky grayed he then heard the attack begin and shuddered inside knowing that people were both dying and having worse things happen to them, and there was absolutely nothing he or any of this group could do to slow or even stop it from happening. Again he thought of his sister and her family and almost cried out in anguish over his helplessness. He knew that the same thing was probably going through the minds of most of the people here. They all had family or loved ones in that city and they could do nothing to save them. Why had this attack come so close on the heels of the fall of the other city? One thing for sure he had his answer. No longer would he have to speculate on what was happening. He now had direct proof.

He and the rest now had to close their ears to what they were hearing. They could hear the screams and cries of the residents of the city as the primitives began attacking the residences. Could they get to the caves before they were discovered? Shayne swept the compound to make sure it was clear, and he remained as the rear guard to insure that all were ahead of him and retreating to the grotto. Even with the chaos within the compound they continued to move quietly and quickly with purpose. For this he was proud of them. It would have been so easy to panic, and to add additional noise to their movement, increasing the chances of being discovered. As he entered the edge of their artificial wilderness he saw some of the primitives coming over the wall. They had gotten out just in time. He hid behind a tree and then sped down one of the many pathways that ran throughout the area. He then came up against the hill turned left, went through a number of heavy bushes, then around a boulder which had a tree next to it. Once around the tree he entered the cave complex and closed the door behind him, and locked it. He then headed down towards the grotto and the growing crowd around him. What had surprised him more than the attack was the number of primitives that were coming over the wall. It appeared to have been enough to equal at least two tribes. And this would have included all the women and children, and old people. Yet, these appeared to have been ones who were male and were of fighting age. Yes something had changed and it bode badly for them and the cities.

He could feel the fear, confusion, and suddenly a sense of anger running through the crowd. Then one of the young members yelled, "Why are we running? They are attacking our city! Are we cowards, just hiding while our families are being killed and who knows what? Come on we have been training for this."

Shaking his head he could understand the sentiment. But if they went back out to meet the primitives then all they would be doing was throwing their lives away and solving nothing. Now the best courses of action was to admit that they would fail here, but hopefully in the end, find a solution, and save others. There was absolutely nothing that could be done to save their loved ones at all. Turning towards the one who had voiced his concern Shayne said. "I understand exactly what your feelings are, but understand this, if we were to go out there, we would just be throwing our lives away accomplishing nothing. If you do not believe this I want you and someone else, someone of your choice, to climb up there and look out onto the grounds and tell the rest here what you see." Then seeing some reluctance on the part of the speaker he then said, "This is not a suggestion this is an order. You need to see for yourself what we are up against. Then with you and the other you can come back down and let the rest know what you have seen. Now go and be back down in no more than ten minutes." We do not know how long it may be before our escape may be discovered." He then watched as the individual with another of his choice headed up the pathway and then up the ladders to the observation point. Once there he watched them pull back the cover and saw both of them visibly flinch. Then he saw their shoulders slump, and he knew that now they also knew that it was hopeless and if indeed had they returned to the compound then they would have either been captured or killed. He watched as the two slowly closed the port and made their way back to the waiting group. The one who had protested spoke in a subdued voice said. "You were right. If we had been waiting and tried to help we would now be either dead or captured. There is nothing we can do. I have never seen that many primitives. We barely would make a dent in the tide if we each had killed ten of them." Then with a look of desperation he asked, "What has happened, what has changed? I don't understand at all. How are we going to be able to do anything against that horde? How are we going to be able to prevent this from happening to the other cities? We are not a warlike people."

Shayne could see the hopelessness showing in the faces of his teams. Then again shaking his head he stated. "I wish I had an answer for you. But I had only learned of the threat yesterday. I have no answers, solutions, or even an understanding of what has changed. But know this, we are going to try and solve this. Solving this is for a future time, now we have to escape and survive. So we will be on the run for a while. This will be hard and dangerous, as we must find our way to one of the remaining sister cities if possible. I am sure the alarm is already been given out since our city has gone silent. We are the fifth. I just hope that we do not lose too many more before we are able to change the situation. It is now obvious that we have become complacent and have allowed something to change. By not being vigilant we have now paid the price. If we are to prevent the ending of our cities and us then we cannot go on as before. Understand this, we are going to escape, and we are going to survive. This road ahead of us will not be easy. But you have to understand this; we must stick together, fight together, and work together. I believe that we are the only chance that the remaining cities have. So we must survive. Now let's work towards the hidden exit . . . and yes we are going to take all of our equipment. I have a strong feeling that we will need it in the upcoming escape, followed by whatever plans we come up with, due to changes in the situation. We need to go with stealth. One last thing . . ." He paused then dropped his voice to almost a whisper before continuing. " . . . When we survive this and then find out what has led to this change, we are going to eliminate the cause, and then hopefully be able to rescue our families and friends that have survived this attack, and of course the members of the other four fallen cities. I am sure that they have been enslaved and their lives will be pure hell, not much different than ours from this point on. We will at least have our freedom, something that they will not. But if we are captured then everything we have worked for and now working towards will be in vain, and the hopelessness of our people will be complete. As long as we are out there they have something to hope for. Now let's move and get as far away from here as we can. Be prepared for anything. These primitives are not stupid, and they live in that world. It's a world that we have only played in. They have the advantage, and as such we must learn quickly or we ourselves will be no more." At this point he turned to his second and said, "Let's get moving. I really have no idea if the primitives will find a way in here or not. I don't want to be here if they do."

At the end of his statement, the teams began the hike through the caves to the hidden exit lying on the backside of the hillside. The exit was located in a dead end canyon where there was a large rock face. At the point of the exit, the canyon was choked with small trees and brush – giving the appearance that it was impenetrable, and nothing of value to make it a place to go and explore anyway. The one danger to this blind canyon lay with its opening. A small group could keep anyone in the canyon from escaping. But since there appeared to be nothing of value here, it had always been felt that no one would ever take the time to even explore it. Then, once beyond the canyon entrance there was at least three ways out, making it more difficult for any that would want to follow, to know the direction they would take. As they neared the exit from the caves they released the small drones that would appear to be nothing more than birds. So if any were actually there the watchers would not give these drones a second thought. As they monitored the drones they saw a single primitive watching up on the ridgeline. "Okay I need one of the better scout teams to go out there and take out that single observer. And be very quiet about it. We cannot afford an alarm to go out." There was a pause and then Shayne continued, "Saige, Shellian, you two are the best we have, I think you two will go out and take care of the primitive. Once you are in position we will send two more out to grab his attention to make it easier for you. Let's get this done."

The exit was opened just enough to allow Saige and Shellian out, then immediately closed. They slowly worked themselves up tight against the canyon wall that would hide them from the observer. Using hand signals they carefully worked their way down the length of the canyon and took the right branch, continuing to keep the primitive out of view. Of course by doing this it meant that they couldn't keep tabs on the observer, so they really had no idea if he was staying where he had been first observed. If he had moved then they could be walking right to where he was and be seen. Luck held with them, as at one point they were able to briefly view the primitive. Since they now were closer they could see that he appeared to be a youth, probably out on his first raid. If they had anything to say about it, it would be his last.

* * *

Kor had been disappointed. At first he was excited when he had been informed that he would join the raiding party. It would be his first, and to be able to join the warriors in battle had always been his dream, and now it appeared it was coming true. He also thought that he might have his first female then also. Yet when they approached the area he had been assigned this duty to be a watchman. A watchman . . . that is a child's job . . . not a warrior's. What made it worse lay in the fact that he was completely isolated, and knew that there would be nothing happening here at all. There was only a flier or two now and then. This place was desolate, nothing to interest one. Why had he been given this assignment when all the action was on the other side of these hills? The sun had been rising for quite a while and it was dead silent, nothing, just nothing was happening. So bored, he glanced around, picked up some pebbles and tossed them over the side to watch them as they cascaded down the side, creating small landslides with the loose soil that rained down to the canyon bottom. He was about to throw another over the side when some movement caught his attention. Unbelieving he saw two females coming down that dead end canyon. Where had they come from? He worked himself up to the edge so he could watch them. He wanted to see where they were going. Maybe he would have his first female anyway, and who knew maybe two. With a wicked smile on his face he concentrated on the pair as they stumbled down the canyon coming closer to his location. Deciding it was time to move he stood up to begin his approach only to hear something behind him. As he turned he felt himself being pushed. He fought hard to regain his balance since he was standing on the edge, but realized that there was no way he would be able to prevent the fall. Screaming once he fought hard to regain his balance, but then slipped over the side and then fell to his death.

* * *

Saige stood there with Shellian next to him and looked down and waved at the two women. He wouldn't have thought to do it that way. But now that he thought about it, it had made perfect sense to send out only women making it appear that they would be vulnerable easy targets, something that a young primitive would concentrate totally on, not thinking that it was an ambush. His estimation in the capabilities of Shayne just rose. By doing it this way they would be out of the area with none the wiser. And with the body of the primitive at the base of a cliff, it would appear to any that he had simply slipped and fallen. As long as they covered their tracks and left no evidence then there would be nothing to alert the attacking force. With a signaling wave the two women headed back to the cave exit and signaled the rest that it was now safe to exit. Fortunately the craft they had were partially hovercraft and as such, would not leave any tracks. Because of the noise they were only used in this mode when there was no other choice. The craft would normally navigate on six wheels. At the back of the group were the trackers with the responsibility of wiping out any sign that they had been here. Now it would become more difficult. Shayne signaled Saige and Shellian to join the teams and then sent out a scouting group ahead of them. He would also have teams of out runners and flankers to both sides and the trackers taking up the rear position. Now once they were in the canyon networks ahead there was a greater chance to escape. Yet, he knew that they were far from safe. After all if there had been a lookout posted here, there was a great chance that there would be others.

No one spoke, and any communications were completed strictly through hand signals. Silence now was their friend, and any noise could compromise their position. So quickly and with stealth they moved into the center canyon. From here this one branched in four different directions. Initially their direction would be west. This would lead them deeper into the wilds. Once there they would have time to set up camp look at their options and figure out which city to head towards. They had to survive, as now they knew what was happening and who generally was responsible for the disappearance of the cities. They were the only ones who truly knew. But were they good enough to avoid the primitives and get this important information where it needed to go? Shayne knew that the nearest city was many weeks away. But it may be that it would serve them better to head for one that was still further away. There had been such a short time between the fall of the previous city and theirs that by the time they could reach the next closest city it may have become a victim of the primitives and could easily have fallen also.

At least with the canyon complex they were working through, the further along they proceeded, with the many additional branching directions they took, the less of a chance they had of being discovered. Shayne, as did the rest of the team, knew it was a desperate time since the primitives could only continue to be successful if the remaining cities were kept ignorant as to what had been happening to the ones disappearing and going silent. While he had these thoughts running through his mind one of the forward scouts signaled back that there was a small force of primitives ahead of them and these appeared to be seasoned warriors, not the young one that had been watching the canyon they came out of. He signaled for one of the forward scouts to come in and let him know what they were facing. Turning to the rest of the team he signaled for complete silence and all of their equipment was shut down. Fortunately most of the craft they were bringing with them was still hidden. Everyone else faded into the surrounding sparse vegetation and waited for the signal to move. There was a heavy tension in the air as they all were aware that their lives were on the line, and they were far from successful in leaving the area unscathed. Shayne, waiting until the scout was close enough that the sign language they used would be easily recognizable, He then signed, "What are we facing, and can we get around them?"

The scout answering back said, "It appears to be twenty to twenty five warriors, and it appears that they were recently in a fight. They seem to be on alert, but presently are not moving."

"Can we move around them without being seen or heard?"

"I don't really think so. They are right in the middle of the main canyon floor where it splits in the four directions. I think we will have to wait until they move. Possibly, if they were not so alert and expecting anything . . . but I suspect they are there to cut off anyone who escapes from the city, you know like us."

Shaking his head Shayne then signed back, "Okay then keep us informed, stay out of sight, and if anything changes let me know. We cannot fight them as it would give us away, and by these primitives believing they have everyone, it is the only way we have a chance."

The scout signaled his affirmative, and then disappeared back the way he had come. Shayne coming back to the team then signed that they were stuck and would have to remain in the stealth mode for who knew how long. He knew that every second they stayed this close to the fallen city the greater chance of discovery. But what could they do, if they attacked the group, they would give themselves away, if they waited they could be discovered which would result in the same thing. So throughout the day they sat quietly, nervously, praying that no one would not come along and check on the one they had killed, and that this other group of warriors would move soon.

CHAPTER FOUR

Keenan was shocked. He was in charge of his section of the communications center that kept the many cities linked, and within two days two additional cities had gone silent. No explanation, no warning, nothing. While each city had their own individual communications, theirs was the hub where all the cities, that still existed, kept in contact with each other. He had his suspicions, but again had no proof. What exactly was going on? At this rate by the end of this annual all the cities could be gone. With no proof he couldn't even put forth his theories. He knew they would just laugh at him, saying something like, "Look at it. Almost all of the cities that have gone silent have been in one area of the continent. So some natural disaster must have befallen them. After all with our technology we are well hidden from the primitives, and there is no way it could be them anyway. We've been able to put the fear into them that we are from their primitive gods so are off limits."

He had to admit that their arguments were valid enough, but these arguments just didn't feel right, and they did not really fit in the pattern as he saw it. Well it was time to go over to the one above him and report the loss. Sighing, and then shaking his head he knew that it would be just filed and he would be told to forget about it. "Sometime soon a valid answer would be found, and please no more of your stupid theories." Had they as a people become so complacent that even with disaster looking them in the face they could not see it? For that he had no answer. He just hoped that what they were saying as the probable cause was correct, and what his theories were, was not. Yet, he had this nagging feeling that he was absolutely right . . . yet . . . with no proof he was just going in circles. "By the gods!" he yelled, "What is going on?" Looking around he saw the startled looks on the ones who worked under him. He then responded, "Sorry team. It's just something is happening to our people and the ones over us are going on as if nothing has changed and nothing has happened. It seems that they are denying all of this. I feel that they are going to do this even if it happens to us. And then wonder what happened?" Shaking his head again he headed out the door to report his findings knowing again that it was futile.

Kellen received the news from Keenan with little acknowledgement leaving Keenan frustrated with the response he received. But there was little he could do about it. With foreboding he then headed back to his section completely at loss as to what to do or where to go. This lack of concern on any of the leaders' part could lead them all to disaster. Kellen, immediately after Keenan left, could see the anger on his face, but he had been specifically told to make it appear to be something minor. Yet he was very worried, and once he knew that Keenan had left he went out with no explanation to his underworker and went to report to the next higher up. Again what was causing their cities to disappear like this? They had been safe and hidden for generations, why now? What had changed? Why was there no communications or at least refugees from these silent cities? Of course the distances between them could be part of the answer, since the portable communications devices were of very short range. Only the major communications centers within the cities allowed direct contact between all of them. So there may not have been enough time for someone from one of the silent cities to get close enough to use the short-range devices or even reach one of the other cities as of yet.

Still it was a worrisome thing, and with little facts and no information what could their response be? And if it turned out to be war, well that would be a bad thing, since they did not even have an army to defend their way of life. There had been no need for such a thing. Their technology had kept them safe to pursue other endeavors. Now if it came down to fighting for their very lives could they do it? He knew that their city, Keahilani, had shut down their wilderness project, oh, at least 10 annuals ago. It seemed to be something they no longer had a need of. Were they wrong? He had to admit he had no answers for any of the many questions that this emergency brought forth, none at all.

* * *

Shayne signed back to the team what the forward scouts had passed on to him. "The scouts stated that a small group of what appears to be warriors just came into the area and appear to be hanging around. Fortunately it was after we had killed the one enemy so they are not alerted at the present to either our location or us. We do not know if they are here just by chance or are here to collect the one we killed. Every moment we have to stay here gives them a better chance of discovering either the entrance into the caverns or finding us. We cannot take them out, as it would then alert the primitives that someone has escaped. So we must just wait, and pray that they do not find us. Keep it silent and continue using sign language." He could feel as well as see the tension and fear in his team. Would they be successful in their escape or be caught?

Time continued to drag as they waited for the scouts to inform them that the war party had moved on, but none had been forthcoming so far. As the morning crept along and nothing seemed to be happening, Shayne could see that many were becoming restless and wanted to do something, anything. The waiting was becoming unbearable with discovery likely at any moment. Finally as they reached mid-morning the "all clear" sign was given. Shayne turned back to the group and signed to them to wait, as he would go forward to confirm. He then left, and again what seemed like an eternity he finally returned and signaled for the team to move out. The warriors had left the area, and apparently were not there to collect the one lookout from here. They then continued to push west through the major canyon complex. Every additional branch of these many canyons increased their chances. They knew by nightfall that they had to be completely out of the area. With heavy hearts and with some distance between them and their lost city they looked back and saw smoke rising. Some of their beloved city was burning, but from the amount of the smoke they could tell that it was not the whole city. Without power the fire extinguishing equipment would not work. It was a sign to them that they would never be able to return here and presently they were a people without a home. As far as they knew they were the last of their city. They really did not know if any of their city had lived through the attack. They suspected that it was a possibility but there was no proof. These thoughts weighed heavily on them as they worked through the canyons further from their home that would be no more.

That night with the day full of avoiding roving groups of primitives they finally found shelter in a small copse of trees and within a small stream ran merrily on its way. But none of the team felt joy in the sounds of the stream as it bubbled over rocks on its way to who knew where. They were exhausted; beat, both physically and emotionally. Had it been only this morning when their city had fallen? It seemed like a lifetime, and that they had always been on the move, dodging and hiding. They ate a cold meal afraid to have a fire, or anything that would give them away. Shayne set up watches for the night wanting them changed every couple of hours. They had to be alert and any member on guard duty for longer than that could become careless. And carelessness was something they could not afford. There was little talk, as most seemed to be asleep on their feet. So after eating most fell into an exhausted sleep.   At this point there had been no young ones to complicate their escape. Although a few of the women that were coupled were early in carrying their first child, and if they went full term before they were able to enter another city there could be problems. Walking among the sleeping team members Shayne was very worried. He knew that the next few weeks were going to be hell. They always had had the city to fall back on and now it was gone. Would they be good enough to be able to completely survive without its support? For this he had no answer, or was likely not to find an easy one. He missed a hot cup of shick. He liked it strong, bitter and very hot. It seemed to help him keep going. But he knew that they would be eating cold meals for many days to come and until they could build a fire he and all the rest would be without it.

Then it came to his mind that now they were going to find out rather quickly if they were good enough to avoid the roving patrols of the primitives. Whoever was presently in charge of these primitives seemed to have some military sense about him. Everything that he had witnessed showed discipline, organization, and precision in carrying out the attacks, the posting of watches, and the roving patrols. It had to be that way or else someone from the city could escape and alert others to what was happening, and thusly change things, making it harder for these attacking forces. *Just what is this unknown person offering the tribes that he seems to be uniting?* Then while on this track of thinking Shayne thought, *we have to find out who this one is the ones who directly support him, and then find a way to either eliminate him, or at least make the rest of the newly aligned tribes to become distrustful.* At this point his mind became too clouded with fatigue to continue so he found a place on the ground and like the rest fell into an exhausted sleep.

It seemed like only minutes when he was awakened, but it was just before dawn and they had to be up and moving out of the area. It was going to be difficult to eliminate any sign that they had been here. They were just too large of a group. While he had them spread out to take care of the morning nature call he knew that with the amount left behind that there would be a scent that could draw the primitives right to their campsite. With that in mind, he assigned a group to cover the wet spots with soil and leaves to help hide their passing of the area. Again with hand signals they headed out, with scouts out front and to the rear, and out-runners or flankers to both sides. It was a cool and very clear morning with a light haze in the distance. It was going to be a very long day. They would be moving from now, before the sunrise, to after the sunset. It presently was the late summer months, and the daylight period was much longer than the night.

* * *

After a week of dodging patrols and putting much distance between themselves and their starting point Shayne finally called a halt. They were presently in a small hidden valley that would provide them shelter for a few days before they continued. Looking around he could see the haunted expressions on many of the faces. There had been too many close calls in their escape. But so far their luck had held and as far as they knew they had been undiscovered. Shayne knew that their luck would fail at some point so immediately had the members practice their combat skills. Then Shayne and Skylar would call in the teams of two and start going over strategies to infiltrate the unknown leader's camp of the primitive alliance. Somehow they had to gather intelligence, and find ways to bring it down. Otherwise their way of life was complete, finis, over, done, or whatever other word came to mind. Plus, now that the escape had been successful, it was time to find an uninhabited area and set up their village. They had to blend in and appear to nothing other than one of the many primitive tribes. It would have to be their base of operation, and it needed to be somewhat close to the alliance but not so close as to make them a target since they were not to be a part of the alliance.

While this was happening they would send out two teams of two to head for different cities and hope that these teams reached the cities before the primitives did. Yet all of this was in the future. As of right now they hadn't completely escaped, close, but not yet. All he could hope for was that the equipment they used would remain undiscovered, and if found by the primitives, it would immediately give them away as being from the cities. Again, because of the short-range communications devices within these units, they needed to be much closer to one of their sister cities so that they could communicate over the airwaves.

This led him to thinking about the differences between the cities and the primitives. Why the two differences? If the history taught in their learning centers had been accurate, and who knew for sure, since history is rewritten over time to fit the present leaders, and the ones who did the writings – yet this written history said that at one time they were all one people. All advanced, with no primitives. There were factions within and eventually somewhere along the time line war had broken out involving the whole world. Some seeing the futility of such an action vowed to remove themselves from the fighting and try and preserve what they had. It is unknown how they accomplished it, but from their actions the cities came into existence and remained outside of the fighting and the death and destruction. Hidden in the desolate untraveled areas, it became *the time of isolation*. As the war raged outside of this isolation they continued to thrive and develop methods that would hide their cities. Then eventually the wars ended and the remnant of those who had fought in those many wars had reduced them back to a primitive way of life. And this way of life had remained as it was presently for hundreds of turns around their sun. It appeared that the primitives would always remain so, with no desire to rise above whom and what they were. So as time had continued, as it always does, the cities remained hidden – observing their once brothers and sisters and remaining unseen.

A commotion brought him out of his thoughts and he quickly looked around to see what was happening. They were under attack! Where had the attackers come from? No time for questions or answers now! It was time to fight or anything they had planned for the future would be naught, and if they did not get out of the area safely, then none of the other cities would ever be safe. As these thoughts ran through his mind he saw one of his team go down under a spear. That was the last direct image head had as it became complete chaos around him as they desperately fought. It seemed that an hour must have passed but he knew it could only be a few minutes in truth. Soon, their training paid off, and they were able to overcome the attacking primitives. He immediately sent out hand signals to search the area and to allow none of the primitives to escape. If they did then their own escape would end here, as the alliance would be alerted to their presence.

As he caught his breath he first wondered how they were found. He thought that they were well hidden. Looking around at the team he was proud of what he saw as without a word they were looking after any that had been wounded in the brief battle. He was glad that these primitives that had attacked them seemed to be a small group. Probably one of the many patrols that this new alliance had working the countryside, and eliminating any competition. What worried him lay in both the discovery of their location, and while yes they had succeeded in overcoming the small patrol, it had proved more difficult than it should have been. They had been lucky. In fact the only severe injury was the first one he had seen before the chaos. The one who had been speared had been lucky, as the spear had missed any vital organs and major blood vessels, but still he had lost a lot of blood, and seemed to be breathing rapidly and appeared to be somewhat pale. The rest of the injuries seemed to be flesh wounds, cuts and scrapes. Turning to the group once it had been confirmed that all the primitives were indeed dead he said. "Okay, I guess we've now had our first taste of battle. I myself did not care for it, but our training seems to have paid off. Still, we were lucky once again, as this was a small force. I believe that had it been a larger scouting party that we would be the dead ones." He let that comment soak into them before continuing. "How we were located I do not know, but it shows that we are not as good as we thought. So if we are to survive, we must get better. Now bury those primitives, take whatever we can from them, as we may need the items, and then prepare to leave. It is obvious we cannot stay here. If we did we would be very foolish indeed. I do not know how much time we have, but I can guarantee that once this group is missed they would be searched for."

"Shayne?"

"Yes Saige what is it that you want to ask?"

"How would the primitives leave their enemy's bodies? Would they bury them as you proposed, or would they strip them and mutilate the bodies? So in their afterlife they could not attack the other spirits."

"Ah I see your point. If we bury them we would be giving ourselves away that we are not a part of this world but of the cities. Okay let's follow what these primitives would do and get out of here."

* * *

The following days and weeks indeed turned into hell as the words he had spoken became true. They found themselves fighting for their very lives as they continued to be pushed further from their goal and deeper into the untamed wilds. Each fight, each ambush left them weaker as some fell to these attacks. In one of the last desperate fights they lost half of their remaining healthy members. Even the leader Shayne was severely wounded. The second in charge had been killed only the previous day. Shayne, before this fight, had then placed the sister and brother, Shellian and Saige as seconds. But if this continued then it would not matter as they would perish and any of the knowledge they had would perish with them.

That evening Shayne called the two to his side and stated that most likely he would not live out the night. He was very pale and his breathing ragged – they could see desperation in his eyes when he knew that he would not be able to continue to lead their small band of refugees. Shellian then said, "Shayne, I know that you have been hurt and your injuries are bad. But you must survive. Who else could lead us? I mean you have taught us how to survive and how to depend on each other. It is you who is the heart, strength and soul to us. You are our leader."

He could see the pleading in her eyes but he felt the truth deep down inside of him. He knew that even with what they had medically, that the wound he had received, in the end would be fatal. Without the access to one of the cities they did not have the means to stop the slow bleeding that was happening inside of him. And he could feel his strength leaving him as his blood loss continued. Smiling up at her, even though it was a weak smile at best, he said weakly, "I have always been a realist. I have been given no special protection or immunity from what has happened to our city and to us. So why should I be any different than the rest of you?"

"But Shayne!" she exclaimed, "You are our leader. If you die how will we continue? We all look up to you. You're the one who gives us confidence, the one we draw our strength from, and the one with the knowledge . . ."

Interrupting by laying his hand on her Shayne said. "Shellian, Shellian, there is nothing I can do to change what has happened." Then catching his breath he continued, "It will now fall to the two of you to take over for me. I do not know what lies on the other side of this physical death, but I do hope there is something. If so some day we will have a chance to meet again. But for whatever reason my time is coming to an end. I believe we are all here for some purpose. I never knew what mine was, and I guess now I will never know, but please . . ." His tone in his voice dropped as they could again see the desperation in his eyes. " . . . Please get any part of this team safely out of here. We are being forced into the mountains and away from any of our other sister cities. It may be that we . . . you will have to survive there for a long time . . ." He then drifted off to unconsciousness without completing his thought. Shellian and Saige looked at each other, Saige being too heavy of heart to say anything at all. This seemed like the end, and for Shayne it was as he quietly slipped from this world as they watched.

Sister and brother looked at each other and neither spoke, as they could not believe he was gone. Shayne had been their leader from the beginning – well at least as long as they had been around. His knowledge and strength seemed indomitable. How could it be that he was to be one of the ones killed as they ran their desperate escape from these primitives? What were they going to do? How were they going to survive? Just what was to be their fate? It seemed that a dark cloud now hung over everything. They had lost two thirds of their numbers on this escape, and had to abandon their mobile units – no longer having the number of members to be able to operate them. Plus it was slowing them down and now speed and stealth was of the essence.

Suddenly they both realized that someone had been speaking to them. Looking up from their overwhelming grief they realized that the woman who had been caring for Shayne and had witnessed his end was asking them something. "Again I ask, now what? What are we going to do?" Looking at her they both could see the pain in her eyes and they reflected that it was probably the same if they could look into a mirror and see their own. Neither had an answer but they both knew that whether wanted nor desired, Shayne's last request was for the two of them to lead the remaining members to safety if at all possible.

Saige then said. "First we must lay our leader to rest." Then breathing deeply and turning to his sister he continued. "Shellian, go inform the others of Shayne's passing. I fear we do not have much time to us and we are going to have to leave this place before the sunrise if we are to survive." Again pausing and then coming to a decision, he realized at that moment that all of the older generation was gone. It was difficult to realize that now they were the older generation here, but indecision here would and could finish them. "We must, as Shayne requested, head into the mountains. It will probably be our only salvation. For some reason that we have never been able to discover, these mountains are a sacred and a feared place with these primitives. They rarely venture into them. When they do, it is usually their holy men only. So it may be that these mountains can be our sanctuary."

Shellian stood there unable to move. It was obvious to Saige that she was on the verge of tears as was the other woman who had been caring for Shayne. He had to admit it himself that he too was emotionally drained. But if they did not get moving and soon it would not matter as they all would be joining Shayne much too soon, and if that happened then they would have failed completely. He walked over to his sister and gave her a hug. She clung to him with her head on his shoulder. She seemed to be shaking and he realized that indeed she was crying. He found that the other woman had joined them and she too had tears flowing. He thought he should say something but could come up with nothing to say that would comfort any of them. So they just hung together for what seemed like a long time. Finally pushing them gently away from him he said. "I'll go out and let the rest know. Please prepare our leader for burial and I will get the rest started in digging his grave. I truly fear that we do not have as much time to honor him, as we should. But in the end I think he will understand." He then turned and left the small shelter they were in leaving the two women alone.

* * *

Had it been just 14 days since they had lost Shayne? It seemed more like an eternity as they continued to be harassed by the primitives. At times it seemed that they had lost them only to be struck by a small patrol. Yet, now they were finally entering the foothills, and the patrols seemed to be less and of smaller parties. But that did not seem to lessen the danger. It appeared that many of these groups were much better prepared and wilderness wise than many that they had evaded when they were barely outside of the city. The city, now it was hard to even remember much about it, as the continual fear, fighting, running and hiding appeared to be their life now. It was as if the other life they had known was no more than a dream. And who knew – maybe it was. And what they were now involved with had been their true life. Saige, looking around to the remainder of the team thought that they had come so far. Although looking at them one would not have guessed such a thing. The clothes that they wore was ragged, torn, dirty and worn. And the bodies wearing the clothes looked no better. Eyes sunken from too little sleep and food, skin dirty from not being able to bath, and a fear that seemed to permeate the group, each wondering if they would be the next to fall. Still they had learned. And Saige thinking back thought that when they were still in their compound that they knew so much. Now he knew that what they knew there had been no more than child's games. So proud of their skills and abilities that they had looked down on the ones actually living in the cities. Shaking his head all he could say now was – "How ignorant we all were. How proud we were of the abilities. How much we believed that we could match the primitives and because of our superior society and equipment that there was no way that the primitives could beat us." Well it had all been proven false. So here they were running and fighting for their very lives.

Saige, crouching down behind a boulder that sat on top of a hill, looked out over the valley that they would have to traverse. Camping down by a stream that ran through the center of the valley was one of the numerous patrols. Shaking his head and pulling back away from the hilltop he signaled the team to head back to the copse of trees. He then joined them and said, "Okay we have a real problem. From what I can see there is only one way through this valley and they are camped right next to that route. I need a couple of you to monitor them, and for heaven's sake, do not be seen. I'm going to send a couple of others to scout to either side and see if there is another way through here. But unfortunately it seems that everything has pushed us here. I know from what we have seen that there is a good possibility that we once pass this point, will begin our trek into the mountains." Shaking his head and breathing deeply before continuing, "Maybe then we will finally be able to take a day or two and just camp and give everyone a time to rest." Looking down at the ground and then at each that was with him he then said, "Still I can hold no promises for any of us." Then pointing at two of the people with him he said. "Okay I want you two to have the first watch, and then I'll send a couple to relieve you. Unfortunately for all of us, we cannot chance a fire so we will all have travel rations. The one thing I know is that we cannot just stay here. So whether we find an alternate route or have to sneak by this group tonight we must continue to move." He then got up and the rest of the team that was with him headed back to the camp leaving the two to watch.

When they got far enough away from the camping enemy he had the remaining team that was with him spread out and recon the area where they were staying. He needed to be sure that they were hidden. This delay was dangerous. It was time they could ill afford. The mountains were so close now, but still completely out of reach. It would be tragic if they came so close to their goal only to fail. Yet there was very little they could do about it. If it came down to it, that the only way through was where the primitives were camping, then they would just have to figure out how to do it. As the day waned away and the scouting teams reported back it became obvious that this was the only way through the area. Thusly, why it was guarded as it presently seemed to be. So how were they going to be able to continue? One thing for sure they would not be able to backtrack and try and different direction. They had barely avoided a number of patrols and to expect their luck to continue was just too much to expect.

"Now what?" One of the members asked to no one in particular. He was answered with silence. Again this had been a question that had been asked over and over again. They were stuck and no obvious solution had been put forth. Then

Steen said, "I don't know if this would work but what if one of us went down there dressed as a courier with a message that stated that it had appeared that we went a different direction and that they could move to a different location to try and intercept us. Then we could wait for them to pull out and go through safely." One of the others then said, "Right if we have time for them to pull out. You know how close we came to being caught just this morning. I really don't think we can wait that long." Silence fell over the group once again as it seemed like a good idea, but the weakness in it became obvious once it had been pointed out.

Saige asked, "Do any of you have any other suggestions? We need to come up with something quickly as has been stated we are out of time and out of chances."

Sahar followed up by saying, "I thought of one but immediately discarded it. Since the way these primitives are, our women would pay the price – and I for one am not willing for that to happen."

"And what was that Sahar?" Saige asked. "Right now we just don't have anything. So maybe putting it out there where we all can hear it might give someone else and idea." Saige then stood up and started pacing. He could feel the pressure building as each minute passing brought them closer to discovery. Their band was now down to 15 and with such a small force they were at a point that once discovered it probably was over.

Taking a deep breath Sahar paused and then said. "Okay, ahhh . . . I was thinking of guards and prisoners heading through to some unknown destination. But I realized that the women would have to pose as prisoners, which meant . . ."

Here trailed off to silence. He did not need to finish, as they all knew what he meant. While like the other idea it initially seemed good until they realized the consequences. Their women would have to submit to the primitives since they were prisoners and be subject to the whims and needs of the primitives in the camp. And with the diminished size of their group there was no way they could prevent it from happening.

"Okay we have had two ideas put forth, and both have strong points and some very telling weaknesses. Let's see if we can strengthen either and try and eliminate the negatives."

About this time as the sun was setting the two who had been watching the camp reported in and stated that it appeared that there were only two guards placed out in a roving patrol. From what they could see they changed them every couple of hours to keep the guards fresh and alert. Otherwise it seemed that most of the remaining primitives remained in camp just lying around.

After they reported in and had given them what they had observed, Saige asked. "How can we put this to our advantage? I am surprised that they are not putting out at least four guards. But maybe it has been so quiet that their guard is down. So they are doing the minimal. Maybe, who knows, waiting to be relieved? This means they may indeed be waiting for a courier to give them new orders. Okay how can we take advantage of what we may be guessing is going on down there?"

Saar, who was their medical person suddenly, looked excited. "Saige what if we take that rotgut alcohol that we stole from one of their villages, spike it with our knockout drug that we extract from some of the native plants, and somehow get them to drink it? Of course the only ones that wouldn't be allowed to drink would be the two guards. But I think it would be easier to deal with just two than all of them down there, don't you think?"

"That's a great idea, and being that they are a patrol getting them to drink shouldn't be a problem. The problem is to keep them from being suspicious. Okay everybody we have many parts here, let's work something out quickly. We need to be moving as soon as we can."

* * *

Stone and Sahar approached the primitive camp with trepidation. Stone was elected as the one to pose as the courier and Sahar his guard. They had observed this enough over time to know the exact process. So that part should be easy. But putting oneself directly in contact with the enemy was not something either of them was truly interested in doing. Well, it was too late to back out now as the guard had spotted them. "Guard! Take me to the commander of your patrol. I have a message of importance that must be delivered – For His Eyes Only!" Sahar remained silent trying to look fierce and suspicious. He was to remain silent, as his grasp of the primitive's language was rudimentary at best. Stone could have easily passed as any of the primitives from his skin coloring to his build. So they hoped that it would not raise any questions as to where Sahar may have been from. Still he was a close second to Stone, but a poor second if one really was honest. Sahar carried the backpack that had the spiked booze in it. As of yet they did not know how they were going to pass it on, but hopefully something would be presented that would make it seem natural.

The guard looked them over, but did not say anything. He then gestured for them to follow him. Knowing now to be silent, they followed the guard to the center of the encampment where the guard then went up to one of the largest members who was sitting by the fire. The guard pointing at Stone and Sahar simply stated "courier", he turned and left and went back to his post. Stone waiting, since by the way it appeared to work from their previous studies he, as a courier, was superior to a simple patrol commander. Slowly the commander stood and both his girth and height made both of them feel as if they were children. It was difficult to keep from flinching, but somehow they hid their reaction. "I have a dispatch from the one in charge. Is there a place we can pass this on – as it is for your ears or eyes only! And yes, before you ask, I do know what is in this, since not all commanders can read." He said this last part in a way that made him appear superior to any who could not read: Again knowing that he needed to do this to play his role.

The commander looked at him suspiciously for a moment then shrugged. He then led them off to one side and said. "Okay, here is far enough. Reading is not important in leading a patrol or fighting." He then puffed out his chest and stated, "I have fought and won many a battle and have worked my way to becoming the leader here. For this I do not need to follow any scratches put upon a skin. What is it that you need to pass on? And since you are here you can take one back from me. I am tired of having to sit here and so is the rest of my clan. Nothing is happening here and I suspect it will remain so. Now what do you have?"

"The ones that we pursue have moved to the West and will not be coming through this area. You are to move your patrol to the West and join up with others to continue the pursuit. None must escape. By keeping our enemy ignorant, only then, can we conquer all. That's all it says." Stone then held his breath to see how the commander would respond worried that they had put something in the dispatch that would tip him off. But then he saw a big smile on the commander's face and knew that they may just be successful.

"I told them they wouldn't come this way, but no, they said that this was the only way through this area and needed to be guarded. We played a game of chance to see who would pull this duty and I lost. Now maybe we will see some action." Then shaking his head he continued. "Now if we only had something to drink and some females to celebrate this."

How had this worked out? The commander was practically begging for alcohol and he happened to have it. Smiling at the commander he said. "I cannot provide the females for your pleasure, but coming this way we . . ." He paused and put a look of conspiracy on his face before continuing. "Well let's say I felt that such a patrol as yours needed something to help celebrate this change of plans. And since no one will know exactly when I arrived to pass on your new orders, then there is no reason not to enjoy the night and leave in the morning."

"Am I to believe that you are going to provide us with something to drink? This is highly unusual."

Careful now, Stone quickly thought, and then said. "Ah yes, these are unusual times are they not? Who would of thought that the many tribes who have fought each other are now allied and working together?"

Nodding his head in agreement the commander asked. "True, true, so where is this *drink* that you are offering us?

Turning to Sahar he said, "Guard please pass on to the commander the supply that we requisitioned."

Bowing to Stone Sahar knelt down, removed his backpack and proceeded to empty it. Stone then said, "I am sorry that there is not as much here for all to get a complete enjoyment from it but it is war and many things are hard to find."

"As you said it is war and we had nothing. So now we have something. Are you going to stay with us since it is almost dark?"

"No, no, can't, as there is another patrol that is to the east of you that must be informed. So I must be on my way immediately   by your leave." Stone then did a short bow to the commander turned around and left the encampment. Trying to make it appear to be as one who needs to be somewhere else quickly, but not so quick to raise suspicions, after all having succeeded to this point and to be too much in a hurry could give the whole thing away. Once a little distance had been placed between the two of them and the encampment Stone stated softly so only Sahar could hear, "I, for one, am glad that we did not go with the other plan that had been put forth. We only have six surviving women with our group now and to have at least 30 in that camp that would want to use them is just too much to think about. I really doubt if they would have survived the ordeal."

"I can't disagree with that statement at all. I have to always remember that as far as these primitives go, women, or females as they call them, have no names, are property, and like the grazing animals are there to both be protected by the males and bred by them. And as far as they are concerned that is as far as it goes." Then shaking his head Sahar continued. "It is a point of view I just do not understand, and probably will never believe in. I mean our women contribute so much overall. To leave part of the race out because they happen to be able to produce offspring, and then figure that's all they are worth just doesn't make sense."

* * *

They continued to monitor the primitives' camp and could now hear boisterous voices, laughter, and see general horseplay emanating from the camp. Then somewhere half way through the night it grew strangely quiet. Even the fires that burned within the camp boundaries seemed to be dying down, as if no one was attending them. Saige then sent down a scouting team to see what had transpired. In too short of time the scouts returned and the leader of the 3-man team reported back. "Saige, they are all dead."

Turning around to their physician Saige asked. "How much stuff did you put in the alcohol anyway? Our goal was to knock them out not kill them, what happened?"

Saar, shrugging, had a perplexed look on his face said. "I really don't know. While I made it a little stronger since they usually are a bit larger than us, I did not put enough in there to kill anybody. Other than that, I cannot explain what happened."

"Nothing we can do about it now. Let's move and I want two of you to take up the rear and wipe out our tracks approaching and leaving the camp so that there will be no evidence that we were even here. Let's move! We've lost enough time and I for one am happy that the pursuers behind us have yet to catch up. Now be very quiet. If we are lucky it may be a few days before the bodies are discovered. Giving time for the wild animals to work over the camp, further confusing what happened here. If things go in our favor it may be that the deaths will be attributed to one of the tribes or clans that have not joined this leader, who, we do not even know anything about as of yet."

Shortly they were working their way through the camp as it had been set up right across the trail leading out of the foothills into the mountains. There was a temptation to search the very silent camp, but moving on was much more important at this moment. Then once through and across the small stream they hid while the final two wiped out their tracks as best they could. In what seemed like an eternity they finally joined them. The plan was a simple one. Now that they were past one of the final obstacles, to push through the remaining portion of the night, then continue through the next day and finally rest the following night. It would be rough but they needed to be at the base or in the mountains by then. Saige looking around in the rising moonlight and then at his small band realized that they all looked like hell. They were dirty – filthy really, and while so far they had gotten this far, there was a weariness that one could see in everyone's eyes. There appeared to be gauntness in all of them also. They had prided themselves on being self-sufficient and were proud of the fact that they could do this better than any in the city. But now he was beginning to wonder if they had been fooling themselves. Now without the city to at least allow some support they were finding it much more difficult.

Of course they had been on the run since they had to abandon the city. So finding the time to actually gather anything had been impossible. Once they had to abandon their machines then the ability to manufacture any food or medicines were lost. So, as they got closer to the mountains, their present goal – and this had become their goal when their way had been cut off from reaching any of the remaining cities – their supplies were almost gone. Now they moved as quickly as the darkness would allow them, with scouts out in front, runners to each side and a trailer to confuse their back trail as best that could be done in the darkness. Tonight it would only be the small moon that would give them light. But it would not be much as he would have liked. But better than the darkness they were now working their way through. He was snapped back from what he was thinking about when one of the scouts had stopped the group. "What's happening?" Saige asked.

"We are going through an area we know very little about – kind of blind here. There's either a camp up ahead of us or maybe a village. We need a couple more to come with us so we can scout out what we are dealing with here, and if there is a way to go around without arousing suspicions."

Signaling the rest to stop and rest for a moment and then looking down in thought before speaking Saige asked, "Tell me what you have seen? Was it a single fire or shelters or what? I'm just trying to get a size here. You know we are not in shape at all to fight. We have to run. But our food is all but gone and if there is an opportunity to add to our stores we may have to chance discovery."

"I don't think that's a good idea. From what we saw they seemed to be on alert. I don't know again if it is another patrol, part of this new alliance, or a clan that has not joined and is being harassed by the others. There is just no way to know."

Shaking his head and sighing Saige said. "We have to know one way or the other." Then pausing for a moment and thinking before speaking again he continued, "Okay, you're probably right. Let's scout it out and see what we face. But make it quick. We don't know how long it will be before the bodies of that main patrol are discovered. I am hoping that it is long enough to hide any evidence of our passing." Then signaling a couple of the other members of their group over to him he then said to them, "Join Staven and go scout out this camp and a safe way around. I need you all back in no more than 2 hours. That will put our time somewhere close to midnight. Again we need as much distance between them and us before sunrise. Now go and as always be very careful. Your discovery by this group could be the end of us all." He watched them leave until they disappeared into the darkness. Now came the waiting, which seemed to be the most difficult. He signaled to the remainder to join him for a moment. And waiting until he was sure they all were there, he brought them up to date as what had been passed on to him by the scout. "Okay, we need to spread out, but keep close enough so that each can see another, and try and get a few moments of rest. We may be here up to two hours, but right now it seems unavoidable." He watched them spread out among the underbrush, followed by small sounds of shuffling about, and then silence.

He must have fallen asleep – not a good thing, but the rest would help. It scared him that it had happened. It meant that he could have been taken and he would never have been the wiser. Yet something had awakened him. So carefully he looked around and shortly saw one of the scouts signaling him to come join him. Curious as to why the scout hadn't joined him he carefully worked his way over to him. He saw it was Staven, "What is it that you have found, and why not come directly to me?"

"No time, will explain it all later. But need a couple of others right now to assist. We've kind of found a windfall but will need help."

With a questioning look on his face Saige asked, "Windfall? What do you mean windfall?"

Quickly, Staven explained. "We've found a place where they have stashed some of their grains, and we need help to move a bit of it for our use. And don't worry we are being very careful and covering up what we take so that it will not be obvious that we are taking anything."

"Okay, but I think I am going to bring the whole group forward so that once we have what can be safely taken that we can immediately move on – just in case." Turning around he signaled the closest to him to round up everyone and meet with him. He waited and then took a head count. In the dark it would so easy to miss someone and leave them behind. "We are going to follow Staven and he will lead us to a place where we will refill our depleted food stores. Once that is accomplished we must immediately move on." Then turning back to Staven he said. "I guess this is some type of permanent settlement then."

"Yup, it appears to be so. In fact there appears to be only one night watchman out and about if you want to call it that. We spotted him right off, and he's staying pretty much in the light and actually looking into the fire that he is using to keep himself warm. It could be they aren't bothered too much as of yet, which is different than we first thought."

"Let's hope he stays that way, or that we are gone before he is replaced with someone who is more alert. We really do need something to break our way for once."

CHAPTER FIVE

Looking back as the morning started graying the skies, and the sudden coolness that seems to greet the dawn he realized that they had a lot of tension while they stole the grains that would hopefully sustain them as they finally made their way into the mountains. It had been a harrowing experience with two constantly watching the night watchman and two entering the small stone building and removing the grain and passing it on to the others. It seemed like an eternity with many stops and starts as at times it appeared the guard had been alerted to something. He really hated to steal, but at this time they had no choice. Once they had their supplies replenished they bid a hasty retreat and continued to move away from the area and towards the mountains. And now that the sunrise was just ahead they found themselves ready to find a way into those unknown mountains. Yet there seemed to be some kind of draw on him that he did not understand. It was like one of those itches that lay just below the surface. One of the types that you try and scratch and where you scratch is not where it truly itches.

As the suns came nearer to the time of showing and it became lighter with the mountains slowly being revealed to them in sharp detail, it was as if they had been here before. But that was all but impossible. As far as he knew there had never even been one of their cities located here. Of course he could never say for sure, but – well, something just seemed to be drawing him. Looking around he could see that it seemed to be affecting the others the same way. At the present they were taking a small meal break before they headed into those mountains. They had built a small smokeless fire to give all of them something hot before the day really began. Shellian, his sister, approached him and gave him something hot to drink. Looking questioningly at her he asked, "What's this? I thought we had run out of our teas and shick a long time ago."

Smiling back at him she said. "Ah that shows you don't know everything . . . actually one of the two who was inside that storehouse found a small stash of this stuff. While I am sure it is not as good as our own it will have to do."

Taking a deep breath and smelling the aroma from the tea he said. "I'm not going to complain. We haven't had anything at all for what seems forever. At this moment it is even hard to remember that we once lived in Sequoyah and had such a different life than the one we have now."

Sitting down beside him with her own cup she sighed and smiled a sad smile, "No truer words were ever spoken. Yet, here we are. I know at times it seems like our life, before the loss of the city, is more like a dream than real. We've lost so much since that day. Not just our way of life, but all those who started the journey with us, and now lie in graves behind us. All of our leaders, friends, and loved ones that are no longer here make it really hard. I mean at times it seems like it would be easier to just give up. There are now only fifteen of us, and only six being women. While I know that we can fight, we have a lesser chance of winning than the men. So really we have nine of you guys and six of us." Trailing off for a moment, letting the silence rise before she continued, "I know, as you do, that if we are caught again that we probably will die. And for us women it will be worse before death takes us. Is all this flight worth it? I know when we started we were to try for another city, but now we can only flee to the mountains as all of the other options have been taken from us. I'm tired and I can see that the rest of us are too. It's easy to understand – too little sleep, food, and constant vigilance, fighting and flight. Look while there is no defeat in our group, yet you can read the weariness in their very souls. I can see it in you and of course I worry. It is part of being a woman."

Thinking for a moment before answering, Saige replied, "Everything you have said is true. I have no answer as to the whys – yet . . ." He paused a moment turned and looked into those mountains as the gathering light revealed them to him. "Yet, for some reason I am finding myself drawn to these ancient mountains. Looking around at the rest who are here with us, I can sense it is the same with them." Then turning to her and looking deeply in her eyes, he said, "See it in you also. It is almost like there is a reason we are heading deep into this unknown. But I don't know why or even understand what is drawing us here. I know it seemed like we were being herded in this direction. And I suspect that camped patrol at the only path through that valley was to be our end. Still . . . still there is something here I don't understand. It seems to be just out of reach – just beyond understanding." Looking down he realized that without thinking about it he had emptied his cup. Then looking up he could see that it was now time to move on. "I guess we will only know what it is when and if we get to wherever this is leading. It's time to move again. I for one will be glad for this night since it will mean we will be able to camp and catch up on some needed rest."

She couldn't disagree with him. She was exhausted and knew that they could not stop until this very night except for a possible cold meal at midday. Sighing and slowly getting up she said, "I wish that I could just wake up and find all of this had not been real. Then we would happily still be in the compound with the city still there and with nothing out of place. Instead we seem to be living this nightmare, where it is all gone, and we are refugees with no home, and no place to go."

He had no answers for her, and knew that really none were needed, as it was just a statement – one that had much truth to it. Standing he signaled the rest to assemble and to be prepared to move on. The Sun was now touching the tops of the hills to the east of them. It would be a couple of hours before the second much smaller sun would rise. Then picking what appeared to be an animal trail he led off. They needed to be away from any civilization by the end of this day. And the fact that the primitives considered these mountains a place of fear was their major hope and refuge, and that the only ones that they might encounter here would be the priests who would be asking of their gods whatever it was they needed, and to leave the tribes and clans behind, and to remain here isolated in these mountains. At this moment he did not send out scouts ahead, that would come later. Right now he needed trailers to watch their backs. Once it could be determined that they were safe from pursuit then he would put out scouts ahead. They just did not have enough surviving members to do both.

The trail they were on seemed to run parallel to the ridgeline, but below the top. It seemed impossible that such a trail should be here as the sides were steep and there was a long way to the bottom of the canyon. He suspected that if any fell that it would be to their death. There did not seem any way one could get up the sides. Yet he knew from experience that these trails, made by the animals, had to lead somewhere and usually did not just end. This he was counting on, as he wanted them to stay off of any of the trails that had been established by the priests and the few hunters that braved the hostile spirits that lived in these mountains, as primitives believed. Still as they worked their way along this small dangerous trail it was a slow and careful hike. By midmorning they were still over the same precipice. The canyon below had continued to deepen and they could hear the roar of flowing water and what they assumed was a waterfall. But none of it was visible to them. As the suns continued to rise in the sky they found that they were beginning to sweat heavily, and still this trail had continued; now slowly climbing towards the ridgeline. If it reached the top they would have to stop and make sure that it was safe to pass over and remain unseen.

From where they were, it appeared that the trail was approaching a large boulder which sat above them. At this moment it looked as if the trail would just end there. If so, they were in trouble, as there had been no place along the path that branched off or even gave them an opportunity to leave it. Once they reached the boulder, they found that again sometime in the ancient past, this monster had been up above them and had then fallen. It must have had a weak point within it. When it had finally struck the ground from where it had originally been, it split in half with the lower portion sliding away and down, opening up an area between the two pieces, and it was here that the trail continued. It was a tight fit but with work they got through. Once through, the trail entered head high brush and then dropped down the other side into a small valley that was completely hidden. Here they found a small stream flowing, with a very small pond where out the backside the water continued to flow out of the valley. There was also a small pasture, so it was a good place for the grazers to come. Now, the question was, did it just end here? Even with no answer to that question, it was a good place to take their break before continuing. It was very quiet and peaceful. He looked at the area regretfully as it would have been a great place to stop and let everyone catch their breath and recover their strength. But it was just too close, and even here as remote as it appeared to be, they still could be found. Well, they would eat their cold meal here. He decided that probably they would now pull in the trailers and put out scouts ahead, returning to as close of a normal setup that they could make happen with their reduced numbers.

Yet, if the grazers came here, where were they? The trail looked used and there had been fresh droppings along the route. Looking around he could see some additional piles here. Yet at the moment there were none to be seen. Maybe they were here, but since it was still close to where the hunters came, they had learned to fear and were in hiding. If so this may not be as safe as he thought. In fact it may be a place those very hunters came to hunt the grazers. Alarmed now he signaled them to silence followed by the signal to carefully search for any sign of the primitives having been in the area. And shortly a couple of the members signaled that they had found something. He went with stealth now and signaled the rest to remain hidden and joined the two. There before them was a fire pit. But fortunately it had not been used in quite some time. But now it was obvious, that as appealing as this place had been, they could not stop here and must immediately continue leaving no trace of their passing. Yet, was this a good or bad sign? It meant that the fire pit hadn't been used in a while, but did that reflect a change of location or just that it was one of the many visited areas the hunters traveled. With no idea of the history of the area they could not take that chance.

He turned to signal assembly and to move out when the two trailers came rapidly over the hill from where they had just come and signaled that a group was approaching. They hadn't had much time to even check the area out but now they had to get out quickly if they were to remain invisible. The valley that they were in was too small to have any hiding places. Flight out of the area was their only choice. So Saige signaled retreat and out of the area. This was going to take a few moments since they had been unpacking to eat a quick meal. One of the trailers finally approached Saige while the other kept a lookout just below the entrance. The lead trailer then said. "We are probably no more than 10 minutes ahead of them at the most. So far they have been making the journey in this direction at a leisure pace. If they pick it up it will be in shorter."

Shaking his head Saige said. "And I almost missed it. The signs were all here, but none of us saw it." Turning around he could see the rest were very busy putting things back together and coming rapidly to form around him. To the ones who had gathered he stated softly. "We have very little time so begin heading out to the upper side and away from where we entered. We need to stay hidden since a group of hunters are approaching. We'll take a head count once we are all outside of this area and away. Now let's go." Then staying with the trailers he began wiping out whatever sign they had left. He knew it would be a poor job, but these hunters were not tracking or looking for anything at this point. So maybe they would get lucky.

Taking a final quick look around, he trailed the others out of the valley hoping that they had done a good enough job. As he slipped through the brush and behind a boulder on the upper side the hunters came over the hill and into the small valley. How much time did they have before they started going after the grazers that had to be hiding in the area, he had no idea. But they needed to be as far away as they could be. The problem was these were hunters, so it had to be done carefully, so as to not alert them in pursing. But again, not knowing the area, they were not even sure what the easiest, safest, or fastest way out of the small valley could be. They, as a group, pulled back deeper into the brush where it was confirmed that everyone was there. Now once again they were on the run with an enemy close by. He had hoped that they had finally left that problem behind, but it was painfully clear that it wasn't that way at all.

* * *

Hours later they worked their way along the edge of a high mountain meadow. The air was cool, crisp, and very clear. From here they could see the valley below that they had escaped, and the one with the dead patrol located at the only path through the area. Yet its distance was great enough that the details of the area could not be discerned. They then hiked around a small outcropping and the view was gone. Here they found that once again they were dropping down into a large ravine, and once there they remained in it, as it appeared to be running in the general direction they wanted to go anyway. He finally pulled in the trailers and ran scouts out ahead, as he felt that they were probably far enough up into the mountains that finding a viable trail and a place to stay for this night was of greater importance. He could see the fatigue in each and every step all of them were taking. They needed a stopping place – one that would provide a respite for them. It would only be one night, but it would be something that none of them had had in a long, long time. As they continued to push his mind started drifting back on their history, as they knew it: They had been taught that they had become separated from the ones they now call the primitives at least a millennium if not many millenniums in the past. From what he could remember there had been a great war and their people had found the desolate as rarely traveled areas and began the process of setting up their cities – using the technology to hide them from the rest of this crazy world. At the time they all had been on equal footing, but it could be seen by the ones who established the cities, that it would not be that way for long. The fighting was destroying everything and once it had finished its destructiveness then the survivors would be starting over. Yet, at this present time, it had appeared that these descendants had learned very little as they continued to fight among themselves.

But something had changed, if only partially. They still fought, and they still killed each other. But now, somehow, they had become more organized, and he suspected it was under one charismatic leader. Then the primitives had discovered the cities and as each one was found it was conquered, destroyed, leaving ghosts and ruin in their wake. Coming back to their present situation, once they were able to establish a place where they could rest and be safe, then they would need to find out who this leader was, and how they could eliminate him. And do it before all of the cities were no more. It appeared that, more than likely, this time the destruction would be complete and all would be brought down to the level of the primitives. He suspected that once this new leader, who seemed to be bringing many if not all the tribes under his banner, died that no one left within the leadership would be strong enough to hold the alliances together, at least that was the hope. He knew that their long-term goal was to eliminate this unknown leader who had brought so much destruction down upon them. But obviously their short-term goal was to survive long enough to be able to get around to that other goal.

The ravine they were in took a sharp right turn then began a steep uphill climb. Here, there were exposed boulders that they had to work over and around. He began to wonder with the depth of the ravine why there was no water running in it. While it was late summer, almost fall, the area here showed signs of plenty of moisture, and this was a large ravine showing much water flow. Again, continuing the uphill trend it returned to its original direction. In the distance they could hear what sounded like a lot of water flowing. It was time to exit this place, so he signaled them to leave and with much exertion, as the sides were both soft and steep they finally stood above the ravine. Ahead of them and shadowed, it appeared that just around a bend in the distance there looked to be a hint of a waterfall. Then as they got closer it was now obvious why the ravine had been dry. The roar of the waterfall now was deafening, and the volume coming over it was surprising. But they could not get any closer, as there was a growing lake between them and the falls. There had been a landslide, which had blocked the flow of the water down the ravine. From what they could see it would be a while before the water level reached the top of the landslide. But it would and then go over the top and break the dam causing a flashflood taking anything and everything that would be in its path. The sight was both breathtaking and very dangerous. They had been lucky that it was still holding. If it had released while they were traversing that ravine they would all have been killed.

The scouts reported in saying that the area around the falls was impassible, and that they would have to work more to the east and around this area. They said that there was another animal trail that was even more precarious than the last one they were on. But it was good enough to use and that it would take them to the top where they all could see the beginning of the falls. That there was another alpine meadow complex before it became a broken land once again and that there was a shallow cave where they probably could finally break. It was partially hidden by the vegetation and if one did not look directly at it, one could very easily miss it. With that information, they followed the scouts finding the description they had given about the animal trail was well understated. He wondered how the animals had even formed this. There was a number of times where in the past shale had slid off the mountainside above the trail and added to its precariousness. They used a rope and tied everyone together so that if one of them slipped and fell it would not be to their death. There was a couple of close moments when some of the shale that they were walking on slipped and fell down the mountainside over the edge and then it seemed like an eternity before they heard it hit the mountainside far below. No doubt about it, if one of them fell they would not survive. When they finally reached the meadow complex all were breathing very hard and were shaking from the ordeal. In fact as he wiped his forehead he found sweat. It surprised him since the area they presently were in was cool. He hoped that they could avoid having to hike that trail again. Going up was bad enough, but going down would be worse. This increased his respect for the two scouts, since not only did they climb up this trail twice, but had to descend to find them. He had to admit he for one was glad it hadn't been him.

Once everyone had caught their breath, the scouts led them across three large meadows then against a rise just before the rough country started. At first he did not see anything at all, but the scouts just kept going and suddenly what he thought was shadow became the entrance. Turning to one of the scouts Saige asked. "How'd you ever find this thing? I mean I was following you and you were making a direct line to the entrance, yet until just now I did not figure it out."

Smiling he said, "It wasn't me, it was your sister. She said that something just did not look right about that. I said, nah it's just shadows. Again she said no, not true. Look it is too dark to just be shadows. Come on, we need to investigate this. And so she dragged me up here to look, and as you can see she was right and I was wrong. We did a quick inspection to make sure nothing was using it for a home, and then once we confirmed that, came back to get you. Good timing too, since we are almost out of daylight. I checked and there is a good supply of dead wood and the cave's location is such that it will not be visible at all unless you walk right up to it. So while not perfect by any means, it is the best we have found. Also scouted for tracks of the primitives and no sign that they have been anywhere around this area. I think we are probably the first to be here. Water isn't real close but not so far away to be a burden. I think also from the reaction of the grazers that they don't see us as a threat – another sign that the hunters have not been here to lead them to fear us."

"I guess you've answered all of my questions even before I could ask them." Looking around he could see the rest of the team moving inside of the small cave and briefly disappearing from sight. Then shaking his head he continued. "I just wish that we had more time. We need a place that we can remain for longer than overnight. Much of our clothes and equipment are in need of repair or replacement. And I must admit like any other male around here seeing our women with less is always exciting, but at the same time it is not a good thing that our clothes have worn that thin. Without that equipment that we had to abandon, and I do hope we hid it well enough from discovery, there is no quick and easy way to do the work we need to accomplish, or repair or replace the items we need.

I guess it is time to chance it and take an extra day, if for no other reason than we need the recovery time. On top of it all we have been on the run and really have no idea of where to go from here. So we need to send out scouting parties and find the best way out of here. While I don't necessarily want to disturb the grazers, we need the meat and time to prepare it for the trail. The grains that we *borrowed* from that last settlement will only last so long and will not sustain us like meat will." Then pausing and looking around in the failing light he said, "Enough on this we need to get things moving before it becomes too dark to see. Besides I need to talk with Shellian and thank her for this discovery." He then turned and went up to their new temporary camp and joined the rest of the group.

* * *

They remained in this area for two days before continuing on to find a more permanent location. In that time they had killed one of the grazers at night so as to minimally disturb the rest. Then they jerked the meat over small fires, packed and divided it among the members, and attempted to hide any trace that they had been there. Still they knew that with the amount of time that they had spent here, that it would be nearly impossible to completely wipe out any sign. The scouting had produced a couple of promising possibilities, and they knew that they needed to go deeper and higher into these mountains. So the decision was made to take the rougher route they had discovered. Guessing that if the primitives found this camp that they would assume that the ones they were following would have taken the easier and more obvious route out of the area. To help further that impression, half of the remaining members worked up that trail leaving easily followed tracks, before backtracking, and heading down the actual trail, which first dropped down into a canyon with high narrow walls extending up and out of sight, immediately placing the entire team in deep shadows. From the narrowness of the gorge and steep sides it obviously was an area where the suns rarely reached with their warmth and light. The chill was immediate and penetrated the warmest of clothing that they were wearing. The time they had stopped had given them the respite to be able to make small repairs and get a little extra rest, something that had been rarc, having to actually lift their spirits. Now instead of feeling dread, and impending doom, or death, there seemed to be an uplifting, and anticipation of what lay ahead of them. Now instead of being just one step ahead of the next fight, ambush, or accident, they had time to be careful and to plan. Yet with all that lay behind them, they had become much better at living in the wilds. Even though their numbers now were less than one third of the original group, in many ways they were stronger, more cunning, and with their abilities tested to the limit, their confidence in what they could do, became very strong. Now with the additional time, hiding their trail should overall be successful. They had to disappear, as if they had never existed. So now was the time to accomplish that. The previous campsite would be the last the primitives should find; it was time to become ghosts, spirits, and find that place to begin the offensive against their enemy. But that was still sometime in the future; right now they were very much on the run with no home or no real destination.

Eventually the canyon walls retreated, opening up to a broken land. It gave the appearance that sometime in the great past mythological giants had been angry and were throwing large boulders around. There was very little vegetation here, and ice was everywhere making footing extremely treacherous. If one did not consciously concentrate on his footing he found himself on his behind quicker than he could react, and it hurt. Yet the animal trail they were following continued to wind around and through both the ice and broken land. This trail had to be going somewhere, as there was absolutely nothing for grazers to eat here. Yet at this very moment it was not obvious. At midday they finally stopped and ate a cold meal. And cold was an appropriate description, as their breath came out in great white clouds. Even though the suns shown down on them there appeared to be no warmth and the breeze that was blowing through this empty land cut right through them leaving them to find the lee of the boulders hoping to have them at least block some of the wind. Looking out across the landscape from their limited view, it appeared that this flat valley just went on forever. At this point they did not know if they would completely cross it before dark. But each knew that they did not want to spend the night here. As cold as it was now it would be deadly at night. That made this meal stop one that was very short and then they were on their way once more.

There was something about this area that felt haunted – as if they were continually under observation. But, it was a silent cold world. No sounds of birds, or the scurrying of the small animals or any movement other than they, giving the appearance that there were no others here but them. Yet as they worked their way deeper into this frozen land their alarm continued to rise. Saige could see it in all of them as each member continued to search the area with their eyes, trying to locate some unseen danger. He could feel the short hairs on the back of his neck rising up, yet like the rest he could find no source to this sense of being watched. He had to admit that this barren landscape, one totally lacking in any vegetation, still had too many places for a predator to hide, surrounded as they were with the piled ice and scattered boulders. If one were able to get up high enough this area overall would appear to be flat. What had happened here to cause this? Looking ahead the wild animal trail continued. Even the trail seemed to pass by areas that would have been easier, it was like the animals that traveled here were sensing and avoiding something threatening.

As the day progressed, and there was no letup in the tension, they found that their nerves were raw and all of them were on the verge of panic. The strength of the feeling could not be denied by any of them. But there was no source that any had found. Just what was going on, what was causing this sense of dread? Unconsciously they had picked up their pace just wanting to be away from this place. Finally needing to break they stopped to catch their breath. Seve standing next to one of the large boulders bent over to get something out of his backpack when something huge, white and extremely quick flashed through and missed grabbing Seve because the animal had expected him to remain standing. With a roar of frustration it was gone. All were standing where they were, frozen in position from the shock of the attack. No one had seen it, and only for a brief moment had it flashed by. Disbelief hit them at the speed of this predator – something that size shouldn't be able to move that fast. Then Saige yelled. "Grab you gear and run down the trail now! We have to get out of here; we have no defense against whatever that was. I don't want any of us here when it returns. And who knows if there is one, there may be others." Quickly they put their packs back together and started trotting out. Now they would again not be able to rest until they were completely away from here. It still was shocking as the speed of this predator. Guessing from the brief glimpse he figured that it was twice the size of any one of them.

"Anybody get a look at whatever it was or can identify it?" Saige asked. There was no answer, just the sound of heavy breathing and feet hitting the ground. He knew from the history of the cities that none of them were located in these mountains so this predator could be completely unknown to them. It may also be another reason why these mountains were off limits to the primitives, except their holy men. But there had to be more to it. Even a beast like whatever this one was could be hunted down with enough hunters. Still what if they had a tendency to run in packs? Now that would be scary. A herd of grazers could be wiped out in an instant of time. He hoped they were solitary. As the adrenaline burned away there came an awareness that once again with too little sleep and too little to eat their reserves were being used up and if there was no respite their bodies would finally just quit and refuse to move.

Looking ahead it appeared that they had much too far to go to get out of this haunted ice and boulder covered plain. Looking back he could not even see where they had entered the area. Then turning back around he saw the group stop and was standing and with the clouds of breath coming from the group as they caught their breath. Catching up he stopped quickly. Before them was a chasm cut by a fast flowing river. Here the trail just stopped. Looking desperately around he wondered if the game trail just ended. But that did not make any sense. Did they miss something in their desperate flight to this dead end? One thing for sure if the beast decided to attack again they had nowhere to go. "We must have missed something. There has to be branch off of this. We know that the grazers do not make these trails that lead to nowhere. With whatever that is behind us we have to search as a group. I do not want any of us separated or alone. We cannot lose anyone. We barely have enough members alive and healthy to be able to survive." They carefully backtracked for a distance, and then returned to the edge; finding nothing – yet there had to be something. What had they missed? "Anyone see anything?" Saige asked. All he could see was the shaking of their heads. Looking down at the ground and closing his eyes he thought hard. There just had to be something they had missed. He suspected that at one time that the trail probably had a passage over the river here and that it collapsed. But the trail still showed use so the grazers had to have found a way around which meant they had missed something. "Okay let's do this, let's split the team in half. No I do not want us to separate. We need all of us together if we have to face that thing again. I want one half to concentrate on one side of the trail and the other half to search the opposite side. Now let's do it."

It took a while, time they had not to waste, but eventually in an area where they least expected it they found where it branched. There was a place where one side dipped away and another split boulder sat in the middle of this dip. When one first glanced at the boulder the split did not appear to be large enough to allow passage between. But upon closer inspection they found tuffs of hair clinging to the sides showing that the grazers had gone this way. The soil here was too hard to leave any tracks or show any depression, but once through to the other side of the crack the trail became obvious. He wondered what had happened to the original pathway across the gorge and how the grazers had located this alternate route. The direction it ran did not seem to lead in the direction that they needed to go. In fact it appeared to head back from where they had started that day. But they stuck with it since there were no other options, and eventually as the level of the trail continued to fall it then made a sharp turn and dropped steeply down. They now could hear the rushing water in the distance and knew that now they were heading directly towards and probably at level with the river. Now the question was, did it end at the river, or was there a way across at this point? With a ridgeline blocking their view they could not see anything of the surrounding area at all. In fact as they had dropped down into this area they once again had walls rising up on both sides of them. If the primitives had been here they would have been trapped since there was no way up the sides and only back the way they had come or forward towards the unknown. Again it was deeply shadowed and quite cold so they continued to press forward towards the increasing sound of the flowing river.

Saige was working the rear guard when the leaders turned a corner and just stopped. And as others reached the same point their reaction was the same. Curious he pushed forward and found that his reaction was just as the rest. Before them the area opened up and there was a large open alpine meadow with numerous trees dotting the area. Off towards the area where they had been stopped by the chasm lay a huge waterfall that had not been visible from above. Sweet smells wafting off the grasses and alpine flowers were quite pleasant and for a short distance the river was wide and slow before narrowing again and heading off over another precipice. Here in the distance and across the river they saw grazers with their heads down and a few looking in their direction. They showed some curiosity but did not have the stance of ones ready to take flight. After seeing nothing threatening these few that had watched them returned to their grazing. Shellian commented, "I think this might be a good place to camp for the night. From the reaction of the grazers I don't think we have to worry about whatever that was, that attacked us up there on that ice and boulder strewn flat land."

Still taking in the scenery Saige paused thinking that they really needed to continue, but there was very little daylight left and he had to admit that there was every sign that she was right. It very well could be that the predator that had attacked them only roamed the area that they had just left. There definitely was something about this particular area that lent itself to relaxing. He had to admit it was almost an idyllic scene. "You may be right. There's not much daylight left and we have no idea what's ahead of us. And I have to agree that we are probably not going to find anything better." Then coming to a decision he said. "Yes, let's do it – but first let's move to the other side of this river. The last thing I would want to happen is for us to get stuck on this side if the river suddenly increased because of some rain that we wouldn't be aware of. Shellian, once we are across, signal camp. Then once its set up we'll get together and see what the others feel and how we should continue."

* * *

It had been a peaceful and a quick night. While they posted guards and rotated them often, the rest slept hard and deep from exhaustion caused by the days of being continually on the run, having to be forever vigilant, fighting and trying to stay ahead of the enemy. The plan had been to be back on the trail by sunrise but it was midmorning before they were moving again. Now they hiked through knee high grasses that were curing in the late summer, early fall. They suspected that both fall and winter would come early to these higher mountain ranges. So they knew their time was short and they needed to find a place where they could winter. It needed to be found soon, because they would have to gather foods and such to carry them through winter, and right now they had little. While this place that they were leaving was nice, it was open and would probably be buried deep in the winter snows and would not be a good place to stay. So they moved on, both to put more distance between themselves and the primitives, and to find better shelter.

Once across the meadow the trail began its climb out and head deep into the mountains. As they continued to climb the trees began to thin out and eventually disappear altogether. Although higher up they could see scattered alpine trees. Looking back across the landscape they could no longer see anything but the mountains. The place they had left was as if it had never been. Now all that was visible was the surrounding rugged wild mountains that may have never seen anything like them. Saar commented to no one in particular. "This surely is beautiful, but I sense very dangerous. None of us have ever lived in such an area, and I being the doctor for this group am worried, as I have no access to anything I am familiar with. I know nothing of the plants, and our equipment that we had to abandon, had the facilities to allow me to manufacture medicines, as I needed. Now – now I don't have anything at all. It really is a worrisome thing."

Saige didn't say anything, as he had no answer. Instead he nodded in agreement. There were many things that they did not have, and would have a desperate need, before winter arrived. The major question running through his mind was, did they have enough time left before winter, and would they find the necessary shelter to get through what he suspected would be a harsh winter? With these thoughts weighing heavily on his mind he really did not see the beauty that now surrounded them. He had been pushed into this leadership role before he *might* have wanted it. He had known that Shayne was working with both he and his sister to be his replacements someday. But that was to be far in the future, not under the duress that had led to he and she, now leading this ragtag remainder of their civilization. He wondered idly if other cities had gone dark. He suspected that *possibly*, was the best answer.

Again remembering the history that had been taught, there had originally been eight families that established the first cities. In the intervening time the cities had expanded to the known thirty. But with at least five now gone that he knew of – which included theirs – that had reduced the number to twenty-five. At least the original city was well hidden and purposely never placed on any of their maps. While most of the maps that existed were kept in the ruling hall he was sure that one might have fallen into the primitives' hands, making it easier for them to locate the rest of the cities. But he really had no proof, since most of the cities existed in similar lands, this alone could be enough, giving the primitives a place to consistently search out for additional hidden cities. Yes it now was painfully obvious that they had become too complacent, too comfortable, and ended up with too much belief in their advantage of technology over the primitives. They were now paying a hard price for such stupidity. Should they have reached out a long time ago and tried to establish some type of relationship with the primitives? Well it hadn't been attempted, so maybe the result would have been the same. Now it appeared that the primitives were bent on destroying all that they could find. Why? Again he had no answers, just speculation, and with nothing to support that speculation he may as well be spitting into the wind for all the good it would do him.

Someone had just spoken to him and because he had been so deep in thought he did not hear at all. Looking to his side he saw Shellian looking at him questioningly. Smiling he said, "Sorry Shellian, but I was lost in thought. I for one was not expecting to take over the leadership so soon."

Nodding her head in agreement she said. "Yeah me neither. But I simply asked you about that plain area we had crossed yesterday. What do you think caused it to be that way? I mean if you look at either side it is heavily forested with many plants and meadows and such. But that area was bare of anything that was living, other than that predator that we really never saw."

"I really don't know. Maybe you should ask Stone since he is our geologist and plant specialist. But my guess would be that sometime in the past that there was a flood through that area. It's the only explanation I can come up with that could create such a place as that. But, I for one am glad that it was only one day's travel to get across. I really would not have wanted to spend the night there, as cold as it was during the day, and then give those predators another shot at us."

She shivered at the thought, "I have to agree with that. All I saw was a flash and in that brief flash the impression was that it was huge and extremely quick. It left me wondering why just the single attempt. I mean it appeared to be something that would have had no problem in coming back and attacking us again."

"I don't know, but my guess is that it had been following us for some time, waiting for the right moment to make its attack, and when it failed, and thanks to the stars that it did, it felt that we would be alerted. Since it did not know what we could or could not do, it may have decided to go after something else. Again not knowing what it even is, I know nothing about how it lives, hunts, or anything at all. So once again it's just a guess on my part."

"Thinking that it might have been following us for some time just sends chills through me." Pausing briefly before continuing, Shellian said, "I mean any one of us could have gone out to take care of nature's call, been alone and vulnerable and then could have been attacked and taken away and no one would have had any idea what had happened. I doubt that there would have even been any real sign left behind for even out best tracker to figure out what had happened."

"Very true, but at least now we know that they exist – even though I would guess that we would have little defense against them. Just not enough is known. So let's just hope that they roam and hunt in that plain and are nowhere else." He then looked at what they were hiking through at this moment and then said. "Not to change the subject but this area is absolutely beautiful. How long have we been climbing? Sorry I really haven't been paying attention, just too much on my mind."

"Really? I would never have guessed oh brother of mine." She answered sarcastically before continuing. "I could see that, but it probably isn't a good thing. I mean we all need to stay alert for dangers – after all this is all unknown to us."

There was no argument for that statement. Yet it had been very difficult not to become deep in thought. There was so much that was unknown behind them and definitely ahead of them. How could one plan at all when he did not even know what question to ask? Looking around the area they presently were hiking through, it was a mix of alpine plants and scattered trees. While the soils looked rich it was also quite rocky. Looking closer at some of the rocks, which were exposed he realized that they were volcanic in nature. His conclusion from that observation was that the mountains they presently were in probably were extinct volcanoes. There sure had been no signs of such activity in this direction as long as he could remember, and as far as their history books spoke. All they stated was quote, "There is a rugged mountain range to the north, which has been little explored." Well, these mountains were going to be explored now – not by choice but by necessity. The air was beginning to take on a chill as they continued along the trail. The breeze definitely had a bite to it. Looking up they could see that in the far distance that there still was snow and it was obvious to them that it probably never melted. Presently they had no clothing that would keep them warm in such an area so they would have to avoid it if at all possible. But the trail continued to wind through the sparse trees and continued its upward climb. Off to the west they could see where a cliff line developed and slowly the trail was working itself towards this cliff edge, eventually reaching and then paralleling it. Looking over it had to be at least 300 meters straight down. It was a dizzying height, and with nothing there to prevent one from falling, it had been difficult getting close enough to even peer over the edge. When they approached the edge they could hear the roaring of a great amount of water, and looking ahead they saw the beginnings of a waterfall dropping over into the abyss, crashing with a roar far below. The trail was heading directly towards it.

When they finally reached the top of the waterfall they could see that the amount of water going over the edge was tremendous. The river – and it had to be called a river – was at least 40 meters wide at this point and was moving rapidly.

There was no safe way to cross it. Like the plain they had crossed the day before, the river was filled with boulders and the water crashed and bounced around these obstructions giving the appearance of anger from the water trying to move these obstructions out its way. There was a heavy mist coming off the water and it cooled the air to almost freezing. It sent a shiver and chill through them and they had to withdraw beyond the mist and find a place out of the wind and in the weak sunlight to warm themselves. Where the light touched the mists, rainbows formed throwing vibrant colors into the air. Here close to water they took their midday break. Saige called a brief meeting to find out how all was doing and what their next move should be. Up until now it had been flight, but with the final flight from the primitives behind them they now needed to find a semi-permanent camp area and the sooner the better. They were in trouble and he knew it. It was late in the season here and looking at that snow on the higher peaks let him know that once winter set in they were going nowhere until spring thaw. "Okay all, we have been doing nothing but running, fighting and reacting to what has been happening to us. There has been no time for planning except for what the situation dictated at the moment. Now that our first danger is finally behind us we now have a greater one ahead of us. We need to be looking for a place to wait out the winter. And while I am not an expert on the weather it is obvious to me that winter comes early here and probably stays late.

"If you look at our food supplies I doubt that we have enough to last out the next ten days let alone a winter. Plus we have no shelter or clothing or anything. What the primitives could not do to us down there, winter up here could. So in the next few days we need to be finding that shelter. I suspect that this mountain and maybe the whole range of mountains here were volcanic at one time. We do not have time to build anything even if we had the tools to do it. So we need to find one of the many caves that volcanoes create and then start working hard on preparing it for a winter stay. That means building a wall at the front of the cave to help insulate it against the cold put together enough firewood to both keep us warm, and to cook by. I suspect that we will be having a fire going all the time. If that is the case think of how much wood that will require. Then we have to face the real problem, even if we solve these first two – food. So we will have to be sending out hunting parties to bring in meat. Then it will have to be smoked and cured so that it will last the winter. And again like the firewood we will need a lot of it since there are fifteen people here. At least with the skins, from the animals we bring in for food, we should not be lacking for materials to make clothes.

"Now when you think about it there are so many small details that will be necessary to accomplish that I have only covered the big ones here and now. You have to think about sanitary requirements, utensils, sleeping areas, bedding, and on and on. We do not have a lot of time to do this so once we find our spot we will all be working from dawn to past dusk. Sleeping I do not think will be a problem." Looking over the group he could see that what he had just passed on to them had them worried. Like him up to this point it had been just survive another day, avoid the primitives and continue moving. Now they had to change their mindset and begin to set up something more permanent.

CHAPTER SIX

As he feared, winter struck hard and with a fury in these mountains that they were unfamiliar with down in the lowlands. It had taken them five days to finally find something suitable to last out the winter that was approaching. Then the work really began and the small group worked from before sunrise to well after sunset. It was hard grueling work and while there were complaints, and many a sore muscle, they all knew that what they were trying to accomplish here would make the difference between survival and death. There would be no in-between here, and in this harsh world they were now living, there would be no forgiveness. There had been little time to really explore the cave they found that would meet most of their needs. Water was close, but not so close that it would draw unwanted animals or people their way. Plus it was partially up the side of a hill so that if the snow piled high they would remain above this snow. It faced at an angle to the prevailing winds so as to keep the winds from entering into the cave and chilling it further. When Stone looked at the cave when it was first found, he felt that it probably was a steam vent from the extinct volcano, and it had vented both vertically and horizontally with the vent hole out the roof being small. This provided a place for the smoke to escape when they built a fire or fires inside the cave. It appeared that in the distant past when this was forming that it blew out the side of this hill placing debris everywhere – giving them ample building materials to wall up the entrance. A few trees also were close further shielding the entrance from sight.

With their group being this small, they could only send out two hunting teams, with each team consisting of two individuals. They had to hunt well away from this area, so if it became necessary, that during the winter they would be able to hunt closer to their camp for additional food. They had completed the transformation before the first flakes of snow began falling. This spurred them on to even greater effort. And if one looked around at the team now they would have appeared to be even more primitive than the ones they had fought. Working the skins into leather for clothing had changed their appearance. Now everyone was in the leather from the game that was also their food supply. While the meat was the main subsistence they also collected nuts and plants to help round out their nutritional needs. This season they could not be selective. Later, if they survived, and with more time, there would be more variety in their foods. Saige, looking at the group working in the camp outside of the cave, as they prepared the meat for drying, reminded him of the holos they would watch in school showing how their ancient ancestors lived and interacted with each other and other tribes. At the time of youth he thought it was fun watching, but since it was all a reenactment anyway it probably was not like what they were being shown. Yet, now he had to admit that the scene he was seeing here was uncannily just like the ones in those holos.

While the opening into this particular cave wasn't very large – one still could walk into it while standing – it was large enough to admit two abreast. Once inside it opened up with the roof sitting approximately 6 meters above and side-to-side 20 to 30 meters. It appeared that as the original magma and water steam headed for the surface; they stopped here, expanded, before finally blowing out in the two places which became their entrance to the cave and exit for the smoke from the fires. Inside they built, using wood and stone, areas for privacy since they were a mixed group. There were a few offshoots from the main tunnel and while not truly explored there were two on opposite sides and deeper inside that they turned into places to take care of their nature calls. And if someone in the group broke the rules they were placed on the duty of cleaning these areas and hauling the waste outside a safe distance away. Not a job any wanted but still necessary. So if all stayed within their rules then all would rotate through the job with none excluded. In another offshoot they found a large bowl shaped by the flowing lava that they converted into a bath.

Close to the area of the cave, they found clay from which they then began to make pots. While they had no way of firing them to proper hardness what they did produce worked. Fragile yes, and because of this they made as many as time would allow. In some of the larger vessels they had created they heated water for the bath. After all with 15 people in an enclosed area for an extended period of time it could get very ripe. They rigged a couple of skins over the entrance to again allow for privacy and set the rule that if it was closed off then it was occupied and off limits until the entrance again was open. When one used the bath they were also responsible for emptying and cleaning it. They had found that one of the plants up in these highlands absorbed water and left a pleasant scent, so the women collected as much of this as they could find. Stating, "It's all right if you men don't mind coming out all wet, but we would prefer to be dry, and the scent from the plants are pleasant too." There had been plenty of dead wood in the area so they began by working the wood that was furthest out leaving the wood close in for later use if they had to add to their supply. So, while a long way from perfect, what they had created was very livable.

* * *

Pulling back the cover they had over the opening to help keep it warmer within the cave, Saige briefly stepped outside and immediately shivered. The temperatures between inside and outside were vastly different. There was a strong wind blowing, but fortunately he was out of it. It had been snowing now for many days and from the looks of the clouds, which were sullen, dark, and appeared to be heavily laden with moisture, there would be many more days of this storm before it broke. Not used to being inside as long as they had, he began to get what he had heard called cabin fever. While there was plenty of room even with the fifteen of them inside he never had to stay this long without going outside to at least see the sky. Once this storm broke they would have to go get more tar for their torches. They had gone through their supply much quicker than they had planned. He also knew that soon they would need to learn the area they were living in. While preparing for this winter there had been little time to actually explore and map the area. If for some reason the primitives were to come up here they would need a quick and safe way out of the area. There was much that needed to be done and it fell on his shoulders, he and his sister's shoulders, he corrected himself – since before Shayne had died he made it clear that the two of them were a team and were to lead as a team.

It still saddened him every time he thought back to that night when Shayne had died, and he was sure it was that way for all of them. He heard the cover being drawn back and turned to see Shellian coming out to stand next to him. Like when he first emerged, she shivered, crossed her arms and hunched against the cold. Wondering why she came out he asked. "So sis why leave the warmth of the cave?"

"Oh I guess like you the cave just seemed to be closing in on me and I needed to get out for even a couple of minutes. I saw you leave and thought this would be a good time to do it since you would be out here. I knew that at least with this storm blowing that you wouldn't be too far, so there would be two of us, *as you have requested,* and not just one."

Shrugging he said. "You got me there. But I was going nowhere except right here and to admit it; I was going stir crazy in there and just needed to step out for a short time. Besides it gave me a chance to see how deep this snow is getting. But I am sure that is not the only reason. I know that Shayne left both of us in charge and with such a small group of us remaining it is not necessarily a difficult task for the two of us. Keeping all of us alive might be though."

With a sheepish look on her face she paused then said, "Yup I guess that's true. Look with all of us so close in there – I know there's plenty of room, but you know what I mean. There are nine of you guys and only six of us. It would have been nice if it was a little more equal, but it isn't. While it hasn't happened yet, I think these inequalities in numbers are going to be a real problem. Now with winter here in full force we will be forced to be together and if things take their natural course we will be having issues with coupling. And for example take Sorrel, she's a big flirt and I don't think she would be interested in settling for any single man. And she is the type that would enjoy seeing jealousies arise over her. Then there is Sabryn, quiet, strong, and not interested at least outwardly in any man. At least outwardly . . . although I suspect she secretly has someone in mind. At this moment I really do not know. With me as one of the leaders I am not confided in as much as I would like. But also being female I know what I see and . . ." Shrugging again and looking into her brother's eyes. "And I could talk about the other three, but their stories would be similar."

"What about you? I noticed that you did not mention anything about your feelings or the direction they are taking? I know for a fact that you have been drawn towards Saar." Seeing the reaction of Shellian he said. "Now don't you deny it! So far he has been oblivious to any of your looks, but I haven't been your brother all this time without learning how to read you at least a little."

Looking down at the snow covered ground before answering Shellian then said. "Okay I am sweet on him, but that's all. Is it that obvious?"

"Probably only to me, since like I said, I know you. Otherwise it would appear to be just a leader's interest in someone under him or her. But you are right. I have only been thinking about surviving this winter, learning as much about this area as we can and trying to keep all of us safe. I hadn't even considered the coupling aspect, and, oh my, that would mean that you or I would have to perform the ceremony if two of them really wanted to become a couple." Now it was his turn to look down before continuing. "Hey sis, I had enough on my mind before you threw this one at me. Thanks a lot."

Smiling she said, "You are welcome of course. But again with so few women that will mean that some of the men will be without and that could further the problems. And no, I am not suggesting that we all start sleeping around and spread the wealth here. All I am saying is that eventually there will be coupling and that will lead to some uncomfortable moments. Oh, by the way, is there one you are especially sweet on? I mean, I usually catch that with you as much as you have with me, but so far I haven't."

"Are you kidding? I've been so involved in trying to keep us alive and together, such a thing hadn't even entered my mind. In fact it probably wouldn't have had at all if you hadn't brought it up. I guess I can see why Shayne wanted both of us to lead. Hey I don't know about you but I am starting to get very cold here and my feet are numb. Shall we go back inside before both of us become icicles?" He could see she was beginning to shiver.

"Of course, I am freezing, but I needed to bring this up because I could see what's coming, and saw that you did not. Now lead us back inside where it is warm. But remember, if you set a rule such as *always a team of two*, when any leave the cave, then it applies to you too."

As he pulled the material away from the entrance he whispered. "Yes mother." and with that they both laughed and returned to the warmth of the cave.

* * *

The storm continued to unleash its fury for another four days before it broke clear and cold. Still, all were eager to get outside and breathe air other than what existed inside the cave. The world they were now seeing had completely changed. With ice hanging from exposed overhangs and trees, the area was completely white. The trees held a heavy frosting of snow in their branches and the world around them, after the winds ended, was silent. It was not known who started it, but suddenly they were all involved in a huge snowball fight. Laughing and acting like children, this continued for a while. It was a sign that finally they could let down a little from the pressures of the recent past. Their breath was coming out in great clouds in the crisp air, and once the initial exuberance had been burned off, they relaxed for a short time. Then as they began to retire back into the cave, each person grabbing additional firewood, to restore their depleted supplies, heading back to the warmth that the cave provided. They smelled of smoke, and when first breathing the fresh air, realized that the cave itself had to smell that way. Having been in it continually they had become used to the odors and no longer even smelled them. Now returning from the outside, it was quite obvious. Storme then said to no one in particular, "Oh this place stinks. I think it would be a good idea to open our front entrance and air this place out!"

"What? And then lose all of our heat?" One of the guys yelled back. "After all it didn't bother you until now." That brought a laugh from everyone.

Saige thought that this was probably the first time in a long time that the spirits of the group were up. It was a good sign, but he knew as they all did that winter here was just beginning. This first storm had dropped enough snow that it was between their knees and the ground. He wondered just how much would fall, and with no experience he had no answer. One of the first things that struck him once the fun was over, was that footing had changed. How did one get around in this stuff? It was something he hadn't even considered, again not surprising since where they were from it never snowed. Then calling for attention he said, "Now that was fun, and it has been a very long time, too long really, since we've had much of that. But something came to me while we were out there. Since we all come from a place where we never see this stuff, especially this close and personal, how does one walk in it? I mean right now it is to our calves and we cannot see the ground underneath. Everything now is hidden under this white stuff, so again how does one hike in it without both hurting and tiring oneself? And this is only the first storm. I don't even know how deep it's going to get before winter is over. But if this first storm is any indication I suspect we will be digging out just to keep our entrance open." These questions quieted the group down and he could see it was something that had not occurred to them either.

Stone replied saying, "There must be a way, since we are not the first to ever live in this stuff. I mean there must be some way that we do not have to break trails through this stuff, you know stay on top of it, but I have no idea how."

"Okay people, I think this is the first real problem that we have to solve. We need to be out here and learning as much as we can about these mountains. We need to be able to locate other areas that we can go to if we need to leave here. We did not have time to find anything else, and if we were found now and had to leave, we have nowhere to go at all. We have left ourselves no safety net, no escape, and I know that we really had no choice given the time limits that we had, but now with winter upon us I do not think we will have any problems from the primitives. So as severe as this is it will be our chance to find those other places that we can retreat to if the need arise."

Then one of them stated, "Now Saige why did you have to go and ruin all the fun. We've been running, fighting, busting our butts to finally get where we are now – and we have lost many a good person along the way. Finally we've had a chance to let down just a little, and then you go and spoil it with what you just said." This brought a chuckle from the group as it was recognized for what it was. It summed up what had happened to them, and then for the first time they had taken a break, giving them all time to forget, even if just briefly. Now before they even had a chance to warm up, Saige was already hitting them with the new responsibilities.

Shaking his head and smiling Saige said, "You are so right, and I am sorry. But since Shayne has placed this position upon both Shellian and I, I just do not want to fail in that trust – not only to him and his memory, but to all of you. If we all die out here, yeah I know we won't know anyway, if we all die out here then I have failed in that trust."

"That's all right." Another yelled. "If we all die out here we will kill you for failing," which brought another laugh.

Shaking his head again Saige continued. "Okay, point taken. We will just take this day off and tackle the problems tomorrow."

* * *

It then took them the better part of the major moon cycle to finally solve the problem of walking in the snow. They had tried a number of different methods, from breaking new trails in the snow, to trying to work a drag to break it up, and none of them worked. Then Stone suggested that they try to figure out how to walk on top of the snow, which brought a laugh since no one could see how it could be done, they were just too heavy. But that got them thinking and they realized that if there was a way to distribute their weight over a greater area then it could be possible. The first attempts were ugly, awkward, very difficult to use, broke often, but it proved the concept. In fact it was almost freeing to be able to move across the snow in this fashion. As time continued to pass, they made small improvements until it worked. They were finding muscles that they never used as working with these "shoes" required learning a new way to walk. Yet they found as the soreness worked out, they could cover a greater amount of territory not having to worry about obstructions as they had, when there was no snow on the ground.

Then one of the women turned up pregnant and neither she nor her lover would admit to anything. With everyone in so close proximity; it was surprising that any could find a place to get physical without being found out. Yet it now was obvious that was exactly what had happened. And it was the flirt Sorrel, so it could have been anyone. Looking at her he could see defiance and smug look on her face. Shellian had warned him and here was the proof that she had been completely truthful and right in her conclusions – now what? Then, in a short time came another shock. One of the two who were out on patrol, searching the areas and mapping it so that they could find a second location, came back into the camp winded and quite excited. Steen yelled. "I need help now! Stone fell through some of the snow that had hidden a crevasse and has fallen out of my reach. He doesn't appear to be hurt but, he appears to be on a narrow ledge and there isn't anywhere he can go but down and it is a long drop." It was midmorning and the two of them had been out since dawn, so there was a good possibility that where he had fallen was not close. No one said leadership was easy, and it just appeared that the problems and near disasters kept coming faster than he, Shellian and the rest could find answers.

Leaving the women in camp, Saige and the six other men followed Steen as he led the way back to where the fall had taken place. As they worked their way to the site, Saige saw that this was in an area that none of them had ever been. As he had feared it took them a few hours to reach the place of the accident. As they approached, he had them slow down and then use poles to check the depth of the snow. They did not need another to join Stone, complicating an already difficult situation. In the distance he could hear another one of the many waterfalls that they had encountered. At least, he mused, there was no lack of water. Now it was time to work out the rescue. Working slowly up to the edge, he looked down and saw Stone standing on a too narrow ledge that just looked like it could collapse at any moment. Then slowly withdrawing, they tied a rope that they had brought around one of the large trees that was close by, and with that anchor worked their way back to the ledge that had been revealed under the snow. But before the rope could be lowered, there came a sound of shifting snow, rock, and soil, and part of what they had just been standing on gave way and disappeared. Had they remained there even for a second more it would have caught all of them. They realized that they had been standing on top of one of the many lava tubes and this one had been thin. It had taken the additional weight of the snow and when they added their own body weight it became too much and collapsed.

Looking down at the fallen earth and snow they could see that the drop even to the piles that were just created was at least ten meters. What next? The collapse was between them and where Stone had fallen. "Now that complicates things." Saar stated. "And if it collapsed here where else does this tube run? And is it just as thin skinned as this portion just proved to be?"

"Hey doc, we have enough problems here without you coming up with questions that bring even more to our attention." Steen commented. "Okay Saige I'll add my own, now what?"

As he looked over the now very dangerous situation, he cautiously peered over into this newly opened area, he shook his head and stated, "I don't know, and I am obviously open for suggestions. This opened a pretty good section and looking at the edges of that lava that was revealed . . . well, it looks as if it would cut our rope to pieces let alone any one of us. And you are right, not only can we not be sure of our footing, but even looking inside this tube we cannot see its true direction and we will possibly see another collapse if we cross it, and it is between us and Stone." Then looking up because it suddenly became shadowed, he saw that clouds were starting to build which probably signaled the arrival of a new storm in the near future. "And if I am reading this sky right we will be having new snow soon. Come on everyone we need to get Stone and get back to the cave." Then yelling he said, "Stone! How are you faring so far?" He then listened hard and heard a distance voice say.

"Getting very cold and I think this may have been a place where that tube that I just heard collapse pushed out the side of the mountain. Maybe the collapse was a good thing, and one or two of you could carefully lower yourselves into it and see if you can find where it pushed out the side. It will be above me. When I fell through I found myself on a smooth slide and my momentum almost carried me completely over. The only way I was able to prevent it was by grabbing desperately at some vegetation that had been growing here. Thankfully it held, but there is no way I can climb out without help."

"You're the expert on this stuff. Okay maybe it's the best answer and right now I do not have any other ideas – okay we will try that." Then turning to the others he said. "Alright you heard him, I want you Seve and you Staven to be the ones to go down. We'll use the rope we have tied to the tree to get you down there and then you two can take one of the other ropes, then see if you can find the side tube that he fell through. We'll keep the rope off the tube's edge so as to not have it cut. But I have to admit that from what I can see, other than where we broke through, it's very dark down there. Did we bring anything that we can make a torch with?" Looking around he saw Seth reaching into the pack he had brought, bringing to light the materials to put together a torch. At least one of them had thought about the possibility of needing one. "Okay let's get moving on this we are running out of time once again, and why does it always seem to be that way?" He wasn't expecting an answer to his final question, but it did seem that every time they ran into some emergency or need that the time constraints would push them into the solution before they had time to truly work it out.

Now working carefully they lowered the two into the tube and watched as they lit the torch and then disappeared from sight. Now all they could do was wait. The rest could do nothing so they pulled back, dug down through the snow to the bare ground and with care built a small smoky fire. While dead wood was plentiful, it was full of moisture, which tended to hiss, pop, and spit as the moisture was forced out the wood as it burned. They could hear the voices of the three but could not make out their conversations. As they waited by the fire they would rotate one member to the tube edge to watch for the other three. Eventually the one who was watching signaled them, and they all then came over to the collapsed area. They could see that all three were now there and ready to be pulled out. Saige breathed a sigh of relief, and once they were out they headed back to the cave. The winds had picked up again and the sky was dark and ominous. Shortly it began to snow once again and by the time they had reached the cave it was snowing heavily. The temperatures had dropped considerably and they were chilled to the bone just wanting to stand around the fire until they felt comfortable again.

Going off by himself for a brief period of time Saige asked himself, "What's next?" He knew that they still had to get out and explore when the weather allowed. If they depended only on this one location they found, and if discovered they would be in real trouble, not that they weren't already. There needed to be at least one other location, and not close by, that was stocked and ready if the need arose. *So again, now what?* They were finding out that this mountain they presently were staying on was riddled with lava tubes and the incident today came close to taking them all out or at least severely injuring them, which was just as bad. Deep in thought he did not hear his sister approach and was surprised when he heard her speaking. "What's going on Saige?" She asked.

Looking up at her since he had been sitting and leaning back against one of the walls in the shadows he asked, "What do you mean? There's a lot happening as usual even for a place and time such as this."

Shaking her head she said. "You know what I mean. It sounded like this rescue could have been much worse than it turned out, and now we have one of the women carrying, and you know that with as much time that we will probably be in here that she may not end up being the only one. Nothing you or I could say will stop that from happening. It's cold and many are showing signs of being lonely. You and I are being kept quite busy trying to lead them, but there is not enough to do to keep all of them active. So they are drawn together for warmth and then it ends up going further than any had planned. But I suspect that there are no regrets. With all the hardships and losses that all of us have endured it is surprising to me that the reaching out to each other hasn't happened earlier. So I suspect even as small a group as we are we will see a rash of pregnancies soon. We have no birth control other than abstinence and that's not going to happen.

"Then once these women start birthing then what? Again we are not prepared to deal with new lives. We have nothing – nothing at all and with only Saar who never was one to take care of women . . . well, you can see where this is going."

Reaching up and pulling her down beside him he said. "I never thought that being a leader could be so hard. It is driving me crazy. We need to establish a second camp yet from the incident today it is much more dangerous out there than I first thought. Yet, we cannot stop looking, but do I send someone out into this unknown knowing that they could fall to their death or injured and die in this weather? Yet, If I don't, then we risk discovery, and if found then there would be nowhere to go and with all of our supplies here . . . Well, you can see there is this problem and now this other one has been brought into the open by the pregnancy of Sorrel, and as you just now pointed out, you are sure it will not be the last. I guess I should have guessed that it was going to go that way, but was hoping it was something that wouldn't. I tell you this if there was some way I could just give this up and let someone else do this job I would. But Shayne put his trust in you and I, and I can see that the rest look to both of us for decisions. So I guess we are stuck." Then looking at her he shrugged.

"Now before you ask, no I am not sleeping with Saar – not that the temptation isn't there. After all, I get cold at night and the thought of a warm body next to me to keep me warm is a temptation – one that I have been able to ignore for now. Like you I'm trying to be an example, and while I know that I'm in charge of the women here, as you the men, and then the two of us together the whole group, it still is something that is hard to ignore. I was just hoping that this wouldn't begin until late into the winter. Then if we had some pregnancies at least when they came to term it would be good weather. Now with them starting this early there is a chance that we may be still fighting bad weather further complicating things. As you have pointed out we have no idea how long winters last up here."

Silent for a moment Saige contemplated what Shellian had just told him, he then said, "And you feel there's nothing we can do about it. So should we conveniently ignore it? Or is there another solution that you have in mind?"

Shaking her head she said. "No, I have no answers for you. Other than the two sexes living in two different locations and not in the same cave would there be a slight, and I mean slight possibility of preventing this. But we are all together in close contact and there is no any way to change that. So no I do not think we can ignore it but I don't know how to prevent or present it either."

Sighing he said. "Okay then, just another of the many problems to face. Not that an increase in our small population is a bad thing. But as you have stated, we are not prepared for the consequences that this will present. And maybe that is the way we need to present it to the rest. Especially now that it's out in the open with Sorrel being the first to prove that there has been coupling going on. After all she cannot deny it since it is the only way one can become as she is."

Laughing lightly even though the weight of leadership was upon her she said. "Oh I am sure she would try, but there is only one other way to get that way and we have no way of providing that service here."

"That's very true. I only hope when she reaches term that the birth is not complicated since we are in no shape to handle complications here. Since our annual is 540 days, and how long does a woman normally carry before she gives birth?"

"Roughly half of that time, give or take a few on either side. But there can be complications that could endanger both the mother and unborn child. That's the greater worry, since we are so unprepared to deal with this." Then shrugging she continued. "But I guess women have been doing this since the beginning so if it was successful, and since we are here, then I guess we can learn to survive – although I for one would not want to be birthing without the pain relief drugs that we use. I've had it described to me by mothers who say it's like being ripped apart down there and that when the drugs hit that it is a welcome relief."

"So, why would one put herself through it more than once? I mean I understand the physical draw and need between the sexes, but to experience that kind of pain and then go back and do it again, that almost sounds masochistic to me."

"Again I have no personal experience yet. Although I know my time will come. But from what mothers have said that once the child is born then you forget all about that pain and are instantly in love with this new completely helpless person who must depend on you totally for everything."

"I guess that's as good as explanation as I'll ever get, and since it is something as a man that I will never face . . . I guess

I will never really know. Oh well, I guess since we are once again snowed in for a while I might as well present our situation to the group. Maybe we should start calling ourselves a clan or something since our birthplace is now gone and in a sense we are starting over far away from our home. And maybe we can start venturing outside our naming and not stick with names beginning with "S" as our city did."

"Do you think that's a good idea? I mean there is a chance that we will be able to reestablish it sometime in the future and our society has always required that the members of any city be named with the primary letter being the same as the city."

"True, true, but we are now without and we have no guarantee that we will be able to rejoin our people and the city was destroyed. This new leader of the primitives has them organized well. I don't know how easy it will to bring him down, or if that does happen, if it will be enough to break the ties that exist right now between the tribes. I suspect that they will break up once he is gone, but I cannot say whether that's just speculation on my part or fact. Anyway that's in the future and this isn't passing on what we just discussed so I guess I better just get to it." He got up went over to the fire where the majority were located, signaled a gathering waited until all were there and then said to all.

"We came close to losing a few of us today. This area appears to have many hidden dangers. It still hasn't solved one of our main problems and that's being located in only one place. If we were found then we would lose completely. We have nothing, no caches no place to go, nothing. So if for some reason the primitives came looking and found us I suspect that we then would become no more just as our city has become. I, like you am hoping that the snows and storms we have been experiencing will keep them out of the mountains. Plus whatever superstitions that seems to make it an area they stay away from, but again at least in the lower areas it does appear that the hunters do come to hunt the grazers. So even with the danger we have to find a second place, stock it, and make sure all of us know its location. This search and subsequence supplying of the second camp will take much of our time during this winter. Yet when the weather is like this we will be doing very little, which brings me to my second concern . . ." Pausing a moment before continuing, he was still a little reluctant to broach the subject but it had to be done.

"Okay all, I know we are a mixed company here, and that all of us that have survived are fully grown and are quite aware of the biology of life." Taking a deep breath before continuing and also looking at each one of them he said. "We are to try and avoid coupling since we are in no way prepared to handle pregnancies, births or any of the many complications that can arise from them. But it has been happening, and I know that it is something that will naturally happen – especially this time of the year when not much can happen and the nights are very cold." He could see the reaction from them and some appeared to have a guilty expression on their faces. So if he needed proof it had been happening it now was proven. "One of our women is indeed pregnant." Waiting to see their reaction he glanced towards Sorrel and still saw that smug look on her face and defiance in her stance. Well he would see how well she handled birthing when it was her time. "No I am not going to put a name to the one, but shortly it will be obvious to all who it is. While it is something that is hard to do all I can do is ask all of you to try and avoid any more pregnancies. We have nothing here to make it easy and we men outnumber our women and we cannot afford to lose any of you women. As it is to *you* our future belongs, and without the proper care when you are carrying we could lose any of you. That's all I am going to say on that subject for now.

"We will be continuing our mapping and patrols once this storm subsides. We have to find another place and soon. While I know from what we are seeing that up here the winters are long and harsh, but if we have not established our second camp before spring then I really believe that we will be in deep trouble. Okay then let's keep the camp we have here well supplied and clean. Our doctor can only do so much and we are responsible for the hygiene of our living areas."

CHAPTER SEVEN

It now appeared to be mid-winter and so far the only known pregnancy was Sorrel's. But whether that was because the rest were being careful or just luck, he did not know. It was time, with the last storm they had just faced, to head back out and explore some more of the area. So far with the few forays into the wilderness beyond their cave that they had been able to do, no second site had been located. On this rotation it would be Saige and Shellian who would be out. When the rotation came around that partnered them Saar would be in charge while they were away. After all, no one wanted to make the doctor mad since he was the only one who could treat anything serious. "Okay Saar I guess that about covers it. As far as the plan goes we will be out at least to dark with a possibility of not returning until late tomorrow − so until sunset tomorrow there should be no reason to worry." Saige shrugged and then continued, "As you know our plan is to continue up from the point where the accident had taken place, go deeper into the mountains and see if there is another location for us."

"Yeah, it's all good . . . but why both of you at the same time? Again I know the answer, since we rotate so that way everyone has gone out with the other members of our group.

But I hate it when it finally comes around to the two of you heading out."

Smiling a teasing smile Saige asked. "Is that the only reason doc?" He knew that Shellian was growing closer to Saar and it was obvious Saar had feelings for her.

Flushing a little from the obvious reference he asked. "Is it that obvious? I mean nothing has been said between us since both she and I have too much going on to have much time to even talk."

"Yes it's that obvious, but both of you are just too responsible to allow something like a relationship get in the way of your duty, at least for now. I just wish the rest would take the two of you as examples of how we need to be, but I guess I am asking too much. Anyway don't worry too much since we were trained as a team and we are close. If you remember – even though it is getting hard to do so – Shayne had continually placed the two of us as the top working team. I don't know, maybe it is because we are siblings, and have worked together for annuals, so I feel confident that we will be back." At this point he heard Shellian say something. He turned around to face the entrance where she was standing. "Yes Shellian?"

"Saige the sun is beginning to break so we need to be going."

"Well doc you heard the boss – see you when we get back." He then joined his sister and they headed outside to a crisp cold morning. Clouds formed each time they breathed out, and they could feel the bite through their clothes, which sent an involuntary shiver through them. "Boy its cold out here!" Saige said.

"You're not going to get me to disagree. I thought we dressed warm enough but now I am not so sure. I am glad we packed heavily though so if we need to add something it's in our packs. Now, since I haven't been where Stone fell to that ledge, why don't you lead on, *oh brother of mine*. I think once we get moving that we'll warm up. It's just the shock of leaving a warm place into this very cold one."

Nodding Saige led off heading deeper into the mountains remembering back to that day when they headed out to make that rescue and almost having to face a second more dangerous rescue. They had been lucky that there had been some warning. Now they were heading back into that area, an area that they had avoided, but since the other directions had produced nothing it was now the best unexplored area that could produce a second campsite. The snow crunched under their "shoes for walking in the snow". "You know we need a better name for these things."

"Name for these things? What are you talking about Saige?"

"Oh these inventions that we came up with, you know the shoes for the snow that allows us to walk on top of it instead of having to break a trail through it."

"Do they require a special name? I think 'shoes for walking in the snow' is just fine. After all it tells anyone just what they do and isn't that what a name is for?"

"Yeah I guess so, but it seems so awkward. Think about it. *I'm going outside, now I am going to put on my shoes for walking in the snow.* Now doesn't that sound funny?"

Laughing at his antics and the way he stated it she said. "I see what you mean. But does everything need some kind of name?"

"Now hold on sis. It seems to me that you women are guiltier of naming everything than we guys. You know assigning pet names to this or that."

"We don't do that . . . oh yeah; I guess we do don't we. Okay guilty as charged sir."

Laughing as they continued their hiking, he found that once they were moving that he was warming up. The views in the cold crisp clear air were spectacular. It was almost like they could see far enough to find their destroyed city – but he knew that was impossible. The landscape they were hiking through was pristine, with the trees having a heavy white layer on top of the green. And where the mists from the rivers drifted, there were sheets of ice reflecting the sunlight in an almost blinding array of color. And where the sun shone through the mists small rainbows formed drifting with them and then disappearing – an area that was just as dangerous as it was beautiful. They continued talking as they worked their way to where the lava tube was exposed. From there he hoped to find a way past and then head higher into the mountain. With the one collapse in that area, a quick survey had identified a large lava flow in the very distant past, and probably the reason for the one huge lava tube that they had almost fallen into.

Yet unlike the cave they were presently living in, there had been no sign of any cave of that size located. Yes there had been a number of smaller ones, but none were big enough to sustain a group their size. Nor were there a number of smaller ones close enough together to be used. It had been a frustrating experience. Once they had begun finding the smaller caves, before they located the one they were living in, it was assumed that it would be a simple thing. Yet it had proven to be anything but. So now deep into winter nothing had been located, although with the amount of snow that was on the ground that in itself was no surprise. At least they were learning the area, which was just as important as finding a second camp. So once they had worked their way past the lava tube they would be in unknown lands.

As it approached midmorning they finally reached the place of the collapse. Shellian said, "So this is it. Hmmm, I thought it was smaller from the description, and the area doesn't quite match the picture I had in my mind. In fact I would never have guessed that this was the area at all. The only real hint is that cliff off to our right. Did you have time to figure out which way the tube ran? I mean I would hate to fall through it again like you guys almost did."

"The best we could determine was that it continues north from here. Kind of in the direction we are going since we are heading higher up. Apparently when this thing was active, it was very active and hot. This would not been a place that I would wanted to be. So, I for one am glad that this one died thousands of annuals ago. And as you can see the trail that we have available to us is limited, so all we can hope is that the tube veers off in some other direction, and we are not hiking on top of it for very much longer. I do not want to tempt fate."

Nodding in agreement she said. "Me either really. So how do you want to do this? Other than *careful* of course."

"I really am not sure. But this was one of the reasons I brought the rope along. I think for a while we will tie it between us so that if the unthinkable happens then at least the one or the other of us can keep us from falling too far."

Pausing a moment before answering she then said. "Okay, sounds like a plan to me, since I cannot think of any other solution."

Looking at his sister in the morning light he thought. *She really is a beautiful woman. Tall, lithe in build. Her skin browned by being outside, green eyes and dark blonde hair that is now down to the middle of her back, but is being bleached by the sun to lighter tones. She moves with the grace of a hunter. You can read the confidence she has in herself and her abilities.* Shaking his head he thought that if the relationship between Saar and she continued he would have a wonderful mate. That was something that was difficult to comprehend as they had always been together and the thought of her leaving to join another man just hadn't entered his thoughts. But he knew that was the way of life and he would be happy for her when that time came – that's if they survived to allow such a thing to happen. Then to cover his thoughts he said, "Then let's be at it, and I don't have to remind either you or me to be careful, since we do not know what this snow is hiding underneath."

He removed the rope from the pack and they tied it between them. He led off using the walking stick he had to probe the snow ahead as they worked their way up a narrow V, which was the only way out from where they were. It was a rugged broken area and it must have been hell when this eruption had taken place. It literally appeared to have blown up. But again this had been a long time ago since trees and plants in the area had reclaimed the land and many showed age. As they worked their way through the V, the trail pushed ever higher and while they were breathing hard from the exertion when they came out of the V and found themselves on top and once again in the open. Once there they had to stop and catch their breath, finding another alpine meadow covering they suspected at least a kilometer. Partially covered in snow, but some areas were bare of snow and it led to questions as to why.

"So I see we have a small plateau here. But why snow, no snow?" He asked. Then before she could respond a heavy wind hit them almost knocking them off their feet and chilling them to the bone. "Well, I guess that explains it." He yelled over the wind. "Let's find us somewhere out of it. Damn that's cold!" Looking at his sister he could see her teeth chattering and knew that it was exactly the same for her. They headed towards an area that still had much of the snow on it assuming that it was protected from the wind and when they got there it was in fact calm.

"That wind just cut through everything", she said. "I was warm and fine until it hit me and then instantly I was freezing."

"Same for me, I think we will stop here and have our midday meal. At least here out of the wind – don't know how far this goes and what if any would be out of these winds. I'll look around and see if I can find us any wood, if you would, see if you could find a place that we can build a fire. He then untied the rope that was around his waist and she did the same, he coiled it and placed it back into the pack and headed off to find wood to build a fire. She went around a small curve in the protruding rock that jutted up out of the meadow, which protected them from the winds, and dug down a short way through the snow and found plenty of rocks to build a small fire ring. He, in the meantime, searched the woods near the open meadow looking for protected dead wood for the fire. They both carried materials to start a fire, but there was no way to carry more than that and still be able to carry their packs. Eventually he found where a couple of ancient trees had died and fallen sometime in the past. There he was able to find much dead wood that was away from the snow. With an effort that left him breathing hard he finally had a large stack and headed back to where they had planned on building the fire only to find that Shellian was nowhere around.

Thinking that maybe she needed to make a nature call, he decided that was not such a bad idea and went back to the tree line to relieve himself. He then returned and she still was missing. Now he began to worry a little. There were predators around, but they had rarely seen any of them. It appeared, like much of the animal life here, at least here in the higher elevations, some of the predators slept through the winter. There was still a little snow where they had decided to break and he then circled their temporary camp to find her trail, and shortly he picked up her tracks heading deeper into the meadow towards a rock face. She had taken her pack so he felt confident that she hadn't been attacked by an animal, but instead had seen something that had drawn her attention. With the air so clear it turned out to be further to the rock face than he expected. When he reached it he then saw Shellian emerging from what looked to be shadows. She turned and saw him and then waved. With concern on his face he finally reached where she was standing. "Don't ever do that again!" He admonished.

"Do what?" she asked perplexed.

"Leave like that. When I got back you were gone. I figured you went off to relieve yourself and thought that it was a good idea so I did the same. But when I got back a second time you still was not anywhere to be found."

"Sorry brother. I really had not meant to just disappear. And you are right that's exactly what I was originally doing. After setting up for the fire I realized that it would be a good time to do just that. So while you were gathering wood I headed off in this direction took care of the need, and then turned to come back when I saw this rock face and something just did not look right to me. So I decided to investigate."

"Investigate? Investigate what?"

Pointing she said. "This."

Looking hard in the direction she was pointing he at first saw nothing, but by looking to either side of where she pointed he found a darker area in the shadows that she had emerged from. "So what is it that you found or thought you saw?"

"Well, like when I found the cave we are presently in, the shadows here looked just wrong. So I thought it was best that I check it out. And since I was closer to this rock face than I was compared to where we were planning to camp I decided to investigate. Come brother I have something to show you." She began to walk back into the shadows, making a quick right, she disappeared.

Shrugging he followed and found that he had just entered another cave. But this one was different. There was a soft glow to the walls allowing him to see the interior with this dim soft light. "What is this place?" He asked knowing that she wouldn't have an answer.

"Don't know." She replied somewhat subdued. "I don't think this one is natural. But it isn't very large. Not large enough for a second location, but, well, it's just different."

That was an understatement. "Tell you what, I'll go back and get the wood that I brought to where we were going to build our fire. Why don't you set up a fire ring at the entrance to this and then after we eat we can really look this over. You are right about the size, but that doesn't mean that it can't be used for a supply location. What do you think . . . we are what, probably about ten kilometers from our winter camp?"

"Actually I think we are a bit farther than that. Remember it took to mid-morning to reach the area where the accident happened. And you had traveled there before so it would seem to be less distance to you than to me because you were familiar with it. So I would guess that it's probably closer to fifteen by the way we had to go. But by one who flies probably no more than five or six."

"Yeah you were always good at estimating distances and you are right the first part of our travels appearing to be short. I'll go get the wood now, see you back here shortly . . . and . . . this time don't wander off."

As he disappeared from sight she went to collect a new set of rocks to form the fire ring when a couple of things struck her about this strange cave. But until she finished constructing the fire ring she would have to wait to confirm what she thought she had observed. In a short time due to the amount of available stones she had a proper fire ring constructed. Saige had yet to return so she prepared to go back inside the small cave to confirm what her mind had shown her. Since she had more time inside, she felt that he would not have had a chance to make the same observations, so before pointing them out she needed to make sure. Leaving the bright sunlight, she reentered the cave and again was struck by the soft glow that the walls were emitting. It did not take long for her eyes to adjust to this softer light. She did a careful search of the cave finding the soils on the floor to be soft and powdery. While doing this she heard Saige approaching and then the pile of wood he was carrying hit the ground. Then she heard him call out for her. "Saige, I'm in the cave. Something struck me as strange about this and I am checking it out. Go ahead and get a fire going then come in here and join me. I think you will find this interesting." She then continued her investigation. Shortly she heard the crackle of a fire and then Saige was inside the cave with her.

"Okay sis, what have you found?" He asked

Signaling him to join her she pointed at the floor of the cave and said. "First there are no tracks of animals in here – small or large, just none. At first I thought that the ground here was hard, but as you can see it is anything but . . . so why no tracks? I thought well maybe a wind worked its way in here and wiped them out. But then I noticed that there are no droppings, no leaves, nothing at all. It's like someone had come in here and cleaned it out. That got me to worrying that maybe someone had and whoever it was, was not far away and would be returning. But the minute I thought that I dismissed it as this place seems to be quite undisturbed for a long time In fact the only tracks are ours."

Looking closely at what she pointed out to him he said. "Okay I see what you mean. I just realized something else. Does it seem to be warm in here or is it because I have been moving out there in the cold and wind and have stepped in and out of that weather."

Thinking about it again she said, "No. No I think you're right. And if you are right where is the heat coming from? Now this becomes stranger by the minute."

At this point both began to search the cave more closely and after a period of time came away with no easy answers. There appeared to be no reason for the light, the heat, and the absence of animal sign inside this cave. "Well this might not be large enough for a second living site, but I see a potential for storage. Since it seems that no animal can get inside here for whatever the reason is, then it would be a great place to store our food, and whatever other items that could be destroyed by animals. But who made this place, what for, and when?" He asked.

"You got me on that one." She replied. "Do you think we should return and report our discovery to the rest so that some of our supplies could be moved here as you suggested?"

"No. Again at first I thought so myself. But we need to finish our exploring. One day or two won't make that much of a difference. And we still need to locate a better place. Not that this is a bad one. But again it's just not big enough to be anything more than a storage area and we need another place to stay."

"Okay then I'll mark it on the map that we are making while we eat and then we can continue up the mountain."

He took off his heavy coat and found that indeed it was warm inside the cave. Warm enough that he could have left the coat off. He shrugged back into it and they went out to the fire with both lost in their thoughts as they ate their midday meal. Finding this particular cave left him feeling uneasy. Maybe whoever had built it was responsible for the primitives being afraid of the mountains and making it sacred and off limits to other than their priests and the occasional hunters. He suggested the same to Shellian, who was deep in thought herself. She was also putting the details on the map they were constructing as they explored. He wasn't even sure she had heard him, but what she was doing was critical anyway and what he had asked had no real answer.

"Saige I just don't have any idea at all. It truly is a mystery. It's obvious that whoever did this did not construct the cave with primitive tools. But to add the light, put up some type of barrier to the keep the animals out, and add heat also. It sounds like something we are capable of truthfully. But as far as I know from what history that was passed on to us in the learning centers we were never in these mountains."

"My conclusions also. But who knows, maybe this is old enough that it could relate to a time before the great wars that led these people becoming primitives. There is nothing in our history books to let us know the true level of technology from that period. But if that is true that means this cave is at least a few thousand years old." Thinking a moment before continuing he said, "I don't see how anything could continue to function for that long."

"I have to agree with you. Unless, like our people, there was a small part of them that survived and took refuge in these mountains – bringing their tech with them. And then over time they just disappeared for who knows what reason. So this may not be that old. Still it could be."

Suddenly alarmed, Saige said, "What if they did not die out or disappear and are still hidden in these mountains?"

Catching his drift she suddenly picked up the same sense of fear and said. "And if they are still around we may be under observation right this moment and never be the wiser."

"Yes, and the way we are dressed we would appear to them to be the primitives." Pausing a moment and thinking he said, "Now wait a minute here. Did you see any sign of anyone or anything at all when you found this?"

"No, but that doesn't mean anything at all. This cave may only be used as a forward point of observation so it would be one that would not be used very often." Still in her voice there appeared to be a small amount of doubt. After all, other than this small abandoned cave, there was no evidence of anybody around, still . . . still that did not prove that there wasn't either. "Okay brother what do you want to do?"

Looking down and taking a deep breath before answering he said, "I'm not really sure. So far there has been no proof of anyone here other than us. But again as big as these mountains are an army could be hidden away and never be found. And just as easily some other remnants from the same war our ancestors survived could have retreated into these mountains and then became completely hidden, or because of the harshness of living up here died out. I guess we will have to continue our exploring, but with the idea that we may be under observation. After all if these people we are imagining *are* real, then with the time that has passed they would be very good at concealment – probably much better than we are since they would live here."

"So you think then if they are here that there is a good chance we may not see them at all."

"That pretty much sizes it up, unless we accidentally stumble across one of their hidden cities, and if there are such things here, I have no idea what to look for, how they would have hidden them, or what they would look like."

"True", Shellian replied, "we've only been here a short time and really only because we were forced here. So we know so very little about this whole mountain range. After all, we both know that we, as a people, live in the valleys and flatlands and did not venture into these or any mountains that I know of. And, as you pointed out we wouldn't be here now if we were not forced to be here – although with as small of group that we have I think we have done quite well."

"Yeah, but remember we have been trained to survive. Had it been some of the regular members of the city and had they made it this far – which is doubtful – they would not have had the tools or knowledge to have lasted this long."

Shaking her head in agreement she said. "Yeah you're probably right. So that brings up the question, if a group from the wars came up here, could they survive if they had no training? I guess part of the answer is here with this cave. But that only proves that for a period of time someone survived, and does not mean that they still are around."

"Well as you said, this is all speculation. So unless we actually find some proof that is newer than this cave we can assume that we are alone up here. But at the same time keep it in our minds that we may not be and act accordingly." Sighing, he continued, "I guess we need to put this fire out and continue on. I think we will stay out overnight and then circle back to our camp. This discovery is such a surprise, and actually a little encouraging."

"Encouraging? Really? What do you mean by that?" She asked perplexed.

"Even with the equipment to construct this small cave it meant that whoever did this had to be up here for quite a while, which means that they survived and that is good news for us, giving us an example that it is possible to do so." Then waving his hand at her as he saw her reaction, he then continued. "Yeah I know we are surviving also. But so far we have luck on our side. There have been a couple of close calls, but no serious injuries, and best of all no deaths. Our party is so small that losing any would put the rest in jeopardy of failure and death. Again, as we both know we do not know how long this winter is going to last, and we have one woman who will be adding to our numbers soon. Who knows others may be joining her. After all, each of these pregnancies, while a good thing in the long run, actually increases the chance of loss – so even this is a very worrisome thing. And, as you also know, we have fewer women than men. So if we were to lose even one of you in childbirth, well it would be something else that could push us to the brink of dying out."

Silent for a moment she said. "Okay I'll concede what you stated, and everything you've just said has more or less been with me also. But there is something you did not think about here. Imagine this. Instead of living up here to build this cave, what if they lived down below and then during the warm season sent work crews up here to build this. I mean that could be a possibility also."

"You're right, but why? I mean this is or seems to be quite isolated. And it's a long way from the valley floor where the primitives presently live. But that doesn't mean it couldn't have been done that way. I just can't come up with a reason as to why – okay, I guess we're ready to continue. Which way would you like to tackle this, sis?"

"How do you mean that? Tackle what? The direction we are going, or to be careful and watchful, or be aware that we could be watched, or what?"

Grinning he said, "Oh all of the above or whichever one hits your fancy. Actually I just meant lead on as we head deeper and higher on this mountain. It does appear that you have an ability to pick these caves up, while the rest of us miss them. Why is it anyway?"

They began to work their way up and away from the discovered cave following a dim path that one could sense more than see. "I really don't know what it is. If I did then I could teach others to do it. But something just doesn't look right to me when I spot them." Shaking her head as she thought about it, "And really that's the best I can describe it. I don't know what the difference is or what is wrong, but to me there just is."

* * *

They covered another ten to twelve kilometers before stopping for the night. Again along the pathway they had decided to travel they did not find a second cave until just before dark. And this one like the last one had been constructed. It appeared, at least from the two that they had discovered, that they were built to cover a specific distance. So, if there had been travelers, sometime in the great past, then these would provide permanent shelters that would require no maintenance. It was a simple solution, but would have required an enormous amount of labor to construct. Again, like the first one they had found, this one was not large, and the floor was covered in loose powdery dirt with the walls having the soft glow and the area warm. Again no animals or animal sign was found within the cave. What was it that the builders had used that prevented wild animals from crossing the thresholds? It was an ability they did not possess even when they still were in the city. Now the question they faced was where did this pathway, one so unused that it was almost invisible to the eye, lead?

As they had continued their exploring that afternoon they finally had come to the conclusion that they were alone. The evidence, as they continued pointed to something or someone from the distant past. The path they were now on, the undisturbed nature of the two caves, the shear feeling of abandonment and disuse lay upon everything. Again, as they had searched the two caves, there was nothing within them either. Nothing had been stockpiled for travelers, such as firewood or even places to sit. It was like a decision had been reached and everything of value had been removed. Then, whomever it was that had built the caves, simply vanished. As they sat close to the small fire before retiring he said, "You know whoever these people were; they may be the reason for the fear and sacredness of these mountains to the primitives."

"Really? How so?" She asked.

"Okay now, let's, for an example, take these caves that we have discovered. For us it is a technology we can duplicate – well most of it anyway. But for the primitives it must have appeared to be magic. I am sure that with much labor they could dig a cave or pit, but to add the heat, lighting, and protection is so far beyond anything they could do that it would mean that maybe their gods had created them. And so far this is all we have found, these caves. I suspect that as we follow this path that we will be discovering much more. Again I think that whoever these people were, they wanted to be isolated. Otherwise why build your civilization in such a harsh and remote place? So if it was also part of their plan, then it is only logical to think that they would then put something in place to scare and keep the primitives away."

"I guess what you are saying makes sense. But what if, instead of wanting to be isolated like this, they had no choice. Now before you say anything let me finish. Look at our cities and us. We have kept ourselves isolated from the primitives for what . . . thousands of years. And part of that reason is we were afraid of what now is exactly happening to us. So what if these people faced the same issues and problems? So the isolation was not so much a choice as a necessity. And then to build in safeguards would only make sense. After all that's exactly what we did."

Thinking about what she said made sense. Yet he knew that either scenario was possible and that they were just guessing. Standing up and then pacing around he said, "I wonder if maybe in the end they suffered the same fate that we as a people are now facing with the primitives."

"No I don't think so. If that were true then these mountains wouldn't be off limits to the primitives. They would have conquered their demons and then they would have been free to travel here – although I wouldn't know why . . . anyway enough of the speculation. We still don't know enough to be able to come up with any real answer. At least with the cave we can sleep easier not having to worry about any wild animals disturbing us or needing to keep a fire going just to keep warm. So right now I am thankful for whomever it was that constructed these caves. And with that I am going to retire back into this one. We have much to do tomorrow so I want to get a good night sleep. There are some mysteries here and I for one would like some answers."

"Okay sis. I'm still too wound up but promise that I will be with you shortly. This surely is a puzzle that we have uncovered. And you're right we aren't going to solve it with the little we know right now." He remained by the fire for a while longer thinking about what they had uncovered and discussed. Now another issue came to mind. But it was too late to discuss it with his sister. That would have to wait until the morning now. This exploration that they were doing was to be only two days, which meant that they should begin their loop back in the morning. Yet, these first pieces of this new puzzle had him intrigued. As far as they knew they and their cities were the only ones to have broken away from the ancient wars and then hidden themselves from the world. So now it began to appear that maybe they were not the only ones to have done that. So they could return back as planned tomorrow or they could continue in their present direction and hope to discover more. One thing for sure, they couldn't split up, with one returning and one continuing. "Oh well . . ." He said softly. "I'm not going to answer this tonight. Better go in and get some sleep." He noticed that the fire had burned down to coals anyway and he did not want to add any more fuel. So with a sigh he got up and headed inside the cave where he heard the even soft breathing of his sister. It was obvious that she was asleep. Well he needed to be there himself. So he climbed into his sleeping sack and tried to find a comfortable position, turned over, and the next thing he remembered was the gray of dawn.

Stretching he looked over to where his sister had been sleeping and saw that she was already gone. Taking a deep breath he crawled out of the warm sack and then headed outside where the air was crisp and his breath came out in clouds. He saw Shellian next to the fire pit coaxing a new fire. "Chilly out here this morning," he commented, "I wonder what the builders used to power these caves. Yes I know that the earth is a natural insulator. But that still doesn't account for the difference."

Looking up from her 'fire starting' she said, "Just another piece of this puzzle. I'm sure that part of the solution has to be some type of a solar collector. But there isn't anything around that I have been able to observe that could be that kind of device. I know that in our cities that such a system got its power from the power unit – not solar. Out here there is no such luxury. So like you I don't know. Besides this wasn't our expertise anyway. If we had an engineer or someone like that then they might know immediately how it's done."

"True, ours is wildness survival, and right now I am glad that it is. If we had one of the city's jobs we probably would be dead right now. Hey I'm going out to make my morning nature call be right back." He then left to relieve himself, and when he returned she had a roaring warm fire going. "That feels great. It's funny how something as simple as a camp fire can make one feel comfortable and safe."

"True, it's really surprising how little it takes to make one feel comfortable. You know after I left you last night to lay down a thought entered my mind . . ."

"Only one? That's a surprise." He said laughing lightly.

Looking for something to throw at him and finding nothing she said. "You're lucky I couldn't find something. Cause I would have done it too."

Still laughing Saige said. "Yes you would have, and I would have had to run because you are very accurate when you throw something. Anyway like you, after you left, I had something come to mind also. Bet cha' we thought of the same thing."

"Okay smarty what was it that I was thinking?"

"First off as a woman most of what you think I haven't a clue. I think that most women are not able to figure out what another woman is thinking. So being a man my chances of even coming close are, oh I don't know . . . maybe a million to one, or maybe a billion to one. But on the serious side, I think that you came up with the same conclusion that we have to decide whether to continue with our discoveries or turn back, finish our loop, and be back to camp by tonight. Does that sound about right?"

"Oh aren't you the funny one this morning. But I cannot disagree with anything you have said. And yes that's exactly what struck me last night. But I did not want to come back out and talk about it then, as I have to admit that I was quite tired and ready for some sleep."

"I had the thought just after you left, and decided that I did not want to bother you with it since discussing it last night or this morning would change nothing, and, well I decided to wait until today to discuss it with you. Now that it seems we, once again, were on the same page, what are your thoughts? Do we finish it like originally planned or do we continue to explore and find answers to the questions this is presenting?"

Looking in her bag and inventorying it she then said. "Okay first of all, I personally would like to continue. While we do not have a lot of food here if we are careful we can probably extend it for a couple more days. I know that they are expecting us back tonight, and by not showing up we will cause undue worry, especially for Saar. But what we have found so far leads me to want to continue. I think if we are back within five days at the most it should be okay. But to be safe for both of us I suggest that we travel on until tonight and then return no matter what we find or don't find. Then we can plan a larger, time wise, exploration and be better prepared. How does that sound to you?"

CHAPTER EIGHT

Saar was worried. Shellian and Saige should have been back two days ago and had yet to make an appearance. He had reluctantly taken over the leadership while they were absent and really did not want to have this position permanently. He had observed both Shellian and Saige while they solved the day-to-day problems and thought for a short time it should be easy. Yet observing verses doing was vastly different. And when he found how petty some of their group was and the small problems that continued and were never solvable he really, really wanted nothing to do with this position ever again. *How do they do it?* He thought. *I just don't understand.* He was their doctor so he was very familiar with responsibility. But there, it was with each, as they had needed his services. So, while overall he was responsible for all of the members, it was only in the role of a doctor, not leader. He was finding that there was a vast difference between the two.

And now it was snowing again. It had started late on the third day and had yet to stop – the only advantage to this storm over others, there were no winds with it. It was dead calm. And when one walked outside in the snowfall it did not feel overly cold. But with the way snow fell and the patterns the mind formed with the falling snow it was easy to get disorientated. *So again where were they? Did something happen that has either injured or killed them?* Oh my how he hoped not. It was not only the fact that he and Shellian were becoming serious, but as small as their group was losing just one more was a bad thing. But two would be devastating. With confirmation now that four of the six women were pregnant, this factor alone would put a large burden on them, but to reduce their numbers by two could be fatal. He found that he continued to watch the opening to outside hoping that any moment they would come through and join them inside the cave.

Looking around to the rest he could sense that they were as uneasy about the situation as he. Again where were they? He saw Stone approaching took a deep breath and when he stood next to him asked. "What can I do for you Stone?"

"Not much doc. I can see that you are worried about our two leaders and I was going to ask yesterday to grab someone and go out and search for them. But first the clouds dropped down and formed a thick fog, and then when it lifted it began to snow. So I knew that you would say no. And while I might have disagreed with you I knew that you would be right. So what do you want to do?"

"To tell the truth I don't know. I would love to be out there trying to locate them, but as you have so well stated, the weather is once again against us. So I guess we just have to wait. Yeah I know waiting is a very hard thing to do, but it would be foolish to go out in this stuff. If something has happened to them then there's nothing we could do anyway. But as you and I know we are experts in living in the wilderness, and before you protest I know it was down where we came from. But much of what applied there applies here also. And because we know what to look for, anything that is different we learn quickly. Think about it Stone, just how much we've already learned up here? And we've been here such a short time overall. Again I know that at times when we are locked inside this cave that it seems to be an eternity. After all we are used to the open spaces and not spending all of our time inside a cave like this."

Sitting down and thinking about what Saar said, he realized why Saige and Shellian had left him in charge when it was their turn to explore. Yet he could see that Saar was nervous about it and really did not like being the leader. Still because of those reservations he probably was a good choice. He knew that a couple here really wanted to be in charge, and he thanked whoever was in charge of watching them from above that when Saige and Shellian left that they did not put one of those in charge – especially Schylar. He could see him pestering both Shellian and Saige all the time to take over while they were gone. It was obvious that he was power hungry. But while he had these ambitions he did not have the skills – not that any could tell him. He had an overblown view of himself and his abilities. If one was around him long enough he would tell you what the two in charge were doing wrong and how he could do it so much better. He had convinced at least one of the women in the group and she was now sleeping with him. And Storme was now pregnant with his child. So it went deeper than just believing what he spouted around the camp. At least that relationship was obvious. Stone then came back around from his thoughts and looked back at Saar and said, "I know what you mean. It is so tough to have to just wait – when it is easier to just go do . . . whether doing is right or wrong. So I commend you on not giving in and allowing any of us to go looking. You did good."

"Thank you for that Stone. Believe me it was one of the things I really wanted to do – you know go and find them. But I realized how stupid that was. Yes we know approximately where they were going. But again that's only an approximate. According to what they've found would then determine if they stayed on the planned route or went a different direction. Heck I know that even extending their time out was included and I am hoping that is exactly what this is. Oh while you are here, sorry different subject here, I am worried with only two of our women not carrying what this will do for the rest of us. I know that you are not involved with any of them so I am not accusing you of anything here at all. It's just as these women come to term it will be difficult for them as well as the rest of us. I think that we are pretty strained now. But when the babies arrive, and from what I can see other than Sorrel, the other three will be close together when their time comes, that these women will be incapacitated for a short time while they are healing and nursing their newborn. I am sure that the men that have fathered these children will be distracted also. It is only right that it should be this way. Of course with Sorrel no one knows who slept with her or who the father is. We may never know other than it has to be one of us. And I am not saying either you or I, since I am sure that neither of us joined her in her bed. But whoever it was, and again I am sure with her personality it was more than one of us she bedded, it will again be a distraction for those men. I know I'm a little long winded here but I see how you kind of observe what's happening so I thought it would be a good idea to bring you up to speed with my concerns. Anyway it means with at least half of our group either out or distracted it could lead to problems, accidents and not enough of us left to be able to provide what we need. Plus I do not have any of the necessary pain drugs to ease these births. I regret it, but we barely have anything at all that I had at my disposal back in the city. Now don't think that you are the only one I am telling this to. I've kept both of our leaders informed. Although I already know that Shellian is quite aware of all of this. I guess I could or maybe should say that it was she that brought it to my attention, even though I was kind of aware of it. Does this make sense to you?"

Sitting down next to Saar, Stone thought a moment before answering. "I know of only one other woman in our group that is pregnant, are you telling me that it's more than that?"

"Yes actually four are, and no, Shellian is not one of them. The only other woman who is not at this time is Seirra. And in her case I don't know if it is luck or if she has been avoiding becoming physical. But it would not surprise me if sometime in the near future that she joined the other four. As far as Shellian and me, we both know our feelings, but for now, we are not sleeping together, besides we are just too busy with what we have to do to find time for such a thing. And to be honest even with this long winter here in the mountains and being closed in like we are I am just too tired by the day's end to do anything but fall asleep when I lay down."

"I knew that doc. Hmmm, so Seirra is one of the only not carrying. In a way I am surprised. I mean she is a beautiful woman, and open, easy to talk to and friendly. With her natural beauty you would expect some of the other women to be jealous of her, but she has a natural way of deferring such things. And in truth I do not think she even sees herself that way. I am sure she has had many suitors here who would be more than happy to be chosen by her."

"I can't disagree with that assessment. I really think she has her eyes on just one male here, and he is completely unaware of it. After all he is so busy trying to keep everything from falling apart that he is blind that way for now."

"Ah I see. You mean Saige don't you. Well if you are right I am sure somewhere along the line she will make it clear to him that he is her choice. In a way I couldn't blame her. After all, our leader, with his sister of course, is a deep thinker, he tries to anticipate, plan, and really cares about what happens to us – just the kind of thing that a woman would really want in a mate. So what are the chances that he will ever notice doc?"

"Not my place to say, but what worries me is that this leaves a number of men on the outside, and that could have dire consequences." Then pausing for a moment, a smile came across his face he said somewhat softly. "Of course with the way Sorrel is offering her charms to any, maybe it won't be an issue. Oh by the way Stone it appears that with the present arrangements that you are left out in the cold. You aren't taking advantage of Sorrel's offers are you?"

Laughing softly and shaking his head Stone replied. "No doc, she holds no interest to me. And yes I know the situation but I am not alone in that area. But you must remember doc that I am a loner anyway, and an observer. That's why I know what I know. But who is actually taking Sorrel up on her favors I really don't know. Although it would not be too hard to narrow it down especially if the other three who are now carrying are in solid relationships. We know that you and Shellian are getting serious even though the two of you try to avoid it openly. And that Saige is too busy and wouldn't take Sorrel up on her offer if she did offer. And I just confirmed to you that I am not involved with her. So let's see here whose left? There are only Sajan, Sojar, and Steen left. And from my observations she has approached all three of them at different times. Oh I know throughout a day she is around most of us, but she seems to linger around them more than the rest of us."

"Something to keep in mind that's for sure. Have you passed this knowledge on to our leaders yet? I'm worried that if she continues as she has, and truthfully I don't see her changing her ways anytime soon – although her up and coming child birthing might give her second thoughts, but I doubt it – that this could lead to open, or maybe not so open conflict between her lovers as they vie for her favors. And from what I have seen she would love it. I wouldn't be surprised if she has already started to hint to any or all of them to manipulate them into doing something stupid."

Both Saar and Stone jumped when another familiar voice answered. They thought they were alone and had been deep in their conversation. "Damn it Saige! Where or maybe I should say when did you get here?" Saar exclaimed.

Standing next to Saige was Shellian, and then smiling he said, "Oh long enough to get most of what this conversation was covering. Parts of it we were aware of but the two of you have confirmed some of what we were not sure of. Now before the two of you start asking questions of us we need to get a little food, and warm up a bit. This storm was a surprise, and while we had clothes enough, when that fog dropped on top of us it changed the look of everything. We had to be careful not to go in circles since all of our landmarks had been obscured. This slowed us down somewhat. Anyway we will call a general meeting once we have had a chance to eat something and relax a little. Until then we will allow you to remain in charge. You can pass it on that we want to talk with everyone. On this trip, well let's say we found something interesting, kind of tantalizing, but for now that's all I'll say. See you shortly." And with that both of the leaders headed deeper into the cave to grab something to eat and to relax for a short time.

Looking over at Stone Saar said. "I almost jumped out of my skin there. I mean I thought we were alone and then to have them both there without either you or I sensing they were here, well you know what I mean."

"Yeah doc I do. But you got to remember that they were the best at stealth. So if any could sneak up on us and leave us unaware it would be them."

"I agree, but we were discussing some very sensitive information here, and had others come close enough to hear us then something might have gotten out to the rest that could be misconstrued, or changed to be damaging. I guess we will just have to be more careful when we discuss this kind of thing in the future. But I am glad that they are back, safe, and I for one will be glad to give them back the reins to this small group. I never wanted it in the first place, but know that I or maybe you will have to do it again once they have to go out again as a team."

"I know that both of us have their trust. And it is something that I don't take lightly, and both of us know that they would never put Schylar in charge, but that doesn't keep him from trying." Pausing for a moment Stone continued, "Again I know that neither you nor I ever want to be the leader here, and I think that is why we end up being in charge when they are gone."

* * *

"Okay all, since it is obvious that we were out a lot longer than the plan had called for there had to be a reason for us to extend out exploration." Looking around to make sure he had the entire group's attention Saige continued. "I think that I will allow Shellian to fill you in on the initial find since, as usual, she was the one who discovered it. I don't know why or how but she has a talent for finding caves – Shellian . . ."

"Okay Saige, simply stated we were taking our mid-day meal break when I noticed something amiss, kind of like when I found this cave, and then went to explore to answer my curiosity. At the time Saige was out in another direction gathering wood for our fire. He came back to the spot where we had set up and of course I wasn't there." She then went on to explain what she had found, and at that point turned it back over to Saige.

"Needless to say we were excited to have found this cave. But as she has stated it was much too small to act as a second camp area. But it's manmade, not natural. So that got us to wondering if maybe some other people had survived the great wars and had escaped to these very mountains. We then became worried that if that was fact they could still be here and we could be under observation. Yet, both the cave and the path showed no use in the recent past. In fact we felt that it hadn't been used in a very long time. The path was almost nonexistent, and we sensed more than saw it." He then went on to explain the finding of a second cave along the path. Here they had made the decision to continue up the path for another full day before returning, knowing that it would extend their time out to twice the planned time. But they had hoped to find an answer to this new riddle. "At least with the way they are protected, we can use them for caches of additional supplies and know that they will be safe. Unfortunately all we found on that additional day of travel were two more of the caves. Yet the pathway or trail continues deeper into the mountains. So as soon as this storm ends and we have some decent weather once again we will continue our search up that pathway. Plus while we are waiting, I want some of our supplies divided out so that we can begin using the closest as our first cache." He then concluded by saying. "I don't know who made those caves only that the technology is similar to ours, but with a couple of advancements I am unfamiliar with. So I am hopeful that at the end of this trail we will have our answer as to who is responsible for this cave system."

* * *

It took another seven days before the quiet storm finally broke. Anytime someone went outside they found a world shrouded in a heavy freezing fog and mist, but with no winds at all. It was a silent white world that completely changed the area from what they were familiar with. Even with the snow that had fallen before this storm, the changes it brought were great. Landmarks now were under a meter of new snow, which was powdery. If one ventured out into it without the shoes for snow they would find themselves up to their waists in the white stuff. Surprising to any who did venture out was that it did not feel cold even though it had to be close or below freezing. Finally on the eighth day the fog finally dissipated and a bright sunny day dawned. But with the fog gone it now became bitterly cold and winds began to blow and the powder drift with those winds changing, once again, the landscape.

Saige, staring out at the scene before him, was eager to get back out and to find where that trail would lead them. But now with this new snow he also knew that it would be almost impossible. So with impatience building that he had to fight down, he had to wait, and probably now with this last storm it might not happen until spring – whenever that would be. He sighed turned and went back inside. As he did he found his sister standing next to him. "Okay sis how long have you been standing there?"

"Oh long enough to see the frustration on your face. I know that you want to get back out there. Well, so do I. But nature decided that we must wait. I know that you have been tempted to go ahead and just do it, but I can also see that you haven't given in to those temptations. Anyway the reason I needed to talk to you wasn't this. Our food supplies are beginning to get a little thin. I suspect that we will probably have enough, but being unsure how long we are going to be stuck in winter I don't know. Stone also informed me that we should probably get a detail together and find some additional wood. Now I wish those caves that we found were larger since they self-heat. We then would only need the wood for the cooking fires. Also with so many pregnant women around I worry about their nutritional needs. We don't have everything we normally would. So I worry about the health of their unborn children. Plus if you haven't noticed they are eating more, which is digging deeper into our limited supplies. So we really need to be prepared to send out parties soon even if there are signs that this winter is over.

Oh by the way I've noticed how Seirra seems to only have eyes for you, and keeps being around you whenever it is possible. I think she really is trying to get your attention."

Looking down with a slight frown on his face he said, "Really? I've been so busy with, oh just about everything like you that I haven't even noticed."

"Yeah I know, and I can see that it has somewhat frustrated her. I think she really wants to be with you."

"Oh come on sis, she'd be better off with Stone instead of me. Even though you and I never thought we would be in charge of this group and Shayne would continue to lead, well here we are. And as such I barely have time to think let alone let another woman in my life."

"Another woman? Who's the first? You're not telling me that you are involved with Sorrel are you?"

Laughing he said, "No sis, she has tried but I have no interest that way. If you think about it then the answer is obvious. The first woman is you, of course."

"Oh. That's right. I mean I am a woman, it's just I wasn't looking at it in that way. After all I am your sister. But I have to admit that does make me a female. Okay that's a relief that it isn't Sorrel, but you had me worried there for a moment. But

I still find some time for Saar. So there is no reason that you couldn't find time for Seirra."

"Easy for you to say . . . by the way did she put you up to this?"

Shaking her head while she smiled she said. "No dear brother, just an observation from that first female in your life that's all."

Raising his hands in surrender he said, "Okay, okay I get your point. But come on I barely have time to keep this group together . . . hmmm so how do you find time for Saar? I know that when we go out that both he and Stone are in charge so that means a little more contact, but at times I find it difficult to breath with all of this stuff. I now often wonder how Shayne did it. And as far as I know he had no woman in his life other than his family. And of course that means his sister, since from what little I knew of him their mother had passed a number of years before."

"So are you trying to emulate him Saige?"

Frowning he leaned forward and asked. "How so, Shell'?"

Exasperated she said. "Okay, *now* think about it. We both respected him. He did a great job of keeping our unit together, and of course our unit was much larger then. He seemed to be able to lead without effort, but I am sure that was just a front. Since we both now are in charge and I for one have found it much more difficult than I ever imagined. So now I have even more respect for what he accomplished. But if I am going to continue in this role I will not follow him down the path of being single. In fact right now it is probably more important than it was then. We cannot say what is happening with our people or the cities. We are completely isolated, without communication, and we have no way to make contact at all. For all we know we may be the last of our people. And that, dear brother, is a scary thought. So for you, even if it is an unconscious act, that you have decided to become even more like him and remain aloof from the rest and remain single, well I think you are wrong." She stood then and put her hands on her hips before continuing. "And as far as finding the time oh dear brother, it's all a matter of perspective."

Interrupting her he asked, "Perspective? How so?"

Shaking her head she thought. *Sometimes he can be so dense.* "Okay it's really simple and I know we all have our blind sides okay? If there is something that we really want to do or get involved with, then for some reason we find the time to do whatever it is. But if it is something that needs to be done and maybe, I don't know, maybe it's disagreeable, or not our favorite thing to do in the whole world, well then it just seems like the time is never available to get it accomplished." Then she said sarcastically, "Funny thing."

He was quiet for a moment. "Okay sis, point taken. But I worry about such a thing and it's another reason I did not want to start a relationship with any of the women."

"And what could that reason be, oh dear bro?"

Breathing out heavily he said. "Look neither you nor I wanted this job when it was given us. But we are stuck, and I know why it was both of us and not just either you or me, or someone else. By having two of us and of the opposite sexes he made sure that there would be a female leader to deal with the females, and a male leader to deal with the males. And that the two leaders would have to be close so that they could talk with each other and keep each other informed. So we were the logical choice. Not only because we are related but also because we have worked as a team for as long as we trained. So we know each other, and we have also garnered respect from the rest of the unit with our skills. And I am sure these were all factors in us getting us placed into this position of leadership."

"Words are all this is. What is it, don't you like her?"

Shaking his head as he tried to explain, and found himself doing it badly. "No, no that's not it. Don't you see that by becoming interested in one woman that I could alienate both other women who may have thought that it would be nice to be a mate of one of the leaders, and the men who cannot because of the number difference, have a mate. It would be like a power play, you know, using the power of the position to get what I want."

"Well guess what. They will just have to deal with it. Besides are you going to allow someone else to control you from afar? And there isn't even proof that any of what you stated is fact or would become fact. Yes I know that it's one of the many possibilities, but only one. So for me, if for nothing else, would you at least talk to her? I can see that by your obvious actions of ignoring her, you are affecting her and I am beginning to see doubts from her, and her confidence in herself is beginning to fail. She doesn't understand why."

"Why? Why what?" He asked perplexed.

Shaking her head she said. "Oh you men . . . What is it with you? At times I think you are just plain dumb. Whether we like it or not, let's be honest for a moment okay?" Not saying anything but shaking his head he signaled for her to continue. "In our society both sexes are treated as close to equal as they can be, but nature has made woman to be a little smaller than man. So she generally has to look up to her man. This immediately puts the man as the more important in the relationship, kind of the one in charge from her point of view. It kind of goes back to childhood when you always looked up to your parents, the ones with the authority. I'm sure it's not meant to be that way, but it is what it is. And I am sure that in many of the relationships that everything is as equal as it can be and others where one partner dominates the other. But generally it is you guys who are the ones in charge. Not that as women we don't run things. After all there must always be someone behind the scenes to keep everything working. And that's not to put, we women, in a subservient role here. Look Seirra is not the type of woman who is going to try and bowl you over with her charms or let you know what her feelings are until she knows what yours will be. So she is being herself and trying to get your attention the only way she knows how. And how have you reacted? By completely ignoring her as if she did not exist. That can't bode well for anyone be it man or woman. Since we all want to feel like we are needed. So when you completely ignore someone like her she begins to wonder if there is something wrong with her. And then that begins to cascade into the many insecurities we women seem to live with."

"Insecurities? You? I haven't seen any Shell'."

"Oh they are there dear brother, they are there. I don't understand why but can guess that it is probably tied to our hormones that seem to control our lives so much. But who knows the real reason, I don't."

"Okay sis, you've given much a lot to think about. And I promise to try and find time for Seirra. But I still worry about what the rest will think."

Glaring at him she said. "Who cares what the rest thinks. Let it take its course. If you two grow to be a couple so be it. If not . . ." She shrugged saying, "Well, so be it also. But at least both of you will know."

* * *

The respite was short and another storm closed down on them and lasted another seven days burying everything deeper in a blanket of white. When any would venture out they would have to clear the entrance. But finally it did break and the suns shone brightly, almost blinding any who ventured from the gloom of the cave. During the time of the storm Saige finally put forth the effort to at least talk with Seirra, finding that she was somewhat shy and insecure around him. He found that at least for the moment these attributes were drawing him towards her. But at least for the time being he kept her at a distance. He really needed to think this through. He still worried about how beginning this relationship could be seen by the others in their group, but shrugged when he realized that his sister had been right. In truth it was none of their business. As long as he was not using his power as a leader to force someone into coupling with him there was nothing any could say. And he was trying very hard to make sure that he avoided doing that.

With the storm over he organized a team to go with him to the first cave that they had located. It was now the plan to move some of their supplies to this location so that if something disastrous was to fall on them here at their primary location that they would have at least something to fall back on. After discussing what they had discovered some speculation had gone on about the possibility that there could be more of these caves closer to their present location. But with all the searching and exploring that had previously been accomplished in the area, and with none found, there was no ready answer. Other questions had come naturally to mind, such as who had built them, why half to a full day apart and why did they seem to either begin or end where they did? Again with so little known there were no ready answers yet. Of course they could be close by, but were hidden well enough that they had yet to be discovered. This first trip would have the purpose of pinning the location for the ones who had not been there. Then when he and Shellian headed out to continue their search Stone and Saar would organize the shifting of some of their supplies.

Saar remained at the cave while Stone was one of the party members with Seve, and Staven to round the group out to five, leaving ten back at camp to assist in the division of supplies. Eventually the group reached the meadow area where Shellian and he had taken their mid-day meal. Like before it was windy and quite cold. So they pushed through and then around to the lee side and immediately felt warmer once out of the harsh wind. Here he let Shellian lead the group to the cave. Like the one they presently were living in, this cave was almost invisible to any who did not know where it was. Stone shaking his head asked, "Shellian, how do you do it? I mean both caves, this one, and the one we live in, is almost impossible to locate, and see, unless you happen to be in the right place, you can't see it. And even when it is pointed out it takes one a little while to find it. Yet, you seem to just do it."

Smiling and shaking her head she said. "Stone I don't have an answer for you. All I know is that when I look at a hillside like this there is something about it that is wrong. I can't even tell you what that wrong is, but once I sense its wrongness then I start searching for the why. And so far it has revealed these caves. So when I figure it out I will definitely pass it on, and that's really the best I can do for now. But now you understand why I have to be on the team that is locating these things. I just seem to be able to find them while none of the rest of you can. And since my brother and I are a trained team, this is why we are the ones who will continue the exploration. We just work very well together. So while we are gone on this next leg of our search, both you and Saar will be in charge. Not that we haven't already explained that, but now that you and the rest of this team has seen this cave I believe it now is clear as to why it is us that must continue on."

Then Saige spoke. "I know that since Shayne made us the leaders that it may not seem smart for both of us to go out and do this and be away from the group for as long as this takes, but Shellian has stated it much better than I ever could. We, she and I, are a team, and as such know how each thinks and reacts which gives us an edge. But I do believe that you Stone, and Saar back at camp, are good seconds. So if the unthinkable did happen and we were lost then the two of you could carry on. I don't know how else to say it."

"Saige, I wasn't complaining about what the two of you are about to do. I just wish one of the other of us were going also. But I understand why. Our group is so small that losing you two would be a burden on our survival, but three could be enough loss especially with as many of our women who are with child now, that we could perish. It's a tough decision however one goes about it."

"True, Stone . . . And I know that you weren't complaining. It's just by you being on site where the first of these were found, you can now understand why we decided as we did. Believe me we do not like the idea of both of us out for the time we figure to be gone and leave the rest of you alone like that, but as you have stated there really is little choice. Shall we go up to the cave?" Seeing no objections he signaled Shellian to lead on.

She led them up to the entrance and then inside with the rest discovering what they had when it was first located. Soft powdery dirt floor, a soft glow coming from the walls, and warmth that was not overpowering but comfortable. A perfect place for any of the small wild beasts in the area, and yet there was no sign that any had ever been inside. "It sure would be nice to know what the builders of this cave used to keep the animals out." Seve said.

"Yeah, wouldn't it." Staven answered. "It sure would make it nice to have back in the cave where we are. We seem to be continually fighting those small creatures. Always into something and we can never find where they are coming from or where they go once we chase them away."

"Well, all of you, you now know where this thing is. Shall we eat before we head back?" Shellian asked. There were no arguments, so they sat in the cave and ate their travel rations before preparing for the return trip. "You know Shellian I surely would like to know how you do it. I know you've said that you don't know yourself . . . but what a talent. If it hadn't been for you and your talent how much longer would it have been before we would have found shelter, and then would we have had enough time to prepare for this winter? Although right now I am beginning to worry a little, since we have no idea how long it lasts up here in the mountains, are we going to have enough food to get us through the rest of the time?" Pausing a moment and organizing his thoughts, Seve continued, "If we were below where we came from I would say that winter was almost over, but up here I just don't have a clue." The rest had to agree. None of them had a clue. They had lived in the lower lands all their lives, and had never even ventured into these mountains. After all the cities were their sanctuaries and up until the primitives found a way into them, the same cities had been their protection.

Thinking back while the others discussed general issues, Saige let his mind drift to a future meeting with Seirra. He had to admit that he found her quite attractive. And again if he thought about it he probably would have been interested in her back when they still were in the city. But at that time their work and training had never brought them into contact with each other. So until this disaster struck the city she was an unknown. He realized that with so few women that it limited one's choices. He laughed inwardly as this sounded to him like he was out choosing some beast of burden, or maybe some type of material or other item he had planned on making his own. Not a real live person, who had their own ideas, rights, feelings, and views on things. Shaking his head he came back to it and realized that in some ways when one of the opposite sex did join with another they both gave up some things, compromised on many, and yet remained who they were essentially. So while there had been very little really said at this point – he really felt that he was walking on sharp stones here – he could see that she was attracted to him. It was something that he had not noticed until Shellian very pointedly stated that he had been blind and that by completely ignoring the situation was really making things worse.

So he began to watch her now and then and found that indeed just as Shellian had stated, Seirra continued to be in places that would keep him in her sight and to be in places where they would "accidentally be in contact". Yet as busy as he had been, and he had to admit to it, *blind*, he really never saw it. He guessed that part of the reason lay in the fact that they had more men than women and because of his position he considered himself outside of the right to couple with any of women. After all that would be an abuse of the power he had been entrusted. And presently while his contact with her had only been brief with conversations never getting past the polite stage such as "Have a nice day", and such he found that his thoughts continued to return to her. Again shaking his head he did not understand it at all. There just had not been enough of anything between them for him to begin to think about her this often. Then he worried that if they started getting serious how would the rest treat her. Since he could not be there all the time to protect her if things became ugly, well it just added another burden and complication to the "what ifs". Again going back to the conversation with Shellian, he knew that she was correct. But human nature being what it is this would not change the possibility that she would become a target, and someone to use against him, or as a tool to get he and Shellian to allow someone to get away with something. Shrugging inwardly, he found that he could come up with all sorts of problems that could happen because of this possible relationship with Seirra. He was then brought back to reality when Shellian asked. "So Saige are you ready to return with the rest of us to camp? Or are you just planning on staying here as a hermit?" That brought a laugh from the rest as he realized that everyone else was packed and ready to head back but he had done nothing.

Embarrassed a little he said, "Sorry. I was deep in thought there and hadn't realized that you all were ready to head back . . . just a sec here and I'll be ready."

Then Shellian hit the mark with the comment. "I am sure we all know where your thoughts were Saige, and I don't really think it was on what we were discussing here."

He smiled and said nothing, not wanting to dig a hole any deeper than it obviously already was. He grabbed his pack and then joined the other four and they headed back to the main camp. Shellian then came up beside him and whispered. "I haven't been your sister and partner all these years not to know how to read your sign." She then continued on ahead like nothing was said. He looked down briefly and smiled. If ever there was a truer statement he hadn't heard of it. He knew that he could do the same with her, so it was only right to know that she could do it also.

It was late in the day with the suns setting that the five made their way back into the camp. When they entered the cave Shellian and Saige found that the rest had been busy working on sorting, and separating their supplies. When the two of them looked at the supplies that were left it seemed like so little. Now alarmed Saige wondered, would there be enough to make this division, and worse, was there enough to get them through this winter. Fifteen people go through a lot of materials, and now with four carrying it increased the need. Looking over at Shellian he could see the concern in her eyes also. But what could they do? Was there someplace that they could find some of the grazers to increase their meat? Or because like them food was scarce during winter, would there even been enough meat on them to be able to provide meat for them? *Great!* He thought. *Now we will have to wait to continue our exploration, and now go and see if we can find additional food. When will this winter end?* He then said. "Saar I see you have been busy while we were gone. I guess the next question I have is, is this all that we have left?"

Shaking his head Saar said. "I'm afraid so. It's a lot less than I thought we had. As one pile it doesn't look too bad. But once you separate it down like this it becomes obvious how little we have left. It is a worrisome thing. I mean we have no idea how much longer until spring arrives. Looking at this I have calculated that if we kept everything here, and I suspect that is what we must do by the way, that we have about thirty to thirty five days' worth of food. And if we ration it a little, maybe extend it by ten to fifteen days, but that's all. And the women who are now with child we cannot reduce what they need or their unborn children and they themselves will suffer because of it – and that is the reality of it Saige. I'm sorry but there it is."

"Okay then, there it is and none of us can change it. So any additional exploring or discovering will have to wait. Does anyone here have some suggestions as to where we could find foods to supplement our dwindling supplies?" Saige thought that since each member had been out and had searched and opened other areas that were unknown to them that there was a possibility they had either seen something or remembered something that could help. But at this moment all he was met with was silence. Looking at each member before continuing he then stated. "We have no choice left to us. If the weather holds, and I cannot guarantee that one, then we are going out as teams of three as hunting parties or teams of two for searching. So that if something is found such as a grazer, then two can dress it out while the other returns to get others so that we can then haul the meat back. I only want two teams out at a time that way if something is located then there will be enough bodies to get the carcass. Any team that goes out must, and I emphasize must, be back by dark whether successful or not. And on that happy note let's just get to the evening. Tomorrow this all begins in earnest. Oh Saar, since you are our only medical help here you are stuck. So I guess I am going to keep you assigned to rationing the food. With the women who are pregnant we need you here just in case something happens with any one of them. Pick a second among our group to assist you. And if I smell things right it smells like food is ready to eat so shall we?"

While eating one of the men mentioned that as they had explored that they had heard a sound that kind of sounded like a whoosh, and had lasted for a little while before growing quiet again. But where the sound had been coming from appeared to be through a narrow deep ravine that dropped out of sight, allowing no view into the area where the sound had originated. He stated that they had stood there for a short while before continuing and had heard other sounds in that area there was similar, but seemed to be more distant. Stone then brought up that since this had been an active volcano sometime in the past that most likely what they were hearing were geysers, and there probably were a number of hot springs in the area also. According to the size of the canyon, it could have a number of protected meadows, which could be snow free due to the heat. Of course by not seeing what had been described he could not be really sure.

"So Staven, do you think you could find it again?" Stone asked.

Shaking his head Staven said, "I'm not really sure. You see that was back at the beginning of winter, one of the first ones I went out on." Turning to Seve he asked. "I think you were with me that time; do you remember where it was, at all?"

Thinking before answering he knew that he had always been one that could easily get lost. Directions such as north, south, east, west, meant nothing and he could get turned around easily. He found that he normally had to depend on the other member of the team to locate a specific direction. "Come on Staven you know I could get lost just heading outside of this cave. There is no way I could take anybody to where that location is. I probably wouldn't even recognize it if I was standing in the very spot where we first heard that sound."

Sighing Staven said, "Okay, I'll have to think about it. But it may take a little time for me to remember. We've been all over these mountains; well at least all over them close to camp. And I have been out a number of times since then and haven't been back close to that area, so I will just have to work on recalling where we were. And before you say it's important, believe me I know. But I didn't consider it so at the time so I did not lock the location in my mind. So right now it could be any number of places. So let me think about it."

Shellian looking over the group asked. "Have any of you heard or found a similar thing such as these possible hot springs while you were out exploring?" Again no one answered. Shaking her head she said, "I guess I can take that as a no then."

Later that night before they retired to their separate sleeping areas, Shellian said, "Saige I really do hope that Staven remembers. You know what may be a good idea is to send Stone out with him. Geology is one of Stone's specialties and maybe between the two of them they can find those, what did he call them, oh yes, geysers. I've never seen one – I bet they are spectacular."

"What", Saige asked, "A bunch of hot water shooting out of a hole in the ground? You think something like that would be spectacular?"

"Oh come on Saige. Can't you see that something like that has to have beauty tied with it? I know that if one was to be foolish enough to be too close when it let loose that it could kill or at least severely injure you, but I really bet that they have their own beauty."

"Could be, but right now that's the last thing on my mind. I can only hope that Staven remembers and that it is as Stone hopes. But with no idea as to where, we'll keep our rotation, and without a location we may, once again be in serious trouble." Breathing out deeply he continued, "Anyway, I'm tired, and once again we have much too much going on even for winter time to find any real time to relax. See you in the morning Shell'." He then turned and went into his area and prepared to sleep. She watched him go shrugged and then retired herself. She thought as he left that he really seemed a bit down. Not surprising really, since it wasn't that long ago that indeed they were still just a brother and sister continuing their training just outside their city, with no thoughts beyond what the next day would bring. Now all of that appeared to be no more than a dream, and the reality they were stuck in now was, at times, crushing. It appeared that when one problem was solved, so many more appeared to take its place. "Oh well", she said to no one in particular since she was alone. She then sighed and lay down to go to sleep. While she had been with them when they went back to newly discovered cave, there had been much going on here also, and the day just flew for everyone, and once again she found herself almost asleep instantly.

* * *

Another storm had struck in the night, but this one appeared to lack the strength of the others that they had faced so far. And by late afternoon was gone. They hoped that it was a sign saying that winter could be close to an end. But when they stepped out after the storm left it was bitterly cold. It had to be well below freezing, and the breeze that was with it just cut right through whatever they were wearing. Exposed skin felt like it was freezing almost immediately, so after an initial foray out of the cave everyone stayed inside. How was it that it looked so inviting and warm outside but was just the opposite? Standing at the entrance and looking out through a small opening Saige wondered if they were going to make it.

There had been so many friends lost during their flight to here, and while presently they were okay, there was no proof that it would continue that way. He could feel the pressure building inside of him, as decisions that needed to be made were not coming to him. Shaking his head he thought, once again that he really had no desire to be put in charge of anybody, let alone this group, but he knew that he could not forsake the trust that Shayne had put in him and Shellian. Shaking his head once again, he thought, *Four women pregnant and one at least halfway through her term. Don't these people realize what a complication this adds? Or do they not care and are looking for whatever comfort they can find?* Well he knew that it was cold here and it seemed that at night that the women were cold and to have a warm body next to them was a comfort. Unfortunately it never remained just a warm body next to them and now without the protection that was available in the cities they were paying the price for these indiscretions. Not that he could blame them. Even Shellian had mentioned that she was cold at night and the thought of having Saar next to her to help keep her warm was a temptation, which so far she had avoided . . . but for how long? He knew that both of them were right for each other, and again only because of the circumstances they remained separate.

That brought him full circle to his own situation and the fact that Seirra was still trying to get his attention. He really did not know what to do about it. So far he had kept his distance by using his position as leverage and what conversations they had were quite impersonal. But he knew that shortly he was going to have to make some kind of decision about her, and truth be told he really had no idea. Up until Shellian had pointed it out to him he had really never paid that close attention to Seirra. But since that time he had observed her, when he felt that he would not be intruding, or because he was one of the leaders that it would appear that he was marking out his territory, he could see her interest. So far he felt that he had been successful. Taking a deep breath he then thought about her. He had to admit that she definitely was attractive, and yet . . . and yet there was this subtle feeling that she did not see it herself – her natural beauty. Just a little shorter than Shellian, she had a lithe athletic build, and seemed to be able to move with a natural grace that most of the other women that had survived lacked. In fact the only other woman that moved that way was Shellian. It spoke of strength, intelligence, and an awareness of the physical world around them. When he thought about it, in many ways, the two of them were quite similar. He was surprised that he hadn't noticed it before. Yet when she was around him she seemed shy, almost withdrawn. It was something he really did not understand.

He realized suddenly that someone was just behind him. Thinking it was his sister he said without turning around. "Shell', what are we going to do?" Then realizing that it wasn't Shellian he turned and saw that the person standing behind and close to him was Seirra. He smiled even though it was a sad smile and said. "Sorry Seirra, I thought you were Shellian."

She was looking up into his eyes and he saw doubt and maybe a little lack of confidence there. "Saige, I saw you standing over here by the entrance and you just looked lonely and somewhat forlorn, and I thought I would come over and see if there was anything I could do to help."

Again with a sad smile he said, "Seirra, are you trying to mother me? I know it's a natural thing for women to want to do. But I do thank you for the offer." Then before he realized he put his arms around her and hugged her. For some reason it just felt natural and right. She had put her head on his chest and sighed softly as she clung to him. He then realized that he was beginning to have another physical reaction that was completely unexpected. And he knew that she could feel it also and at that point she clung tighter to him. At this point he knew that she knew, but before anything could be said they heard a heated argument between two of the women, he released her and left to see what was going on and if he or Shellian would have to intervene. Having four pregnant women around was not the easiest of situations to deal with. It appeared that their emotions were always on the raw edge, and anything would set one or another off on some tirade. While the cave system they were living in was not necessarily small, this constant chaffing from these imagined slights made it seem much too small. He arrived at about the same time as Shellian and they saw two of the women, Storme and Sabryn, ganging up on Sorrel. At the point where they had arrived, the argument or fight, had become quite loud, and anger had flared between the three of them.

It was obvious from the vindictiveness that was being thrown at Sorrel that they did not like her lifestyle and were letting her have it. He suspected that because Sorrel was free with her body that maybe she had coupled with their men. With no proof other than the fact that the two men in question had probably looked at Sorrel, it was still enough to make these women suspicious. He was pretty sure that nothing had gone on, and Shellian had been monitoring the situation closely. But Sorrel had one of those bodies that men just naturally looked at. And of course she knew that, and had taken full advantage of it. And because she liked an open free relationship she had not settled on any one man – making her the target of the three women who had. Plus it appeared that as the women got deeper in their pregnancies and their bodies changed to accommodate the growing fetuses so did their emotions, doubts, and it never took much to bring these doubts out. So looking over the scene he finally had to raise his voice to be heard. "Storme! Sabryn! Sorrel! Enough! Let's end this here and now. Listening to the two of you, Storme and Sabryn, I think that you are making accusations where you have no proof, and we, Shellian and I have been watching things." Storme interrupted and said. "Right, and if you have watched things as well as you say you have then who is the father of her child? For all I know it could be my man Schylar or hers", pointing at Sabryn. That way she throws her body around I wouldn't be surprised if she has coupled even with you Saige."

Before he could say anything Seirra said with much emotion. "No he has not coupled with Sorrel!"

Storme turned and faced Seirra and asked. "Why is that Seirra? Have you been warming his bed at night?" And with those questions asked Seirra's face flushed red. Then in triumph Storme said. "So that's the way it is."

"No Storme that is not the way it is." Saige answered. Although he knew that they would not believe him. But from

Seirra's reaction he now knew that she had wanted to share his bed, and that Shellian had once again been correct. "In fact, it seems that you are accusing any man including yours, of sleeping with any of the women, so is it you who is cheating on Schylar? Since I have found that the ones who usually make such accusations are usually doing it themselves, and because they are, they suspect that all are guilty of doing the same thing. Is that what it is Storme?" After asking he could almost see the truth in what he had asked. But he suspected that while it may be something she may have contemplated, he felt that it was something that she probably could not be successful at doing. Since she had a tendency to want to do what Sorrel had done so successfully she then felt that all would be that way, and because she couldn't or wouldn't, it frustrated her more that some other woman could, and then have such a physical draw on her chosen man. "This ends now. We are not going to be throwing unproven accusations around just to heal our hurt pride. You two have no proof of anything you are accusing Sorrel of doing." Seeing the rebellion in both of their eyes, he continued. "No, it ends here and now. We have to live together and while I cannot keep you from disliking each other, these confrontations are to end now."

"So what are you going to do if we don't want them to stop?" Storme asked defiantly.

Smiling at her he said, "Very simple Storme. It really is. You see we have no choice here. So if one decides that they don't want to live with the rest then we simply will put you out. In this case it would include Schylar since the two of you have decided to couple. And with the discovery of these other caves there would be a place to send you. Does that answer your question Storme?"

Looking at his face and then at the faces of the rest that were now present she could see that he was quite serious but wanting to get the last word she said. "That may be so, but this isn't over, and there may come a time when you and Shellian are no longer the leaders. I think then Schylar will be, and we will see who is put out." And with that statement she turned and left, leaving Sabryn standing there by herself, with Sorrel still standing defiantly across from her. Saige had to admit even with her late in her second third she still was a beautiful woman, and would still turn the head of any man. Then gently he asked, "Sabryn, do you understand what was said here? Do you understand that with the way we have to live right now that it must be this way?"

With her shoulder slumping in defeat she just shook her head, sighed and then said. "Yes, Saige . . ." Then looking across at Sorrel she said with strong emotion. "But she!" Pointing her finger at Sorrel, "She had better stay away from my man!" Then a little more softly she asked. "You two aren't coupling are you?", as she pointed to Seirra, and he.

"No . . . no Sabryn, we are not coupling. Although from Seirra's reaction here I suspect that it is something that she would like to see happen eventually." Once again Seirra's face reddened. He took a deep breath and continued "I have not coupled with any as I have felt that it would look like I was using my position as one of the leaders, and to be truthful I have been just too busy to even consider a relationship at this time – *so even the accusation of me coupling with Sorrel is really a joke.* If any member of this group is under scrutiny it is Shellian and I. Since we are the leaders we are constantly in contact and observation by everyone. Don't you think that if something was going on that all would be aware of it in a short time? And as far as Seirra goes, at the present we have barely had a conversation, let alone discussed anything about coupling or becoming a couple, so put that out of your mind also."

At this point Sabryn just shook her head, and then like Storme turned and left the area where the confrontation had begun. Shellian looking around at the rest still standing there, with most looking down at the ground, she could tell that the rest were uncomfortable, she then said gently. "Okay, I think this is over for now. So let's get back to whatever we all were doing before this outburst." Then seeing little movement from the gathered group she said. "Let's move, unless one of you wants to discuss something here and now?" Then looking around and making brief eye contact each shook their heads and then slowly drifted off. Shellian looking at her brother said. "I was afraid that something like this was eventually going to happen. Something about 'we' women who are emotional anyway, it becomes much worse during pregnancy. So I would be surprised if this did not happen again in some form or another. *So dear brother be prepared.* I suspect it will be very tough a number of times between now and when we will have new lives joining us. And then it probably will get worse."

"Worse? I thought this was bad enough. How could it get worse?"

Smiling she said. "I can see you haven't been around too many babies. The ones who will have these new lives will have their lives run completely by them. There will be too little sleep, distraction when they are away from their children, tempers, arguments as they come to terms with their offspring."

Laughing he said. "You make it sound like it's the worst thing that one can do."

"Yeah I guess it does sound that way. But from what I have seen, well I know you have never been allowed around at birthing time. But all of us women share it. At that time there is much work, after all it isn't called labor just for fun, much pain, and they say it is like trying to eliminate a large rock, and actually some tearing of the tissues, so don't be surprised to hear screaming when it comes to that time. But after it is all over and the child is born then you can see that almost immediately that what the woman has just gone through is forgotten and all she can see is that child and the love for it just pours out of her very soul. I don't know if I can explain it better than that, and I haven't gone through this yet so I can only tell you from what I have observed."

Silent for a moment as he took in everything she had just told him, Saige said, "Ouch! I guess we men are just on the sidelines and, well how can you women want to go through such a thing? I mean I understand why coupling. It is the way of life. After all if it hadn't happened in the past we wouldn't be here now. But knowing that you are taking a great chance to be on the road that will lead to being uncomfortable for the time that you are carrying the child inside of you and then knowing that sometime in the future you cannot avoid all that pain and suffering . . ." Shaking his head he continued, "Well I just don't know if I could do it."

"It's all there, but there is also wonder . . . and I guess I really can't quite come up with the word for it. But from the beginning, when you have sickness in the mornings letting you know that you are pregnant, which fortunately goes away in the first third, then in wonder you watch your body begin to change. Of course we are not necessarily happy about that, but it is part of life. Then comes the time when you first feel the baby move inside of you. It is an unbelievable and happy time. You know that your baby is alive and now you actually can feel and see it move. But as you reach the end of your third-third, you are tired, you feel like a large fish, you cannot keep cool, and because the baby is taking so much of the inside of you, you find that nature calls are very frequent. At this time you are very ready for this to be over, but still fear that time. So I guess that's just about it. Well, then the labor starts, and you are scared, because you know it is time, and you cannot stop this until it's over, and you have your new child in your arms."

"Well for not finding the words I think you did a pretty good job. And you are looking forward to this sis? In a way it sounds like something that should be avoided."

Laughing at him she said, "I think when it finally happens to me, and of course to whomever you eventually couple with, that you will have a different view."

CHAPTER NINE

Seirra sighed as she looked across the cave to where Saige, Shellian, Stone, and Saar were in deep conversation. It was at least seven days ago when the two of them had finally made the first physical contact, and Saige had briefly let down his guard. Then came that fight and since then he had avoided her. When he had held her it just felt natural and good and when he had the physical reaction to her closeness it had surprised her. And when she looked up she could see the surprise in his face also. But even that felt right. Now he was cold and distant. She remembered what he had said and realized that it was something she hadn't considered – that any leader was under the watchful eye of the group more than any other individual. So somehow she needed to find a way to move this relationship further along. The one thing she knew for sure, that after her first real physical touching of him, and then the way he and Shellian handled the situation afterwards, made her more determined that he and she should be a couple. But now with what had been revealed could it ever happen? She took a deep breath and continued to work the skin into clothing and was at a loss as to what to do next. She had to find a way . . . she just had to.

But she now also knew that it was obvious what her feelings for him were. Shaking her head she thought. *If I could only have controlled my emotions and not have blushed like I did. And I know it had to be really bad since my face was hot both times. Now not only does he know but so does everybody.* And while it was true they were not a couple and they had not slept together, from her reaction, the rest, even with the denial, could easily assume that she had. Again what could she do?

Glancing over briefly from their meeting Saige knew that he wasn't being fair to Seirra, but he felt that right now he had to keep his distance to reinforce to the rest that there had been nothing going on between them. But the rumors of their relationship kept coming back. *If only she hadn't turned so red when the accusations were thrown out,* he thought. But at least he now knew what Shellian had told him was quite true. No doubt that Seirra wanted to be with him. But for now it just couldn't be. Turning back to the other three in the group he said. "Sorry, a little distracted, what was it that you asked?"

Shellian smiling back at him said, "Never mind dear brother. We can see that you are distracted, and you have been through much of what we have been discussing. So why don't you just go over there and talk with her. It's out in the open anyway. Not that anything has really happened between the two of you. But with the rumors and stories flying around here, the two of you have been coupling for quite a while. So why not just make those rumors come true? It was obvious to all that she really does have feelings for you. And your denial, while I know it is true, didn't fly with the rest. No, I'm not talking about Stone or Saar who are our seconds here, but the remaining ten, well I don't know if all of them do, but the majority appears to believe it. And Storme, with the encouragement of Schylar, is pushing it for all it's worth.

"It's obvious that Schylar is trying to drive a wedge between you and the rest. And while we all knew it, this is the first time he has come out in the open to push like this. If you think back to when the attack first came back at the city he was the one who was questioning Shayne. Of course Shayne had confronted him and made him go up and view that attack. But he has always been a pain, and he has always wanted to be the leader. Although I know that it would be a disaster if he led anyone."

"Yeah", Stone said, "he is the greatest of leaders in his own mind, that's for sure. But it would scare me to death to have him in charge of anything. Incompetent really is too weak of a word, but it's the one that comes to mind right now."

"Anyway this is off the subject. We need to get our teams back out and locate that possible geyser area. It quit snowing about two days ago and so far the suns have been shining. But there has been no heat in them up here. So I am hoping that shortly it will warm enough to allow the next team out. Hmmm . . ." She said as she was looking at her notes. "It appears that Sojar and Steen are due to be the next exploration team out. So where do we need to send them? I know the information that we got from . . . ahhh . . . you know who, was pretty vague. But at least we know the general direction they had traveled since it is written in our logs. Of course this trip out is to try and locate those possible hot springs. If found and the grazers are there, then we can send in a hunting team. Any that we have sent out so far have come back empty."

"I think we probably should have them go out in the morning. We can't wait very much longer. Food isn't an issue yet, but from what we have discovered it will be soon and I don't want us to reach that point. Do any of you have any better ideas?" Saige asked

Pausing a moment, Saar asked, "So how long should they be out before reporting back in?"

"Good question. It seems to me that we were running one-day explorations at the time, so I would guess two days only." Looking around at the others Saige asked, "Does that sound good?" He looked around at the other three once again and they nodded their heads in agreement. "Okay with that solved what do we do with this deteriorating situation here in the cave?"

* * *

With it announced at the supper meal, Sojar and Steen prepared their supplies to leave at first light. Looking around at the rest of the group Saige could see suspicion on many of the faces. Shaking his head, he really had no idea how to defuse the growing animosity against both he and Shellian. Yet somehow it had to be done if they were to stay together. Again shaking his head he wondered if maybe it would be easier to just let the team fall apart. But he immediately put that thought out of his mind. Shayne had trusted the two of them to keep them together, and no one said it would be easy. He knew that there was only so much one could do when trapped within a cave for this long winter. So it gave time for such rumors to fly, to build, and to be believed. It did not matter that there was no truth, if repeated often enough, they took on a life of their own and became the truth. So he knew that for the present that he could not, would not, make any move to reinforce these rumors. That left Seirra out in the cold so to speak, and he hoped that she understood why he had to do this for now. With the coming of spring and the work that spring would entail he felt that much of this would just flow away as the ice did when the spring rains hit – something about busy hands, if he remembered correctly. Tired he decided to go to sleep. While there may have been idle time for many there had been none for him and he had to admit he was tired. Tomorrow would bring a whole new set of problems, and they hadn't cleared the ones from today. *Oh well,* he thought, *tomorrow is another day.*

He was up before dawn to give last minute instructions to the outgoing two. Pointing out on their rough map he made sure that they knew to cover some of the earlier explored areas. They had to find where the grazers spent the winter. Standing outside the cave in the cold morning air with their breaths coming out like smoke, created by the crisp clear air, he watched them until they were out of sight. It would be two days before they returned. Then it would be time to put out the next team. So far they had been lucky. Other than the incident of falling into that old lava tube there had been no serious injuries. All he could do was hope that with winter nearing its end that it would remain that way. This first winter here in the mountains had been rough. They barely had time to prepare for it, and now with winter still upon them, they were beginning to pay the price of insufficient preparation. Even though it was very cold out, for the moment, it really felt great to be out and in the fresh air. It helped clear his mind, and since the cave had been closed up it had begun to take on an odor all its own. And it was not the best of smells, but he found that one got used to it. It was only when one came out into the fresh air did one really realize how bad it had gotten inside the cave. One thing for sure when spring came, there would have to be a major cleaning and airing out. Right now it stank of bodies not bathing enough, urine, dirty clothing, smoke, and who knew how many other things. So lingering outside to watch the suns rise over the horizon, he finally chilled enough that he needed to go back in to get warm.

* * *

The next two days flew by, and that truly was a surprise. But it had remained clear and cold, and from what they could see it might remain that way for at least a few more days allowing a couple of additional teams out. While not desperate he had the short supplies on his mind constantly trying to come up with some solution, and he knew that he was not the only one. It was to main topic of conversation anytime people got together to talk. They all realized their plight. He heard one of the women who was outside scream, and then heard her yell for Saar. The whole camp spilled outside to find out what had happened. Once outside they found Steen bloodied and broken, without Sojar. It was obvious from his condition that he barely made it back. Saar arrived and immediately took over the care and signaled for a few of the men to carry him in and place him by the fire. Steen's breathing was ragged, and there was a slight froth on his lips. He was immediately placed by the fire, and then Saar did a quick examination while he ordered some items, and then he shooed everybody away saying that until he had a chance to really check the injuries that it would do none of them and especially Steen, any good to hang around. Turning around to leave Saige spied Sorrel and she was white as a ghost. Looking over at Shellian he saw that she was looking with concern at Steen and was about to leave. Going over to her he said. "I think you need to go talk with Sorrel. She looks really bad right now and I think she's going to need some support."

"What do you mean? She's been really strong throughout this . . ." Turning and looking at Sorrel she said. "Oh . . . I see what you mean. Of course I'll go comfort her." She then left immediately and was at Sorrel's side with her arm around her shoulders. She led her away and then out of sight. He knew that when she found out what was going on with Sorrel she would pass it on to him. Right now he needed to know what had happened out there, but knew that it would be some time before any answers would be forthcoming. He glanced over where Saar was working on Steen and then at Steen and realized that he was out cold. Shaking his head, he needed answers and he needed to know where Sojar was.

* * *

It was hours later when Saar came to see Saige. Shaking his head Saar said. "I tried to save him, but without my equipment that I had available in the city there just was no way. He had internal bleeding, and I think a broken rib had punctured one of his lungs. All I really could do was comfort him while he slipped away from me. It's a miracle that he got back here at all."

"Did he tell you anything at all? I'd really like to know what happened."

"It was pretty garbled, but I think I got the jest of what he was trying to tell me. First off he said that it was their fault that it happened. Both of them got careless since they were getting close to the camp. I think that's why he made it back. They were only less than a half-day's hike and were eager to get back. He said that they didn't find what they were sent to locate, but that there had been a great number of tracks from the grazers, which in his mind meant that they were on the move. Plus while he had to admit that he had coupled with Sorrel it had become plain as time had continued that she was favoring Sojar, and he her. So he thought that soon Sorrel would not be offering her body to anyone but Sojar. He said that they had stopped and had not considered where they had stopped since they had felt safe. Then like down below when that predator attacked us and missed, another one or maybe the same one attacked them and had grabbed Sojar, and at the same time it's shoulder had hit him hard in the chest. He said all he got was a glimpse at the creature and it was huge. He said that it was gone and he heard Sojar screaming as the predator disappeared and suddenly the screams just stopped, and he knew that Sojar was dead. When he tried to get up he hurt everywhere, and he felt broken up inside. He knew that he was severely injured and was trying desperately to get back here to both get help, and to hopefully live. And that's about it. After that he sort of just went back to sleep, and never woke up."

Looking down at the small fire he had built, Saige thought. *We've been so careful. We made it this far without any serious injuries or death, and winter is almost over. Now in one incident we lose two. I wonder if that predator was following the herds and saw the two of them. Heck all of this winter we haven't even seen any sign of the beast. Other than the large tracks we found lower down we've never even seen one. Now what?* "Thank you Saar. I know that you did the best you could." Shaking his head he asked, "Why now? We have almost beaten our first winter here." Then more softly more to himself than Saar he again asked. "Why now?"

"I know that you really aren't asking me that, and even if you were I have no answers for you. I've been asking that question . . . what's that?" He asked when there appeared to be a sound of approaching people. Their tone was ugly.

Schylar came over from the far side of the cave with eight others of the group. There was triumph written all over his face, and with a sneer he said. "We've put up with you, your sister, and you Saar, and even though Stone isn't here he is included in this." He then pointed to Seirra and said. "You, since you have been sweet on him can join them," which she quietly did. Saige could see the fear in her eyes and realized what was coming down. Schylar had convinced the rest that it was time for a change in leadership and any who had been in the inner circle of the present leadership would have to go. "We've not liked the way you have been leading us for a long time. And now your leadership has caused the death of two of us, so we decided it was time for a change. In the morning the five of you will leave and never come back."

Softly Saige said. "Don't you mean that you've decided Schylar? It has been obvious all the way back when the city was first attacked that you did not like the way Shayne had done things. And he then proved to you that he was right. But even that did not sit right with you. It has been obvious from the beginning that you have wanted to be in charge. Isn't that it?" He then looked over the rest that stood with him, giving them a hard stare." He could tell they were uncomfortable with the action, but at the same time were unwilling to go against him. Then to the group he said. "So that's the way it is."

Schylar answered. "Yes Saige that's the way it is. If I had my choice I would have put you out tonight to fend for yourself, but they convinced me to wait until morning. So at first light you will leave, and from that point on you will not return under threat of death. It's just that simple."

Saige knew that they were outnumbered even if four of the group were women carrying. But it would do no good to start a fight since it was obvious that sometime earlier that they had taken all of their weapons so that they were now unarmed. It would serve no purpose since Schylar had somehow convinced the rest that he would be a much better leader. So taking him down now would not change the feelings that had grown against them. "To prevent any others from getting hurt we will do as you demand." Then turning to the rest again he said. "I really hope you know what you are doing. Because I think you are putting yourselves in a very bad situation." Then turning back to Schylar he asked. "Are at least going to allow us our share of the food, and some of the weapons, or is that going to be denied also?"

Sneering again he said. "Of course, and that has already been done, and as far as I am concerned you're getting more than you should. I would have put you out with nothing."

Looking at him in pity now Saige said softly, "I'm sure you would, I'm sure you would. Anything to cement your power, and it would be easier just to kill us off, wouldn't it?"

"Enough! Everything that needs to be said has been. We will see all of you out of the cave in the morning. Until then have a good night, your last in this cave." He with the group who followed him turned to leave when Saige interrupted them once again.

"Sorrel," He asked gently, "You can join us and leave in the morning. I believe you would do better this way – would you do that?" Looking closely at her he could see that she was still quite white. She didn't say anything, but the accusations that he was responsible for the deaths were in her eyes. She just turned and left. He knew that Storme had been working on the other women, and there would be no help or mercy there.

Shortly Schylar with the rest turned and left them alone, but they knew not totally alone. They were sure that there would be someone spying on them all night. "I hadn't realized that it had gone that far." Saige stated. "Did any of you sense it at all?" They all looked at him and just shook their heads. Taking a deep breath he continued, "I guess we have no choice. So gather your gear and join me back here. I do not think it is a good idea to be apart tonight. Just because we have been promised that no one will be hurt or killed we cannot be sure of it. So from this point on we need to stay together. And that is everywhere including nature calls."

When he had stated it, they realized that he was probably quite correct. That any one of them could become victims and their injuries or death could be chalked up as an accident. So quickly they went as a group to each of their sleeping areas, collecting Stone and then gathered their equipment and returned to the area where Saige and Shellian were. "This is such a big mistake." Saar said. "I am the only doctor. Don't they know what they are doing to themselves?"

"No doc, I don't think so." Stone answered. "But when someone like Schylar makes this type of move he believes he is so much better, but we know that they have just doomed themselves."

"I know . . . it's just that I took an oath to heal and protect life, and they have knowingly just thrown all that away. I worry about these women, but even more about their unborn children. Yet, they all have thrown in with him." Then shaking his head he continued, "I just don't understand . . . not at all." None of the others had any answers to give him.

* * *

The next morning at sunrise they were all outside the cave. Saige looking at the group could see no change in their expressions and knew that there would be no way to change their minds. Sighing softly, he shrugged and with the others headed away from what had become their home. They had been given only their knives; all other weapons had been kept. At least the five of them had a destination, the caves that they had located. But since the ones who had just thrown them out knew of the first, they would continue on to the second. Again he and Shellian felt that the ones who would remain here would not go far to find them, or spend the energy locating the almost invisible trail that they had followed to the other caves. Once again the weather appeared to be ready to change. It had been sunny now for a few days, but now it felt like snow. They needed to hurry if they were going to arrive at the first of those caves before the snow began to fall again.

They pushed through the morning and as midday approached it began to snow once again. Fortunately they now were just a short distance from the first cave. But if this storm turned out to be severe then it would delay their move to the ones further along. Plus new snow would make it easy for any to track them if they so desired, and it was something they did not want or need. Nobody spoke as they made their trek up and deeper into the mountains. They all knew that with what had happened that their chances of survival had dropped significantly. Thinking about what happened Saige felt that now he had failed Shayne. Had they been a little more alert to what had eventually happened, maybe, just maybe it could have been stopped. But as someone had once told him, "You can 'what if' yourself to death, and that doesn't change a thing. What is done is done and there is no way to go back and change it. So get over it and live with it, and do the best you can." He had to admit it was good advice, but it still was hard to live with this apparent failure.

* * *

Once inside the first cave they broke down what gear they had. Saar turned to them shaking his head saying. "I just don't like it. I know I am repeating what we talked about last night, and I am sure we all are thinking it right now. But I just don't." Pausing before continuing, "I know I know there's nothing we can do about it at all. But I am a doctor and all of my instincts say that I should be there if there are any complications with those women, and I won't be, can't be . . . oh I know it was their choice, their decision, but they are wrong, so very wrong." He could see that there was no disagreement from the rest of them and fell silent.

Saige signaled Stone to join him and then the two went back out into the snowstorm. "We need to gather some wood – at least enough to put a meal together. I still haven't figured out how this cave is heated, but at least we won't need to worry about a large supply to keep us warm. We need to be on our way to the next one as quickly as we can."

"Yeah I agree. I can't say that they will come after us, but I want to be sure that if they do decide to do that, that we are where they cannot find us. Darn! Now we have two enemies to worry about, and one of them are our own people. Saige, I wish I had seen it coming to this point also. I mean we had discussed the fact that there were some problems but how did he and Storme keep it such a tightly kept secret? Usually in such a small group nothing is kept hidden long."

Shrugging Saige said, "Wish I knew. Why he was one of the ones who had to survive all the way here I don't know. There are so many others who either died or were captured that deserved this." Shaking his head he continued, "I will never understand how this works. I mean we lost so many good people coming here, and somehow one of the worst ones survives and now have divided us further. I just hope we can survive now. I was worried about our chances when there were fifteen of us. Now it's just the five of us. I don't know, maybe it gives us a better chance. And now I wonder if we will be able to do anything at all for our people. That's if any of our cities have survived these attacks. I mean I hate just not knowing but again there is nothing I can do about that either." They continued through the wooded area picking up firewood where they could find it. Again much of it was buried in the snow. After finding a sufficient amount, the two of them returned to the cave, dropped their load outside and returned to the warmth within. While they had been gone the remaining three had made the area within the cave as comfortable as they could for the short time they were going to stay here.

Shellian said, "I know, before you say anything that our plan is to remain here as short as we can. But that doesn't mean we can't be comfortable while we wait. I, for one, do not want to tackle the next part of this journey with a storm blowing out there. And yes I know we will want to go before the storm blows over so that the snow will cover our tracks. But I think personally that we will be safe today, and should just spend the rest of today here, and then have all of tomorrow to reach the second cave. We discussed that while the two of you were out gathering wood and concluded that it would be a good idea. Well, Seirra listened more that said anything." Looking directly at her she asked, "Seirra you have been awfully quiet, is there something wrong?"

Still not saying anything, she just shook her head in the negative. But anyone looking at her could see that she was upset. Well, truth be told, that probably applied to all of them. "Anyway I think that Schylar and Storme will be too interested in making sure that they are in control than pursuing us." Silent for a moment she continued, "I do hope that they like their choice for a leader back there. But I think everything is just about to come unraveled. I really think that they are not going to survive. He has never been a leader no matter what he thinks of himself. And that is going to haunt them and I believe destroy them."

No body disagreed with her assessment. In fact if there was anything that they could agree upon it was that Schylar would destroy the ones who threw in with him.

* * *

The next seven days passed rapidly as they had continued up through the caves that Shellian and Saige had discovered. Until they had reached the final one that they had discovered, and here they had made their base camp. The storm had lasted three days, and had allowed them to leave no trail behind them. So if Schylar decided to pursue there would be no trail for him to follow. Here once again they needed to follow the almost invisible path to its source. Worry was with them since they had been given much too little food to be able to last more than fifteen days. They began to ration the food to extend their days, and they knew even then it would not be enough. They had to find something and very soon.

They continued their exploring deeper into the mountains, following the almost invisible path that had been placed who knew how far in the past. They discovered six additional caves, all constructed, and all with the same unknown heating system and dim lighting. But here they just ended, or begun, they did not know which. But as each new cave was discovered they would move their camp into it until now they were days away from their original camp. Saige, thinking out loud, said. "I just don't understand this. These caves have me stumped. I mean look they are at half-day intervals. The first one you found Shell' was where we made our first camp, and this one just seems to be either the last or first. Either way we should be within half a day of either the end of the trail or the source, I don't know which. It just seems weird to me that there should be nothing but these caves. Yet we have searched both sides, the first one that we found we searched for additional caves and there were none. Not to say that we could have missed them, but the faint trail that we followed to find all of them disappears beyond this one, and beyond the first one."

Listening as he talked it out Stone then said, "I agree. It is a puzzle that's for sure. The trail that we followed is very ancient and like you and Shellian stated you sense more than see it. But to have nothing at either end just doesn't make sense. And from looking at them they were never constructed to be more than a safe stopping point along this route. So where do these things lead us? Right now I have to admit the answer seems to be nowhere . . . but why nowhere? Why waste your time constructing these things? I just don't know or understand the logic of it all."

"The one thing I do know that if we do not find some additional food soon the rest is a moot point anyway. We are down to just a few more days, so either we find some of the grazers to provide meat or we find something else. Right now we cannot be particular in our choices", Saar added. "Yes I know that as we found these caves that we have been searching, but not the location of where the grazers, which stay in these high areas are hidden, and these mountains are huge so they could be anywhere."

It was dawn and all had eaten far too little, but had no choice. Breathing out heavily Saige said, "I guess today then we all should go out. I think our gear is safe here. I think that we will form two teams with Shell' and I on one and you three on the other. We'll work northwest, and I'd like the three of you to work northeast. We all need to be back here tonight, so keep that in mind – half day out and half day back, just that simple. And yes I know it's never that simple climbing around these mountains, but with our group now down to what it is we just cannot be out longer than that for now, at least until we have some additional food. Okay then, let's head out, and we will see you tonight." He shouldered his pack and headed outside of the cave and waited for Shellian to join him. They needed to find something before the food completely ran out and they became too weak to search.

As they explored the area that they had assigned themselves they found the going rough. The area was a broken land. Yet whatever had caused it was long in the past. Again because the area had been volcanic, they assumed it was the old volcano. Breathing hard as he pushed through another large crack in one of the many broken boulders he stopped to catch his breath. "Shellian this area is rough. I haven't even seen any sign of the animals that live up here. And there doesn't appear to be any game trails, paths or anything. Do you think that maybe we should abandon our search of this area and just move on to another one?"

Shrugging she said. "I don't know, I really don't know. But we are not far from mid-morning so let's push through to at least that. Boy is this land broken. I can't see very far in any direction and setting any landmarks are difficult. It had to be an explosion of some kind to fracture these boulders like they have been, and then this brush, tough with wicked thorns on them. The stuff doesn't even want to break. It's like it's made of iron or something similar. I have a feeling that we really haven't gotten very far from our cave. I hope the others are having a better time of it than we are. And I have to agree I've seen nothing to indicate anything as far as animal life goes. Okay, I've caught my breath shall we continue then?"

"Yeah, this brush is tough but did you notice that it seems to have a lot of spring in it also? This stuff, because of its strength, might make good bows. And we do need to make new ones since Schylar and his group confiscated the ones we had. But it's something we can check on later, if there is to be a later. Okay I guess I'm rested also." Then with a sigh he headed back out and pushed through another section of the brush. Here between the broken boulders the brush forced him to move to the right. As he stepped he found nothing under his feet, screamed a warning to Shellian, and felt himself falling. There had been no warning of a drop off or cliff but it had been there, hidden. He felt that he had been falling for a while but suspected that it was just an illusion, but he could see trees rushing up at him and then he struck them near their tops, falling through them as the limbs broke his fall somewhat, but when he finally struck the ground he remembered nothing.

Shellian hearing her brother scream and warning her, crawled through the brush, up to the edge and caught a brief flash of him falling and then lost sight of him. Looking desperately for a way down to see if he was injured, or worse killed, she could find nothing. Now what to do? Now what *should* she do? There had to be another way down there. But did she chance it or should she go back for help? The problem with that was the other members would not be back until dark, and then they would have to wait until morning to get back here and that might be too late. She yelled down to Saige hoping that she would hear and answer from him but all there was, were silence and the sounds of the breeze blowing through the scrub trees and brush. Again she searched desperately for a way down and found none. Then making her decision she marked the location and began to head back to their present base camp. She needed help and knew that with a prearranged signal the other team would return, cutting their exploring short. It was something they had arranged just in case of an emergency. It was a last resort as it would identify their location and it was something they had wanted to avoid if at all possible. But now there was no choice.

It would be after midday when she got back to their camp and lit the signal fire and then throw on it some green boughs to produce smoke. Once there all she could do was wait for the other team. But in the mean time she could put together some items that she thought they could use.

* * *

He returned to consciousness and just lay there for a moment trying to get himself together. He remembered falling and desperately trying to grab anything to break his fall, and then hitting those trees and falling through the boughs. He remembered the sound of breaking branches and then he had hit the ground and had passed out. *I guess I should try to move.* But again he just stayed there and didn't, afraid that he may have broken something. Glancing up he saw his path through the trees, and then looking around he saw that he had landed in a deep bed of needles that had fallen over time from the trees in the area. He now knew that through a combination of luck and this deep soft surface that he had landed on was the only reason he was alive. It must have been close to a thirty-meter drop, and the trees he'd fallen through had to be close to twenty meters tall. Finally taking a deep breath he slowly sat up and inspected his body. He found that he hurt just about everywhere and that he was bleeding in a number of places from the cuts and scrapes he received from the branches as he went through them. With a careful check of his body he found that there was nothing broken. He just could not believe his luck. That fall should have killed him, but here he was alive if not hurting, but alive. *Now where is here anyway?*

Finally, gingerly he stood and found that he was favoring one of his legs. Pulling up the pants leg he saw a large ugly bruise that covered most of his thigh. He must have struck one of the larger branches with this leg and again if that is what happened he was fortunate he did not break it. Looking up as he hobbled around he saw where he had fallen and now could see the trap he had stepped into. From above, this small valley wasn't visible and where he stepped off was a rounded end that appeared to sit just a little higher on the side he had stepped off. Searching carefully he could find no way back up, at least at this point. *So how long was I out?* He had to admit he had no idea, and with much of this small valley in the shadows at this point he had no way to judge. Then he remembered that he was with Shellian at the moment of the fall. He then yelled to see if she was still around, but there was no response. He had to assume that she went back to get help. Looking around he found a dead branch that he could fashion into a walking stick. He was finding it difficult to walk with that bruise. It must be very deep with the amount of pain he experienced every time he put weight on that leg. *Guess I better look around . . . if she went back to get help it will be a while before anyone could get back here anyway.* Then he realized that something here did not feel right. At the moment he could not place what it was.

It was silent. Other than the breeze that was very gentle here at the moment, there were no sounds of birds or the scurrying of the small animals, just the wind. At least it felt somewhat warm here even with the heavy shade. Then he realized that there was very little snow on the ground. It was winter and late into winter besides. There should be a lot of the white stuff but there was just a dusting. Again looking up he could find no reason for the lack of snow. There was nothing above to block it from here. He realized this as he looked around, while he had been standing and leaning on his walking stick, he then began to explore this strange place. As he limped away from the point where he fell, he worked towards what he hoped would be an opening into this valley and a way of escape. But in a short time he had reached the other side and found a pond with a waterfall providing the water for the pond. But there seemed to be no exit from the pond, and while the waterfall was not large it was large enough to require the water to exceed what this pond could hold. So where was the excess water going?

Once again he realized that something wasn't right about this pond also. But what was it that was wrong? Then two things struck him at once. First while the pond was not huge the edges were far enough away from the disturbance caused by the waterfall that it should be frozen, but was not. And secondly the pond did not look natural. There was something about it that said that it had been constructed. But what that was he could not say at the moment. He bent down and put his fingers into the water finding it quite cold, in fact cold enough to numb his fingers. Looking into the water he found it crystal clear and he could see all the way to the bottom. While not especially deep he could see that as he looked further from the edges that it continued to drop in depth. And he thought that he could see fish there also, but with the shadows could not be sure. *At least I won't lack for water, and if I have to remain here for a while probably won't lack for food either.* As he continued to work his way around the valley he was beginning to believe that it would turn out to be completely surrounded by cliffs – making it a trap for anything that fell into it and maybe the reason for no animal sign.

Working his way to the side with the deeper shadows he stopped and stared, then looked hard once again. Then shaking his head he thought. *No that can't be what it looks to be.* But it did. From where he was standing it looked to be the edge of a building – one built out of the native stone but looking so old that it almost looked to have been here since the beginning of time. Shaking his head again, he thought. *This has to be an illusion. After all why would there be such a thing in the valley? And if indeed it is a building how was it built and by whom?* He slowly worked his way towards what he thought could be a building and as he got closer he could see it begin to take shape. There was no doubt now, his eyes had not deceived him, it indeed was a building. Now excited he limped up to the corner that he had seen and stood and looked at it. Indeed it could have been here since the beginning it looked that old. But at the same time there should have been signs of decay, of it returning to where it came from. Yet it did not. How was that possible? If there were no one here to maintain it how could it continue to exist?

* * *

With no answer from Saige she made her way back down the mountain towards the cave they had made their base camp. With the other members of their now reduced group also out exploring she would have to use the signal fire to call them back. From her initial scanning of the small valley she could see no way down. Her impression was that it probably was an area that collapsed when the volcano was still active. Then over the years after the volcano died it become a small hidden valley with no way to get to the floor except by using ropes. She could see a point opposite where a small waterfall cascaded over the edge and entered a small lake below, but with the amount of trees she could not see much more. She knew that it would be hours now before she could make it back. But she worried that with the troubles that they had with the rest of the group that by sending up the smoke signals that she would be giving away their location. So that meant that once they had determined what had happened to Saige they would have to move. There just was no choice. With their location compromised they would be open to attack if Schylar decided that he would want to just eliminate them completely. She did not feel that he would since they were pretty even, with very little chance of surprising her and the others with her, plus there had been time for them to replace the weapons that they had lost, but one could just not be sure.

It was between midday and dusk when she finally reached the camp and had to stop and catch her breath as she had almost run the last portion. Sitting on a large rock just outside of the cave she contemplated lighting the fire or not lighting it. Was she ready to let the world know where they were? She knew that they had arranged the fire as a last resort and had discussed it for size and visibility. They had felt confident that no one in the valleys below would be able to see the smoke, and if so that it would be so faint that it should raise no suspicions from any there, just their local group would be affected. Knowing in her heart that this could be the only chance that Saige could have she took a deep breath and then went ahead and lit the fire. Once it was burning well she added a couple of green boughs. These immediately began to steam and smoke changing the almost invisible smoke to white as the moisture burned out of the boughs. It then briefly turned dark as they were consumed. Once the boughs were consumed, the smoke cleared once again and was a very light blue, almost invisible. She waited for a short time and then repeated it, and once again for a third time. Once the final boughs had burned she extinguished the fire. Now all she could do was wait and hope that they had seen the signal.

She knew that it probably would be a few hours before they returned so she began to go through what they had. Yes they did have rope, but would it be enough? And if not what did they have that could be used? Stretching out the rope she thought that maybe it would be long enough for them to be able to reach one of the trees, and then climb down that way. She could tell now that it would be the only way they would be able to descend into that hidden valley. Time dragged as she waited for the rest to return and she continued to pace, looking out in the distance a number of times thinking she had heard them approaching only to be disappointed. She also looked back down the mountain to see if maybe Schylar and his group were heading their way, but she knew that was foolish since it was at least a four day hike to here from that original cave. But she couldn't stop herself from checking now and then. After all she had just compromised their location so she worried that the others would show up immediately. Eventually she heard crunching on the gravel that was surrounding the cave. They had suspected that it was material taken from the hillside to create the cave. And shortly Stone, Saar and Seirra arrived. They were breathing hard and had a worried expression on their faces. When they had set this signaling system up they really thought it would never be used. "What's going on?" Stone asked, as the other two caught their breath.

He had pushed them hard to get back and had actually made great time. But now she could see that the other two were quite winded and it would take a little while for them to be ready to travel again. Quickly she outlined what had happened and that they would need to move out immediately if they were going to get back to the area before dark. It also meant that there would be a good chance that they would need to spend the night close by the valley since the area they had been searching was treacherous. There were many places one could get hurt.

"We need to hide anything we don't take with us. If all of us are going to be gone then it would be easy for the others", Saar said, "now that they should know approximately where we are, to come here and destroy what little we have left."

"True, very true. I didn't think about that. What if we just take all of it?" Shellian asked. "After all we carried it here and since we would only be going a shorter distance it should not be too much of an issue." She could see a little rebellion in Seirra's eyes but she didn't say anything. Once she had found out that it was Saige that had fallen she wanted to go there as quickly as they could, but now with what had been said Seirra knew that it would delay their departure.

"Saige could be seriously hurt. Do you think it's a good idea that we take this additional time to get our stuff when he could be dying?" Seirra asked.

"It's been hours Seirra, and it will not be easy to get down to where he is. When I sent those signals out to get you back here it probably alerted the others to where we are. We can't afford to lose what little we have so we really don't have a choice. We must take everything or risk losing everything including our lives. It really is that serious. If it means we end up losing one of us then there is very little we can do about it, but by not covering ourselves here we could find ourselves at the end also. Yes I do know you care for him, we all do, but we can do him no good if we do something stupid that will end up destroying all of us. After all he is my brother and we have been close all of our lives. I hate the idea of delaying but Saar has made a very valid point, and once he did, I happen to agree with him. So let's see how fast we can get this stuff together and then I'll lead us back to that hidden valley."

Looking at the positions of the suns they realized that by the time that they reached the valley once again that it would be close to dark. But it was something they would have to face once they arrived. After a day of exploring, returning to their camp and then once again heading out they found that they were tired, which meant that they would have to be doubly careful. It would be much easier to make a mistake and not recognize it until it was too late, when one was exhausted, and the snow that was on the ground did not make it any easier. Even though the trail that she had taken was plain to see, it was obviously not an easy path. As they struggled their breath came out in great clouds of steam. It was also cooling rapidly as the suns began to set, and the sunset that was displayed as they continued the climb, was spectacular. It was absolutely clear with no sign of any approaching storms. Probably a good thing, but it provided another problem. Clear skies at night meant extreme cold, and they would not have the heated cave this night. As they continued their trek Shellian began to wonder if they should have waited until morning, but immediately put that thought out of her mind. That could be too much time and might ensure that her brother would die. So what if they were a little uncomfortable tonight if it meant that Saige would survive.

It wouldn't be the first time since this whole mess began, and she suspected that it would not be the last. And if they were unable to stop the primitives then there would be other refugees heading to these mountains. But with the failures that they had faced she wondered if they could have any impact at all, or even if they would be around to try. Considering the size of their group originally and what it was now it did seem impossible. Feeling the cold beginning to penetrate and the shadows lengthening she picked up her pace once more. Once again time seemed to be against them. She slowed as they got close to the area. She did not want to repeat what had happened to Saige, but was stopped in her tracks as standing before her was Saige. At loss for words she just stood there and stared.

Smiling although it hurt Saige said, "Now don't just stand there with your mouth open say something."

"Sorry. Ah, but, I saw you fall and from what I could see that valley was completely walled – especially on this side. There was no way out of there. So how'd . . .

"How did I get out sis? Is that what you are asking?" He then turned slowly around and said to all of them. "Just follow me and all will become clear." He then began to limp off in another direction beckoning them to follow. Shocked by seeing him it took a moment for the rest to react and begin to follow. Since he was moving slowly because of his injuries he was not that far ahead of them. Saar looked at Shellian and said. "He obviously has some injuries, but for someone who fell as far as you said he did, he seems to be in remarkable health." Saige appeared to be heading straight for a rock wall. There appeared to be no reason for this action as there was no trail, and the area was somewhat exposed. Shrugging they tried to catch up only to watch him walk right up to the wall and then disappear from sight. It surprised them enough that they stopped in their tracks once again, and again stared. What was it that Saige had discovered? They quickened their pace and then when they approached the same area Saige made an appearance as if he had walked through solid rock and then asked. "Does something about this appear to be familiar?"

"Yes." Saar stated. "Yes this appears to be something similar to what we are using in the cities to hide entrances. But why would such a thing be here?"

"A very good question and one I think will need some time to confirm. But my initial impression is that this, although obviously much older, is of the same technology that we use in the cities."

"No. No can't be. There's no record of any of this here in these mountains. Yes I know I'm the doctor, but I always enjoyed history and it has been my hobby. Well, at least until our world fell apart."

"Understood Saar, but before we really get cold let's all step inside. I think that there are many surprises awaiting all of us." He then turned and once again disappeared. This time they followed and found that they were standing on a large platform sitting above a large open cavern, and it was warm. When the warmth hit them they shivered a moment as the heat penetrated. "I haven't had much time to do any real exploring here. And I know it is almost a miracle that I am even walking let alone standing before you. And I'll explain my side of this adventure, but let's take the ladder down to the floor. I can see by the size of your packs that you've brought everything with you. Would that be because someone lit the signal fire?" He saw them nod their heads. He then gingerly climbed down the ladder to another platform, and then continued the process through two other platforms before finally standing on the ground. Even though the light was dim, the whole cavern was bathed in the soft light. It was huge, and looking around there appeared to be many areas that had been modified for storage. One thing about it, whatever this was, it was not a small operation. It would have been easy to put their whole compound in here and still have room. Then it came to them that the volume of this area was enormous and yet the whole area was warm. That took some power and yet there was no sign of any. Looking down they could see Saige's tracks from his earlier walk across the dirt floor. These tracks led away into the distance towards what they suspected were the valley that he had fallen into.

"Okay some explanations are necessary." He said as he led them across the floor in the opposite direction of his previous tracks. "When I fell I thought I was dead. But after falling for about ten meters I was fortunate enough to fall into one of the many trees. The boughs of the tree broke my fall, and I broke many of the branches on the way to the ground. Then when I hit the ground it knocked me out. I don't know how much time passed before I was conscious. But the first thing I noticed was the tree I had fallen through above me, and then realized that I had also fallen into a deep pile of needles which further broke my fall. No, as you can tell I did not come off unscathed. I have many cuts and contusions, with some of them deep, but at least none of them were close to a main artery so they scabbed over pretty quick. I have a large deep bruise on this leg and it's why I am limping, and to be honest I hurt just about everywhere. Later Doc you can check me out to be sure nothing is worse, but overall I feel very lucky. I then searched this small valley for a way out. Found some things that just did not look quite natural and then found the corner of an ancient building, which led me to this huge cavern and then hearing all of you. I wasn't sure of the way out so I climbed up and saw that there was an entrance there at the top. And for now you know the rest."

They stopped briefly looking around the enormous cavern. Its height disappeared above them and it seemed that it went on forever around them although they knew it was an illusion. Near some of the walls there appeared to be small structures. Guessing, they felt that at one time these structures were probably a place where supplies had been stored. Again looking at them from a distance one had the impression that the owners had just temporarily stepped out and would be returning at any moment. Yet at the same time the place had the feel of age laying on it. "What is this place?" Saar asked to no one in particular. "And who used it and built those structures?"

"You got me Saar", Saige replied. "As you know I have been here just a little longer than you, by no choice of my own I might add, so I truly know no more than you at this point."

"Really just thinking out loud Saige," Saar replied, "I'm sure that all of us are wondering the same thing. This building that you found, where is it from here?"

"Well before we stopped to admire the sheer size of this place I was heading to it. Very little of it shows in the valley and I was surprised when I found the entrance to it. I expected it to be just a home, a place for a small group to live, but . . . well instead of just telling you, follow me and you can see for yourselves." He then led them across the floor of the cavern to another wall that again appeared to be solid. Yet looking down they could see his tracks disappearing through the seemingly solid wall. Again another barrier like they were familiar with – identical in fact to the ones used in their cities.

Contemplating what little had been revealed so far Stone said. "I wonder . . ."

"Wonder what Stone?" Shellian asked.

"I know we have seen very little yet, but what we have appears to be very familiar. I don't know or understand how all of this could still be functioning after all of this time, but it is. So there has to be some type of auto maintenance going on here. Otherwise it would have quit a long time ago. Still . . . still this feels like we are home, in one of our cities that are down below."

"Yes, I think you are right Stone." Shellian said. "It is, well it was like the moment we came inside that we immediately felt comfortable, safe, and yes like we were back in one of our cities."

"That's quite a conclusion being that we have seen so little of this place", Saar replied. "But yes I can understand it and really have to agree. And truthfully, I cannot even tell you why."

"Ready?" Saige asked. He could see that they were and so he went through the illusion and they then followed him. Before them was a set of double doors, which they went through. Once through they stopped again in awe with what was before them. Here they found a large area that could easily have been an administrative section. There were places to handle whatever supplies that would arrive in that cavern, and a section with cubicles for whatever business needed to be carried out. Behind the cubicles were a few rooms with standard doors identifying ones who were probably in charge of the operation. All of it laid out neatly making the different areas easily accessible for any that required the services provided.

"What is this place?" Seirra asked, "This is just huge. Why here in the mountains? There's nothing here for something this size?"

"I can't disagree. When I came into the building it stopped me in my tracks. I've really had very little time to explore it, but from what I have seen we are just touching the very beginnings of this place. Before coming into the building I realized that there was another problem and it was the trees. There was something very wrong with them. I don't mean that they were damaged or dying or anything like that – well, other than the damage I did falling through one of them. But they are subtly different than any I remember seeing and are living around these mountains. That's not to say that that they don't belong here since plants and trees are not my specialty. Well, as we finally get back outside, inside that valley you'll see what I mean." He then led them down a hallway, which had a number of closed doors on either side. Finally ending at a set of double doors, which he opened, and walked into what looked to be a large dining area, and off to one side, an area that appeared to be a large kitchen. Then on the opposite wall a couple of doors that looked to be entrances into public bathrooms.

"You know what; I think I could use that." Shellian said, pointing to the door for the woman's restroom. "I wonder if it is still functional after all this time. And if it is it sure will beat using the bushes for our nature calls." then turning to Seirra she said. "Shall we go find out?" They both left and entered the restroom leaving the men standing there.

Shaking his head Saar said. "Now that is something I will never understand."

"What's that Saar?" Stone asked.

"Why is it that any time a woman wants to use a public restroom that they always must go in packs, or at least two of them? After all when we use them we just go. Sometimes it's with another guy, but most of the time it's just us, one at a time. But if there are at least two women, then they always tag team it."

"I've never thought about it", Stone replied. "But you're right. I've never seen any of them go to one of these things alone."

They sat at one of the tables that were anchored to the floor waiting until the women made an appearance from their trip. With no one speaking initially and all just looking around. "I would say that this place could seat maybe fifty or sixty easily", Saar said. "And I suspect that whoever was here probably worked in shifts, so that means that this place could have had at least one hundred to one hundred and fifty people, if not more. What's off in the other direction from that administration area Saige?"

"Don't know really, didn't have time to explore it yet. But my guess is, that's it is the main way through. It wouldn't make sense for the main thoroughfare to go through a place where people eat. But to have a place to eat close to the working areas makes total sense."

"True, but working areas for what?" Stone asked. "While I know that we more or less just walked through that cavern I didn't see anything that would constitute work."

About this time Shellian came out of the restroom and quickly joined them at the table. "Hey! Guess what we found?"

"I hope an operating restroom." Saar answered

Laughing she said. "Yes, and so much more. Care to guess?"

"Well a working restroom is plenty for me." Turning to the others he asked. "I wonder how they did it. This place hasn't been used in what seems forever. Yet so much of it appears to be in working order."

Placing her hands on her hips and shaking her head she said. "You men always are looking at how things work, instead of just appreciating that it just does. Okay since none of you want to guess I'll tell you. These restrooms are equipped with showers. The real thing and like everything else they appear to work and there's hot water also. So I don't know about you but I am tired of smelling like smoke and I for one am tired of smelling dirty bodies. So I suggest that the three of you go check it out and if yours are so equipped go clean up. Oh by the way there seems to be supplies of towels and believe it or not some type of clothing that whoever worked here used. So we can also get out of these skins and into something a little more comfortable." She then turned around and headed back into the restroom.

Looking at each other for a moment they then got up from the table and headed into their public restroom. Pushing through the door they found a large area with the standard urinals, toilets, and sinks. But further in there was a section that held supplies of toweling and clothing, and just beyond that there were showers. Not waiting they stripped down, looking in one of the cabinets they found something that could pass as soap and went into the open shower area. Later, with the clothes provided in the restrooms they emerged feeling clean for the first time in what seemed like forever. But even though they had started their showers later than the women, the ladies had yet to emerge. "Wonder what this material is?" Saar asked idly, as they waited for the women to make their appearance. "You know I've forgotten how good a shower feels." The rest had to agree, and to be out of those skins, which had needed cleaning for a while, but with nothing to change in to, they had to make do. Looking at the clothes that they were in, they found that it changed their looks, now not appearing to be a part of the primitives. The items were one-piece coverall style – making it easy to get in and out of. The material could have been paper, so they were a one-time use and then probably recycled. In the supply lockers all of this clothing was a simple light blue. It appeared to use some type of magnetic closure so there were no buttons or other type of fasteners. "I don't know about you . . ." Stone said. "But I think I want to go check out the kitchen area. If this place is similar to the cities then they probably have food processors in there. I really don't think that this would be an easy place to grow food. Although I bet with something this size they probably have hydroponics somewhere." Looking around they saw that the women still had not emerged and so agreed with Stone. They all got up and headed into the kitchen area. The first thing that hit them was that everything was spotless, and no dust lay anywhere. It was obvious that it had been shut down with the idea that it could be a long time before anybody returned. "This will take some time to figure out." Saige said. "This was a careful shutdown and it appears that the equipment has been mothballed, but with the idea that it can be brought back quickly if needed – which makes sense, as this would be one of the first places I would reactivate after returning."

Shellian and Seirra finally emerged from the restroom and saw that the men were not around. "Now we couldn't have beaten them out", Shellian said. "After all I've never seen a man take a shower that he wasn't out way before any of us. So I wonder where they went?"

"I think I hear voices over there towards the kitchen." Seirra said as she pointed in the direction.

"I do think you're right. Shall we go and join them?" They headed into the kitchen and found the men once again in deep discussion about something. "Okay guys what's going on?" Shellian asked.

"Wow! Look at you two." Stone exclaimed. "Oh while we were waiting it was decided that we'd come in and check out the kitchen. After all we are just about out of what we brought with us. So it was a good time to check it out since we really didn't know how long the two of you would be. But personally I can say the wait was worth it."

Looking at Stone with askance Shellian asked. "Now what is that supposed to mean?"

Laughing at her look he said. "Now Shellian you have to admit that with the way we have had to live that none of us looked the best that we could. I am just saying that I appreciate the change. Besides it appears that you and Seirra had more choices in the one-piece outfits than we did. We had the choice of, oh let me see, one color, while I can tell there was a much greater selection for you – and I have to admit that they fit rather well also."

Shellian had picked an outfit that was pale yellow and with her tanned skin it worked very well for her, while Seirra had found one that was a darker shade of green and again had done her justice. Stone continuing said. "It's nice to be really clean again, and if I cannot appreciate what it does then . . ." He shrugged looking to the two other men for support.

Laughing Saige said. "Don't look at us Stone. It looks like you're doing a great job of digging your own grave right now, and besides I've never succeeded in winning when sparing with words with either Shellian or Seirra. So leave me out of it."

Saar looking around at everyone just shook his head. "Okay guys not to change the subject, but to change the subject, we do need to figure out how to get this back on line so that we can use the facilities here."

"Breathing out deeply Stone said, "Thank you Saar, and you're right. But I think that Saige should continue to show us what he has found so far. Then we can come back and try and get this and anything else we need back on line. So Saige, if you would?" Stone then stepped back and gestured for Saige to continue.

Looking around at the other four Saige said. "Okay? If you are ready, let's do this. Like I said before we were interrupted . . . not that it was a bad interruption." He added hastily as he headed through them and led them out of the eating area through a set of double swinging doors and into a hallway. Looking down the hallway there were a number of closed doors on both sides. He turned left where there was only one door at the end. And like the one they had just gone through it was double swinging doors. Once through the door they found themselves in a large room with a single table and many chairs around it. There were some small cabinets around the perimeter and on the walls that the doors attached to. But the opposite side was all windows. But at the moment, with the soft light that was in the room, they could not see through them. It was now nighttime and completely dark out. So the only things visible were their reflections on the glass, or whatever the windows were constructed from. Glass first came to mind, but then they realized that unless it was tempered that regular glass would probably been destroyed by now. "Well I was going to show you the outside portion, but that looks like it will have to wait until the morning. I guess we should explore in the other direction from the cafeteria, dining area or whatever you want to call it, and see what exists in that direction. So far I haven't found any living areas, but I suspect with the size of this place, there has to be."

No one said anything other than nodding in agreement. So they turned around and headed back through the areas they had just left, then through the administrative work area and then once again through double swinging doors. Immediately the atmosphere changed. It was obvious that this was the area where the living area had been built. The first doors they saw were marked for single men on one side and single women on the other. As a group they went inside of both finding that the side for the men was generally open with cabinets that divided the areas from each bed and chair arrangement. The cabinets were spacious and allowed each one who lived here their own space. On the far side was the common bathroom with the normal items including the open showers. Seeing the arrangements Seirra then said. "I just don't understand this, and I never will. I could no more shower in such a place, then run around without my clothes. How do you guys do it?"

It was a question none of them had ever thought about. As a group the three of them shrugged. "I have no answer for that as this is the way it has always been and it doesn't bother us at all. Why would it bother you?" Saar asked.

Shaking her head Seirra replied saying, "I don't know it just does. Shall we go look at the other one, you know the single woman area?"

"Why not" Stone replied. "I've never really been in one of those as such places were always off limits to us. So lead on if you would Seirra."

"Okay I will. And I think you will see that it is quite different. Oh by the way, I think I am beginning to believe that our ancestors built this place. There are just too many things that are the same. If the other side turns out to be like I suspect it will only strengthen my beliefs." She then led them out and then across the hallway and into the single women facility. Immediately it was obvious that it was set up completely different. Each area where the single women would live had "L" shaped walls blocking any view from the next area, giving each woman almost complete privacy. If there had been doors on the front then it would be so. But instead there were curtains hung in the openings. Once inside the cubicle they found dressers mirrors and cabinets that would hold infinitely more than any they had seen on the men's side.

"Wow! Is this the way it was in our compound back at the city?" Stone asked.

"Pretty much so", Shellian said, "But I am sure there are some differences, but I think I have to agree with Seirra now. This could be close to what we are used to. But until I look at the bathroom here I'll hold my judgment."

"Okay then, why don't we?" Saige asked. They made their way into the bathroom and were immediately met with the differences between the two. All toilets had stalls, and each shower was also enclosed. Everything based on privacy and just the opposite of the men's unit. "This is so different. I didn't realize that you women took your privacy that seriously."

"Well, we do Saige", Seirra said. They as a group then left the area and then continued down the hall. Here they began finding what could only be called apartments. These obviously were for the coupled members. While not large they at least were comfortable.

After some additional time had passed Saige said, "I think I would like to continue this, but I don't know about you but I haven't eaten for a while and my stomach is complaining so let's go back to the cafeteria and eat. We can discuss what we have found so far and then actually retire to a real bed. I know what a concept. But I suspect that we won't sleep too well on them anyway. You know strange bed, strange environment, and strange noises, all leading to poor sleep. Tomorrow we can do a better search and maybe get the kitchen operating again. I suspect that there may be some emergency supplies around somewhere. So if we can find those it will at least give us something until we have this facility up and running again." Then with a sweep of his hand he asked. "Shall we?"

Laughing Stone said. "Call me anything but late to a meal."

* * *

It was entering the middle of the night and like a prophet, he found that indeed he could not sleep. So Saige headed out of the large room past the silently working bots that appeared only at night to clean. He suspected that there were similar bots that did the repairs. Breathing deeply, and with eyes that were burning, he headed off through what they had believed was the admin area, then through the lunch room, out the other side and into the large glassed room that he suspected was used for executive meetings. Pulling one of the chairs back he sat down staring at the opaque windows seeing only a reflection of the interior from the soft glow of the lighting. He did not know how much time had passed but he suddenly realized that someone else was entering the room. Looking back at the entrance he saw Shellian coming in. She, seeing him smiled, but it was a sad one. "I see you couldn't sleep either. Seirra was out cold so instead of staying there and maybe waking her I decided to go and walk. I really needed some time to think, and you?"

"I don't know, maybe it was the sound of those bots going about their business. You know a different sound. And since it has been very necessary for us to always be on the alert for danger . . . well it's a different sound. Then knowing I wasn't going to be able to sleep both for that reason and the fact that I hurt just about everywhere I decided to come here. Don't ask me why it just seemed like a quiet area that one could look out from. But of course I forgot that these windows are built somehow to prevent any light from the inside to be seen from the outside. So all I could see was a reflection of this space."

Coming over and then sitting across from him Shellian said. "I wonder if Seirra is right." Then shaking her head she continued. "I know right now there is no way of knowing. We've seen so little of this place. I guess it's just idle speculation on my part. But . . . but it just feels right. I don't know how else to explain it, it just feels like us."

Sighing and then shaking his head Saige said. "I just don't know. I have so many questions. Like why is this place abandoned? Obviously from what little we know right now, this place was shut down with the idea of returning someday. Yet no one ever did. And yet the bots have continued their work, again for how long is anyone's guess. It is the only reason that I can see that this place is in the condition it is. It looks like whoever was here just stepped out yesterday. Yet there is a feel of age on this place – a feel of real age, like it has been here for thousands of annuals. And if that is so can we solve the puzzle as to why someone left a perfectly good facility and never returned? I don't know." For a short period of time both were lost in their thoughts as these puzzles lay before them. Finally restless once again Saige said. "I have to get up and move, I just can't explain it but something about this place really bothers me. So I'm going to walk a little and probably try to get back to sleep. I think that tomorrow some of our questions will be answered as we search this place. I guess then I'll see you in the morning sis." He got up and left the room leaving Shellian alone with her thoughts.

I can understand it. She thought. Then looking down at the huge oblong table she got up and idly walked around the room opening the cabinets that lined the walls – finding pitchers and glasses in some and pads of paper and writing implements in others. It established for her that this was a place for meetings . . . but what kind of meetings? There was nothing left to give her any hints at all. Finally weariness began to overcome her once more and she got up to head back and try and get some additional sleep. She sighed, shrugged, and then left the room leaving it vacant and silent once more.

CHAPTER TEN

The next several days they explored the facility finding many important areas including the nursery, learning center, hydroponics, and security. With the location of the nursery and learning center found, just down from the apartments, this confirmed that there had been children of different ages here. This only deepened the mystery as to why the abandonment. With families now confirmed, and from personal experience of what lay outside of this facility in these mountains, why place themselves in this environment and the hardships that existed? Something really terrible must have happened . . . yet . . . yet there was nothing to indicate a problem or disaster – nothing at all. The discovery of the security office excited them all. Since there they would be able to find information on the facility. But the greatest find within the unit was the monitors. Once again they still functioned and through the rotating images they got a view of the whole facility. And then to their surprise, each of the caves along the pathway came into view. So somehow even these were under constant surveillance. It took about half a day for them to figure out the basic system, although manipulating those images was well beyond them. And now armed with maps of the facility and images generated by the security system they began to get a real feel for the layout. Surprising to them was the similarity to the layout of their city. But all could easily be racked up as coincidence. It was decided that one of them would stay in the security office and monitor the rest as they worked their way around. Again like before they worked in teams of two. Then by accident they found that there was two-way communications with the security section and anywhere they were within the facility.

That got them to wondering if it was the same throughout the network of caves that had been located. There apparently were thirty of these caves, allowing these people to travel far down the mountainsides in just about any direction. By having the caves monitored these people would know if it was safe, which led them to believe that like the facility, that there had to be voice communications within the caves. After all it made sense so that if there was danger detected, then the travelers could be warned. Of course it could also be that the travelers carried some type of device that allowed them to communicate, but if it was anything like they had presently it would have been short ranged. Not allowing for the great distances and line of sight problems that they had to deal with.

On this day Saar drew duty in the security office while the two women worked their way through the school to see if they could find out what was being taught there and to compare it to what they had learned in their own educational system. Nothing had been located as of yet to identify the people who had built this place. And while the clues stacking up still pointed to their own ancestors, they had no proof. The two men were working the large cavern where they had first entered. Since that time they had located three other entrances or exits from this hidden facility, but still used the one Saige had found when he first left. "Everyone!" Saar stated. "I need you all to report back to the security office now. Something is developing and we need to be together on this."

The two women looked at each other and Shellian asked as she looked up into the area where the camera was located. "What's going on Saar?" But he just repeated that they needed to come to him directly.

Hearing the request as it echoed in the large cavern, it took a moment before they understood what had been asked. They stopped immediately and at a fast pace headed back. In a short time they had joined the other three there since the two men had the furthest distance to travel. They saw the others looking at a couple of the screens intently and began to ask what they were looking at when a movement caught their eyes. "What the heck is that?" Saige asked.

Saar not taking his eyes off the screen said. "This is the view in the area of the third cave. And I do believe that what we are seeing here is Sorrel."

"Sorrel?" Stone asked. "What the heck is she doing out there, and from what I can see alone?"

"How can you tell doc? The image is still distant from the camera location. I can tell that whoever it is that this person is definitely female, and pregnant – quite pregnant, but other than that I don't recognize her." Saige said.

"Give it a couple and I think you will. Being that I am the doctor for this group I've become pretty familiar with all of you."

Laughing and lightening the moment, Saige asked. "How do you mean that doc?" This immediately brought a chuckle out of the rest while Saar's face reddened a little.

"Now hold on there! You know what I mean."

Patting his shoulder Saige said. "You're the one who said it not me." Then pausing briefly he continued. "Yes we do know what you meant, but it was the way you said it that made me think that way. Anyway I'll take your word for it. I know that from a distance I can recognize Shellian from the way she walks and her movements, and I know it is the same for her since we have worked and trained together for most of our lives. It can mean the difference between living and dying. So I trust your judgment. If this person keeps on heading in her current direction then she'll be very close to the camera shortly and we'll have it confirmed. Have you seen anybody else out there, or any who may be following her. You know something to lure us out in a trap of some kind?"

"No. Once I saw her I began looking at the other cameras that are behind or in the direction we originally came from. And then looked ahead just in case they would be ahead of her, but she appears to be quite alone."

They all watched fascinated with the image as it approached the camera's location. Shaking her head Shellian said. "She looks like hell. I wonder what happened." Then pointing at the screen she said. "Look how dirty she appears, and the clothing looks damaged." Then Sorrel passed the camera's location close to the cave. There she stopped and looked desperately around. They could tell from both her body language and her haggard look that she was near to the end of her endurance, and that she had lost all hope. Then Shellian asked, "What has happened back there? I mean this woman we are watching is in her early third-third, and yet she is risking everything to be away from shelter. With the amount of snow on the ground and the way she is dressed she has to be cold, and she'll find no sign of us either. I'm surprised that she's gotten this far. So what do we do about it, and is this some kind of trap? I know Saar, you've been making sure that it isn't, but that doesn't keep me from worrying about it."

"Look", Saige said, "if she continues as she is, she will almost naturally be heading in the right direction for the next cave. It doesn't look like she's carrying a pack or anything extra. This looks like a decision that she made quickly, and did not have time to prepare."

"You're right." Stone answered. "And that's not a good thing. I mean when one has the equipment with them to make such a journey and not be carrying then it's not too much of an issue. But here with this she is in very real danger. Not only to herself but also to that child she is carrying. I say let's go get her before she gets into any more serious trouble." Looking around he could only see agreement on the rest.

Saige seeing the response of the others said, "Okay, I have to agree and I can tell the rest of you feel much the same way. Shell, you come with me and we will go and meet her. I would like the three of you to continue to monitor the situation from here. Run it in shifts. I know at this time we have yet to figure out the voice communications for the caves, but keep working on that. There has to be something here that allows it. After all whoever built this place has the devices all over the facility and also visuals. And since we have visuals at all the caves it is only reasonable to assume that there is voice also." Then turning to Shellian he asked. "Shell', shall we go?" And then turning back to the Saar he said. "Yes I know you being the doctor would love to be one of the ones to go. But if this turns out to be a trap we cannot afford to lose you. Just be prepared to take care of her if it isn't." Then looking one last time at the screen he shook his head and said. "She really does look like hell." And with that statement, turned and left the security office with Shellian close behind. "Shell' grab those communicators so that we can hopefully be in range and keep in contact with whoever is in the security office. I'll grab some of the food, and weapons. We'll meet at the ladder in that large cavern." If she was at the third cavern from the original direction that they had come from then it would take them over a day to reach her, unless they pushed hard.

* * *

The two of them had pushed hard to get down to Sorrel. At the same time they continued to test their portable communication devices to be sure that contact could be kept. Sorrel had shown up on the screens about mid-morning and it had taken another thirty minutes to get everything together. They fairly trotted to the first cave covering the distance in only a couple of hours, but the day was advancing, and they wanted to find her before night where it would be much too easy to miss her. Again, what had happened back there to make Sorrel take off with nothing but what she was wearing? And how had she been able to follow the almost invisible trail that had originally led them to the hidden facility? However she had done it, could she continue to do it? So far the information they had received back from Saar, who remained on duty back there, stated that she had found the cave and was presently inside of it. He then reported that the other two were attempting to figure out if there were listening devices set up inside these caves and tied into the security system, but so far they had been unsuccessful. So there was no way to really know what Sorrel's condition truly was. But the images they were receiving did not give him much confidence. Sorrel looked pale and drawn, and from the images her breathing was heavy and ragged.

Saige and Shellian continued to push as the day rapidly flowed past them. Then Saar contacted them. "I think she has passed out. She hasn't moved from that cave and she appears to have slumped over. You need to hurry! I really don't know how long she has. I'm also giving this over to Stone so he will be your contact. I need to take a break and then go to the infirmary and prepare for your arrival. If it was only she to worry about it would be bad enough, but she is carrying a child, and with the stress she's putting on herself right now, there is a good chance that she'll lose it. I want to do all I can to prevent that from happening. Stone will keep me informed of your progress, and Seirra is preparing some meals while we are busy here."

"Okay, this is Stone so I have it now. So how far are you from reaching the second cave?"

"I don't know for sure", Shellian replied between the breaths as she tried to catch her breath. "But I would guess that we are between the first and second from this direction, which would put us between the third and fourth from the other direction. We are still a few hours out, and with us trotting we are covering a lot of distance, with a lot to go, but we think that we will be there just before dark. I really hope she can hold on. What really sucks here is that we haven't found any way to let her know that help is on the way. Yes, and I know right now she is unconscious so it wouldn't matter anyway. But it's just that if you know that someone is coming for you it gives you hope where there may have been none before." Turning and looking at Saige she could read the determination in his face. She figured that hers looked much the same. "Well brother shall we pick it up again? At least there has been no new snow so that it won't be hiding any new traps for us."

"True, but I just thought of something that worries me. Like you, I have really enjoyed this nice weather, and am hoping that spring is just around the corner. But Sorrel is leaving tracks that will be easy to follow. And we are now doing the same thing, which means we will be leaving an easy trail for any to follow right back to the facility. And with this situation being desperate, we will not be able to cover any of our tracks. So we will be giving away our location."

"Yeah, but what can we do, leave her to die out here?"

"No, you know me better than that. But this is putting us back at risk. It's just another one of those things that makes it so much more complicated. I almost wish for a storm now to cover both her tracks and ours, but what will be, will be right now. She is more important anyway. Okay, done with our brief break let's push on through this time. I think if we continue alternately walk and run that we should just about make it before dark. Darn!" Saige exclaimed, "I wish we had figured out if there is a way to communicate with the caves, it would make it so much easier."

As they trotted there they received no new updates and hoped that no news was good news. Finally as the suns began to set and the shadows overtook them they could see the location of the cave in the distance. At this point the portable communications devices were becoming inconsistent. But at least they were able to make one final contact so that the ones at the facility would be aware of their approach. Of course they knew that shortly they would be visible on the screens as they came into the hidden camera's range. And then finally, they saw the mouth of the cave. The communications from the security center now was almost unintelligible, but they could at least tell that they now were visible to them. Taking a deep breath they walked into the cave and found Sorrel half lying on the floor unconscious. She looked worse than the images had shown them back at the facility. Looking at each other Shellian said, "Now what? We won't be able to move until the morning. Look I'll set up a bed for her. Why don't you go out and gather some wood and start a fire. I think we are going to have to nurse her back a little before the morning, and from what I am seeing here we will probably have to watch her closely tonight."

"You'll get no arguments from me Shell'. From what I see here if we are able to move tomorrow I suspect that it's going to take us all day just to move up one cave instead of all the way back." He began his way outside stopped, turned and then asked in a tone that showed he really wasn't expecting an answer. "Shell', I wonder what happened back there after we left? It had to be something really serious for Sorrel to take off like this with no preparation." He then left to gather some firewood and to light a fire.

Once he had left, and under her breath more to herself she said, "Yes, Saige, I do wonder."

It was a sleepless night for both of them, as Sorrel remained unconscious and continued to look pale and drawn. They had tried to get some broth down her but were unsuccessful. This was a very serious situation and now once again they were too far out to be able to communicate. If indeed they were able to move tomorrow then once they came back into range they would have to let them know of the seriousness of the condition. "Saige, do you have anything that we can write on? I know with our need to leave it was something I did not even consider."

"Why sis?" Then he just said, "Oh." He thought a moment and then shook his head. "No I don't remember seeing anything like that. Maybe we could take one of the burned sticks and use the charcoal on the end to write on something. Then we could at least let them know what we need."

"My thoughts exactly. Now, we need something to be able to write on, any suggestions?"

Looking around inside the cave neither could see anything that would work. Knowing from the view of the cave on the security screens they looked at the wall across from its probable location.

Studying it for a moment Saige said. "I wonder . . . be right back." He then headed outside where the fire was burning grabbed a burned stick or two then returned inside. "Now let's see if this can be seen." He then tried marking the cave wall and with the soft glow and some experimentation he found the size of letters needed to be visible. It was going to take a few more sticks, and he knew that the message would have to be very short and to the point. Turning around he could see

Shellian studying both him and what he was trying to do. "What do you think?" He asked.

"Well it's a little hard to read but I guess it will have to do. What do you want to say?"

"This is a little more serious than what we first thought. So I was thinking that we need Saar to meet us at the next cave. It's not something I really want to do, but neither you nor I are doctors and her condition is beyond us. I just hope that we can move on in the morning. I really have no idea if any of the others are following her or not. I just don't like this."

"You want to say all of that?" She said as she interrupted him.

"No just thinking out loud here, sorry, just these few words. 'Need Saar at first cave tomorrow', I hope that's enough."

"Me too." Then turning back to her patient, when Sorrel moaned softly, she said again with a slight edge of desperation in her voice. "Yeah, me too."

* * *

The twin suns were rising in the sky and Sorrel had yet to wake. Her breathing had eased and she appeared to be resting now, but sometime soon they would have to try and wake her and move on to the next cave. They had no way to know if the message they had put on the wall was received at all. So once they began the journey back they would continue to try to make voice contact once again. The problem with these devices was that they were line of sight only. And in these mountains there were few places where it was line of sight. Both of them standing by the entrance looking outside were deep in conversation when Sorrel said in a very weak and surprised voice asked. "Where . . . where did you come from? When I found this cave I thought that it was the end. I was scared to death, but I had nothing left – just nothing left at all." She then began crying softly which shook through her whole being.

Shellian immediately went to her side, put her arms around her shoulders and said, "It's not important Sorrel, not important at all. We are here and we are going to do all we can to get you through this." Turning to Saige who was still standing at the entrance she said. "Well, just don't stand there Saige, get us something to eat. See if that broth we had prepared for her is still hot from our morning fire, we need to get some food into her now, and then move."

"Sorry sis, I was just surprised that she was awake. Be right back!"

* * *

It was mid-morning before they could begin their return trip. Both Saige and Shellian took turns in supporting Sorrel. There was no doubt that the trip just to the next cave would take them all day. Sorrel had no strength at all, and leaned heavily on the two of them as they continued their trek. It was a miracle that Sorrel had made it as far as she had, let alone finding the path that led by the caves. The trip back to the next cave was an ordeal. Sorrel was now running a fever and ranged from semi-consciousness to short periods of ramblings about nothing at all. They half carried and half supported her the whole distance. It was now obvious to them that if they had not come to rescue her she would probably have died in that cave. It saddened both of them with that thought. There had already been way too much tragedy and death in their group, and to be close to that once again was something they did not even want to consider. Eventually close to dusk they saw the location of the cave in the distance.

As they got closer they saw two emerge and come towards them. As they got closer they relaxed recognizing Stone and Saar. Not that it was likely, but there had been a slight possibility that it may have been someone from the other group. Stone arrived first and said. "Here let me take over. I'll carry her and Saar will monitor as we move." Then looking close at Sorrel he continued saying, "She really looks bad. I hope we've gotten to her in time. I wonder what happened?" Then Saar joined them with deep concern on his face he studied Sorrel for a moment.

"Let's get her inside. She really is much worse. We really need to get her back to the facility, but it is almost dark and we haven't located any of the lights that we could use to see our way. So I guess we are stuck here for this night." Then looking at Saige and Shellian he said. "You two look like your all done in. Look we have a fire going and food already hot. Why don't the two of you go get something, we can handle this for now. I think we will be carrying her on a stretcher tomorrow." Shaking his head he said. "I really did not think she was this bad. The screens surely did not do her justice that's for sure."

That night she never regained consciousness, and the next day they carried her on a stretcher, for which again, she was totally unaware of anything. Eventually, with all four of them rotating the job of carrying her, they finally reached the facility early in the afternoon. There they took her to the infirmary and Saar began to work on her. Seirra stopped by briefly before returning to the security office. Since she had been the only one left at the facility, she had locked herself inside the security office while they had been gone. Once the chaos was over they would again work it in shifts. Now Sorrel's survival was in the hands of Saar, and in the inner strength of Sorrel. Saige, Stone, and Shellian headed for the cafeteria area to get a meal and to relax for a short time. "I really wonder what has happened to force her out like this." Shellian asked.

Shaking his head Saige said, "I know you did not expect an answer, but I have no idea. Something must have gotten pretty desperate down there to make her leave."

"You mean she didn't tell the two of you anything at all?" Stone asked

"She was only coherent once and since then has either been unconscious or delirious. When we showed up she was out cold, and it wasn't until later that she opened her eyes and asked how we had gotten there. But that was just about all. We all but carried her all the way to the cave where we met you and Saar. And from there she never regained consciousness. So in reality you know just about as much as we do." Shellian said quietly. They all were silent for a while, and then Saige got up and started pacing. It was obvious that there was restlessness there, but the other two remained silent.

"I wish we could have seen it coming." Saige said.

"See what coming Saige?" Shellian asked.

Waving his hands in the general direction from where they had come from, he said. "Oh that conspiracy that split us up. If we had then there is a good chance that we all would be here, and all the women who are carrying now would be better for it since there is better food and actually a place to take care of them. Instead we have what we have now – no idea what's going on down there, one of the women running away from it and endangering her life . . ."

Shrugging she said, "Well we didn't. And unlike some of the exercises we did back in the compound, we can't go back and try again to get it right. We've been over this again and again, and we probably should have seen the signs, but we didn't or if we did we ignored them with too many other things demanding our attention – so, quit putting yourself down for it. We have to live with what we have now and we cannot change a thing."

"You're quite right. I keep seeing Shayne lying there on his deathbed staring up at us, pleading that we take care of what was left of our small band, and then to have it end up like it has. I just feel like we have failed him, and ourselves."

"I can understand that. But remember we are not the mother and father of the ones who are not here with us. So they had a right, at least as far as they were concerned, to do what they did. If they felt that our leadership was so poor, then they should have made it known. But as you know they didn't. Instead they chose to do it the way they did, and any bashing you do of yourself is not going to change that at all. I know it's a difficult thing, but we need to move on. We still haven't been able to find out what caused the primitives to do what they are doing, and that was originally what we were to do. Instead we have been fighting just to stay alive. We've now been here almost through this long winter, and being isolated as we are, I have no idea what has happened down below. As far as I know all of the cities may have fallen by now or maybe only a few more. I think . . ."

Saar entered as she was finishing her statement and interrupted. "Shellian I need you now, and I've already grabbed Seirra. I think that Sorrel is going to lose the baby, and there's nothing I can do to stop it. I need both you and Seirra's help now if I'm to save her life. Hurry!" He then turned and left leaving silence and concern behind him. Shellian got up quickly and headed out of the cafeteria to head for the infirmary, leaving Stone and Saige alone. Saige, shaking his head, said, "I don't understand it, I just don't. We were doing okay and had made it through most of the winter when the breakup happened. While things were not the best, we were doing okay. Now there's a possibility that we will lose another one, and from the worry on his face I'd say it's a guarantee that she'll lose the baby." Then taking a deep breath he continued. "Well Stone, I guess it leaves you and me to keep the watch in security, so why don't you go and take the first watch, and then later I'll relieve you. I'm sure whatever the outcome from the infirmary we'll know as soon as they know."

Stone rose from one of the tables, and nodded in agreement, but did not say anything, heading out and towards the security office, leaving Saige completely alone. Once again taking a deep breath he thought. *What's going on? Is everything going to continue to unravel? Or will there eventually be some good news out of all of this?* Looking around, his thoughts continued to flow. *Well, I guess I have to admit that by finding this place that this is something in the right direction. But even finding this place was a complete accident.* Then laughing and shaking his head as his train of thoughts continued, *Yeah, an accident caused by an accident. Enough on this I've got to figure out what we need to do from here. I mean we really know very little about this place as of yet.* He got up, and with no clear destination in mind, walked out of the cafeteria, and then found himself in what they were calling the executive meeting room. Sitting there at the large table he stared out through the windows to the outside world, finding that he couldn't sit, got up and went outside to walk the small hidden valley to try and gather his thoughts.

Stone reached the security office and found the door wide open and the room vacant. He had expected that, and so entered and began to monitor the area. He saw Saige leave and then followed him as he entered the meeting room, and watched him as he exited that room to go outside. He hadn't said much, but it worried him that Saige had felt so personally responsible for what had happened. He could tell that it weighed heavily upon him. Shaking his head, he knew that he had no answers and from what was happening in the infirmary, the tragedies were still coming. While he knew from observation that Sorrel appeared to be a strong woman, he did not know what the loss of her child, following the loss of the one she apparently loved, would do to her. While, from what Saar had said, she would lose her child, would they then lose her too? He looked back up at the numerous screens and then consternation furrowed his brow. Could it be? Turning to the intercom system he paged Saige to come to the security office, and continued to monitor the screens while he waited.

In a very short period of time Saige arrived breathing hard. "What's up Stone?" He asked.

Pointing to the monitor that had rotating images from the cave system on it Stone just said, "Watch. It will take a moment for it to come around again but I need you to confirm what I thought I saw. I think this is the first cave past the one we wintered in." They both waited while the images of the other caves flowed past and finally the one he was waiting for flashed on the screen. "See!" But then the images moved on. "Darn! I haven't figured out how to lock this on the images I want. Do you know anything about it?"

Shrugging Saige said. "No, not yet, but remember we've not been here very long and really haven't had much time to figure anything out yet. But I think I saw what you did. We'll wait until it comes around again and see if they are still there."

"Do you think that they could be looking for Sorrel?"

"I don't know . . . just not enough information here – but from the brief look I think there are only four of them and two of them are women. Again because it was so brief I cannot even tell you who they are. Wait . . . it's coming around again." They both concentrated on the monitor as it once again flashed briefly on the cave before moving on to the other cameras. "Yes definitely four of them. Darn! Wish I knew how to stop this so we could really look."

"Know what you mean Saige. Now what? I mean we don't know if they are out just to hunt for more food, or are they trailing Sorrel, or what their intentions are at all."

Shaking his head before saying anything, he stated, "Okay Stone, I guess all we can do is continue to monitor their progress and see if they head our way. The only good thing we have right now is that we are equal in numbers with that group, and they have no idea that we can watch them or that this facility even exists."

"That's true, but it hasn't snowed and I'm sure the trail that Sorrel left will be plain as day, and then when our tracks show up, they will know that we are out here and that we came and picked up Sorrel . . ."

". . . Which means that they would be able to follow our tracks right back to here, great! Another problem while we are dealing with this serious health issue." Shaking his head Saige continued. "Okay, point taken, but for the life of me I don't know what to do about it right now. At least the way into this place isn't obvious. I'll go up and brush away any of our tracks leading to the entrance up top, and I guess all you can do is keep monitoring them. They are a couple of days away yet, and there's still a chance they will just turn around and head back. At least we can hope."

"Do you think we should inform the rest of them?"

Thinking for a moment, Saige shook his head. "No . . . no, they have enough going on right now, and really do not need anything distracting them. I know that Saar has turned off the camera and mic in the infirmary so I would have to go in person. I suspect that what is happening there does not need to be observed. And it is why he asked for Shellian and Seirra to assist him. No unless they appear to be a threat, we will just keep it to ourselves for now . . . Ah, anything else before I see what I can do to wipe out our tracks?" Stone just shook his head no. "Okay then, I'm on my way to clean up the tracks. Don't know how long I'll be gone, so I guess you have it here until I get back." Saige left and headed out through the large cavern – a cavern they had yet to discover its true purpose – up the ladders and then out through the hologram.

He returned several hours later glad to enter the facility. The air still had a bite to it and to be back inside where it was warm felt wonderful. He immediately headed down to the security office to be updated by Stone. Walking into the office he found Stone waiting for him. "Saige glad you're back!" As he continued to monitor the screens, Saige looked and was surprised. "How'd you do that?" He asked.

"This time, with the amount of time I would be spending in here, and knowing that there had to be a way to set this monitor to watching a particular cave, I just started checking things out. Actually found a manual buried deep in one of the cabinets over there. Fortunately it was a training manual that somehow had been left when they abandoned this place. Anyway the way this system is built, it's set up to be able to stop at any particular cave you want, and when you do that, one of the other monitors takes over the role of scanning the rest." Then pointing to the screens to make his point he then continued. "I've been watching the next one in the series that leads up here once they went out of sight from where I first saw them. Interesting stuff in this manual, I think we all need to read it. And I mean we *can* read it. This is another confirmation that we are dealing with our own ancestors here. Unless there was another common language on this world then this is just too much of a coincidence."

"Yeah I know. I've kept trying to resist it and be skeptical, but there is just too much evidence that this place was built by our ancestors. But as to why I just don't know. And was it built before the war or after . . . . And why in the Sacred

Mountains? There are just so many unanswered questions. So I guess the real question now, since I've been gone long enough, is . . . have they shown up at the next cave yet?"

"No, but it could be any time. I've been going between the two of them – the first one where I saw them and then the next one in line. Oh, it says in the manual, that at one time there were more monitors set up to watch the trails, but eventually they were removed since the primitives appeared to avoid the mountains except for an isolated hunting party now and then."

"Okay, any word from the infirmary yet?"

"No, and no one has left it either. The monitoring system is active in the hall and has shown nothing at all. So I guess whatever is happening in there has to be very serious."

"Okay Stone, I'm going to get something to eat and then come in and relieve you so that you can get a break. When I come back you can show me what you have learned. I'll be in the cafeteria or lunchroom or whatever we are going to call it. If anything new shows up or the infirmary contacts you let me know." He then turned and headed out. He hoped that the work he had performed outside would be enough. He almost turned around and headed back to the security office when he realized that he should have asked if the caves were wired for sound, but thought better of it and went to get something to eat.

Sitting alone there, all he could do was shake his head. *Don't things ever get easier, and why does it seem that the problems just continue to pile up?* Well he had no answers for that. So with the meal finished he headed back to the security office. Stone hadn't contacted him, and with silence from the infirmary he could only hope that it meant that it was still good news. As he entered the office he saw Stone staring intently at the one screen that had the cave system on it. "What are you seeing Stone?"

"I'm not sure as of yet, since the camera angle isn't the best. But I thought a caught a flash of something . . . there! It happened again." Looking harder and closer at the screen and with Saige joining him Saige asked. "Can you bring this up on one of the other monitors?"

"Yes, yes I can. Give me a sec here." Stone then fiddled with some of the controls that were part of a pullout shelf and then on the far side one of the monitors that showed the valley changed to reflect the same image that Stone had. "There, now you can see if you can catch whatever it was I saw."

"A pullout", shaking his head and smiling, "Something I wouldn't have even considered. Well, I guess it makes sense considering how tiny this place really is." He then took the seat on the opposite side of Stone and began staring at the screen. Presently nothing was happening and then like Stone he caught a flash. Glancing over he could see that Stone had seen it also. Then before their eyes the four came into view. The two of them looked at each other and Saige said. "Well I guess we can now say that they are definitely coming our way. Okay for now I have it, so go get something to eat. Then when you are finished come back and show me how to make all of this work."

"Ah, Saige I don't know how to work all of it yet. In fact I've barely figured out what I have so far. But I must admit that getting some food would be nice. But this is becoming serious. I'll go get something and bring it back here then I can show you what I have learned, and you can at least read some of the manual also." He handed it to Saige. "See you shortly and no not a word from the infirmary." Stone left and headed for the cafeteria to put together a small meal and when he arrived he saw Seirra sitting there. She appeared to be beat and down a little. She hadn't seen him enter as her back was to him, so not to startle her he made some noise. She then turned and faced him. Yes, no doubt about it, she had a defeated look on her face, with puffy eyes showing that she had been crying. "Seirra, can you fill me in, or has Saar decided to wait before passing on anything?"

Shaking her head as she sighed, she then took a deep breath. "Stone, this is so tough – probably more for a woman than a man, since we carry the lives inside of us." She began crying softly again just for a moment and then got her emotions back in control. "She's definitely going to lose the baby. She's still unconscious and not doing very well and she has gone into labor. I think it's a situation where it will be either her or the baby and her body has made the decision that it will be the baby. But from what she looks like I can't say that we are going to save her either."

Coming over to her he offered her his arms, which she gladly accepted. Then once again while in his arms she began to cry all over again. They stood there silently while the tears flowed, and finally when they stopped she said. "Thank you, thank you Stone. I really did need a shoulder and someone to hold me. And Saige wasn't here." Then taking a deep breath she said. "Look, if Sorrel survives this she's going to need some serious support. I know that both Shellian and I will be there, but I suspect that someone like you would be a good thing also. Now don't give me that look that you don't think so, I know better than that. It will be a shock to her when she learns of her loss, and it is something that could cause her to give up completely. We . . . we can't have that. There are so few of us now and to lose any more of us would be so devastating."

Silent as Seirra talked, his first thought was, the last thing he needed was to become involved, but as she talked he realized what she said was very true. He also suspected that when she finally met with Saige that she would say much the same thing to him, if Shellian didn't beat her to it. So taking a deep breath he said. "You're right, and I, we, can't afford any more losses. I'm sure the reason you are here is to take a break and get something to eat. Well, so am I. I'll go get something from the kitchen for both of us. Once I get back I need to tell you something also which is not going to improve your mood." Seeing her about to ask he held up his hand telling her to wait, and then headed off to the kitchen to get something for them. *It just goes from bad to worse. But there is nothing we can do but see this through. Oh well, Saige was right in worrying about the others trying to find us and now with a pathway almost to our door, and with everything that's been happening – well I don't know if we will survive this. Enough!* Shaking his head he needed to keep his thoughts more positive. From one individual set of skills and as a group they had survived and would continue. Grabbing the disposable plates he brought out the food to the two of them. "Seirra here you are, and I'll grab a couple of glasses of water. Look, the situation may be getting worse. We, Saige and I, are tracking four of the group who threw us out. And with the trail that Sorrel left and then when we went and rescued her . . ."

Shaking his head before he continued. "A baby could follow the trail that we left. So it will be no problem for them. Saige went out earlier and tried to confuse the trail up to the entrance on the top, but how successful it will be I just don't know. So when you go back into the infirmary pass it on. I'm sure that the three of you are taking breaks one at a time. And from what you have told me this appears to be something that will involve all of you for quite a while. So Saige and I will continue to monitor the situation, and if it gets serious, not that what's happening now isn't, then we will come in and inform all of you or at least put it over the system. But until then just pass this on and worry about what the three of you are trying to do." She picked at the food, eating a little of it, but he could see that everything that was happening was bothering her. "Look you need to eat, just as I do. If you don't then you'll start to weaken and then you may find yourself in the same situation as Sorrel. No not pregnant and about to lose your child, but if she wasn't as ill as she is then there could be a great possibility that she wouldn't – lose her child that is. So if you don't eat you could become just as ill. Besides if you don't I'll sic Saige on you." He finished the statement with a smile. He had just finished his meal himself. "Okay, I've got to go back to the security office. We both are there, so if something comes up, you or any of the others can find us there." He left and entered the security office and then related that he had met Seirra in the eating area taking a break and that he had passed on to her what they knew at this moment. "Anything new since I was gone?"

Shaking his head he said, "No, nothing. I've not learned to read lips and they are only facing the camera now and then anyway. Plus I haven't taken much time to scan this manual yet. It's quite thick, really thick. Anyway the four of them appear to be arguing about something. You can tell from the animated movements and the facial expressions. I don't know if it has to do with staying there before continuing or something else. It really sucks not having any voice. It sure would make this easier and either increase our tension or make it go away. We really have no idea of what their intent really is, and that is a real bother. I guess at least at the moment with them still at this cave we know that they are still far away from us. So again, what did Seirra relate to you?"

"First let me say that she was depressed, and it's understandable. Sorrel is deathly ill, and right now it is touch and go. She stated that Sorrel has gone into labor and it's much too early, so she will definitely lose her child. But as bad as that is, Saar is worried that she may not make it either. So from what I could gather, the three of them will be in there with one taking a break now and then, until she either dies or the crisis is over. So we will be on our own – I know great timing. So once again because of the pending situation we are once again outnumbered by our opponents."

"I know I said it earlier, but does it ever get any easier? Here we find this facility and I feel that finally something has broken our way only to see that once again we are facing unknown dangers and unpredictable problems. I just don't know why, and I just do not understand any of this. Okay Stone, I guess enough on this, look I'll continue to cover this for a little while longer. Head out and get yourself some air, and maybe relax for a while. Come back in four hours and then with that change we'll continue to switch off every four hours. That way at least we will be more alert. Does that work for you?"

"You're the boss, and I think it will work out fine. Maybe in that time you might find out more about this security system."

Smiling and shaking his head once again Saige said, "One can only hope . . . yes, one can only hope." Then taking a deep breath he said, "Now go and get away from here for a while. See you back in about four hours then." Stone nodded in agreement turned and left the office and was gone. Saige then turned back to the monitors and saw that the four, who they had been monitoring, seemed to reach some type of agreement. From what he could see it appeared they were going to stay there. It made sense really – as the day was close to over and there was no need to be traveling in the dark. But not knowing what had been said or why they were there he had no idea what their need or agenda really was.

* * *

For the next two night and day cycles the ones in the infirmary continued to minister to Sorrel. While Stone and Saige continued to monitor the group heading their way. At this point they had traveled to the last cave. From there they were less than half a day away from the facility. As he suspected, the tracks that had been left in the snow made it easy for them to follow. And it would have been obvious to the group that at some point that Sorrel would have picked up some help. At the time that the two had rescued her, there had been no thought of or way for them to cover their trail, and now it was coming back to haunt them. He knew that once they had reached the final two caves those additional tracks would reveal more of them. So with Sorrel at this point, there would have been at the least, five sets of tracks. He had backtracked to the first or last cave earlier and tried to hide the trail that he and Shellian had taken on that fateful day of discovery, and later that same day the rest of them, to this hidden valley. He tried to make the path that Saar, Seirra, and Stone had taken to be the one they all had taken. But with some work it would not take the four of them long to figure out that, that was a false trail. All it really was more of a delaying tactic. And once they figured out the correct direction both he and Stone would need to be in the better position offensively.

Still no final word from the infirmary, and the brief contacts they had still placed Sorrel on the edge of death. She had finally aborted and her stillborn child had been a girl. He could see with the brief meetings with the two women that it had affected them deeply. Both were crying at the loss, but really couldn't say much – *From such a good beginning another tragedy*. Just when would they end? Maybe with the death of all of them, and then the silence of this facility would return, quietly waiting until it once again was rediscovered. Watching the monitors both Stone and Saige could now see that the ones they were monitoring had met once again back at the cave after following the false trail and were now heading in their direction. All the delaying actions were now over. At least the trails leading into the facility had cameras covering the whole distance. They would know when to be ready to face them, and it would be today and towards evening. Saige sent a voice message to the infirmary to bring them up to date, and then a tired Saar answered voice only. "I think we are close to a resolution here. There have been some subtle changes that could mean that she is going to recover. But it is still very much in doubt. I wish I could send you some help, but this still requires all three of us. And to be honest one of the girls is asleep right now, and the other is quite exhausted. There has been absolutely no chance to be away from Sorrel. It's just that close. If we were not here, then she would have died, not that that outcome couldn't still happen, because it could. But at least she has a chance now. But I just don't know how she will be mentally when she finds out all that has happened. I know, but we've got to get her body healed and then face that later. Good luck and I mean that. All of us in here are counting on what the two of you do. And when this is over I think I'll sleep for at least a day myself." He then signed off and it was quiet once more.

The two of them looked at each other for a moment. Stone had to agree it would be nice to have all this nastiness over with but it continued to be with them. "That's good news, I think. I mean at least there is a slight sign that she's made the turn to recovering. Okay Saige how do you want to handle this?"

"I really have no idea. I think taking *a wait and see* position for now is the best. If they come up and do not find the side trail that leads through the hologram, and just head up to the edge of the cliffs, then they will probably just head back thinking we had to have gone in a different direction, no matter what the tracks show. Since the other side was a false trail, they might come to the same conclusion. After all we were exploring in many directions when this place was located by accident. Whoever placed it here knew how to hide things. I did notice that there are a couple of places built into this facility that allows defenders to be above any hostiles. So if it looks like they are coming this way I guess you and I will have to go there. Until then . . ." He trailed off and shrugged. So far the four that were approaching had only been seen from a distance, so no real intent could be assessed. Why only four instead of the full seven? Again, no answers. "Stone, I'll cover here for the next couple. Head out, relax, get something to eat, or whatever. Then come back and I'll take a break. Once they get close we'll both be here and monitor the situation, and if it appears they will be heading for the facility then we will go and meet them."

* * *

Evening was approaching and after monitoring the group up close and personal, Saige felt that they were not looking to attack anybody. In fact they looked tired – whipped actually. There was a sense of depression that lay on the four. Their body language seemed to say, we give up. What had happened back there since they had been kicked out? Whatever it was couldn't have been good. Since right here in this facility they had Sorrel and she was in serious condition, and now these four, while healthier than Sorrel, did not look much better. Turning to Stone he said. "I don't know about you but I don't think they are here to attack us. They look like hell, defeated, and at the end. Go up to one of those points for defense. I think I am going out to meet them and see what I can find out. No I'm not going out into the open where I can become a target, but something is just not right here. I mean look at them."

"Yeah they look pretty bad. But it could be a ruse."

"And that's why I need you to be where you can watch the whole thing and defend both me and the facility if need be. If one of us doesn't make contact and they continue to work the area, then they may discover this place when we are not quite as prepared as we are now. Yeah I know, just two of us is really some preparation."

"Got a suggestion Saige, let's send the image to the infirmary since both of us will be away from the security office, and that way they will know what's happening."

"You can do that? I didn't realize that these images could be transferred."

Shaking his head and smiling Stone said. "Yes, it's in the manual, although it wasn't easy to find. I think whoever worked here in the past probably was trained for it, so some of what is in the manual is not explained, but assumes that whoever is reading it is familiar with the subject."

"Saar, this is Saige. The ones outside are close. We are leaving the security office now, and Stone will transfer the images from here to the monitor there in the infirmary so that you can watch from there. Hope to be back shortly." Stone and Saige then left the security office not awaiting a response from Saar, and headed for their different positions. Saige would wait until he got a signal from Stone saying he was in position before heading out. And then carefully make the approach to the ones outside. At no point did the group of four approach close enough to a hidden camera to be recognized. Both Stone and Saige thought they knew who the four were, but until Saige was close enough to positively identify them they would wait. Saige waited at the top of the platform until he got the signal from Stone that he was in position, and then waited for the signal that he could see the approaching group. He knew that they were getting close, but not so close that they would be there immediately. So the waiting dragged on for what seemed like forever. Then he got the signal from Stone and left the facility through the hologram and carefully worked his way towards the main trail, if it could be called such, which he and Shellian had followed in what seemed so long ago.

With the countryside being as broken as it was here, there was no problem finding a place to remain out of sight and to be able to observe the trail. Shortly he heard a conversation and knew that they were now approaching his position. He continued to observe as they came in sight, hiked even to where he was, and then continued on apparently completely unaware that he was there. What he saw disturbed him. They, on closer inspection did look like hell. He recognized them immediately. Although he had to be sure he was right. As they were quite dirty, appeared to have not eaten well, and the two women in the group both pregnant looked drawn and tired. This definitely was not a war party. Taking a deep breath Saige asked." What are the four of you doing here? And do not turn around as we are watching and have you covered with weapons."

He could see their reaction in the scrunching of their shoulders, but then when they recognized the voice their shoulders slumped. "Saige? Saige is that you?" Starr asked. There was a trembling in her voice and he could tell that she was close to tears.

Then in a softer, gentler voice Saige answered. "Yes, yes Starr it's me."

"Thank the stars and heavens!" She exclaimed. "We have been desperately looking for you or Saar or any of you. Can we turn around?"

Looking them over, he could see that none of them had their weapons even out of the sheaths. And from his observation there did not appear to be any interest in bringing their weapons to bear. "Yes, but just be careful. I don't want something to happen to all of you because one of you got careless."

"No problem Saige . . . and we understand." Seve responded. The four then slowly turned around and faced Saige and he immediately saw their surprised reaction when they saw him. After all, he was no longer in the animal skins but the disposable clothing from the facility. He obviously was well fed, and clean. Silence reigned for a short time while both sides sized each other up. Once again Saige could see the poor condition that they were in. "Okay would one of you please explain why you are here?" Sabryn stepped forward and before any of the others could say anything she signaled them to be quiet.

She then said, "Saige, first off let me say personally I am sorry for what transpired back in the cave. Storme and Schylar convinced us that they would be the better leaders. Every time any of you would do anything he or Storme would show us how it could have been done so much better if only they were in charge. Eventually they convinced us and then the five of you were ejected. Now looking back I can see it was a mistake. From that moment on the two of them did nothing but demand that we wait on them hand and foot, and continually remind us that they were in charge. They started to be more demanding and put more pressure on Sorrel and were demanding that she and Sajan live together. Sorrel wanted nothing to do with it. It was then, as retaliation, they began to hold food from her. So in desperation she left, snuck out. We wanted to go and get her, but now the three of them demanded that we stay. Somewhere and somehow once again they ended up with most of the weapons and we were at their mercy. Then once again they started rationing out the food with the three of them getting the greater amount, while the rest of us got next to nothing. No matter how we reasoned or pleaded it was to deaf ears. So the four of us got together when we could, and decided that like Sorrel we had to get out of there. So, on some excuse each of us went outside of the cave at different times on different errands and then never returned. As far as I know the three of them are still there in their kingdom with no one to rule. I, for one, am glad to be away from them.

"Then once away we could only go in the direction that the five of you, and we suspected that Sorrel went. But all we ever found were tracks in the snow. Some of them newer, which we assumed were Sorrel's, and others that were much older which we guessed, were you and the others. We were afraid that we would come upon Sorrel's body because at the time she left she was in pretty bad shape. Her tracks confirmed that also, since they weaved a lot. And we just followed the tracks and here we are now facing you."

At no point during the story, as it was passed on to him, did Saige interrupt. Then shaking his head he asked. "So what is it that the four of you are wanting of us? After all you were part of the group responsible for kicking us out. Why should any of us care what happens to any of you now?" He was asking hard questions, and he knew it but he needed to know if they could be trusted enough to be able to bring them inside the facility, or just to leave them to themselves and the elements. There was silence and a look of defeat on their faces. He waited and still silence. Then taking a deep breath with his hands on his hips he asked. "Well, is anyone going to answer me or are we going to just stand out here and enjoy the sunshine?"

"What is it that you want us to say Saige?" Seve asked. "We all have paid a heavy price for our belief in Storme and Schylar."

This angered Saige. "No, not close to the price that Sorrel has paid. All of you have cost her, her child and maybe her very life. Right now she is fighting for that . . . and how she will be after this ordeal is anybody's guess. So, not one of you have come close to paying the debt that you now owe at least to her." He was mad, and wanted them to know it. So as he had stated the facts he put as much of his feelings into the statement as he dared. He could see them flinch under his hard questions and statements. "Again why should we bring you back into our group? What is to prevent you from doing what you did again once you have recovered?" Again he could see the complete slumping of their shoulders as his hard words and questions struck them. If they had appeared defeated before, it was nothing to how they looked now. They looked at each other and without a word turned to leave, with no obvious place to go. It struck him to his very soul to see it. Should he invite them in or just let them go to what he knew would be their deaths. He watched them as they began walking away with indecision riding him. Did he just let them go, or what? He had no answers. And because of this indecision riding him and the war within himself as how to solve this dilemma, he was frozen to inaction. After all they had come close to killing them, and now if he let them go he would be putting the sentence of death on them. *Damn, what I am supposed to do? I really don't want them to die out here. We were put in charge of these people, but they rebelled. But if I bring them in they could again.* They were almost out of sight as they headed back towards the cave again with complete defeat in every step they took. Not once did they look back. For them it was over, finished, and they could not change anything. This warring going on inside of him continued to freeze him into inaction. One side saying, that they were only getting what they deserved, and the other saying, that they had learned their lesson – why let them die?

Stone, from his position inside the facility, could only see the interchange between Saige and the group. From the animated movements the conversations had to be somewhat heated, but suddenly he could see complete defeat in the four, and defiance in Saige, and then something else. He could see the four leaving and from a brief view of one of the women he thought he could detect a tear running down her cheek. Just what had happened out there? Saige appeared to be frozen where he was standing with his arms crossed. Once they were out of sight he quickly got down from his position and headed outside to find out what happened. As he approached Saige he saw that Saige was just staring. There was an obvious battle going on inside of him, and Stone was not sure that interrupting him right now would be a good thing. But he needed to know – what happened out here? Standing there he could see that Saige was not even aware that he was there, what to do? "Saige," he spoke softly, "Saige what happened? I could see all of you but could hear nothing. Why are they leaving and having the look of death on them?" Expecting an answer all he got was silence. And still Saige stood there silent and far away.

So are you going to lower yourself and become what Schylar and Storme did to you and the rest that are with you? Saige thought. *Or are you going to admit that you are wrong here and go get them. You do know that you just sentenced them to death. It was obvious that they had nothing, no food, no additional clothing, and no real weapons, almost like you did when you were thrown out. Does this revenge really make you feel good? After all that's all it is. And if it does what does that make you?* He was so deep in the internal fight that he did not even see or hear Stone approach. Finally through the fog of the inner struggle he heard Stone ask him something. Seeing him stand there made him jump slightly. "When did you show up? He asked in a distant voice.

Not quite sure as to how to respond Stone paused before answering. "Saige, I've been here for a little while. Just what is going on here? I mean I could see all of you but heard nothing and now they are gone looking like death warmed over and you are like this."

Sighing Saige said softly, "I sent them away.", as he stared once again off into the distance. *Why are these decisions so hard and why am I having this internal fight? It really sucks to be in charge, and have to make the tough decisions. It would be so much easier to just follow. But I wasn't given that option. And I guess the real question is was I in the right to do what I just did?* "I just sentenced them to death . . . they have nothing at all and winter is not over . . ." Was he really seeking revenge, or maybe retribution for what had happened to Sorrel? But the longer he thought the more he felt that the decision that he had made was wrong. These people had once looked up to him for their direction, but with what he just did he was no better than the leaders who led the conspiracy. Shaking his head he said. "Stone, I just don't know. When I sent them away it seemed right at that moment, but now . . ." He trailed off once again.

Helpless and not sure what to do Stone stood there and waited. He knew that if they did not go after them shortly that there would be a good chance that they couldn't catch them, and with night approaching they would be easy to miss. None of them knew the area that well, and the cameras were not set up for night vision. So once the suns set and darkness arrived, then there would be no tracking or viewing. He knew that they would probably try and push through to the cave but again he knew that it really was too far to go. Especially in the condition the four of them appeared to be in when they slowly passed by his hidden position. "Saige, we need to go get them before they completely disappear. We need them as much as they need us. Just what did they tell you anyway that led you to send them away?" Looking at Saige he could see that he wasn't going to get an immediate answer since that faraway look was still in his eyes. Stone could tell that he was fighting something deep inside of him.

Saige looked up and then at Stone and asked. "What did you ask? Sorry Stone but I am trying to make this right in my mind – to understand what happened here and to come to a right decision."

"That's all well and good. But if we wait too much longer then we will have lost the opportunity of going after them and bringing them back. And losing that opportunity in the end may weigh heavier on you, then you standing here frozen out of any action at all. Come on! Let's go get them, unless there is a specific reason or danger from them that you haven't told me. Is there?"

Shaking his head he said. "No."

Grabbing Saige by the arm he said. "Okay then, let's go and prevent another tragedy here, and one that we would in the end regret." He needed to get moving as too much time had passed and with each passing moment the four were getting further away and increasing the odds that they would miss each other. Then Saige seemed to have come to a decision, looking into the eyes of Stone and said. "Okay, Stone, you're right. Let's go find them and bring them inside."

* * *

When Saige had refused them it was a complete shock, although not completely unexpected. In silence the four of them, feeling death upon them, left. Not one of them turned around to see what Saige might be doing. Now time was against them. While winter would be over soon, it wasn't now and they needed to find shelter for the night. They were too far from the cave to be able to get there and traveling at night in this unfamiliar broken land was not an option. So they began to search for a place off the trail where they could get out of the cold winds that were beginning to blow. The two women had quietly been crying the whole distance, and there was little the two men could do to comfort them. It was over – finished, and who would have thought that it would have ended this way? Shortly they found a likely place to pull off the trail that was surrounded by boulders that at least broke the wind. Plus here they were almost invisible to any of the night predators that roamed these mountains. Seve and Staven left their temporary shelter to get firewood, while Starr and Sabryn stayed. The two women went through their meager supplies, and knew that they barely had enough for this night, let alone the time that was left until the end of winter.

Eventually they had a small fire, and by choosing this location they and their fire would be invisible unless someone was very close. With a voice filled with failure and dread Sabryn said. "I was hoping . . ." Then taking a deep sobbing breath she said, "I was hoping that they would take us back. It really was our last chance." It was silent for a while as no one wanted to speak, and what she had stated summed it up quite well.

"Yeah, I know. But what did we expect? I mean we threw them out, so why should they care about us? Are we not getting exactly what we deserve?" Staven asked, not expecting any answer. Again it was quiet. Now what could they do? There was no food, and no place to go. No time to find their way back down the mountains where they were sure it was now spring, it appeared to be completely hopeless, and thusly the deep silence each with their own thoughts. Again with the silence both Starr and Sabryn began to softly cry. With all the strife, and difficulties that they had endured up until now they had been ecstatic when they found they were carrying new lives inside of them, but now it wouldn't matter.

Whoever these new individuals were, they would never become, live, or have a chance in this world, and these thoughts were tearing the two of them apart. Staven and Seve could only watch helplessly as their women cried. And to know why, and to be able to do nothing to change it, ripped them apart inside. It was as if a dark fog had settled over them and even the light from the fire could not penetrate the despair that the four of them felt. Let it end, and let it end quickly, but even here they knew better. They were not the type to take their own lives, but ones to fight on to the very end. What truly was to become of them?

It was now fully dark and the cold closed in on them. With inadequate clothing and bedding they got as close to the fire as they could, but the fire did not appear to be putting out much heat as they shivered with the increasing cold. The wind had increased and every time a gust would find them they would try to huddle even closer together. It was going to be a miserable night and none of them were going to get much sleep. They felt that if they tried that there was a good possibility that they could die from exposure anyway. Maybe that would be the easy way out. Just let the cold take them, but once again they knew that they would fight – fight for life. But why . . . why not just let it end here? There had been so many more when they had started on this journey, it would be easy now to just join the many who were no longer with them, the ones who had perished along the way. They had thought that they knew so much, and would be able to go through anything and come out alive, but now they knew better, so why not let the cold take them? It was during these thoughts that they suddenly realized that they were no longer alone.

Turning around they found on either side of them Stone and Saige. But even seeing them stand there initially did not register. They were too deep in their misery and self-pity to realize what they were seeing. "Are the two of you real?" Starr asked incredulously.

Stone and Saige looked at each other and then at the four and then Stone said softly. "Yes we are real. Now gather what you have and follow us. It is much too cold for any of us to be out here tonight. We have better shelter not too far away. Would have gotten to you there earlier, but we could not find the place where you had left the main trail up here. In the failing light of dusk we missed your point of leaving so had to carefully backtrack once we realized that you had."

Still not believing what they had both seen and heard Sabryn asked. "Are you sure? Are you sure you want us to come with you, and that both of you are nothing more than a wish for something different and that I'll wake up and find it all a dream?"

"No Sabryn", Saige said softly, "this is not a dream, although it would be nice to find out that this whole adventure that we are living was no more than a dream, and I would awake back in the compound thinking – wow it seemed so real. But it is real and so are we. Now let's get moving before it gets any colder."

CHAPTER ELEVEN

Summer began with the temperatures rising, but remaining cooler than the lands that they had left. There were two new lives in the group now – a boy from the union of Starr and Staven, and a girl from the union of Sabryn and Seve. Sorrel had recovered, and with the loss of her child, had clung to Stone as he tried to comfort her. As time healed the wounds she and Stone grew closer together. And it was obvious that now she looked to his strength to help her through. She was no longer the open and defiant one, but quiet and almost afraid to do anything. With her confidence completely shattered by the ordeal that she had lived through, she looked completely to Stone for approval. Stone took the role of protector and healer seriously and slowly there could be seen a change in her as the past was slowly slipping away from Sorrel. For the longest time she isolated herself from the rest, but eventually with a lot of work from both Saar and Stone they were able to get her involved once again. And if truth were told, it was probably the arrival of the two new lives that was the deciding factor. Yet even here, you could see the yearning, and the hidden tears, from her personal loss. For the rest it was a time of discovery and understanding. This facility was indeed a place of their ancestors, and they were learning more with each new discovery or reactivation of the equipment, machinery, or computer systems within the structure.

"Okay all." Saige said, as they sat in what they still called the meeting room. Everyone was there today including the two babies which were contentedly asleep on their mothers' laps. So as not to wake them, the conversations were kept low and soft. "What have we found out so far? First off, I'll start by saying that I have now investigated the waterfall and the system that brings the water into the facility, and have to say that it is completely manmade. I know that it looks natural and I think that was the plan, just in case any of the primitives got past their fears of these Sacred Mountains and investigated. It's a masterful job and only because we are from the same society and level of technology I found it. So Staven, have you been able to get the main computing system up yet?"

Shaking his head he said, "No. No not yet. It is still password protected and I have yet to figure out what it is or how to find it. We have much of the system that is automatic and accessible, but where the important records are, is still inaccessible. I'm sure that from the way this place was still operating when you and Shellian found it that there probably had been a plan to return here, if not permanently, at least periodically to check up on things. So I suspect that there is something that is kept within this place that has that record. But so far we haven't found it. But on the positive side, we were able to get the educational programs running and they seem to address children from just about toddler to young adult. While we haven't observed much of the data yet, there are some things we have seen that we feel just can't be right. But there was also a large library of digital readings, so we feel that maybe what we are observing is a fictional story or something like that."

With a look of questioning on his face Saige asked, "How so?"

Taking a deep breath trying to get his thoughts together before continuing Staven said. "Well, if we look at what we have been taught in our educational system we have been in our cities since the Great War a few thousand annuals in the past. And it was that Great War that caused the ones we now call primitives to abandon the technology that we use and become what they are presently." Looking around he could see the rest of the group agreeing with him. "Okay, from what I get from the teaching computers they completely contradict that. So that is why I question it."

"Contradicts what part?" Shellian asked.

Pausing for a moment before continuing Staven said, "Pretty much all of it, and that's why I question it." He could see with that statement that all of them were looking closely at him.

"Are you sure?" Sabryn who just looked up from watching her sleeping daughter, asked.

Again taking a deep breath and pausing before answering Staven said, "As sure as I can be right now. But until we can access more than what we can right now I can only question it."

"Okay then, I guess all we can do is continue to get more of this facility operational and then some of these new questions might get answered." Then turning to Stone, Saige asked. "Have you and Sorrel learned any more about that large cavern, where we first entered this facility, was used for?"

"First off," Stone began, "It is much larger than we first thought. And if you go back to the distant end of it you can see where it has been sealed. We haven't been able to discover if this sealing is because of danger beyond that point or whether it was just a good place to seal it off, or whether there is really anything of importance beyond it. There doesn't appear to be any doors, holograms or hidden entrances beyond that point, and the lighting just sucks by being almost absent. Plus back there the cavern curves around into a little cul-de-sac. Here we found large, well, what I could only describe as tanks and equipment to operate them. From the little investigation we have done they appear to be empty at this time, and no these tanks did not hold water or anything like that. In fact they have the markings that show that whatever the contents had been that it was poisonous. From what we have observed so far, it appears that our ancestors took advantage of one of the extinct volcanoes to build this facility, thusly shortening the time necessary to build this place. But we've only explored in the one direction, and there's so much more. And that's just about all we can say right now. Again we have more questions than answers, Saige."

"Okay, how about the hydroponics Starr?"

"Again, just like everyone else, the system is automatic with little need of us doing anything. We haven't figured out much, but really don't want to tinker with it since it is our food supply. But we can see that it actually sits lower than the pond so it just uses gravity to feed the water through the system, and the lighting that is used is both natural and artificial, with the lighting being directed by skylights, and where it doesn't provide enough then the artificial lighting takes over."

"I guess that just about covers it then. While we have found out some things there is still much we do not know at all. I feel right now that we are more visitors here on a tour than actual guests who are part of this place. There is still so much we don't know, and until we do there is very little at this point that we can do to help our cities. We can only hope that the primitives do not know the location of all of them and that ours falling so quickly after the one before was just coincidence. So keep working on this and we'll meet again in a couple of days. And if my stomach is telling me anything I think it's time for lunch. So let's go eat and then get back at it. Thanks for the updates, and now we all know everything that is known." Saige then pushed back his chair and headed for the cafeteria. He had to admit he was hungry. Still it was frustrating to have been here to the end of winter and through spring, to now at the beginning of summer and still know little more than they did when they first entered here. Yet, at the same time to be in the best shape physically and mentally that they had been since the fall of their city and the harrowing flight so long ago. Now if they could only learn why this was here and if it predated the existing cities or was just a part of the network.

After lunch Saige headed for the security office, as it was his shift to monitor the cave system and approaches. But with the arrival of the four other members there had been nothing but the local animals that would periodically show up. The three who were behind the conspiracy were never seen again. Either they stayed at that first site or returned to the valleys.

Stone, who had a knack of discovering how much of the equipment worked in the security office, would be there with him as they continued to research this hidden place. As he watched the many screens Stone asked more to himself than to Saige. "What's this? Hmmm, now that's interesting."

Half listening and half watching the monitors Saige asked. "What's interesting Stone?" As he looked down on Stone, who was under the consoles and built-ins, which housed the equipment and was generally out of sight except for his legs sticking out.

Stone backed out and sat on the floor looking up at Saige and said. "I think there is a hidden door down here. Probably requires a key or something to open it – not very large, but in a place where one would normally not look for anything. Do you remember that set of keys that we found here, and do you remember where we put them? There's a possibility that one of them might unlock this thing." Again more to himself than to Saige he said. "I wonder why one would put something like this here? It's not easy to get to, or find, and there is very little space to work down here. There isn't any access to the equipment from here and it just looks like a place to put one's legs and feet while working here." Then shaking his head he continued, "Just doesn't make sense to me."

Getting up from the chair he was sitting in, Saige went over to the cabinets where they had first found the key rings. There had been many and they were both color coded and identified for the different sections of the facility. Opening the large cabinet that was attached to the wall he looked over the keys and asked. "Okay Stone, we have, oh I don't know how many keys here, which one do you want to try?"

Getting up off the floor Stone came over and joined Saige as they looked over the vast array of keys there. "I keep forgetting that this facility is large and there are a lot of doors, and all of them have locks. Which makes me wonder, why so many locks? I mean we are guessing that there probably were roughly 100 or more people here, and there appears to be just as many keys. Were they that untrustworthy, or was it to keep the others from getting into anything if they found a way into the facility?"

Shaking his head as he smiled, Saige said. "You got me Stone. I know that in the compound where we trained and worked there were few locks. But I know that in the city itself that all the residences and places of business had locks. So maybe it's just something that is common with us. By the way, how are you and Sorrel getting along? I know that at first she just needed to support and someone to help her rebuild her confidence in who she was, but I think that it's much more now."

"Yeah, it's much more now. At first I was reluctant to be the one to help her, but it has worked out well for both of us. Hmmm, now if I was one to want to lock something up, and yet have a key available in the security office to be able to open it in an emergency how would I place it?"

"Hey, isn't there a second set that wasn't in here", Saige said. "In fact I think that we had to use them to open this key cabinet. Now where are they now?" Both of them started searching the small room, since the keys in question hadn't been touched since they had first opened the locked cabinets within the security office, and after about an hour of fruitless searching Saige said. "Ah, here they are."

"Where? I don't see anything?"

"Well, believe it or not, since we haven't used them, and all of us have used this office as we each shared monitoring, somehow they got knocked to the floor and . . ." He laughed and then smiled, "They ended up on the floor under these consoles and in one of the corners where they probably were kicked – right next to where you found that hidden door." Then pointing to the very corner he said, "See . . . right there."

"Okay I can see them now. Okay, keep your monitoring up and I'll retrieve them and then try the different keys to see if any of them work." Then grabbing the ring he said, "Even with this office being small there are a lot of keys on this thing. They can't all be for here. Okay this is going to take some time since the keys are all similar and only the color coding identifies different areas." Sitting on the floor once again Stone began to study the ring of keys. He leaned back and placed his back against one of the walls as he looked at each key. "I would suspect that it would be one that is used rarely, but that is only a guess." Again saying this more to himself than Saige, "I wonder . . ." Then deep in thought he quietly said, "I wonder if this hidden locked door is for emergencies only. If that's so, then using our color scheme I should try the ones that are for the highest danger." Looking closer he found three keys marked that way. Then crawling back under the unit he grunted as he shifted to get into position to be able to try the keys. After a couple of attempts he said triumphantly. "Got it!" Saige could hear the turning of the lock and the squeaking of the door as it complained from being opened. "There appears to be a few manuals and stacks of papers in here. It's too dark to make anything out. Here I'll hand them up to you." He then handed Saige a large stack of paper, and a few thin books and then crawled back out from underneath and joined Saige. "So what do we have here?"

In his hand Saige saw that there were complete schematics of the facility, and then to his surprise on this was a statement identifying the large cavern as a spaceport. He looked at it questioningly, a spaceport? But as far as he knew they never had been in space. And there had been nothing ever taught to reflect that possibility, yet what else could this mean? Meanwhile Stone was going through another stack and then said, "Jackpot!" Saige asked, "Jackpot? What do you mean?"

"Saige look at this! This booklet here has the emergency override codes for everything here including the main computing system. With this we should be able to finally get into it and find out what this place is all about."

"This is great news, but I have something here also that needs some understanding. Look here, this map or schematic of this place lists the large cavern as a spaceport. My first thought was outer space with space ships landing here, but we never achieved space flight, right?"

Stone thought a minute and said, "I don't think so. As far as I know we have always been here on this planet. We know that most likely there are other intelligences out there, but from the observations that have been made; the distances are so great that it would be almost impossible to travel them and survive. And that doesn't include the deadly stuff out there that our planet protects us from. Yeah, now what did they mean by that? I mean as large as that cavern is I guess you could have a space ship land there – a space ship, wow. Are you sure you are reading that right?"

Handing it over to Stone, Saige said. "Here you look at it. See, plain as day it says spaceport."

Stone couldn't deny it. But did it mean something else. "I wonder if we will find the answer once we get into the main computing system."

"Good chance. I think I'm going to call another meeting since this is important, and all of us need to get right on it – Especially if the overrides that you found work."

* * *

Indeed! The emergency override codes allowed access to the mainframe and they were finally able to learn much about not only the facility, its beginnings, purpose, and why it was located where it was, but it was the part about themselves, and this was the most revealing and shocking revelation. They learned that unlike what they had been taught, that this facility had only been in existence for somewhere between two to three thousand annuals around the binary suns. It was the first on this planet. Its location had been carefully planned and located, to make it easier, both to hide, and to provide access to most of the species of this planet. And they were not from this world at all, but their ancestors had come to study these primitives and remain completely unknown to them. Their ancestors were anthropologists, sociologists, scientists, and such. Their ancestors were from a distant world called Earth, and the war they spoke of in the histories of the cities had nothing to do with this place at all, but one that involved their home world. Whenever it happened, the ships no longer came to this place to bring supplies, and other vital equipment. The war had been a surprise and there had been no time to leave. They had become isolated and had no way to return to their home world, thusly beginning a *time of isolation*. Eventually even the communications network went silent and they knew not of what had happened.

Over the next, what they called a year around the twin suns, they worked on trying to reestablish any communications with their roots, but all they got was static and silence. So it was decided that they would need to move from these mountains and establish a number of hidden cities using the technology that they possessed to keep these cities invisible to the primitives and to continue to study the people. Once they left this hidden facility it would be powered down to the minimum, and all of the automatic equipment placed in the maintenance phase and set an automatic signal to alert any from their own home world that they were here. As this history became available to them, they continued to look at each other as one surprise after another was revealed. Everything they had been taught, everything that they had believed, was a lie. While they were similar to the primitives, that was as far as they could go with it. Nothing else was compatible. There could be no children from the union of the two different species no matter how similar they appeared. From the surveys that had been performed, at least the fruits produced by the vegetation and the meat from the animals, were edible and would sustain them. But even here they relied more on their hydroponics than on what the world could provide.

Here they learned that part of the plan had been the signal, one that continually pulsed out to space – an SOS for any who might travel close by. Then if they responded to that signal it would set in motion another signal and operational plans for the cities to return here. But either the signal failed or no one passed by this remote region of space – because, as far as they knew, the signal was never answered. And so the cities grew and the truth disappeared over time. The histories changed to reflect only this place, and the true origins were forgotten. Stunned to silence they could only look at each other as the information continued to scroll across the monitors. And while it explained much, it still left much too much out. And still the information continued, and when it finally reached a breaking point Stone paused it. Taking a deep breath and looking around he said, "We started reading this in the morning. I think if you all look around you will see that it is now dark. We have been here all day, with brief stints to the restrooms and taking care of the children, but other than that this day has flown. I think we need to break, eat something, and then absorb what we have learned here today. I have to admit that what this has revealed makes me wonder if any of it can really be true – or is this some type of cover story if the primitives ever found this place. Yet, I feel that what we have just witnessed is true, so very true. I am worried about what it hasn't said." Silence followed.

Shellian then said. "I have to agree Stone. This is almost too much to take in, let alone accept. So let's all go eat something in the cafeteria, and decide while we are there, if we want to continue this tonight or wait until tomorrow. This changes things."

With his brow furrowed Saige asked. "Changes things? How so, Shellian?"

"Well, think about it Saige. If what we just sat through is true, then we are the interlopers here, not the primitives. And while our people had done a good job of staying out of the way of the primitives, and not interfering with their way of life, other than to observe and record, which is what we in the scouting unit did, and is what our ancestors were doing anyway, then do we have the right to interfere, even if it means the destruction of our cities?"

"Good point and that really causes a dilemma. Okay we aren't going to answer any of this right now, let's go eat as Stone as suggested. I really had not realized that this much time had gone by." They got up as a group and left the meeting area and headed to the cafeteria much subdued, and silent. Shellian had made a valid point, did they have the right, or should they try to just let the cities die and bring as many as they could back to this hidden facility?

It was decided while they were eating, that since the information was going to be still available later that all would take the rest of the night off, and come back after the morning meal to continue to see what else this facility and computing system had to tell them.

* * *

"I've had all us of gather once again this morning, not that we weren't going to do this anyway. Last night I couldn't sleep for the longest time and so not to bother Seirra, I got up and went to the terminal that we had, and read some additional stuff on what our ancestors faced. So I have marked it on all of your monitors to read as I read it to you. But before I do that I need to bring all of you up to date on what they were thinking." Pausing a moment before continuing, he stood up leaned forward to make his point before continuing. "With the news of the war, and unfortunately they never learned with whom, they knew from the received communications that there would be no one coming to get them. And what made it worse lay in the fact that a supply ship had only been there a short time before the announcement of the war, and would have been ample in size for all of them to leave and go home. It wouldn't have been a comfortable trip, but quite workable.

Then for the longest time they were in a quandary as to what they should do. You know should they stay here in this facility, should they try and make real contact with the primitives that they had been studying, should they leave? But as each question was answered the only real answer was to build the cities in the valleys, and lowlands, in places that the primitives would not normally want anything to do with. And that was how and why our cities came to be. So with the decision finally made they planned to make the move at a time when the primitives would be staying within their villages and camps, and to assist each one of the new sites until they were up and running, and all the security measures could be put into place. Even with the equipment they had it took about five annuals around the suns to accomplish. They established twenty-six cities, which eventually expanded to thirty, each with a name that attached to the letter of the alphabet that they and we use, with the names coming from our home world. That's why they are so different from the names that the primitives have attached to places, lands, mountains, and such – different culture, different beginnings, and truthfully a different world. Some of the cities were empty, but they knew that eventually that there would be enough population to begin to fill them. The other decision lay in how people in each of those cities would be named. By doing it this way they would know immediately which city one came from and its location. At least that was how it was planned. Thusly that is why all of our names begin with an "S". Of course, the first people in our city had names that started with any number of letters. But, I guess at the time of the decision it made sense to them. Anyway that kind of brings us up to date with our beginning history. I've skipped over a lot here and tried to just cover the highlights. Now here is what the leaders said at the time they prepared to leave, and I quote."

"After much thought, discussions, and deliberations we have decided that it is necessary for us to leave our hidden facility in the mountains and establish cities below. Since we are not of this planet, and had only originally come here to study the people it has been decided that we must keep ourselves separate from the true owners of this planet and let them advance as they naturally will. With that isolation each city will become one onto itself. While communication between cities will exist, there will be minimal travel so as to avoid alerting the primitives of this world of our existence. While we plan for the long term, it is hoped that whatever this war is, that for us it is short, and not terribly destructive, and that in the near future we will have a ship arrive to rescue us and then at that time be able to return to the Earth our true home. Until then we will live, and remain isolated from this world and its peoples using the technology we have to essentially become invisible. We have set a beacon, a signal to any passing ship that we are here, and where we presently are located on this planet. We have planned for the long term and truly hope for the short. Below is a map and marked locations

of all of our newly established cities. So that if any do arrive here and find the facility empty they will know that we are here, alive, and well. This will be the last communicate that I have placed in the system as my last act as administrator of this facility. It has been a great assignment and we have learned much from our studies, but all may be for naught since in the end we ourselves may become natives of this world with no knowledge of our true past."

When he finished reading Saige remained silent for a short time to let the words of the last administrator of the facility sink in. "Okay all, there you have it. If any of you doubted it at all, here is the final proof that originally we were from somewhere else, a place called Earth. It's obvious that he and the people who were here were looking forward to returning, but whatever this war was, it ended any such hope, and we are here because of their work and planning. Now what do we do? As you can see the original plan was to remain isolated from the primitives and allow them to continue on their own path. But now we have been discovered. Do we just let this continue and save a few by bringing them to this hidden facility or do we somehow bring an end to this sudden gathering of the tribes by bringing down their leadership? These are tough questions and we need to answer them quickly. We are few and so we will not be able to bring an end to this by any direct means. And we really have yet to even establish where this leadership is located. So for now I leave you with this and later today we will get back together and discuss it. Thank you all for being here this morning and now let's get to whatever we were to do before I called this, and yes I know that originally we were going to continue here.

But for now we need to continue to learn all we can about this facility."

Before any could get up to leave Sabryn interrupted and said. "Before we go, a couple of things hit me when we both read and heard what the administrator said. So if you will wait I would like to see if any of you see what I just saw."

Saige looking over at Sabryn said. "Hey if anybody has any additional input I'm all for hearing it. What do you have for us?"

"Well, in truth I'm still thinking this out. But what he left here explains a lot." Then taking a deep breath before continuing she said. "Look, if we really compare this place with our cities there really isn't much difference. I mean we were able to come into this place and everything about it was somewhat familiar, you know just like in the cities. Does it strike anybody that there have been no improvements or inventions in the cities to help?"

"What are you getting at?" Saar asked as leaned forward placing his arms on the table.

Clearing her throat she said, "I think it explains why that was so. Our ancestors were waiting for someone to come and return them to our home world, this place they called Earth. So there never was a time where they had planned on staying here. The cities were just a temporary refuge while they waited out whatever this war was. And as far as we know right now, no one has ever arrived to pick up any of our people. So that brings up a more worrisome thing, and it's this. While we have no proof one way or the other, we could be the last of our species. We could be the last that ever could have called this Earth home, the place where we came from, our mother world." As she finished it brought another silence to the meeting as each contemplated what she had just stated.

Shellian, looking down at the table, thinking for a moment and then looked up at the rest at the table said. "I guess that's a valid assessment, and I did not even think about it that way. So from what you just said, and again we have no way of proving it one way or the other, we could be it – we and our cities that is. We have no idea what the war was about as the details are basically nonexistent. We don't know if maybe another spacefaring race found the Earth and started a war or whether it was our own people. Either way I guess it really doesn't matter, since no one showed up to collect the scientists and their support staffs. So it would be easy to then conclude that we are it, we are the last. So with those thoughts it now strengthens our need to find a way to break this alliance, or alliances, and have things return to like they were before. But I have to admit that this discovery we have made will make it impossible to return to anything close to the way things were before the primitives began destroying our cities. So I guess this makes it more imperative that we find a way, not that it wasn't before. At least it reinforces the need to interfere instead of just letting the primitives have their way with the cities." Then taking a deep breath she asked, "There's much to think about here, is there anything else that any of you want to bring to our attention?" She looked around the table and saw that none did. "Okay then as my brother said earlier, let's get about our day's work and we will meet back here again with the evening meal."

They broke up at this point and headed out in different directions. Except that Seve approached Saige and asked. "I know whatever we decide we will have to do it indirectly, since we are so few, but something came to mind while we were in here. If our ancestors were anthropologists I'm sure at some point that they had to contact the primitives to get closer, which means somewhere they would have to had pack animals. But so far there is no sign of any such thing here at all. And all the maps have shown just the facility and this valley. So where would they be? I feel that they would have kept and bred their own so that they would know them. Plus it would be something to use for trading. After all to be a real observer, and still remain apart from these people the perfect role would be a traveling merchant. So where is anything on this?"

Shaking his head, Saige had no idea at all. "You've raised some valuable questions, Seve. See if you can follow up on those if you can. There has to be something in the system on the methods they used to study the primitives, and there you might get a hint to where these animals might have been kept. Personally I would say that it would have to be close by – again, someplace hidden, but not so far a way that it would provide undue danger to either the animals or the people either tending them or picking them up for an assignment. Since Sabryn, your significant other, brought out those other points, the two of you can research it together. I guess you probably could leave your daughter with Starr since she's got the duty today of searching the schooling records. Since she will be in the playroom area anyway with her son, then adding your daughter should both help as the two infants could be watched at the same time. Plus I think it only fair if Sabryn periodically checks in on them and assists anyway. I know she will anyway since both she and Starr breast-feed their babies. I've pulled the security detail today so if anything comes up that is where I'll be. And good luck, I think that you're right. It makes sense to do it that way. Now all we have to do is find the proof, and then hopefully the location of where these animals were kept. Although I doubt that any of them could still be around after all of this time. Yet, this facility is fully operational, maybe the place where these animals are kept is also under computer control."

"So you think that maybe there would be a chance that there would still be some of the animals around today? It has been an awful lot of time that has passed since they abandoned this facility. And we are truly just guessing that it is one of the methods they used to contact and study the population."

"True, but once you mentioned it, it makes perfect sense. That way they would not have to be from or live in any one tribe. They simply could say that they were beyond the mountains and that they are trying to open new trade sources. And by studying them like we did from a distance, they would have had a pretty good sense of what would have worked and what would not have – not that it didn't have its own share of risk, but I think it would be less than if they had joined a tribe. Then there could have been problems when one tribe attacked another, which as we know is quite common – at least until recently."

"Yeah, I guess so. Okay we'll get right on it and be back here with anything we find with this evening meeting." Seve turned and left to take this new assignment. Saige then headed off to the security office to monitor the facility and the surrounding area.

As the day progressed and with nothing showing on the screens Saige was becoming bored, but knew the importance of continued diligence, and then thought. *I wonder . . . If these screens are covering the facility, the surrounding areas, is there a way to see if the system checks other areas also? If an animal husbandry area does exist one would think that it's under the same system.* Standing up and pacing, he knew that Stone had become the expert, and while the rest of them could operate the equipment, it was not to the expertise Stone had demonstrated. Well, all he could do was try. Turning to the now much used manual, he began to leaf through it to find out if there was a way to view alternate locations that may have been on the system, but did not require full time monitoring. But after a couple of hours of frustration he was no closer to finding out if there was a secondary, lower priority monitoring system in place. If there had been it could have been general knowledge, and something that the security personnel were trained for, and thusly it had no need to be included or required to be in that manual. After all, the manual was more of an instruction manual on the operation and repair of the equipment, and probably was a standard manual for any security facility wherever it might be. Not something that covered the different possible circuits unique to each facility that as they could exist.

He knew that Stone was out in the hidden valley, searching for alternate accesses and also working in the hydroponics section. While yes much had been automated, there were some areas they found that required their assistance. In fact some of this portion had shut down and was awaiting a human hand before continuing operation. So he and Sorrel was there, with her being exclusively in the hydroponics. "Sorrel, are you there?" Saige asked. He had the one of the monitors covering the hydroponics and at this moment no one was in view. Not surprising really, considering all that was in there, and with only one security camera there were many blind spots. After a short time period he asked again. Then he heard some light laughter, and then he saw Sorrel come into the view of the monitor.

With a smile on her face she asked. "What do you need Saige?"

Smiling back, he thought. *It's good to see her smile again. Stone has been good for her.* Instead he said. "I'm looking for Stone, is he with you right now or is he out in the valley?"

With a look of devilment on her face she said. "Oh he's here. Do you want to talk with him?"

Then it hit him what had been going on, and quickly said. "No, no that's not necessary. But when he can I would like to have him come to the security office. I need his expertise, and he may be able to help me solve a possible problem." Then smiling he said. "The two of you can go back to what you were doing." He then cut the connection. He had to admit that it really was good to see her smile again, and to have those looks that could just drive a man crazy. And he knew once he saw it that she and Stone were involved physically at the moment he had tried to find him. He then laughed quietly thinking. *Isn't that the way of it? You decide it would be nice to get as close as the two of you can, only to be interrupted.*

And it's something you really don't do a lot when comparing it to a full day. But for some reason when you do there always seems to be something to interrupt it.

* * *

"That is a problem Saige. It's something I didn't think about. But you're right, there's a good chance that there is a secondary non-critical section that the security office here could switch to just to make sure everything was okay." Glancing at the panel Stone just shook his head. "I'm going to have to think about it. You said that you looked through the manual right?" At which Saige nodded his head. "I guess I wouldn't expect it to be there, but one could hope. Hmm . . . I think I've tried most, if not all of these different switches at one time or another . . . but, haven't gotten around to labeling them yet. Well at this moment you got me." He got up and took a deep breath, leaned on the ledge that served as a desk staring at the monitors thinking.

Saige leaning back in one of the chairs looking up at Stone asked. "Do you think that what I am suggesting could exist?"

"Yes, once you suggested it, it makes perfect sense. I know that it's important to be able to have the priority areas always monitored, but there has to be secondary areas that just did not require constant surveillance, so either they are on passive systems, and if a sensor went off alerting the security office, or there is a way for them to check into those areas now and then. You've definitely given me a problem here Saige, not that there aren't constant ones anyway."

"Yeah, ain't it true – and so many discoveries about our past and us. I really wonder what this Earth looks like, or maybe looked like. I mean, after these people being informed that there was a war on, and since then, there has been no communication, no contact, no nothing and that isn't good in my way of thinking. And only a couple of things come to mind when I think about it. Either the Earth was destroyed, or the records that we are here were lost. And after seeing how this place operates, in my mind it would be the former before the latter. But again with so little to go on who can really say what happened."

Shaking his head Stone said, "Not me, I mean just a short time ago I was happy and dumb in my ignorance. You know, working in the compound and thinking just about learning what I could. And now that life seems like a dream, unreal, like it never happened, and now this present life being the real one. Oh just an FYI here, while I have been exploring this place I can see where the first section was built, and then over time others added to it. Most of it looks like a common plan – prefab would be my guess. In fact I would say that if our people were on other planets in other solar systems then these are probably what they lived and worked in."

"Makes sense I guess. It would make it easier to transport, or build, or however they did it, if all the pieces were made to fit together with minimal effort. I mean, could you imagine having to build here in this hidden valley by scratch?"

"Not really", Stone responded. "But some of the stuff outside is actually native. So I guess that they were here a long time. I mean think of the work that went into redirecting that small river into this valley. Hey I have a question. Have any of us figured out where it goes once it leaves the facility? I mean it falls over the cliffs into that large pond where it is used. But there is no way that we could be using all of that water coming into this valley, and during the spring melt there probably is much more and yet the level on that pond never changes."

"No, never really thought about it, but it's a very good question. So what does that panel over there do?" Saige asked as he pointed to a small panel that sat by itself in one of the corners of the room. "By the way the reason I'm trying to figure this out is because of something Seve said to me. I have him researching it right now, but your question makes me wonder if this is where that water might be going after leaving the main facility."

"What the heck are you talking about Saige?"

"Sorry, Seve suggested that one of the ways that our ancestors probably contacted the primitives, to get up close and personal, was to become traders, which meant that they would have to have pack animals somewhere, and thusly where the water is going. So I figured that if they did, these animals would have to be close by, and probably were taken care of by the automated equipment or systems. So I thought that these animals would be on a lower priority circuit, thusly why I had you come here to help and see if we could find one."

"You don't think that they would just have haggled for them do you? It would be easier than trying to keep your own herd."

"True . . . but there are some other considerations that would make sense in keeping their own herd. For example, they could, as we did before we found this place, use the hides to make clothing that would match what the primitives wear, they could provide meat to supplement the vegetables that the hydroponics section produces. From what I have seen so far there are no replicators for foodstuff. Just those large ones we found in the maintenance section."

"True," Stone responded, "but while all of that could be a fact, we really have no proof yet."

"I know, but we really haven't been here long enough to even do a cursory search of the records, let alone a complete one. I just think, from my own point of view, and I realize that we are talking about a great distance of time between when they were in this facility, and now, that it really is the easiest way."

Stone had moved over to the questioned panel and studied it for a moment. "I don't know. There really is very little here – nothing labeled, of course that's not a surprise since most of the stuff in here wasn't labeled, and really only this dial." Looking closer at it he could see that it had different graduations marked outside of the dial itself. A closer inspection revealed a white mark on the dial nob, which corresponded to one on the markings outside of the dial. "I wonder . . ." Stone reached down and turned it to the next mark on the panel, and turned to Saige and asked. "Did that do anything?"

Saige had been watching Stone and quickly turned back to the monitors and was silent for a moment. "Stone come here and look. I think you found it, but look at what's on the monitors right now."

Stone came over and was surprised to find that now they were watching the base of the mountains and all of the approaches. Again like the other view that showed the direct approach to the facility where there were more cameras than monitors, two of them rotated images. On one of the areas they could see hunters working the herds. "Let me try a different setting and see what we get", he said excitedly. But before they could, the monitors changed their views. "Wait . . . what's happening here?" They both watched as the monitors shifted their views with one automatically taking over the views of the priority circuit and then another taking over the views of the secondary circuit they had just opened. The rest of the monitors went blank as if waiting for something. Both Stone and Saige looked at each other surprised by what had just happened.

"Stone, let's put it back in the first position and see if things go back to the way they were. I'd hate to lose this because of something we did."

Nodding, Stone had to agree. He then turned the nob back, and in a short time all the monitors were back to the way they were before. "That's a relief. So it looks like, at least from the first experiment here that each position changes how the monitors work and what they then receive. Okay, do you want to try the other positions on this switch to see what is here?"

"I guess, now that we have confirmed that once we reset it back to the original position that it works like it did when we got here – yeah go ahead." Stone switched back to the previous setting that they had just tried, waiting, while the monitors adjusted once again, to the new command. Once there, he moved it to the third position. Here the two monitors that sat in front of the chairs showed signs of picking up something, and what they presented was a complete and unexpected surprise. "Can this be real?"

"You're asking me? Come on here, how would I know?" Stone responded. They both stared at the two monitors as the images changed. "It surely does look like it's coming from above our world, but look at the quality of those images, and look there; you can actually see a really large herd on the move. This has to be real."

In awe Saige just stared at the images. There was no doubt that they had to be coming from above their world. It meant that their ancestors had placed these cameras in orbit, and from the views they were seeing it had to be an orbit that kept them in the same location monitoring a large swath of the planet's surface. To see their world from space made them appreciate the beauty of their world, well, their world now, since they knew that they originally were from somewhere else. "I wonder what our home world looked like from this type of a view." Saige asked. "I've never really seen anything like this and it really is beautiful."

When Stone had placed the switch in the third position another panel lit up that sat between the two monitors. They both looked at this panel that until now had never been active, and saw that there were twelve active switches, and on either side was a small stick like device that they all had played with but until now, seemed to serve no function. Again looking at each other both seeing the same questioning look, Stone asked. "Okay, now what?" He could see Saige just shaking his head and shrugging.

"I guess we should try one of the buttons that just lit up on this panel, and since you've been the one to discover this, I'll let you do the honors, Stone."

Not sure it was such an honor since they were treading unknown territory here he hesitated, then reaching a decision shrugged, and pushed the first button and immediately both monitors settled on only one image from above. Saige then reached for that stick that had been standing next to the panel, and there were two, one on each side, and moved it. Immediately the image moved in closer to the surface, and as he continued to move it, it continued to get closer. It almost felt like they were falling towards the ground from a great height. He quickly let loose thinking that he might be bringing something down on them since the image they ended up with was of the mountains where this facility was located. But once he released it the image returned to its original view. "What the heck was that? I mean, you did see that didn't you, Stone?"

"Yeah I saw it, and like you I thought, what did we just do? Did we bring something out of the skies that was going to fall on us? But when you released it everything returned so I'm thinking that somehow it, whatever it is, doesn't move, but enlarges the area its viewing so that one can get a closer look at something that it can see. Let me try the one I have on this side and see what it does." Stone pushed a different button then moved his stick and the image changed location. This apparently let the operator shift views, and so between the two sticks they could bring an image in closer and then look around. "Why not use your stick again and I'll see if this one can change the angle of our view." So Saige pushed the stick again and brought the image in closer to the surface. Then Stone moved his and indeed it changed the perspective. It allowed them the freedom of searching a complete area that was under the view of this camera, wherever it was located.

Again once they released the sticks the image returned to the original position. Now both were excited with the prospect of what these images could do for them. They looked at each other and both began to speak, stopped, and then laughed. "Go ahead Saige, I think we just came to the same conclusion."

Smiling Saige said, "Probably. But before we jump to any conclusions let's try some of the other buttons." Which is exactly what they did, and each provided a different view of their world. "This is great! I think we can use these to find out where this alliance is, and it will provide a great way to monitor any of us once we really learn how to use this tool. Is there any more settings on that nob?"

Stone turned back to the original nob and then said. "Only one more, but I really don't know what would be left since what we just viewed kind of covers everything."

"True, but try it anyway." Stone set it to the last position, and immediately images of areas around the facility that normally didn't show up on the priority channel came into view. As they watched the images flow by one of them showed a meadow with a herd in it. "I wonder . . ."

"Wonder what Saige?" As the new images continued to flash by on the monitors seeing areas they had never witnessed before.

"I bet you that scene we just saw is the herd we have been looking for . . . Now if we can only figure out where it is."

"I don't know if there is a way to lock on just one image yet, when they just rotate like they are now. There, it came around again. Nothing about it looks familiar to me, not that I know whole heck of a lot about these mountains yet. This range is huge and I can see why our ancestors would have picked it. It's a place where it would be easy to hide something so it never could be found, and with all the natural caves, caverns and such, it's an ideal place to use for exactly what they used it for, hiding this facility."

As they watched, the images continued to rotate, Saige said, "It really cannot be too far away. They'd need access to it from here, and we really don't have any idea yet how many teams they would have sent out. But again looking at the size of this facility, and the number of different tribes or clans that are out there I bet there would have to be many teams. And I would guess that a team was a minimum of two – one that would go in, and then one would monitor the situation from a safe distance. You know kind of like how we were doing it before the city fell. And since we now know that there never had been plans on staying here, I suspect that very little has changed. And the way we have been doing it probably came from our ancestors originally."

* * *

That night at the group gathering and meeting both Stone and Saige went over what they had discovered, with Seve and Sabryn adding to what they had researched and discovered. But the discovery of being able to see their world from space excited most of the team and they wanted to see it for themselves. So after they finished with the meeting they all filed into the small security office where with all of them there, there was barely standing room. Then Stone and Saige demonstrated what they had found and how it all worked. He had Stone also go to the last position so that the other members could see the secondary areas that could be monitored from the security office, and had asked the rest if they had recognized the area where the herd animals appeared to be. Unfortunately no one did, so the location was still a mystery. Then each member wanted to try the new settings and as the night continued to advance, eventually one by one they left until only the one who had the duty there tonight remained, and for the first shift that would be Staven.

Saige now undressed and ready for bed talked with Seirra who was already in bed. Breathing out heavily he asked. "What do you think about what was located today?"

She was silent for a moment and then said, "I think we have much to learn about whom we really are, and that goes double for who our ancestors were. Now come to bed, I need you close to me tonight. It has been a surprising day."

"Surprising? How so?" He asked as he continued to sit on the edge of the bed.

Shaking her head she said tiredly. "Oh come on Saige. It made sense that they had security set up to monitor everything close to this facility. But to have set up everything else that we've seen took some time and effort, let alone the cost. And then to do whatever they did to be able to see the world from space. All these things were unknown to us, and in my mind unexpected. Think about it Saige, if we knew that we could see any part of this world from space, don't you think we could have had a better warning that our cities were going to be attacked like they were? I mean we're beginning to have a larger mystery here as to why none of this was known by the cities or the ones in charge. You'd of thought that this information would've been there somewhere in all of them . . . Yet, not a word, not a hint, just nothing. Now enough of this, come to me now would you?"

Her questions were thought provoking, but those would have to wait, as he then climbed into bed and got really close to Seirra.

* * *

After a communal breakfast the orders of the day were quite simple. Find out where this other area could be. The research that Seve and Sabryn had performed the day before had really turned up nothing new as far as the location of the husbandry area. They were able to read many of the field notes left by the researchers, and the mention of going and picking up an animal as they prepared for the next portion of their research. But for the ones who had written these notes the area was a known. And from the tone of the notes the area wasn't too far away. With time moving much too fast, and not really knowing how many other cities had been located by the primitives, and then attacked, they needed to move. There, of course, was still much that needed to be done. They really wanted to find a way they could return the favor to the alliance that had formed. It now was obvious, either they survive, or perish as a people. And they wanted the former not the latter. Yes, if all the cities were lost then their small group might, and that was a slight chance, survive and be able to begin to build again. But with only ten of them would it be enough variety in the gene pool to avoid genetic problems? As this was not their field of expertise, none of them could truly say.

Staven, Starr, Seve, and Sabryn would search the main facility to cover areas they had not searched before. With Saar and Seirra working the Security office, at least through the morning to early afternoon, Stone and Sorrel would continue their search of the large cavern, which they now knew as the spaceport, where the shuttles would bring in supplies and take out the research data and whatever other items that were slated to be returned. Saige and Shellian, because they had been trained as a team, would work the valley itself. This was to be the most thorough search of the facility they had made to date. And yes, while there were both maps and schematics of the facility, not every area was properly represented. The maps were more a fire or emergency evacuation plan, than a detailed layout. Again, they suspected that, somewhere within the computers that information existed, but so far none of them could find it. They also suspected that the layout was something that was commonly used throughout any of the areas where their people needed to set up both a working and living area. It only made sense to do it this way. By using a modular system, then all that would have to be done beyond this would be the standard stuff like water, waste disposal, and foundation, and there was even a possibility that only leveling of the ground may have been required. Yet from what they had seen so far, these units were also built to last. Of course the maintenance bots could have something to do with that. Yet they also sensed that once a project had been completed that these units could then be pulled out, serviced, and placed in storage or sent out for use somewhere else.

As Saige and Shellian worked the valley Saige asked, "Shell', how's it going with you and doc? I mean with it as busy as it is we haven't had much of a chance to just talk, other than business I mean."

"It has been crazy hasn't it? And here we are now in summer, although I have to admit that summer here in the mountains is more like a cool spring day down below – and it rains a lot too. I think even with the heat I prefer the lowlands where we came from. But to answer your question we are quite happy. Of course it would be a better situation if we didn't have to deal with the possible extinction of us."

Stopping by the man-made pond, and picking up a small flat stone Saige skipped across the water until it sank out of sight. Then taking a deep breath he said. "Yeah, there's always that. We have Saar and Seirra trying to locate the base where the alliance is working. And if they don't find it, then the rest of us will continue to use the surveillance system until we do. But right now I still haven't a real idea how we are going to be able to stop or break up this alliance with so few of us. I know that everyone is trying to come up with something that will work. I suspect that we will only get one chance at this. So whatever it is that we do it has to work the first time and be totally successful."

"Gee, you don't want much," she said as she laughed, "but you are right. We are not going to get a second chance." Then smiling Shellian said. "No pressure here. We must pass this class with a perfect score, and tell me Saige, how many classes that we have taken over time have we've passed with a perfect score? I was good in some of them – actually great in one or two, but perfect, never happened." *But what choice do we have? Our people are out there dying, and they really don't have a clue. This alliance has been successful because they haven't let anybody escape.* She thought. *Well until we did, and right now we are almost useless anyway.* After this brief stop, both left the pond to continue their search of the valley floor for something that may have been overlooked or missed.

* * *

"This cavern is really big," Sorrel said, "and there just has to be better lighting somewhere."

"Probably, but I suspect that there is really only lighting in the work areas. As you said this place is huge. And if they only used a portion of it why light the whole thing? I know that they had portable lights, but none of them work now, and none of us are really good at working those industrial replicators, so we haven't figured out how to make new ones. So I guess we just will have to search in this gloom. At least there is some lighting; otherwise I suspect that it would be pitch dark in here."

"Yeah that's probably true, but wouldn't you think that there would be some type of emergency lighting just in case they had to come here? I mean even though there's a little light here; it's so dim that one could easily get hurt by stumbling over, or into something that can't be seen." *Yeah I know you mentioned the portable lights they could carry, but there has to be something better than that.* "I guess all we can be is careful. I don't need something else to happen to me. That last time I was close to death, and I for one do not want to repeat it."

"How much do you remember of that anyway? I've meant to ask but, something always came up or I would forget. But if you don't want to talk about it that's okay too."

"I really haven't thought about it a whole lot. I remember leaving our first cave, sneaking out without anything. I felt that it would be too dangerous to try and steal something to help. I knew where the next cave was and headed for that one. But by the time I reached it I was weak and I could feel a fever coming on. I had no choice once I got there but to continue. I was desperate. I couldn't go back and I didn't know where you guys had gone. Sometime after I left that cave the fever hit and really don't remember much of anything – just waking up in the infirmary, and being informed that I had lost my baby, and that I was lucky to even be there at all. When I found that I had lost the baby I was devastated and really didn't want to live. Well, from there you know the rest." She shrugged before continuing. "I don't know, maybe not remembering is the mind's way of protecting us. But that's the best I can do, and who knows, maybe later more of it will come back. But at the same time, it may never."

Looking down at the dirt floor he thought once again. *She's really is a strong woman. And maybe it is good that she doesn't remember. I know from what Saar stated, she had almost died at least three times, but something in her, some hidden strength kept her going, and now I find that I have grown close to her. So I for one am glad she is alive.* "You're right it's probably a good thing, a way for someone to protect themselves. After all if you don't recall anything, it can't come back to haunt you and give you trouble later on." They continued on quiet both in their own thoughts walking carefully through the twilight that the cave provided. As they proceeded the cave began to narrow, and they finally located the far wall. From there they moved along it briefly in both directions finding nothing to tell them that it went any further, they turned around and began to retreat back but then stopped. Out of the corner of their eyes they caught what looked to be another dim light in the distance off to their right. It was so dim that at first they were not sure if they had indeed seen anything. It might even be a crack admitting sunlight from the outside. Turning to Sorrel, Stone asked, "Well, what do you think? Should we try and find the source of that light I think we are seeing, or just head back?"

"We were sent out to try and find out more, so I guess we should just go ahead and look. I suspect that all we will find is a crack and its light from outside. But if we don't check it then I guess we really haven't done our job," She looked down in that direction, "I must admit that it's pretty dark in that direction and it would be easy just to skip it."

"My thoughts also – okay then we'll go do it, but very carefully." With hands on the wall they headed in the direction of the dim distant light. Shortly the wall on their left closed in and they found themselves in a narrow passageway that if arm in arm they could reach out and touch both walls. Still it was close to pitch black as it could be with only the dim light ahead of them in the distance. At first it appeared to be receding from them, but that was impossible so it had to be an illusion, a trick of the eye. Finally it appeared to brighten a little, but not enough to light their way, so they continued their careful approach. Then her hand brushed against something and instantly the area they were in lit up, temporarily blinding them. "Ouch! That's really bright! What did you do Sorrel?"

With her eyes screwed tightly closed and watering from the change in light, she whispered. "I really don't know. But I can't open my eyes yet, it's just too bright."

"Know what you mean." He then found that he could slowly open his eyes without it hurting too much, and finally they adjusted to the brightness, and he breathed out a sigh of relief. "That's better. Now let's see what happened." Turning around and looking back from the direction they had just traveled he could see that the passageway they had just entered in the twilight was now lit. "I wonder where the switch is on the other side, since it only makes sense that there would be more than one. It would suck to have to come all the way here in the dark just to turn on the lighting."

"True. Look there it is, a panel built into the wall here. It's what I must have put my hand on. And look ahead of us, doesn't that look like a door?"

Before going to that closed door, Stone retreated to where they left the cavern and had entered the passage, he then said. "Sorrel come here, you've got to see this." She had briefly remained behind as he had retraced his steps not knowing exactly what he was trying to do. She then joined him and then shook her head. If they could have found the companion switch to the one she had accidentally found, then coming to this side passage would have been a breeze. On the floor of the cavern was a double row of lights shining up from the ground towards the hidden ceiling above. The lights formed a path that led directly across the cavern floor to where the bright lights in the passageway were presently shining. As she looked closer she could see that some of them were partially buried under the loose soil that made up the cavern's floor. "That would have been nice if we had found the other switch that's for sure. But now I am wondering where that door leads?"

Shrugging and smiling he said, "You women, always curious. I guess we should go and find out, now that we can see everything. Lead on, oh lady of mine." He then bowed to her and motioned with his hands for her to lead. She giggled slightly and took the lead back into the passage, with a stately walk. They both arrived at the door at the same time, as there was room enough for two to walk abreast and still be comfortable. Looking at the walls as they proceeded towards the closed door Stone said. "You know this looks like it was widened. I suspect that the original passage was a steam vent from this old volcano, but there definitely are signs of additional work here and see as we approach the door the area has been enclosed and constructed so that this ending wall and door would fit." Shaking his head he thought. *This really is fantastic work. And considering how old it is, it really was built to last. If I didn't know it's age I would have thought that it truly was not that old. Hmmm, I really wonder what other secrets this place holds.* They stood there staring at the door not sure if they really wanted to open it or not, but finally Stone reached out, turned the handle and opened the door.

* * *

"You know Seirra, I can't get used to this feeling that I'm falling every time we adjust our views from wherever these things are located. It almost makes me ill with; I guess you could call it motion sickness. And I swear whatever this is, that it is falling out of the sky – yet . . . We've done this a lot and they're still there. So logically I know that they remain wherever they are. And this still makes me wonder what happened in the cities so that they forgot about this. I mean we all have seen the records here and now know the truth. But it has been so skewed in the cities and the way it is taught in the learning centers, that none of the truth is known." Saar complained.

Smiling at him for his minor complaints, she really couldn't blame him for his thoughts. And she had to agree that when they used these small sticks to adjust their view, it really did feel like she was falling. But what a tool, what a view, and it really showed her the beauty that this world had, albeit somewhere above this world. She'd been dazzled by the shear variety that she'd been shown. And also the sheer size of their world – well not their world even though they had lived here for a few generations – really was a surprise. It was not surprising then that they had yet to find out where the alliance was headquartered. She felt that they could probably be here for days upon days and do nothing but search and barely touch all that was being revealed to them. "Well Saar, I know what you mean. It does take some getting used to that's for sure. Hey, it surely is a great view. This world is just gorgeous, I never realized that at all, and so large. I haven't even begun to recognize everything we've spotted so far. There has to be a better way of doing this. Not that I'm complaining, but we cannot even be sure at this point where we are looking. And I am worried about our people who still are living in whatever cities that haven't been located by the primitives, and of course for the ones who have been captured, and probably been made slaves or worse."

"Yeah, I know, but there's really little we can do. After all, considering what this alliance has accomplished so far, well whoever is in charge has successfully gathered many of the tribes and so far has been able to hold them together, has accomplished. We, who now know, what's going on, well, you can count on the fingers of your two hands of those who know, and we are supposed to defeat that? I think the odds here are a little one sided, don't you think?"

Looking down at the floor and then at him Seirra said. "Yeah, I know all of that. But what can we do? I mean, somewhere here we have to find an answer. We don't know what happened to our own people. I am meaning the ones from our own home world, and it they were annihilated, wiped out, then, as far as we know, we are all that's left. So somehow we've got to find a way to break this alliance, and finding it is the first step. So I guess instead of talking about it we should be a little more diligent and at least locate the area they are working from. Then we can decide what to do from there. I wonder if any of the other teams have found anything as of yet?" She glanced once again at the screen that was in front of her and noticed the small letters and numbers that were displayed at the bottom of the screen. "Saar?"

"Yes Seirra, what is it?" He asked quietly as he studied the images on his screen. He had to admit that she had been right. This world was much larger and varied than he ever imagined. When this search had started he thought it would be a simple thing. Since they could see from the sky it should be a snap to just see the gathered tribes. But he had been proven wrong. And all of them had been going over and over the images produced so far with no apparent success.

"Has anyone figured out what these letters and numbers mean yet?" She asked.

"Not that I have heard of. In fact someone guessed that it might just be a way to tell you, you were looking at a different image from wherever they are coming from – in space I guess. Why? Is there something about them that seems important? Or are they in your way, because if they are, I've been shown a way that you can remove them, or make them larger or smaller."

Shaking her head she said. "No, no that's not it. They are not causing me any issue at all. It's just that there has to be a reason that our ancestors put them here, and I feel it's not something to do with which view we are seeing. Look, if I shift the view to a different portion of this world from the area I am looking, then numbers change. So it has to be something more than just a way to identify the view we are seeing."

"Ah, I see what you mean. But what it means I really have no idea. Maybe it's something you can bring up tonight when we get together. It could be that one of the others has some idea, and right now I think I'm going to get us something to eat. Be right back, we can eat here while we continue our search." He then pushed back his chair got up and headed out the door. On his way out he asked. "Is there anything special you would like me to bring back?"

Without turning around and continuing her search she said absently. "No, no not really . . . surprise me."

* * *

Sabryn and Star, because of their children, worked the facility around the areas of family living and schooling, while Staven and Seve concentrated on the areas that dealt with maintenance, and operation. Not that there would be a true chance of finding the area where the pack animals were kept, but there could easily be a reference to, or an alternate way, that could be located somewhere within the facility. Part of the reason for the search in these areas was to be able to say that they would have searched everything and covered every corner once they finished. And if in the end they came up empty, then there was a good chance that this idea of an alternate entrance was incorrect. "Whew! I think you just loaded your pants little one." Star stated. "I guess we need to take a break here and change your pants." Fortunately at the time they were close to what they had determined was the daycare area, and immediately headed that way. While there, Sabryn decided she would check her daughter's diaper also. It probably would be a good time to feed them and put both down for a nap anyway. One of them would remain with the children and the other would move over to the terminals in the schoolroom and at least continue to search the files. "So Star, is everything going okay with you and Staven?"

"Yeah, no complaints. He helps where he can, but is a bit clumsy around the baby. But he'll get better. Like all things it just takes practice – After all these things do not come with instructions. So it's an on-the-job training type of thing. And as you know if you get it wrong, the boss here will let you know in no uncertain terms."

Laughing she had to agree. If her child did not like what was going on she would let them know her displeasure immediately. "It's funny how that works. You would think that because we are the parents that we would be the ones in charge. And that's so far from the truth. Okay that's done. I guess I'll feed her now and then put her down, stay long enough to see her asleep, and then go do the searching – actually if both of them go to sleep, then we could prop this door open and both of us could work. How does that sound?"

"Like a good idea to me. But we'll see if he will go down. At times it just seems like all he wants to do is go." Starr responded, "But it doesn't allow me to do much when he's like that."

* * *

Staven was covered in the grime from the pump house. Shaking his head he found that after complete search, he determined there was just the one door and that was it. After crawling through the numerous pipes, pumps, unknown equipment and searching all of the hidden areas, he had come up empty – other than the fact that he had skinned a knuckle or two from slipping and falling. He hoped that Seve had better luck, and he thought that he had better join him since the area he was searching was both the electric and steam room, separate of course since electricity and water did not mix. One thing for sure it was easy to tell that the whole thing was modular in design. It would have made it very easy to set up, and to repair if it needed to be. And he was sure that this probably had been repaired a number of times over the thousands of annuals that it sat here empty. He knew that after the two of them finished here, they would move on to the maintenance section, but between the two areas they would head back in for a bite to eat, before continuing. So far nothing had been found to indicate a way to the pack animals, if there were any at all.

Seve, once he had entered the electric room, just shook his head. This place was huge, and while the task was daunting, it wouldn't get done if he just stood there looking at it. He knew that as soon as Staven finished in the smaller pump house that he would join him. With that in mind, he thought that probably the best thing for him to do was to either work the steam room, which provided heat and air conditioning to the whole facility, and provided the push for the turbines, or to concentrate on the electrical. Obviously for safety's sake the two were separated, but since the steam room required a substantial power source it was only smart to locate it close to the generators. He knew that the generators used a number of sources including solar, water, and yes even the steam that was generated in the next room. It also used materials that could not be recycled, and vented any of the smoke, which was almost invisible, out through one of the many chimneys that the extinct volcanoes had created in the distant past, effectively hiding its location. In his hand he had a schematic of the room, and there were numerous doors marked, but not all of them were identified as to what they were or where they led. Which probably meant that whoever worked here was familiar with this standard layout and did not require a full labeling.

Thinking about it he decided that he would work the steam room because it was smaller. He headed off that way, with his reasoning being that it was much smaller of an area, not really much larger than the pump house – he should be finished in about the same time as Staven. Then when Staven showed up from his search of the pump house they could both work the electrical room and all of the doors. He opened the door into the steam room and immediately felt a blast of hot damp air. Shaking his head he thought. *It surely is named right. I really would not want to be assigned this section if I had been here back then.* He thought that most likely the bots handled most of the work anyway, yet moisture was the enemy of the bots, so he couldn't be sure. But at the same time, felt that it had to be inspected and confirmed that there were no problems. So even if the previous owners had to come here only once a day to confirm things were okay, it would still have been a miserable visit. Looking through a small steam cloud that appeared to be venting, he saw the entrance to the small operations center. It sat higher up and had what appeared to be windows that overlooked the entire facility. He worked his way there, climbed the metal ladder to a small platform that led to the door. Opening the door and entering into the control room he saw a panel that allowed the operators to manually override any portion, and to completely shut it down if some emergency required it. There he found on the back wall a drawing that showed the emergency evacuation routes out of the facility with this area highlighted. It was really hot and humid here and he wondered how and why this equipment didn't rust. After all, with the constant attack of heat and high moisture, it should show signs of rust and damage. Yet from the condition of everything there, it could have been placed there yesterday, and not the thousands of years in the past that he knew was fact. *What did they construct this stuff out of? While I know that something like this isn't my specialty back in the city, I don't think our stuff held up nearly as well as this.* Shaking his head at these thoughts he continued to look around the small room. *I guess even though we thought we were advanced, what this place has shown me so far, is that we have lost some of that knowledge that this place has demonstrated so competently, and it has been shown by the way we have found things. So much of what we don't understand our ancestors took for granted . . . and how do I know that? Because they did not label something, because it was common knowledge, so it did not require labeling, that's how.* "This isn't getting this place searched. I guess I should just use this evacuation sheet and check it against the doors it has people leaving by." He said quietly to himself.

He took out a small notebook and drew a rough copy of the emergency evacuation plan and then headed back off the ledge to the floor and in among the pipes, heat, humidity, and steam and then looked at the floor. He, to his surprise, found that the floor had large markings on them. He followed one around the corner and found a large arrow painted on the floor with the words emergency evacuation written within the arrow. Shrugging he thought, *why not*, and headed in the direction the arrow pointed.

* * *

Later with an unsuccessful search of the steam room, he met up with Seve and they first went to the showers to clean up, and then headed to the cafeteria to grab a bite to eat before both of them searched the electric room. When they entered the cafeteria by chance they found Starr and Sabryn had arrived just ahead of them. "What a surprise." Seve said, and Staven couldn't agree more. So far the day for them had been unsuccessful, but not completely, since they now knew more about the facility, its layout, and construction. It once again, gave them insight into their distant ancestors and how they thought, lived and worked.

* * *

"So Stone, what do you think? Do we continue, or do we take a break and get some food?" Both of them were standing in front of the closed door. Neither had ventured, as of yet, to open it and see what lay on the other side.

Taking a deep breath, Stone had to admit that he was getting hungry, but at the same time curiosity was driving him forward. "I guess what we can do is open it and see what's there, then before we go past this point, go back and get something to eat. That will leave most of the afternoon for us to continue our exploring. And I think that we need to locate the switch on the other side so that we aren't stumbling around in this semi-darkness. There has to be one. Now I wonder if they are timed or motion sensitive – which could be the case also, since that way, once a master switch was thrown, anybody walking in this direction would turn the lighting on. And since this cavern is part of the natural landscape here, it would have been something that would have been added at a later time – I'm speaking of the work on this steam vent or lava tube, and possibly what's on the other side of these doors." He paused knowing that he was delaying, as he shook his head. "Let's just do it." He reached for the handle and gave it a twist. At first nothing happened, and then he realized that he had been pushing on the door, so he then pulled and it opened. Looking through the now open door they could see what looked to be a small lighted room. They entered looking around. On the right wall they found another door and this one had a small glass insert which allowed one to look inside. Peering through, they could see steps heading up and out of sight.

The wall opposite of the door they had entered through was solid. But the left wall had two double doors, which had no handles. Between them was a small panel, which had two buttons on it, the top with an arrow pointing up and the bottom, which just said basement. But that bottom button also required some type of key for access. "I wonder what's down there, if anything." Sorrel said, then continued, "Probably not important anyway, but what does this other one do?" As she asked she reached out and pressed it with her finger. Both of them jumped as both sets of the closed doors opened revealing another small room in each. Again both were frozen in position with indecision as to what they should do. In that time of delay both doors closed again. They both looked at each other and Stone asked. "Now what was that all about?" In the cities that they had grown up in, all the buildings were single story, and the ones that had basements used stairs to access those areas. This was something they had yet to encounter. "Tell you what, before we go any further let's get some food in our bellies, and think about this."

"Works for me," Sorrel said. She was no more eager to go into a small room that had no apparent exit than Stone was. And once the doors closed and they were inside could they then get out, or was it a trap of some kind? They turned back to the door they had entered this room through, opened it, and saw that once again it was dark. "I guess that confirms that these lights are at least on a timer. Do you remember where that switch that you hit was located Sorrel?"

She nodded her head and then stepped out into the passage. As soon as she did the lights came back on. "Looks to be motion sensitive. So I guess the switch I accidentally found was a master switch. Still like you, I think there has to be one on the other side somewhere. But maybe it isn't important now. Shall we go eat something then?"

As they entered the cafeteria they ran into the four who were searching the facility directly. They were well on the way to devouring their meal when Seve looked up as they entered and asked. "How's your search going so far? We've been unsuccessful overall."

"Let us grab something then we'll fill you in to what we've found so far, and maybe it's something that will help – don't know really at this time, but ran into something strange, or at least different." He paused there and then went and grabbed a plate of food for both himself and Sorrel. She had gone to get them drinks, and then joined the others at one of the larger tables. Once they sat down Stone then continued, "First off let me say that that cavern is really huge. From what I can determine it's mostly natural. I really wouldn't have wanted to be here when this volcano let loose. It's no surprise the primitives fear these mountains. Anything close would have been wiped out, and the amount of smoke and ash this thing had to put into the air would have put the fear of the gods' anger in such a people. And with no lights, other than a few to keep it from being totally dark, it was difficult just to walk across the floor, let alone see anything. But when we got to the other side" . . . he then went on to explain what they had found and that before continuing they needed to eat.

"Wow, that's more than any of us has been able to find so far." Staven said. "Are you planning on going into one of those small rooms, or what?"

"No don't think so right now. I think instead we'll just climb those stairs. I suspect like the ladders we used to first enter here, that it is another way in and out of this place. Once we check it out, then tonight like the rest of you we will fill everyone in. Then with more of us we can figure out what those two small rooms are all about."

* * *

"So what do you think Sorrel? Should we see what those small rooms are all about – you know if one of us stays on the outside and one of going inside, or should we just take the stairs?"

"Well, I don't know about you, but the stairs are something I know about. This other thing I don't. So until I know more I think I'll stick with the stairs, thank you."

Laughing lightly Stone said. "You know what; I have to agree with you. Maybe later." He then bowed and swept his arms in the direction of the door that led to the stairs and asked. "Shall we?" Smiling she curtsied and together they entered the stairway. "I think we'll take it to the top to see where these things end, and then explore the different exits as we come back down. How does that sound to you?"

"Works for me," Sorrel responded. They looked up and could see that it appeared that the stairs went quite a ways up. So they began the ascent. It appeared that at each level the stairs would switch back and make the rise and that it took one switch back to make what they guessed was a floor. After ten such switchbacks they came to a platform and another closed door. On the way up they had really only passed two others and they guessed that some of the area was no more than the walls of the natural cave. Catching their breath before opening the one at the top they reached and opened the door, stepped out, and then caught their breath once again. Before them was a panorama of both the mountains and views that appeared to just go on forever. Here, the area had been worked and some type of material laid that was impervious to destruction by nature. They saw tables, chairs, and some additional sealed cabinets similar to the ones they had found in the facility. Plus there appeared to be facilities for cooking meals, a small stage, and other items that they did not immediately recognize at the moment. The next thing they noticed was that there was a wall around this area that probably kept anyone, such as the primitives, seeing into this place. "Wow, this is beautiful!" Sorrel exclaimed. "And chilly after the cavern!"

Shaking his head and smiling Stone said. "If you want me to disagree with you it's not going to happen. And this place is huge. It looks like most of everyone who worked and lived here could be up here at the same time and it's invisible to the rest of the world. And it would give the support staff some place to go to get outside for a while. I bet now that we've found this place that there are others. Some place where the children could run around and play that let them burn off all that excess energy they all seem to have." They walked around quietly and inspected things as they went. Close to where they had emerged they found a double set of double doors built into the side of the rock face that was similar to the ones with the two rooms at the bottom. And here between them was a single button with an arrow pointing down. With a look of curiosity on his face Stone speaking low said. "I wonder . . ."

Looking up at him she asked. "Wonder what?"

At this point he reached out and pressed the button, which immediately lit up, and then both of them felt and heard a slight rumbling which slowly got louder. It stopped suddenly and there was a loud ding, followed briefly by a second one, both unexpected sounds making them jump because of the silence that had surrounded them. Looking up above the closed doors a light showed and suddenly the doors opened which made them jump again. And before them were the same two rooms they had witnessed at the ground floor. Frozen for a moment, Stone then started to enter one of the rooms, and as he did the door began to close on him. Instinctively he reached out to block it and found that as soon as he put pressure on it the door reopened. After a few seconds with him standing partly inside the door attempted to close again and once again it reopened when he pressed on it. "I guess we can say that whatever these things are, you can't accidentally get crushed by them. And I guess that would make sense by what we have found so far. Hey let's have you stand here and you can block the door and I'll check it out." And while they had been involved with the one side, the other set of double doors had closed.

Shaking her head, she said, "You're not going to get me to do that. Besides I'm smaller, let me get by you and I'll check it out." And without waiting for him to answer or argue she pushed past him and entered the room. First thing she noticed were the handrails, which were located on three of the walls, and then she turned to face Stone and then a panel caught her eye. "What's this?" With the way that Stone had been blocking the door his back had been to that side and he leaned around to see what she was looking at, lost his balance and fell inside the room with her. The doors immediately closed behind him and both of them were now inside the closed room. For a moment they looked at each other and then fought a little bit of panic and then she said. "Now you've done it, we are both inside of this thing, and now what?"

"I don't know, but at least it's lit. Well now that we are in here, let's look at this panel that you were pointing out to me. She reached down and helped him off the floor where he had landed when he fell inside. "Look this has buttons similar to the one we saw outside, and look there are two more one stating doors open, and the other doors closed." He pressed the one for opening the doors and they miraculously opened. He then followed it by pressing the other and the doors closed. Looking at her he said, "At least we aren't trapped in here. And I guess we don't need to panic either." Breathing heavily out and giving his head a slight shake he continued. "Okay then, let's scc what this thing is all about now that we have, well, fallen into it."

She laughed and said. "Don't look at me. I wasn't the one who *fell* into it, as you just said. I was just standing here minding my own business when you stumbled in here and the doors closed." They looked around the inside once again and she continued. "I guess you probably could fit oh around twenty to twenty five people in here at a time. And if I remember right the other side was larger. Now why would you want to do that?"

He studied the panel and noticed that the bottom button stated "Ground Floor". So he reached out and pressed it. A number of things happened at the same time – first the button lit up, followed by a small clunking sound and then they could feel themselves descending, as the floor seemed to drop. She screamed in surprise as both of them reached out for the rails. For a moment it appeared that they were falling faster then suddenly it slowed down and came to a stop. As it stopped they looked at each other and she had that look that a mother gives her child when he did something he wasn't supposed to do. Then the doors opened once again and they found themselves in the area where they had first entered. "Wow, it just took us from the top to the bottom and no stairs to climb. Does it work the other way also?" She asked

"It must, as there are only three buttons here, and the one on top just states "View Deck". But the middle just has a number two. So I wonder if that is where that other door that we passed as we climbed the stairs on the way to the top. Well I guess we aren't going to find out unless we try it." He then looked at her and asked. "Would you prefer that we go back to the top, or do you want to see what this other area is like?"

Looking down at the floor for a moment she said. "We do know what the upper area is, and we are here trying to find out all that we can about this place, so I guess we should go there. Not that I haven't had enough surprises for one day." She reached across and pushed the middle button. The doors closed once again. They, at first felt nothing, and then they could tell that this room was ascending back up the way they had just come. But this time the ride was much shorter, they heard that chime again and the doors opened into a room similar to the bottom floor. They quickly stepped out and noticed that again, like the bottom or ground floor, the doorway to the stairs was located directly across from the doors that they had just exited. "At least that's consistent," he said. Looking to the right all he saw was a solid wall, but looking to the left he saw double doors, and then looking back as Sorrel he asked. "Shall we?" She nodded in agreement and both of them headed for the double doors.

* * *

"This electric room is huge, and I think I've confirmed that it uses steam from the steam room to drive these turbines here." Seve, looking around at the sheer size of the room they were in, shook his head. "I bet this is the largest of the modules that they had to bring in. In fact, I'll bet this consists of at least two of the buildings that they used. Then these generators – all four of them, would have been individually delivered. And that steam has to be geothermal. I know that back in the cities they used more solar and wind than what we are seeing here. But it must be based on what is available in the areas where they set up. In fact, now that I think of it, I can see similarities in the structures in the old section of our city, to what I am seeing here. So most likely, they used some of the modules to initially set up the cities. It would make it quick an' dirty."

"That could be true." Staven replied, "But if they had done just that, then why is it that this place appears to be complete and still working? I would have thought that they would have cannibalized this place to build the initial cities, but here it stands."

Again looking around at the large space, Seve shook his head. "I don't know, maybe they used those industrial replicators to produce them. But who knows, maybe it was important that this place continue to operate. After all, it was here that this research team had been placed, so by leaving it here, then if anybody did finally return, they would know that there were survivors, I think."

"I don't know about that." Staven responded. "I mean if I returned here and found it empty then after doing a planetary search I would conclude that the primitives had wiped out everyone."

"That does pose a dilemma doesn't it? How would you let any rescuers know that you were still here, when you knew that it would be necessary to abandon this place? As you just stated, leaving it empty and running would not prove anything one way or the other . . . unless . . ."

Looking closely at Seve, Staven asked, "Unless what? What have you come up with here?" He could see now that something was beginning to excite Seve.

"Look, and I think it's something that we have completely overlooked – if you were going to abandon this place and still at some time in the future hope for rescue, then you would have put something in place that would allow the rescuers to know that you were still here and alive. And not only that, but you also would have put something into place that would allow you to communicate to them from your cities. So I think that this is something we've completely overlooked, which means if I'm right, we can contact the cities from here and warn them. Let's go and find Saige, I think right now this is more important than finding what's here. After all, the remaining cities need to be warned, and as quickly as we can do   it.

CHAPTER TWELVE

Eight cities had gone dark. Rumors flew, but there were no hard facts. And while the city of Keahilani was considered the pivot city, the one all communications passed through, the knowledge they presently had wouldn't fill a thimble. One would have thought that by now something would be known, and they could begin to solve the puzzle that had been presented. And while it was not his place of expertise, Keenan knew that somewhere there had to be a reason for this to be happening. Especially since all of the cities that went dark, did so, in the exact same way, and approximately at the same time of day. These facts alone spoke strongly of a correlation, something in common, but for the life of him, he couldn't figure it out. There was just too little known. The one thing that he could lay his finger on was the overall nervousness the permeated the air here. He suspected that it was the same for the rest of the cities. Well, his shift was almost over and soon it would be time to return to his residence. As usual, except when the cities disappeared, all the communications traffic was normal, routine, almost boring in fact. Standing at the railing that overlooked the floor he saw his people preparing to leave their shifts and the replacements waiting quietly to replace them. Sighing deeply he thought, *Yep, another normal day . . . Not that one cannot see the tension that is flowing through everyone, but, other than that, a very normal day.*

* * *

Seve and Staven headed back to the security office. At the moment they couldn't remember which section of the compound that Saige and Shellian were searching. Once there, Seve asked. "Saar, where is Saige right now?"

Looking up from their search he turned around and was silent for a moment. "Has something come up? Have you finished the area you were searching or what?"

Shaking his head no, Seve said, "No. No, but something occurred to us while we were working our area and we need to run it past Saige and Shellian. We feel that it's important enough that we run it past them right now."

Turning back to the equipment, he first looked at Seirra and said. "Seirra continue if you would. I'm going to switch this so that I can locate Saige and Shellian. If they are close enough to one of the speakers then I'll contact them." Then turning back to

Seve and Staven he said. "They are searching the grounds, and that would mean that the meeting area would be closest. So why don't the two of you head there, and when we get their attention we will, or I will, send them there." At this point Seve and Staven nodded and headed back out of the security office. "I do hope they find them quickly. And yes I know it can wait, but we really need to be pursuing this, as well as everything else we are doing, and I have a feeling that the place to set such a thing up would be the security office, or the office of the one who had been in charge here. But it just seems like the security office would be the most logical place." Staven commented, as they reached the meeting room and waited the arrival of their leaders.

* * *

"You know Shellian, we've been over the grounds a whole number of times and so far we haven't really found anything new. I mean other than the fact that some of these trees are different, and that small area, where it appears that they used some type of climate control to allow the residents here to cultivate plants that wouldn't normally grow in this climate. I'm sure there are a few things like that that we have overlooked, but nothing on the scale that we are trying to find." They continued their search of the grounds and were heading back towards the main building that Saige had first found when he had fallen into the hidden valley. Shellian couldn't disagree with him. Everything he had said was true, and she was beginning to wonder if what they were trying to locate really existed. *It seemed so plausible at the time. After all, it would have been an easy way to make contact and observe, without raising any suspicions on the part of the primitives.* Shaking her head slightly she continued her thought process. *I would have sworn that our ancestors would have done this. But so far we have no proof at all, other than a brief statement or two saying that it was a viable option.*

"Saige, Shellian, this is Saar. Can you report to the meeting room? Seve and Staven want to discuss something with you, and they felt that it was something that needed to be brought to your attention immediately." Snapped out of her thoughts she asked, "Now what could that be about?" Not realizing she had said it she turned to her brother who just shrugged before answering her. "There's no way I'm going to know sis." They picked up the pace since they were heading back in that direction anyway, and in a short time entered the room from the same entrance where he had the first time. Once their eyes adjusted to the dim interior lighting they saw Seve partially sitting on the edge of the table and Staven looking out through the windows. Both turned towards them as they entered the room.

"Okay you two, what's so important that you needed to see us immediately? By some chance did the two of you find something?" Saige asked.

Seve and Staven looked at each other and the Staven said, "Well Seve, it was your idea, go ahead and tell them."

With a slight pause Seve got up off the table edge and said, "Yes, and no. No in the sense that so far in our search we have come up empty. But as we searched the two of us were discussing some things and then from that we realized something."

"Okay, you realized something and what would that something be? I mean we were not privy to your conversation so we really have no idea."

Smiling, and shaking his head Seve said. "Sorry Saige, it's just I was trying to set it up so you could see how we came by this. Anyway, we began to ask ourselves that if our ancestors had to abandon this place, like they did, and then set up the cities, like they did, then they had to have put in place a way for any rescuers to contact them. I mean, think about it. If rescuers found this place abandoned, would they just leave, or would there be something in place that would allow them to know what happened, and then have a way to contact our ancestors from here."

Quiet for a moment as the implications of what Seve just said really sank in, he sat down and put his arms on the table and then leaned forward. "That's an interesting thought Seve. And it makes total sense. But what would they have done? I mean . . . I'm sure that it is something that was standard, but standard for them not for us. Now all we have to do is figure out what that was." He laughed bitterly before continuing. "And since we are far removed from that time, and from what we have discovered here, we know that we have adjusted facts and our societies have changed, and with no known information left, I haven't a clue." Then turning to the others in the room he asked. "Any of you have an idea what they would have set up?" Once again there was silence and he could see that the rest were just as much in the dark as he was. "So in your thinking Seve, did you have some ideas as to where the rescuers might first go if they found this place empty?"

"Yes, that was the easy part. At least once we found out how this place was laid out and how it worked . . ."

"Let's keep the explanation short if you would. After all you've already convinced both of us, and I have to admit that I can kick myself for not thinking about it."

"Sorry Saige, I think either the administrator's office or the security office, and of the two I believe that the security office would be my first choice."

"Again I have to agree with you. So I guess we need to head there, and I know that all of us can't fit in there very well, but we can get a feed from there into this meeting room which allows communications in both directions, so Seve, you and I will go, Shell', you and Staven can monitor from here and give us any ideas and suggestions that need to be addressed." Saige then signaled Seve to precede him out the door and both of them headed directly to the security office. Once there, Saige said, "Saar can you set up a complete feed to the meeting room? Seve has come up with something critical and we are going to need all of us to figure out the solution. By the way has anybody had contact with Stone and Sorrel?"

"Yes." Seve replied, "We met them while eating the midday meal. And they may be on to something. Anyway, they had found another way, which they thought would lead out of here, but hadn't had time to explore it yet. I suspect that we will know much more tonight when they come back. As far as the rest of us, we've come up empty."

"That may be true, but what you've come up with here, Seve, may be the most important thing so far. I mean once you presented it, then it was just obvious. Is that feed set up yet Saar? Oh, and add the area where Starr and Sabryn are working, if you please."

"Yup." Then pointing to one of the larger monitors he said. "See, there they are." And as he said that the ones in the meeting room nodded their heads in response. He pointed to another one and they could see the women.

"Okay, can all of you hear us in there?" Saige asked. Again they nodded yes. Smiling for a moment before continuing he said. "Now come on, would one of you please speak so we can adjust the volume in here."

Laughing, Shellian approached the monitor and said. "No Saige we figured we would pantomime the whole thing and make you figure it out. So how's this sound?"

At about the same time Starr whispered. "Sommer is asleep, so we are going to remain quiet."

Nodding he said, "Fine." Turning back to Saar and Seirra he said, "I'm going to have Seve repeat to you what he told us, and I should have thought about it at the time he presented it to us, and then all of you could have heard. But then again, I had no idea. Seve, if you will?" Then Seve gave a much shortened version of what they had covered in the meeting room.

Seirra then asked. "I wonder if these letters and numbers that keep coming up at the bottom of the screen when we are searching from the sky mean anything."

Looking over her shoulder Saige asked. "What are you talking about Seirra?" She then pointed at the screen she had been studying and said. "Right here, Saige."

He then looked closer and saw what she was pointing at and asked. "Do they stay the same?"

"No silly, if they did that I wouldn't have thought anything about it. If they had never changed, I would have assumed that it was probably some serial number or such that had to do with what we were using, but it changes according to what I am viewing. Now watch and I'll show you." He watched as she changed the view and as she had stated the numbers changed but the letters did not. Seve came over to join him and paused a moment. He had the look of concentration on his face as if he was trying to recall something. "I think we need Sabryn to come in here. She commented that she had found both in the computers and in the administrator's office in hard copy, something similar to this."

Looking up at the other monitor Saige asked, "Sabryn, can you come here now?"

She nodded and tiptoed out of the room and away from the camera, obviously heading to the security office, leaving Starr to watch Sommer.

* * *

"These double doors are really large." Stone commented. "Hmmm, did you look at that other room that moves and see if it might have been the same size or maybe larger than the one we rode?"

"Why do you think that something like that would be important Stone?"

Gesturing with his hands he said. "Look at the size of these doors. I mean there has to be a reason for them to be this big, and the moving room that we just left isn't big enough to require doors this size. So I'm wondering if the other one is larger that's all."

She turned around and pushed the button on the wall that activated the moving rooms and waited until both the sound of the ding and the panel above the doors lit. She stood in front of the one that was to the right of the button and waited while the doors opened. She then peered inside and said. "Yup, this is at least twice the size of the one we were in, and if I am honest, these doors are larger also. So what do you think it means, Stone?"

"My guess is that it's a way to move large things, maybe supplies, or whatever, out through those double doors. So, it could be that where this leads, is a storage area and that would explain the size. But until we actually go through them it's all conjecture – shall we?" He pushed through the doors and found that they were in a small room with a second set of doors similar to the first. But unlike the first set these were not manually operated. Try as they may, the doors would not push open. Looking around Sorrel saw a square silver plate on the wall closest to her. She reached out and pushed it and then the doors swung outward allowing them to pass. Stepping through the doors they found themselves in another tunnel, again, he suspected that originally it had been a steam vent caused by the extinct volcano. Still, he could see that it had been modified to accommodate whatever their ancestors had used this area for. Along the floor and ceiling there was recessed lighting which turned on as they approached, and on one of the walls, an identical panel to the one Sorrel had pushed to open the doors. "Must have some type of motion sensor for these lights – good way to conserve energy, to only have them light when they are needed. And doing it this way means that someone cannot accidentally leave them turned on."

The tunnel changed in direction bending to the right in a gentle curve and then coming back to the original direction. Up ahead, in the distance, they could see what appeared to be another set of doors. Once there, like the first of the double set, they were able to push through them, only to find once again a set that required pushing a plate. When the doors opened they were hit with a blast of fresh cool air, but from what they could see, they were not yet truly outside. Walking through the doors they found themselves in some type of building. Yet the floor was a mix of dirt and straw, and looking around they could see some the areas had concrete floors. Just past the entrance, and looking up, they saw a pulley system set up that could hoist items and move them around this building. Above they could also see shelving and platforms for storage, and presently most were vacant. There was a musty smell and they could hear the bleating of animals somewhere in the distance. After leaving the warmth of the compound it felt almost cold and both shivered in response to the change in temperature. Both looked at each other and then Sorrel said. "I think this place is probably where they take care of the animals, and obviously they used it for some type of storage. But since this seems to be open to the weather, I don't know what that might be?"

"I don't know either; shall we explore this before we go outside? You know it really doesn't feel like this place stays open all the time. I bet you that when the suns set those large doors close down for the night. I suspect that like the sensors that turned on the lights as we approached, that there is something similar set up to close the doors when night falls or the weather gets really nasty." Stone stated as he looked around. They slowly walked around the interior of the building and found many stations positioned at different locations, most they had no idea what they were used for. "Well, I am really starting to develop an inferiority complex here. I mean, the ones who built this place were our ancestors, and obviously they knew what all of this was for, and I haven't a clue."

Nodding in agreement, she looked down for a moment and said. "Enough of this, let's go outside and see what other wonders our ancestors left us." They headed out through a huge opening, stopping briefly; Stone noticed the opening had a huge door, which was on rollers, which would allow it to slide to cover the opening. Studying it closely he could see that that the rails that the rollers tracked in showed signs of usage. He commented. "See, the tracks show signs of usage which means that they probably do close and open." Looking up, he saw that he was alone and that he had been talking just to himself. *Now where did Sorrel run off to?* He raised his voice and yelled, "Sorrel? Sorrel where are you?" Looking around the area he presently was in, he noticed that there were at least two more buildings to his left and on the right arose a volcanic wall that he suspected was another cone from one of the extinct volcanoes. Not getting an answer, he headed towards one of the other buildings that were a little distance from where he was. As he walked he could hear his footsteps crunching on the gravel. He looked down and realized that this whole area had been covered in gravel, and it extended around the other buildings as well. With no response he was getting worried that something may have happened, but realized that there was little chance of that actually happening, and got his emotions back in control. He went around to the right of the furthest building and stopped and caught his breath. Before him lay a large meadowland and surrounding it completely, rising to a great height, was the volcanic walls. Again he marveled at the sheer size. And again was thankful he hadn't been here when these mountains had exploded with volcanic fury.

As he surveyed the beauty before him, off in the distance he could see Sorrel standing and staring at something. He then made his way to where she was standing, and was about to admonish her for getting separated, when he, following the direction she was looking, became distracted himself. Out in the distance was a large herd of what he knew was the herd animals that the primitives used for their milk, their skins, meat, and for transport of materials. He saw that like the two of them, these animals, well at least a number of them were watching them also. "Well", he said softly, "I guess this answers the question, as to whether our ancestors had their own herd or not." He was then silent as the quiet beauty of the place settled in on him.

She turned to him with a sad smile on her face and said. "Yes, I guess so." *It's just so sad to realize that sometime a long time ago our ancestors worked and lived here. Had created all of this, and then because of something we really do not understand, had to abandon it. And then it lay sleeping, awaiting the day when someone would rediscover it.* She gave herself a mental shake and continued saying, "Let's go out there and see what there is to see. One thing for sure, with the natural walls around this place, these animals can't leave, and it protects them from their natural predators also. There has to be some type of a water source out there, and from looking at how green everything is, I bet that this place has either a high water table, or our ancestors set up some type of irrigation system to keep it this way."

"You're probably right, and I'd guess that it's sub-irrigated. But seeing what we have found so far, it would not surprise me to find that they artificially irrigated this place. And I agree with you, we need to walk this out and explore it. One of the main reasons we need to do this, is because, they had to get these animals in here in the first place, and I guarantee it wasn't the way we came. So there has to be another outlet where they could take them out of here. Plus, I feel that it needs to be far enough away from the main facility that there is no hint of where the facility is located. And again you are so right; this place is just so beautiful. Who would have guessed that such an area as this existed here?"

Looking at him she said, "Well then, the day's flying by, let's do it." They headed off towards the wall on the right figuring to follow it around, since it would logically be somewhere along one the walls that the exit from this place should be. Looking up at the sky he saw that they really did not have much time. While summer days were longer, they had entered this area late after lunch, so the day had been more than half over when they discovered the meadows. Unconsciously he picked up the pace. She found that he was starting to pull ahead of her slightly and said. "Hey, this isn't a race."

Smiling slightly he said. "Sorry Sorrel. Didn't mean to do that, but we're running out of daylight, and I guess I just unconsciously picked it up to try and get around this place before darkness fell. I mean, look at this place. It's huge! I'd guess we are looking at a circumference of oh, I'd guess around ten kilometers, and I suspect that it will be pushing dark thirty by the time we head back to those buildings."

* * *

"Can you watch Sommer for me?" Sabryn asked. "I don't know if I can help, but it sounded urgent."

"No problem, after all, there seems to be an excitement in Saige's voice. I wonder what's come up. I know that we haven't found anything that we didn't expect here where we are in the facility. Maybe one of the other teams found something."

"You know that could be it. Anyway I just fed her and put her down for a nap and she fell right to sleep, so if you just look in on her a couple of times it would be appreciated."

"Oh you know I will. We do this all the time for both of our children, and I'm not too far from doing the same with my son – feeding and putting him down for his nap. And I think that like your Sommer, Shayne will be down for at least a couple of hours. That will allow me, and maybe you, if they let you go, to continue to search the records."

Smiling as she went out the door Starr heard her whisper, "Thank You", as she disappeared from sight. Sabryn hurried down the hallway, at the moment she was almost on the opposite side of the compound, and it would take her a little time to get there. As she hurried along her way, a smile came to her as she thought about her sleeping daughter, and wondered what the future would hold for her. *One thing for sure it will be different in so many ways. Even if we are able to break up the alliance, we now know that the past, as it has been taught, is completely wrong. I really wonder when it got changed to what we were taught. And where is our home world? There's absolutely nothing in any of the records even identifying its location. But I guess I can kind of understand it. That means that if something happened to one of the outposts, that the information on its location could not be compromised. Still, I would really like to see it if it still exists, and there is just no way to know, is there?* She reached the security entrance and found that other than Starr, who she had left with the children, Stone and Sorrel, everybody was here at the security office. "This is a surprise." She said, as she saw all of them there. "Are we having a party or something?" This brought a chuckle out of the group. "Would you like me to come in, or just wait out here? It's getting a little tight in there, and I don't know if I could fit comfortably with all of you in there."

"No, we do need you in here. Seirra wants to show you something, and see if it looks familiar to you. Seve thought that you had either seen, or mentioned that you had seen something similar, and that it might hold the key to solving another of the many puzzles we've found since this place was discovered. And while it's a little crowded, it's really not that crowded since I believe that if we needed to, we probably could put everybody in here. But instead it's just a few and I know you were just jesting anyway. The rest of the team will head back to the meeting room where they can continue to monitor us." They began filing out and headed back leaving plenty of room for Sabryn to enter the security room. She watched as they left and stood silently for a moment before entering the security office. She looked around briefly and then at Seirra, who was looking back at her.

"Okay, I'm here. What's so important that you pulled me away from our search? Not that anything new has been found, but I really did not figure that we would be looking at anything else until we had finished the searching."

"Seirra showed me something and again, as I said, Seve thought that you had seen something like it, so if you would?" Saige then gestured for her to come forward and look at the screen.

She came forward and looked over Seirra's shoulder and asked. "What is it that you want me to see?"

Seirra pointed to the bottom of the monitor and said. "It's these letters and numbers that change when I or any of us change the view." She then demonstrated. "See what I mean."

"Yes and no. The letters stay the same; it's just the numbers that change. Hmmm, let me think." She was silent for a moment and thought. *They are right. I've seen something similar to this. But what is it and where?* Shaking her head as she continued to think, *I've been through so much stuff lately just where is it that I saw this?* She could feel the pressure mounting as the silence in the room grew, but at the moment she didn't have a ready answer. "He's right, I did mention something about letters and numbers, but I'm drawing a blank right this moment. Just let me think about it, okay?"

Saige shrugged and said. "At least it was worth a shot. So you do remember something, but not much more at this moment. Okay keep thinking about it. Tonight I want all of us back together to go over what we have learned, or not, and maybe by that time you will have come up with something."

Again shaking her head, Sabryn said. "I'm so sorry. It's just we have been researching so much stuff lately that it just escapes me for now." She saw that Saige was nodding his head, and signaled her that she could return to what she had been doing.

"At least we may have an answer soon." Then looking up at the camera he continued. "Remember we all need to be in the meeting room after dinner so that we can compare notes, and has anyone heard anything from either Stone or Sorrel since the midday meal?" All he got was silence. Breathing out heavily, he finished by saying. "Maybe they had better luck, so I guess everyone can go back to doing what they were before this interruption. We will look at what Seve suggested, and hope that Sabryn can remember. I think somehow it is all tied together. See you all later."

* * *

The suns were dropping down behind the horizon by the time Stone and Sorrel reached the buildings once again. They had at one point cut across the meadowland to at least check part of it out. But to do a thorough search would require another day, if not two. The first thing that they noticed was that the pack animals were heading towards the buildings also. "Maybe they spend the nights inside one of the buildings." Sorrel suggested.

"Yeah probably", Stone responded. "It probably provides not only protection from the weather, but from the predators also, even though there has been no sign of any. I bet that these doors on the large building close at night also."

"Really? Why would you think that?" She asked.

"Well think about it. If you remember what the entrance looked like, there was no soil buildup or signs of disuse on the rollers and channels. To me, that speaks of constant use. That way, in the cold of winters it would provide protection for the beasts of burden. And I suspect that once they are here that there are bots that monitor them and probably are also responsible for thinning of the herds so that they do not outgrow their food."

"And that's probably where the meat is coming from." She was silent for a minute before continuing, "I think we need to hurry back. We've still got a ways to go, and I'm finding that I am actually hungry – haven't done this kind of exercise since we've been here. And we can truthfully say we found where the beasts are kept. I know, it still doesn't explain a lot, but it surely is one step closer, don't you think?"

He had to agree, and he reached out and took her hand, and then hand in hand they retraced their steps from earlier in the day, as they headed back into the facility.

* * *

"Has anyone seen either Stone or Sorrel?" Saige asked as they began sitting in the meeting room. Looking around, he saw that overall that no one had. He wondered what had delayed them. He knew that from what had been relayed to him, that they had found stairs that climbed out of sight, and a couple of enclosed rooms. From the brief description that he had received, the area was a place that he did want to visit, and the feeling he got was that most of the others here were of like mind. "I guess they will show up when they get back from whatever they have found. So let's open this up with each of us passing on what we have found, or not found today, and I'll start it. Shellian and I searched the grounds completely, and overall nothing has changed. We found a small greenhouse sitting back in a hidden corner that we felt was there for the use of the staff. You know, for things like growing flowers, or plants, and I think that it was also used for school projects, as there was a section that was separate that had a sign stating *education* – other than that, nothing at all new. Seve, Staven, your turn." He sat down and Staven got up.

"Both the steam room and the electric room were completely searched, and other than learning that most of our system is based on geothermal and solar, we have nothing to report. Everything there was as expected. While there, of course, Seve came up with his ideas that were then presented, and I think Sabryn now has the answer to the question that was asked of her after lunch." At this point Staven sat back down, and turned it over to Sabryn.

"Once Seirra had shown me those letters and numbers I knew that I had seen something similar, but where and what I couldn't remember. But before I get to that, I need to say that our primary assignment was to search out the immediate facility, and nothing new was found, and the maps and schematics of the place are accurate. Now, onto the other, I now remember that there are three places that I remember coming across those combinations of letters and numbers. In the system it describes these as longitude and latitude. It is a way to locate something anywhere on this world. So when they were looking at a certain place on this world from those views it was automatically providing the longitude and latitude. The measurements that are used are degrees, minutes, and seconds. And don't ask me why, I'm not the one who developed the system. Longitude measures through the poles and latitude measures from the equator. With these two, and the breakdown, any place on this planet can be located. Once you realize that, then it would make sense for someone to leave information on the locations of the planned cities. So once I understood that, I went back through the records that existed in the computer, and found a reference to a source in the administrator's office, and a second tied directly to the security office. It required one to go to the admin office, to get first, the list of the cities, their names, and such. Plus there was a password there to use in the security office that would then release not only the locations by this system of longitude, and latitude, but emergency frequencies to contact them."

"You mean that there might be a way that we can contact each of them directly? Wow this is great news." Saige stated excitedly. He turned to Seve stating, "I guess you're right, and when you presented it, it made sense." About this time the doors opened with Stone and Sorrel arriving.

"Sorry about being late." Stone said, "But we have some very important news to pass on, and while on that subject, did we miss anything?"

"Only the fact that we may now be able to contact the cities, and let them know what is happening, that's all . . . Anyway Sabryn, are you finished with your report?" She nodded and sat down. "Okay then Stone, since you are standing, go ahead and let us know what you have found, other than the area that you had talked about over lunch of course."

"Simply put, we found it. Well at least part of the puzzle anyway. As you know, the stairs led up, and we climbed them to the top. We discovered, albeit accidentally, what those rooms were also. Since we never had a need of them in our cities, it would never have occurred to us that it was a way to move between floors, without walking. They transport one from one floor to another. It is a different feeling when they begin to move. If they go up at first you feel heavier, and quite the opposite when you go down in them." Catching his breath for a moment, he leaned forward supporting his weight on his hands that he had placed on the table. "While that is a nice discovery, the question is why would they need such a thing? It turns out that there are just three stops that we could get to. There is at least another, but that one requires a key, which we did not have. But I would guess that it is another supply area. The ground floor is at the level of the cavern, and the top floor exits to an open lunch slash meeting area, beautiful really. But the one in the middle empties into a room that has large swinging doors, big enough to move large crates through. So initially we thought it could be just another supply area, and when we went through it, there was a worked steam vent and . . ." He went on to describe all that they had found, and apologizing at the end, since they had been unable to do a complete search. "My feelings are that there has to be an exit on the far side, somewhere that would not compromise this compound, and besides I can't really see anyone bringing those animals through the area where we entered. And for now that's all we have."

Smiling Saige said. "With the way things have been going I was getting very frustrated on the lack of progress, and now all in the same day things have moved so quickly that we will be working hard on solving the problems that have now been presented. Oh, one more thing Sabryn, did any of that information include locations for the primitives?"

Shaking her head she said, "No, the notation stated that since many of the primitives were nomadic, and had no real permanent location, that only full descriptions of their lives were included."

"I guess we can't have everything, but that sure would have been nice. Okay, it looks like we have a lot of work ahead of us, so in the morning, normally Seve and Sabryn would have manned the security office, but I am adding both of you, Seirra and Saar back there. There's room for that many in there. We need to get that information and figure out how to contact the remaining cities, and of course the first one we need to contact would be Keahilani, since it is the pivot city, the one that maintains all communications traffic between the cities. They could get the word out quicker than we could. The rest of us will head out to this place that Stone and Sorrel located, and see if we can find that exit. Truly we are running out of time, and so far we haven't been able to locate the alliance headquarters. But we do have, or will have shortly, the coordinates of all the cities, so we can narrow the search area down a bit by comparing the times when the cities we know were taken by the primitives, and by looking at the differences, come up with a much smaller area to search. If there isn't anything else, I for one have to admit that it has been a full day." He looked around and saw that the rest agreed with him. "Okay then, we is done here. Let's all meet for breakfast in the cafeteria and then we can go as a group to our different areas. And I'm going to take a chance and not have anyone monitoring the security office tonight. So far, we haven't seen a primitive within kilometers of this place. We need everyone for what is happening tomorrow, and all to have a full night's sleep. So, good night all, and thank you for all of the effort that has gotten us to this point." He watched as the members filtered out of the meeting room. He saw that Seirra waited until all the rest had left and then came over and joined him.

"I agree I'm really tired tonight. Do you really think that we will be able to contact the cities?" *I really do hope so, there has already been too much loss here, and if there is a slight chance that we can alert the rest to what's happening, then maybe they can come up with some way of keeping the primitives out.* "I know there is no way you can answer that right now, but I had to ask."

He reached out and hugged her and then took her hand and said. "I really never, well Shellian and I really never wanted this job, and to answer your question, I don't know. After all, all of our training was to spy on the primitives, and not repair the equipment. That was for other members, and none of them survived our flight to here – so all of us are flying quite blind here. And while everything seems to be working because of the bots and replicators, I just don't know." Taking a deep breath and shrugging he said. "I really wish I did, but I have to be honest, I just don't. Enough on this, I'm tired, lets head back to the apartment and call it. I have a feeling that the next few days are going to be extremely busy, not that most of them haven't been, but we now know so much more, and I do hope we can use what we learned to stop the slaughter and slavery of our people."

"I do love you, you know that?" She asked as she looked up into his eyes and smiled.

Smiling back at her, she could see softness in his eyes as he said. "Yes, I do, and I knew that for a long time. It was just that back in the cave I couldn't show any favoritism towards anybody, and especially you, but I have to admit that I am in love with you also.

You have become very important to me in so many ways."

Then smiling mischievously she said. "Well, let me show you tonight how much I appreciate you." And then she laughed as they headed for their apartment.

* * *

Keenan stayed long enough to make sure that the shift change went smoothly, and then headed out to grab something to eat before he went home. He was in a dark mood, and really did not want any company tonight. The word coming back from the council was nothing but political mumbo jumbo saying absolutely nothing, and the information being passed down by the over-bosses was just as bad. In other words, nothing was known, and nothing was being done. Was this paralysis to continue, until, for whatever reason, the light would be turned off here? Again he had no answers. He wanted to do something, anything, but again by not knowing what had happened he was frustrated, and had no real direction to go. He was a man of action, one who wanted to delve deeply into the problem and get it solved. And this was the reason for his dark mood. *Yeah, it's obvious that nobody knows anything, and is just saying what sounds good. Why isn't someone out there trying to find out? Instead all we get is talk, talk, talk!* Breathing deeply and shaking his head slightly his thoughts continued unbidden. *I just don't get it. Why haven't they sent someone out to at least check on one of the cities that have gone dark? Yeah, I know, not one of the cities is that close to each other, but if I remember correctly, there was supposed to be some type of special team to do just that.* Now with a bit of sarcasm his thoughts continued. *Oh that's right. Budget cuts, since we never had any need or use for that department it was eliminated as waste.* Chuckling inwardly he just stared out at nothing in particular as he headed for his favorite restaurant. *I guess tomorrow will be another day, and maybe, just maybe, someone will do something – yeah like that's going to happen.*

* * *

Morning came too quickly, and all of them filtered out to the cafeteria for breakfast. Looking around, Saige could see that most looked blurry eyed and somewhat drug out. *At least I'm not the only one that looks that way right now.* But it was little consolation, since they needed to be fresh and alert today. He really wanted to be able to make contact today, and to completely explore the meadowlands that had been discovered yesterday. Looking around he noticed that the women were missing at this moment and realized that it was their day for kitchen duty at the meals, and as he realized that, the women began to bring in the food and as the smells reached him he realized that he was quite hungry. Smiling at them as they piled the plates of food in the middle of the table he could hear his stomach rumble in complaint and anticipation. The women then went back briefly to the kitchen and brought out steaming pots of coffee. It had been something they had discovered here, and all of them had found, that like their ancestors, they were living on the stuff. It was different than the *shick* they drank back in the city, and he had to admit, better. Once the coffee had arrived they sat down and Shellian said. "Well, dig in everyone while it's hot. I do not like cold food." Someone replied. "My parents raised no fools; you don't have to tell me twice." This brought out a general chuckle from everyone there. Then all that anyone heard was the moving of plates, silverware, and cups as everyone concentrated on the food and drink.

* * *

It had been a restless night and Keenan was short tempered and in no mood for the normal political crap today. So he knew that he had to keep his mouth shut, and to be careful, so that he did not say something that would put him on report. Things had been building for quite a while now, and if something did not happen soon, it would not matter, he would blow up anyway. It seemed that all of the ones above were avoiding any mention of the problems that were now confronting the cities. *As if ignoring them would make them go away.* Yet, as he looked around on his way to work, everything was just too normal. Shaking himself inwardly he thought once again. *Eight cities gone, and still no one to explain why, and no one who will take responsibility for trying to discover the reasons why they have gone silent.* He knew that right now he was too old, and had too many minor health problems, to be one who could do the discovering. It was another point of frustration for him. Back in his youth, he had almost joined the ones who were active in keeping an eye on the primitives, the research, and advancements that they made. And yes, even the fighting between the clans and tribes. All of this was important, but before he could join, the council disbanded it as unnecessary. So here he was all this time later close to the age of no longer working, to have this crisis show its face, and no one willing to do anything about it.

He knew that the city of Sequoyah had been the last to maintain the unit that worked out in the field, who had trained continually to be able to work among the primitives, if it came down to the need, but Sequoyah was one of the cities that had gone dark, and so any chance of discovery went out the window with them. He looked up and realized that he had reached the central communications center, and wondered how he had gotten here so fast. It appeared to him that he had just left his apartment. At least if something happened to this city there would be no family for him to lose, he mused. He had been coupled twice, but it had never worked out. And in those short unions no children and his parents had died a long time ago, as had his one brother and sister. Oh if he searched he probably had a couple of nieces and nephews but he truly did not know. Looking up at the large clock he found that he had time to get something hot to drink before beginning his shift and headed for one of the machines before relieving the last shift.

* * *

As they walked the large cavern towards the entrance to the stairs and moving rooms, the lights turned on automatically, as they came into the range of the hidden sensors. Before them, lay a pathway of lights, shining up from the ground towards the ceiling that was high above them. This area had to have been a large pocket of magma, that had disappeared, leaving this cavern here a very long time ago, and it was huge. Sorrel and Stone led the way, and they shortly arrived at what Stone felt was originally a steam vent. Making the turn, the passageway lit up as the floor had, and before them they could see the closed doors leading into the room where the stairway and moving rooms were located. "The stairs are on the right through a door, and on the left is the other rooms, and straight ahead is a wall," Stone commented as they reached the door. As they prepared to enter, the rest could see that there was wired glass to allow them to look into the room. Sorrel then held open the door and with a flourish, waved them through. As all of them entered, the room was exactly as they had described. Stone then went over to the doors on the left and pushed a button that was between them. The doors opened immediately causing Saige, Shellian, Staven, and Starr to jump. Laughing softly Stone said. "Sorry about that, I didn't think they were going to open that quickly. But hurry everyone inside. These doors only stay open for a short time and they will close again." Hesitantly the four of them joined Stone and Sorrel inside. And as he had stated the doors did close. Stone then turned towards the panel and pressed the button for the top. He could feel the tension in the air, since the other four did not know what to expect. There was a soft whirring sound and suddenly the room was moving upwards and they briefly felt heavier, then just the opposite as it slowed and then came to a stop. The doors opened and they now were outside of the facility. "Quickly now – these doors will close again. It really isn't a problem, as you can keep them open by blocking them." Stone then demonstrated, as the doors had begun to close and he blocked them and they opened again. "The other moving room is much larger, and I suspect that it is the one the used to move freight up and down."

They took a quick tour around the area and had to agree with the assessment that they had been given the night before. Again, it was obvious, that from the trails on the mountains that this area would be invisible. And the views from here, as described, were spectacular. "I can see that this would give any of the support people a place to go that would be safe and still be outside. Yes, I know that they probably walked the small valley, but this area gives you vistas to stare at, and one does not feel closed in at all. It is just beautiful." Saige said.

Stone then led them to the stairs, and they descended to the middle area and the large swinging doors that marked the passage into another worked steam vent, and out into the buildings that led into the meadowlands beyond. Once there, after a brief stop in the buildings Starr exclaimed as she saw the area. "This is so big, quiet, peaceful, and really, really beautiful too." Then turning around and looking at the rest of them, she could see that all of the rest were in agreement with what she had said.

Sorrel then stated as she pointed out into the distance. "We ran out of daylight, and unlike the buildings which seem to have a dusk-to-dawn lighting system, there are none out here at all. We were only able to get less than half way out there and had to return. Stone figures that this place has to be around ten kilometers around." Then she pointed towards a different area and said. "Over there is a small lake. We didn't have time to figure out whether it was natural, or something that our ancestors had built. But we were able to confirm that this volcanic wall goes completely around it, protecting the animals that are in here."

"Were either of you able to get close to the pack beasts at all?" Shellian asked

Shaking her head Sorrel said, "No, they were still out towards the other end of this giant bowl, but as night approached they were beginning to head back to those buildings. But we were out of time and needed to get back. Yet, from a distance, they showed more curiosity than fear. But whether that's because there is nothing for them to fear here, or because the bots have worked with them, I really don't know."

Turning around and facing the group Saige said, "I guess even with your description I didn't think this would be as large as it is. Okay, here is what I would like to happen. Staven, you and Starr take the left wall and follow it out. Stone, you and Sorrel, since you have been here, work up through the middle of the meadows, and then Shellian and I will work the right wall. We should be able to see at least some of the others as we work our way around. Then we will meet on the other side, and see what we find. We can then break for lunch and continue. You all know what we need to do, so let's get to it."

* * *

"You all know what we are here for today. Seve, you and Sabryn search that manual and database and see if there is any mention on how we tie what you Sabryn found to anything here in the security office." Turning around and facing Seirra, Saar continued, "Since you were the one who actually discovered the locations being placed at the bottom of the screen, maybe you can find out which of these, I guess you can call them, eyes-in-the-skies that will get us closest to Keahilani. And since part of our job is to keep us safe, for the first part of the day here I will monitor the area. We'll all switch jobs later. And as Saige said, we are in a critical situation, and time is, as usual, running out on us and our people."

Seve turning to his mate said, "You've been great on searching the database, and if Shayne becomes fussy or needs to be fed, you can slip out to the nursery and take care of his needs and probably be able to continue the research."

Smiling and shaking her head she said. "I have no problem with that, but we created this child and we *will* share in everything. Of course, since I am breast-feeding him you cannot take part in that, but I expect you to go with me with everything else, and that includes helping me put him down for his nap or change his messy pants. That's the way it was in my parents' house and that's the way it will be in ours." She looked over lovingly to the sleeping baby that was lying in a small portable bed, oblivious to what was going on around him. "It appears that Staven is totally into fatherhood, and he is carrying Sommer on his back, as they are exploring that meadow."

"Yeah I know. It's just something I have to grow into. In the house I grew up in, mom and dad stayed within their roles. Mom took care of us and dad did the rest. I think probably it had to do with the fact that they worked closely with the primitives and that's how the primitives that we observed sort of lived." Then putting his hands out in front of him in defense he continued. "So it was the way I thought it was supposed to be, but I can see that it is so much better to share in everything. But it is going to take me some time to change the way I was raised."

Saar then interrupted saying, "Now that we have had our family discussion, can we get on with this?"

Both turned around and realized that was exactly what they were doing, and apologized profusely. When Saar turned around he saw Seirra smiling. "So what are you smiling at?"

"Oh them. The one thing everyone forgets when they get into a relationship is that both are coming from different places, have different views, and have different experiences. So, there is much the two of you have to overcome, and it's really surprising that anybody actually stays together. But I guess we all learn to adjust if we really care."

As he thought about it he had to agree. Even he and Shellian had had some growing pains, but both of them were willing to work on it. Shellian was a very strong willed woman and one who had confidence in her abilities. And he had to admit that she had earned that right. "I guess that's very true. Oh well, I guess the show's over, so to all of us, let's get to it."

* * *

Keenan, looking over his workers knew that they had sensed his mood, and were being very careful to stay out of his way. They all had been, at one time or another, on the receiving end of his displeasure, and it was not pleasant. So they all walked on eggshells and avoided direct eye contact. Yet, all of them had to admit that they would not want to work with anybody else, as their boss even when he was in a foul mood, made sure that all were treated fairly. They knew that as much as he would not put up with anything from them, he was the same way with his own over-bosses. So they, in some ways, were able to do more and have a little more freedom than the other shifts. Still, they could sense the electricity in the air, and now was just waiting for it to discharge, and hope everything would return back to normal. But this had been something that had been building for a while, they knew it had to do with the cities that had gone dark, and the weak excuses his over-bosses were passing on to him.

Shaking his head as he paced back and forth on the raised area in the back of the center, he felt as if something was about to happen, and he hoped that it was not another city going dark. But the morning passed quietly, and all appeared to be much too normal for him. And even with this semblance of normalcy, he still sensed that something was very wrong. So with a deep sigh, he headed for the midday meal, and looked for a table that would isolate him from the rest of his peers. He was in no mood for company. As he sat down with his food, he looked across the cafeteria and saw Kiley approaching his table, and he looked up at him and glared, and almost laughed as Kiley stopped dead in his tracks, changed direction, and headed for another table.

Later, back on shift, he thought that other than supporting his body, that the midday meal was worthless. He couldn't even remember finishing it and leaving, let alone tasting anything. Looking over the workers again, everything appeared to just be as it should be, and yet, he felt that it was just wrong. How it was wrong, he had no idea, but he just could not put down the feeling that it was. He turned his back and stared at the wall deep in thought, trying to come to terms with this foreboding that appeared to penetrate his very soul. There was a crisis, but looking around one would never have guessed. Maybe that was why he was feeling this way. Everything appeared to be very normal, and it was anything but. "Sir?" He barely heard it and then thought. *Sir is it? How I hate to be called that.* Then shaking his head inwardly, *Yeah, I know it's a sign of respect, but I always figured that it belonged to my parents or someone older than I am. Okay, who asked?* Turning around he saw Kacey standing below him. She had worked here for about eight annuals and was very good at what she did. She monitored the little used channels, and he had tried to get her not to use *sir*, but she had insisted. With a mental shrug he asked, keeping the tension he was feeling out of his voice. "Yes Kacey, what is it?"

She paused for a moment not sure how to continue, and the indecision was plain on her face. She looked down at the floor for a moment and then said, "I'm not sure what to make of it sir . . . ." She immediately paused again when she saw him glare at her for using *sir*. "I'm sorry, but I just can't change the way I was raised."

Looking at her, he could see a nice looking woman, not pretty by any means, but one who could be attractive if she dressed a little differently and wore her hair in a different way, but she preferred to keep things as plain as she could, while working. As far as he knew she was still single, and he tried to stay out of his workers personal lives, unless it had an effect on their work. "Yes, yes, I know, but as you know, I've never cared for it." Sighing, he continued, "This is getting away from why you are here, now please continue."

She nodded her head and he could see that she almost said it again but paused. "Okay, I just received a communications from a channel that has never been active."

"You mean active while you've worked here, right?"

Shaking her head she said. No, no as far as I can see, and I've checked the logs as far back as I could, it has never been used. And this channel has our highest priority color attached to it. And the signal is weak and scratchy, but I think I can actually hear someone trying to communicate with us."

"Are you sure?" Then shaking his head he said. "Of course you are, sorry about that, but it is a surprise that's all. What does the monitor tell you?"

"That's the really weird part; it's saying that it is originating from point Alpha."

He looked perplexed for a moment and then glanced over at his monitoring panel and saw that one light was flashing, and like at her station this light had never flashed in his twenty-five years of working here. "What the heck is going on?" He thought a moment before continuing. "Okay Kacey transfer it to my station and I'll take it from here, and please set up for record, we want an accurate recording of this, and if it turns out to be some type of hoax, then we'll have it all down. And please monitor it with me so that if something comes to mind that you want to either ask or add you can." He glanced up at the clock and it said 1433.

* * *

"Look, when we pushed this button that is marked with the highest priority color, then this happened." The other two stared at the center panel than now was lit up. A message appeared on the monitor that sat above this panel and stated, "Ready to Transmit". "Who'd of thought it would be that easy?" Saar asked. He looked around at the rest and he could see the surprise in their eyes also. "Okay now what?"

"Now what, what?" Sabryn asked.

"Well, as far as I know, we were just supposed to figure this out, and then report back to Saige and Shellian on our research, not actually make a connection." Saar responded.

"I guess it's too late for that now." Seirra replied. "It looks like it has sent out a carrier wave, and set itself up, and connected to Keahilani."

"Which means", Seve said, "that some type of confirmation would have happened there, so they would know that someone would be trying to contact them." They could now feel the excitement building inside of them, as well as nervousness, as they realized what was happening. After all this *time of isolation* they were finally going to be able to talk to a city.

Saar, looking around at the rest asked, "What should we say?" He could feel the tension in the room as the other three shrugged. "Take me to your leader, doesn't work here," he said, trying to ease the atmosphere. And it had its effect by a series of small nervous chuckles that the statement evoked. They all jumped when a scratchy but understandable voice came out of the panel.

"Who is on this priority channel?" The voice asked before continuing. "If this is some kind of joke or prank we are not laughing here. And if it is, then there are serious consequences for operating on this channel." The voice said with strong authority.

They looked at each other for a moment and then Seve said. "You'd better respond, or I guess the better question is, have you figured out how to respond?"

"Ah, this is Saar."

"Saar? Who the heck is Saar, and since you are connecting through point Alpha why is your name beginning with an "S"?" Keenan asked.

"Point Alpha? Look, whoever you are, since you haven't identified yourself, if you happen to really look, you will know that on any of the circuits or maps for that matter, there is never a mention of this place, point Alpha as you called it." And it was true, this location had never been on any map and the list of cities never had one that began with "A". And because it had never been there, there never had been a question as to why. Now their little band knew why, but nobody in the rest of the world did.

"True." The voice agreed. "But for some reason it is on my panel, although I've never seen it activate or become active in any way. And I am Keenan, the leader of this shift." Again he couldn't keep the suspicion out of his voice.

"Keenan is it? Okay then, there is a reason for that, and if what happened to our city had not have happened, then all of this would not have happened, or had become known. Anyway, I am a doctor, and as you have guessed, we are not from here or there. Our city *was* Sequoyah." That brought silence for a moment, as if the speaker on the other end was trying to assimilate what he had just been told.

Then in a softer tone Keenan said, "Sequoyah is one of the cities that went dark." Then with the realization of what had been just relayed to him he continued. "You aren't trying to pull some type of prank here are you? Because if you are, then I personally will be sure to see you pay for it."

Saar looked around at the rest of them that were in the security office and just shook his head. He then took a deep breath before speaking again. "No, Keenan. In a way I wish it were so and our city still existed. But it is gone as are the others, which have gone dark. And on that subject just how many have gone dark now?"

"Have you been out of the loop or something? Everybody knows that we've had eight cities go dark. How is it that you don't know that?"

"I guess you can say that we have been in isolation for somewhere close to or more than a full annual. And let me say that we know why it is happening, and that every city that still exists needs to know this information, and all of you need to figure how to fix it now."

"Okay, right now all you are doing is talking in circles. You've given me no proof of who you are, and how you got on this channel, or even what this channel is for. I don't think I've even heard anything about it at all, and I don't remember any mention about it in the archives."

"Okay, okay then, what is it that you need from us to prove that we are legitimate and not someone who is trying to pull off some big publicity stunt?"

"Good question, give me a moment and I'll get back to you. I've got to find some info on your supposed city, and then I'll ask the questions, you then can give me the answers, and confirm that what you are telling me is true. Be right back." The mic then went dead.

Saar, looking around at the rest shrugged. He had to admit that he thought it wasn't going to be that hard to get things moving once they made contact. But it was turning out to be much more complicated. Turning around he asked to no one in particular. "I wonder what that is all about? After all it's not like we are all jokesters here, and just love to put something over on any who are gullible. So what's the problem here? Is there something I did or said to make this guy suspicious?" He could see that everyone in the room had no answers for him, so all of them just waited until this Keenan made contact with them again. Yet, at the same time, there was an excitement building. Now they knew for sure that other cities had not received the same fate that theirs had, and there were still ones of their own species around. Saar, thinking, *I need Saige and Shellian here, but there is no way. As far as I know they are half way across that large meadow by now and we will have no contact with them until they return tomorrow. They have planned on camping if necessary so that they could do a thorough job of exploring, and possibly finding the exit that they are sure has to be there. So I guess, since I've been in charge in the past it is all on me.* "What do you think he needs to know?" Saar asked the group. Again shrugging, as he turned back to the console, when he heard the crackling as someone on the other end was picking up a headset.

"Are still there?" The female voice on the other end asked. This is Kacey; I'm the one who monitors the less used channels. Keenan said that he would be with you in a moment. And since I do monitor these channels I heard the conversation between you and Keenan. Is it true that you are from one of the cities that went dark?"

Smiling, as Saar could hear the barely concealed excitement in her voice, said. "Yes, it is quite true. But I am sad to say at the same time that we are very few."

"Oh, here he is, and to let you know everything that is happening on this channel is automatically recorded."

"Thank you, that's good to know." Saar replied. He waited as the mic went dead once again, and then heard a different one being moved. He turned around placed his hand over his mic since it was voice activated, and said. "I may need help with whatever questions this person has, so listen well."

"Okay, Saar is it? Right. Saar, you say that you were originally from the city of Sequoyah. If this is so, who was your present head of the council at the time your city went dark?"

At least that was an easy question. But if he really admitted it, most likely, he would not have known, since they had more or less isolated themselves from the city to be able to work and live closer to the way the primitives did. And he had to admit that was probably why any of them were still alive. When the crisis had arisen it had been the leader who had contacted Shayne and then everyone in the compound knew. "His name was Sione. And I say was because I do not know of his true status, but from what we observed, there is little chance for any to have survived."

"Survived?" Keenan asked. "What do you mean survived?"

"Look, we can go into all of this later, have I not answered correctly? And if you have any additional questions please ask. Time is short and what needs to happen needs to happen yesterday, especially if you don't want to lose another city. And it's really that simple."

"Okay, you did, and I did have others but I'll accept what you have told me, but just one more thing, where did you and your over-bosses work?"

Laughing a bitter laugh Saar said. "We were the last of the scouting units. We had learned that all the other cities had dropped the units. We feel that if that hadn't happened then what has transpired may never have occurred. Look, I was told that our conversation is being recorded, and if that is so, you need to transmit a copy of what I am about to tell you not only to your council, but to every city that still survives. Our very existence depends on it, and it is that serious, do you understand?"

Still with suspicion in his voice Keenan said. "Oh come on, you're telling me this and expect me to just jump and do? Get real here."

Saar then interrupted Keenan and said. "Look we can argue this all day, and still not solve anything. When this was first brought to Shayne he was given the color yellow."

Then interrupting Saar, Keenan asked, "Shayne? Who is this Shayne that you are talking about?"

"He was our leader, but was killed during our escape. But that is old history now, and I am giving you a color that is rarely given as I feel it is that critical. And that color is *Black*." Now there was only silence on the other end for the longest of times. Then he heard a deep sigh.

"Okay Saar. You do know that using that color has, as far as I know, been used only once in our entire history. Are you sure you want to invoke black?"

Then in a quiet voice Saar said. "Yes." Then he let a few seconds of silence go by before continuing. "If there was something higher than black I would use it. This is that serious."

"Okay then, as you know we are recording this."

"I was told, but now I have a question for you. Can this be put to your council live? And if so, how long before they can be gathered?"

"I don't have that kind of authority!" Keenan responded.

"Then run the color black against whoever you need and let's move on this."

"Okay, I'll see what I can get done. In the meantime work with Kacey, and let her know the details so that there will be a small part that can be presented while the council is getting together."

* * *

The information passed through the cities like a wild fire. Now the cities that remained were on full alert, knowing what had happened to their sister cities. But no one had any answers as of yet, as to what they could do to stop the primitives. Saar was thankful that their *time of isolation* was over, that they had found that many of the cities had survived. But there still was a long and twisted road ahead of them as they came to grip with this alliance. But with knowledge, many times a solution could be found. And with point Alpha rediscovered, their true history would be known throughout the cities. And Saar for one would be glad to let Saige, Shellian and the rest of the crew know that contact had been made and plans were progressing. Still he knew that this was only the beginning, and there was much work ahead of all of them. Including the search for their home world, and whatever it was that had left them isolated here, on this distant world.

To be continued in the novel Desperate to Survive

ABOUT THE AUTHOR

F.D. Brant always wanted to write, but life got in the way. Finally after retiring he got his chance.

Storytelling and writing has always been F.D. Brant's passion, but responsibilities took preference. And because of those responsibilities it took retiring to allow those passions to come to fruition. Since retiring he has written 9 books, and maintains a weekly eclectic blog, Words in the Wind.

Growing up in the backcountry he learned the appreciation of "doing things for yourself". Because it was impossible to call in someone to repair anything one either did it themselves or went without. This led to the appreciation of the natural world, and the daily struggles that one faced as nature threw problems at the family that had to be overcome, leading to confidence and self-sufficiency. This led to the strong characters that populate his stories and books. And his female protagonists are strong willed and confident – something that he saw in both in his mother and sister.

www.ingramcontent.com/pod-product-compliance
Lightning Source LLC
Chambersburg PA
CBHW050609170726
48283CB00001B/176